THE CROWN PLONKED QUEEN

Book 4: The Western Lands and All That Really Matters

ANDREW EINSPRUCH

DEDICATION

To Billie and Tamsin

Everything of greatest value that I've learned, I've learned from you.

CROWN PLONKING

The Venerable Prelate Herself, a berobed tapir whose prehensile snout made sermonizing a tedious affair, sat awkwardly on her haunches and held aloft the Gumballic Heraldic Crown for all in the chapel to see. The GHC featured beautifully wrought filigree metalwork in gold and silver, a deep maroon velvet that covered its thin steel structural arches, and 3,271 individually set jewels and precious stones, including the Sapphire of Wishful Thinking, the rare Ruby of Righteous Indignation, and to top it off and draw the eye, the magnificent Liver Spot Diamond. The early afternoon sun flooding through a high window caught the crown, sending a dazzling shower of refracted brilliance splashing in all directions.

Eloise Hydra Gumball III, who was, at least for a couple of minutes more, the Future Ruler and Heir to the Western Lands and All That Really Matters (before she became its actual ruler), knelt on an unpadded, oak prayer kneeler and gawped up at the crown and the prelate who held it, and tried not to wonder if tapirs had armpit hair.

Her stomach clenched into an acid knot, burning like a prize-winning habanero, and she hoped her shaking wasn't visible to the crowd behind her. Her mother was just two days dead and lay in state with thousands of mourners walking past her open casket. Yet Protocol insisted a Crown Plonking ceremony be held, so the realm had an official queen wielding the royal scepter. Her formal coronation would be three months later (at least). But for now, the seventeen-year-old wore the Raiment of the Queens—a musty, uncomfortable, too-long hodge-podge of a gown that had been altered to accommodate the plaster cast on her broken right wrist and the bandages covering the burns on her back. The garment suffered from a teeth-jarring mismatch of styles and a collar ruffle that would have embarrassed a frill-necked lizard.

This is too soon, Eloise thought. *Much too soon. I'm not ready to be queen.*

The Venerable Prelate Herself's snout waggled hypnotically as she droned through the interminable ritual prescribed by Protocol. "With Divine Çalaht witnessing from the heavens, I present for all to behold this symbol of the sovereign's rights and obligations."

Eloise wondered how long the prelate could keep holding the crown up. The tapir had four splayed toes on her front feet—each like a little horse hoof. Not exactly designed for gripping. The prelate had to hold the crown by pressing on its sides, and her forelegs shook with the effort. At least she hadn't dropped it. A crown hitting the deck would not have been a good omen; that would be like breaking a mirror while walking under a ladder in a blood-rain beneath a black moon.

The Venerable Prelate Herself addressed the crowd. "Will you accept she who wears this crown as your sovereign?"

"Yes, by Çalaht," replied everyone. "We will."

"Rightio," intoned the prelate.

Eloise tried to gauge their enthusiasm. On a scale of "rote" to "exuberant," she'd put it somewhere between "ritual" and the subdued side of "measured." That would have to do.

Arms trembling, the tapir set the crown back on its velvet cushion. She spoke to Eloise, casting her nasal voice loud enough to be heard by all.

"Are you willing to take on the throne as Queen of the Western Lands and All That Really Matters?"

Eloise had been asking herself that very question, not just for the past hour and a half, but in every free moment since her mother had breathed her last. If she was being honest, Eloise had been pondering that question on and off for four years, ever since her Thorning Ceremony, when she'd been named Future Ruler and Heir.

"Yes." Eloise croaked out the word. She quietly cleared her throat, and tried again. "Yes, I am."

And it was true. She was willing to. She just wasn't sure she'd be any good at it. And the habanero in her stomach seconded that doubt.

The Venerable Prelate Herself gave a graceful upward wave of her front foot. Eloise braced herself on the pew's handrail with her unbroken left hand and hoisted herself, the ludicrous dress, and the Habanero of Doubt up toward the prelate. Surreptitiously, she patted the wooden box tied to her hip under the gown. It held the Star of Whatever, the most powerful and dangerous magical object in all the realms. Eloise would not leave it behind, not even on a day like this. *Hey, Sparky,* she sent to it silently, but there was no *Hey, Loulou* in reply.

The chapel overflowed with people of all species, its pews crammed with Court nobles, hangers-on, and important functionaries. Those who could do so held a scroll with the ceremony's text. Eloise gave her audience a quick scan. Her fraternal twin, Princess Johanna Umgotteswillen Gumball, sat in the front row. Eloise felt sad, knowing Johanna would be gone soon, heading back north to the Half Kingdom where she'd continue wrangling to be named its next queen, succeeding their late uncle.

Next to Johanna was their father. Chafed Motley Gumball née de Chëëëkflïïïnt's eyes were bloodshot from crying and his cheeks sunken in profound grief. When Eloise's mother died, her father had lost the privilege of sitting to the queen's right, and worse, his entire purpose in life. As the dowager king, he was now little more than a footnote at Court.

To the other side of Johanna was Eloise's champion, Jerome Abernatheen de Chipmunk, holding paws with his mother, Court Seer Maybelle de Chipmunk. Eloise felt tears spilling from her eyes. The late queen had never been one for holding hands, but Eloise had reached out and held her mother's as she lay dying. Eloise would never again share a moment like the one Jerome and Seer Maybelle were having right then. Her grief, shunted aside in the whirlwind of the past two days, snuck up on her. Embarrassing that it happened right then, but all she could do was sniff twice and dab her eye with the heel of her unbroken hand.

She blinked back tears and saw Guard Lorch Lacksneck standing to the side. He'd been part of the journey that had taken her to three-and-a-half of the four-and-a-half realms—along with Jerome, Hector de Pferd (Eloise's Equine Designate, although that role would get murky when her crown got plonked, as it was associated with her being a princess), and Lorch's Guard Horse partner, the always-silent Nameless One. Together they'd protected her, guided her, transported her, planned, plotted, and schemed with her, set her broken wrist, fixed her dislocated shoulder, brought her back from the brink of death from the Soldier's Cold, and saved her life over and over.

Lorch had found a spot near the front, and Hector and the Nameless One stood in a vestibule designed for larger species. It was reassuring to have them all there.

Toward the back, Eloise spotted Odmilla de Platypus, who'd been her handmaid since her Thorning Ceremony. Next to Odmilla sat RoyLee, the young wombat who'd returned to Brague with Eloise from their travels, and to whom she'd promised a role at Court. There were others in the crowd she knew well enough to speak to, like First Advisor Leccino Ligurian and the Other Places Advocate Bërnädïce-Ändrëä Thëjëts (who went by Bënnïë-Änn). But mostly, it was people she always figured she'd get to know someday as her mother groomed her to be queen.

Now, "someday" was here, and not enough grooming had happened. Not nearly enough.

The Venerable Prelate Herself interrupted Eloise's survey of the audience by raising both forelegs toward the crowd and asking the ritual question, "Will you accept this woman as your queen?"

Scrolls rustled as everyone in the room stood and gave the ritual reply: "Yep."

"Will you follow her guidance, accept her judgments, and bend your knee to her wisdom?"

Everyone with anything that resembled a knee knelt and said, "You betcha."

"Will you support her in fostering a realm that lives in peace, one that goes into the future hand in paw in wing in hoof in cilia in pseudopod —together in harmony, and free from the ravages caused by bands of ransacking marmosets?"

As one, everyone reached for their neighbors, clasped hands (or equivalent) and chorused, "Uh-huh."

The Venerable Prelate Herself stage-whispered, "Apologies for this slight against marmoset-kind. Protocol is slow to change."

Reading from their scrolls, everyone whisper-replied, "We understand that marmosets had a lengthy anti-social period around the time the *Livre de Protocol* was written. Such is Protocol."

"Such is Protocol," repeated the Venerable Prelate Herself. Then, back at full volume, she said, "Be at rest."

Everyone sat, except Eloise, who turned to face the tapir.

The Venerable Prelate Herself held her forelegs wide, like she was ready for a hug. "Eloise Hydra Gumball III, are you prepared to take and sign the Queen's Oath?"

"Yes," she said. But the word caught. Eloise swallowed. Blinked. Swallowed. "Yes." Her voice was clear this time.

The prelate took a scroll from her robe, unfurled it with a flourish, and then proceeded to ignore it, reciting the oath from memory: "Will you solemnly promise and swear to govern the people of the Western Lands and All That Really Matters, no matter the number of their limbs, their odor, their color, whether vertebrate or not, whether sentient or not, whether pleasant or not, according to the realm's laws and customs, with particular consideration of the *Livre de Protocol* and the *Scrolls of Çalaht* and its commentaries?"

"I so solemnly promise."

"Will you, to the extent of your power, cause law and justice tempered by mercy to be executed in all your judgments?"

"That I will."

"Will you, to the utmost of your power, maintain the teachings of Çalaht and the spirit of her ways? Will you help her devotional houses flourish so that the worship of the Divine One may never flag?"

As queen, Eloise was also official head of all Çalahtist sects in her realm. Her mother had been a ceremonial figurehead at most, and no one in her family would be mistaken as devout. Making this last promise was a stretch, but it had to be done. "All this I promise."

The chapel's devotional house minder appeared from a side entrance carrying an ornate copy of the *Scrolls of Çalaht*. He carried the oversized scroll by its two handles, balanced against his chest and shoulders. He crossed the altar to a slanted reading table. His assistant, a gibbon wearing burgundy vestments, slipped off the embroidered cover, and the house minder laid the holy document on the table. He and the assistant then twisted the two handles to wind the lengthy scroll back to its beginning. With a new queen, the lessons and readings would reset to the start in devotional houses across the realm (unless one belonged to one of the contrarian sects, in which case, they scrolled to the end and worked backward).

Eloise took a step forward, but her foot caught on the hem of the ridiculous Raiment of the Queens. She righted herself before she stumbled, delicately hiked the garment so it cleared her feet, and made it to the reading table. She extended her hands above the scroll and said, "These things which I have promised, I will perform and keep. May Çalaht be my guide."

"So be it," said the Venerable Prelate Herself.

"So be it," echoed the gathering.

Even though one was never supposed to touch the holy scroll, there was one exception, and this was it. Eloise leaned forward and planted a series of chaste kisses across the sacred, revered, mystical opening verse of the *Scrolls of Çalaht*:

There once was a gal named Çalaht

Who suffered in life quite a lot

But when she was dead

The people all said

"A holy one! That's what we got!"

Eloise's lips glanced from line to precious line. The scroll's papery hemp parchment felt dry and ancient—not unlike the teachings of Çalaht themselves.

The Venerable Prelate Herself spread out the oath scroll next to the unfurled *Scrolls of Çalaht* and offered Eloise an albino-white peacock feather quill provided by the Quill and Quillery (Yes We Know They're Not Related Concepts) Guild. She dipped the sharpened tip into a pot of ink that, like the absurd Raiment of the Queens, had been used by every Gumball queen before her, and signed her name to the oath.

That formality completed, Eloise returned to her prayer kneeler and knelt.

The Venerable Prelate Herself gestured toward a dish held by the devotional house minder. "These are the anointing oils," said the tapir. "Cassia for dedication and devotion. Salvation Cedar for strength and protection. Holy Fire for purification and empowerment. Myrrh for grace and peace. Pomegranate for blessing and favor. Spikenard for worship and praise. And patchouli because it smells rather nice."

The prelate dipped her largest hooved toe in the oil dish and dabbed the mixture on Eloise's right cheek, left cheek, and the wisdom eye of her forehead—the same pattern as a Western Lands kiss. A small trail of the oil dribbled down her face, and it was all Eloise could do to not wipe it off with the back of her hand.

Next came the investment of the royal regalia. These were brought out by the Crown Jeweler, a toothy brick of a rhesus macaque, whose ruddy face and deep-set eyes made him look like an ancient drunkard. A procession of other macaques, all wearing maroon vestments and white sashes adorned with the Gumball coat of arms, assisted him.

First was the Queen's Robe. Eloise stood and a stack of three macaques piled on each other's shoulders draped it across her back, while the top macaque on another stack fastened the clasp at her throat. Next came the Orb of Alleged Omniscience, the Scepter of This is Much Better than the Stick They Used to Use, the Coronation Spork, and finally the Scimitar of Great Bodily Discomfort If Employed According to Specification, which Eloise was pretty sure her mother had used as a back scratcher.

Finally, it was time for the crown to be plonked. Eloise knelt, inelegantly holding the cumbersome regalia. The Venerable Prelate Herself hefted the Gumballic Heraldic Crown from its velvet pillow, held it aloft for a second time, then said the words enshrined in Protocol: "And heeeeeeeeeere we go!" Then she held the crown half a dozen weak lengths above Eloise's head and let it drop.

Plonk! New queen.

Sweet Çalaht seeking insufferable succulents, Eloise thought. *That sucker's heavy!* The crown sat on her head like an ill-fitting watermelon, pressing down on her neck and shoving her head forward. It was loose, and Eloise feared it would slip off at any second. She should have thought to ask someone if she could practice with it beforehand, but that would have broken a thousand rules of Protocol.

"Arise, Queen Eloise!" exclaimed the Venerable Prelate Herself. "Arise, Queen Eloise Hydra Gumball III, and greet your people!"

Again, Eloise braced on the pew's handrail with her good arm and stood. She kept her head level and her neck rigid, balancing the crown and juggling the regalia. As she stood, so did everyone in the room, just as they had any time her mother had gotten up from a chair.

That would take some getting used to.

"Behold, our queen!" called the Venerable Prelate Herself.

"Behold, our queen!" chorused scores of voices.

"Honor to the queen!" cried the prelate.

"Honor to the queen!" echoed the crowd.

"Honor to the queen!" called the prelate again.

"Honor to the queen!"

Eloise's cheeks went pink. It seemed so heartfelt, but crown or no crown, she didn't feel any different. She certainly didn't feel like a queen. But the external recognition was heartening.

Thank Çalaht, the Crown Plonking was basically over. All that was left was to lead those in the chapel to the Throne Hall for a small reception dinner in her honor.

The Crown Jeweler and an assistant stepped forward, and Eloise returned the spork and the scimitar. She kept the Orb in her broken right hand, as she could just grip it with the tips of fingers, which protruded through her plaster cast, leaving her left hand free to hold the heavier scepter.

Eloise carefully stepped away from her prayer kneeler, aimed herself up the middle aisle, and started walking.

Her mother's head must have been bigger than hers. Or maybe it was Gwendolyn the Irritable with the larger skull, since she was the one who had the GHC made. No one had measured Eloise's head so the crown could be fitted, and it felt like she was wearing a salad bowl made of marble.

As Eloise approached the aisle, Jerome began clapping. His outburst sounded odd in the chapel—one didn't normally applaud in the hall of holiness (not that the Venerable Prelate Herself ever said anything that earned it). But Jerome ramped it up, and his enthusiasm was contagious. Johanna joined in, then her father, and then everyone else. Encouraged, Jerome put two claws in his mouth and let loose an ear-splitting whistle, then yelled, "Honor to the queen. Whoo-hoo! Honor to the queen!" Clapping turned to heartfelt cheering, and Eloise couldn't help but break into a huge smile. The Habanero of Doubt in her guts eased, transforming into a smaller Jalapeño of Possibility.

As she reached Jerome's pew, she mouthed, "Thank you," and winked at her champion. Jerome gave her an exaggerated, hand-wavy bow. Eloise acknowledged this with a small, regal nod.

The nod was a mistake.

So was taking her eyes off where she was going.

As she nodded, Eloise's foot caught the hem of the Raiment of the Queens. The newly crowned monarch tripped, stumbled, and felt the crown slip forward over her eyes.

Without thinking, Eloise reached up with her right hand to steady it, forgetting that she held the Orb of Alleged Omniscience. She clunked herself in the head with the pearlescent sphere, which went flying, but not before knocking into the crown and sending the GHC toppling off.

The Orb of Alleged Omniscience landed with a denting thud and a smattering of gemstones. But no one noticed the damage to the royal relic, nor did they pay any attention to the scepter flying off in the other direction. Instead, they were transfixed by the sight of their freshly minted monarch lurching forward, bobbling the Gumballic Heraldic Crown like she was a hockey sacking changer snagging a fumble.

Fortunately for Eloise, all those years of hockey sacking paid off—she caught the crown with her left hand and clutched it to her middle.

Unfortunately, the Raiment of the Queens was not made for athletic endeavor. Her legs tangled in the ancient, overlong garment, and the crowd gasped as their monarch's first act as queen was to flop face-first toward the chapel's flagstone floor.

Eloise threw out her right hand to break her fall and protect the box with the Star of Whatever. She landed hard, jamming her broken wrist, crushing her plaster cast, and re-cracking her fracture. She cried out in pain as the rest of her body kathunked a moment later, her full weight smashing down on the Gumballic Heraldic Crown.

The realm's most revered symbol of royalty—its highest representation of authority and power, of propriety and legitimacy, of divinely inspired governance and triumph, victory, honor, and glory—flattened like a week-old blancmange left in the sun and struck by a sledgehammer.

The chapel was shocked into silence. The only sound was the Scepter of This is Much Better than the Stick They Used to Use clattering to a halt.

❦ 2 ❦

PERCUSSIVE MAINTENANCE

There was a long moment of frozen horror.

Eloise felt the misshapen twist of metal and gems poking into her sternum. That wasn't good. She was going to have a crown-shaped bruise on her chest. It felt like her nose was broken, and the pain in her wrist made her want to scream. Eloise wondered if there was some way for her to melt into the stone floor, or maybe evaporate and disappear—either would do—so she could avoid the shame of having to stand up and go on with the rest of her life.

They're going to call me "Eloise, the Crown Crusher," she thought.

Lorch was the first to move. He rushed forward and knelt at Eloise's side. "Princess El— Sorry. My queen. Are you alright?"

Jerome, Johanna, and her father also came to her side.

"Do you think anyone noticed?" whispered Eloise.

"It's possible they might have," said Jerome. He made a show of looking around. "There's a bit of murmuring going on. So, yes. It would appear they did."

Johanna put a hand on her sister's shoulder. "You OK?"

Eloise rolled off the flattened crown and sat up. "Ow. Ow, ow, ow." Her wrist felt like it had been stabbed. The damaged crown snagged on the collar ruffle and dangled at her front. Some of its jewels dribbled into her lap.

"Goodness, sweetie," said Chafed. "Your nose is bleeding. Here." The dowager king pulled a white handkerchief from his tunic pocket and handed it to his daughter. "It was clean fairly recently."

"Thanks." Eloise pressed it to her nose for a moment, then looked at it. A large, bright red stain soaked the cloth. She glanced down at the Raiment of the Queens and saw that it, too, now had blotches of red. "Fantastic. I look like I just lost a boxing match."

"What do you want to do?" asked Johanna. "Do we need to get the apothecary? Or a healer?"

"Oh, please. Let's complete my humiliation, shall we? Maybe carry me out on a stretcher." Eloise shook her head. "No, I'll be OK."

"Are you sure?"

"I'm sure." Eloise tried to stand, but it was difficult with the stupid dress, the mangled, dangling crown, the broken wrist, and her good hand pressed against her nose.

"Let me help you," said her father, taking Eloise's left arm.

"My queen, if I may be so bold," said Lorch, taking her right.

"On three," said the dowager king. "One, two, three…"

They hauled Eloise to her feet, accompanied by the clatter of loose precious stones. She thought she heard chuckling from the crowd, but was too embarrassed to look around and see who it was. "Thanks. I should be good."

The Crown Jeweler rushed up from behind, his pink face flushed darker than normal, and gasped when he saw the GHC up close. "Goodness!" said the macaque. "The Gumballic Heraldic Crown! It's… It's rui—"

Lorch put a hand up to stop him. "It's going to be fine." The guard reached forward, and at a nod of assent from Eloise, detached the crown from her frill. His eyebrows shot up. "That sucker's heavy," he said. Lorch looked at it like he was assessing an iron mace damaged on the head of an enemy. He turned it over and over, nodding to himself, considering every angle.

"What do you think?" asked Eloise.

"I think it needs a little percussive maintenance."

"What?"

Lorch turned the damaged crown so the narrowest side was upward. Then he used his fist like a hammer, bashing it back into a circle. He twirled it slowly, considering it again, then whacked the crown with several more strategically directed wallops to finesse the shape. Finally, he gave a satisfied nod. "That should do."

The Crown Jeweler looked like he wanted to faint.

Lorch held the crown toward Eloise. "Prin— Sorry. My queen, if I may."

Eloise nodded. The guard stepped forward and placed the crown on her head. "Behold, our queen."

"Behold, our queen," said Johanna, Chafed, and Jerome.

"Thank you, Lorch." Still holding the handkerchief to her face, Eloise jiggled her head, feeling how the crown sat. "Actually, that fits much better. Well done, Guard Lacksneck."

Lorch's face reddened. "Thank you, my queen."

Eloise looked at the others. "I think I've provided enough spectacle. Shall we go to the reception dinner? Not that I feel like it, but it remains on the agenda."

"Yes, my queen," they all said.

Jerome reached down and began gathering the loose gems. The Crown Jeweler joined him.

Chafed found the Orb of Alleged Omniscience beneath a pew and held it out for Eloise. The pearl-like sphere had a chip out of it, and the gold encasement had been severely damaged. "They'll have to rename it the Flattened, Dented Oblong of Alleged Omniscience."

Eloise smiled thinly. "That has a ring to it. Perhaps you could do me the kindness of carrying it for me?"

"Of course," Chafed said, then added, "My queen." He positioned himself a few paces behind Eloise, ready to be part of the procession.

Lorch had retrieved the Scepter of This is Much Better than the Stick They Used to Use, and with a bow, offered it to Eloise. "Thank you, Guard Lacksneck," she said. "I'd be grateful if you could bring it for me."

"Yes, my queen." Lorch took a spot behind Chafed.

"Right then," said Eloise. "Shall we?"

"Just a sec," said Johanna. She stepped behind Eloise and gathered the Raiment of the Queens and the Queen's Robe and held them like they were a bridal gown's train. "That should keep it from underfoot."

"Thanks, Jo."

"You're welcome, Queen Eloise."

Then, for the second time, Eloise aimed herself up the middle aisle and started walking. She stared straight ahead, not wanting to see any mocking eyes or amused expressions, not wanting to think about what sensationalism the gossip heralds would reap from her Crown Plonking misfortune, and strode out of the chapel with as much dignity as a bleeding nose, a refractured wrist, and a bent crown allowed.

3

WAS IT YOU?

Eloise walked from the chapel to the Throne Hall without further incident. This struck her as an incredible triumph, given what had just happened. The GHC fit better after Lorch's attentions, but the weight of it still pressed on her. Her mother must have had a neck like an ironwood stump. At least the thing stayed on as she led the procession past the Salon des Champions, around the wintry, snow-caked Culpability Courtyard, lit by the last rays of dusk, through a couple of internal hallways, and to the Throne Hall itself.

Peering in, Eloise saw that the hall looked lightly decorated, which was appropriate, since the official status was that Court was in mourning. Normally, she'd have expected to see dozens of white banners embroidered with the Gumball crest (a weasel on a bushel of onions and a one-eyed otter holding a fire poker). Instead, there were a few somber black ones with the crest in shades of maroon and silver. Adding a splash of color were orchids brought out from a hothouse for the occasion. Half the banquet tables had a vase with a golden disa orchid, its bright yellow blossoms bringing a touch of sunshine. The other half had a small orchid with tiny purple flowers that somehow smelled of lime zest and talcum powder.

Eloise quickly tucked the hanky into her sleeve, hoping her nosebleed was done. As she stepped into the hall, a herald announced her. "Her Majesty, Queen Eloise Hydra Gumball III. Long may the crown-plonked queen live!"

Everyone stood, turned, and looked at her. Eloise wondered if they all knew what had just happened. It was safe to assume they did, since gossip traveled faster than a longwalker with his breeks on fire. Her cheeks flushed pink as she imagined them all sniggering about her as she walked past them.

Eloise strode toward the center of the room, allowing everyone to bow or curtsy as she passed. On the dais, a single throne—her mother's—stood by itself. The rest—hers, her sister's, and her father's—had been cleared away. Flanking the throne were small tables, one with the golden disa and the other the lime-talcum orchid. As she walked, she heard the rustle of those who'd been in the chapel filing in behind her.

She paused at the step up to the dais and drew a breath. Eloise flexed the fingers on her right hand and winced. Her wrist would need attention sooner rather than later. She readied herself to step up and sit on her mother's throne for the first time.

"I'm letting go of your train now," said Johanna. "Please be careful, Queen Eloise."

Eloise turned and looked at her sister. "Come on up, Jo. Keep me company. They can bring another chair. Or even your throne. I can ask them to do that."

Johanna shook her head, then subtly moved her hands in the private sign language the twins had developed when they were young. *I don't think that's such a good idea*, she signed. *Plus, it's against Protocol in about a dozen ways.*

Eloise's shoulders drooped. She signed back, despite the throbbing in her wrist. *Right. Such is Protocol.*

Johanna nodded. *Yes, such is Protocol.* She gave her sister an encouraging smile. *This is your moment. It's the start of your reign. People need to see you as you, not as one of the two of us.*

I guess you're right. Eloise lifted a shoulder. *I just don't feel like a queen. I feel like a goofball in a dumb outfit pretending to be queen.*

The first time in front of everyone was always going to be weird. Johanna nodded toward their mother's throne. *It's all yours. Have a seat. Go be queen. Everyone's waiting.*

Eloise nodded. *Thanks, Jo.*

You are most welcome, Queen Eloise. Somehow, Johanna conveyed just a hint of joshing with her hands.

Eloise smiled, hiked the hem of the Raiment of the Queens to a safe height, and headed for her mother's throne. She stopped in front of it, carefully turned to face the room, and spoke the words her mother had used to open hundreds of gatherings: "My friends."

"Our queen," chorused the voices as one.

"Please be at rest."

People relaxed, but no one sat.

"Right," said Eloise. "Got it." She sat on the throne and tried again. "Please be at rest."

Everyone sat at their banquet tables, keeping their attention on her.

At a nod, Lorch and her father mounted the dais. Chafed placed the Orb of Alleged Omniscience on the table to Eloise's left, careful to position it so the chipped, dented side faced away from the crowd. Eloise took the Scepter of This is Much Better than the Stick They Used to Use from Lorch and laid it across her lap. Chafed and Lorch bowed and left her alone. Her father took a seat at a table in front with Johanna, First Advisor Ligurian, Other Places Advocate Bërnädïce-Ändrëä Thëjëts, and a few others. Lorch marched off at attention to stand at the side of the room.

Eloise sat there for a minute, surveying the room. It looked a lot like every other time she'd sat up on the dais with her family. The angle was a little different, since she was right in the middle instead of off to the side. And it was a little lonely. But otherwise, it felt normal.

But nothing about this was normal. Certainly not with the crown sitting like a granite basin on her head. She wasn't sure how long she could stand wearing the thing.

Plus, there was something wrong with her throne. She wriggled a little, but it was still there—an uncomfortable lump in the seat cushion. Eloise stood, being careful not to let the Gumballic Heraldic Crown topple, turned, and fluffed the seat cushion.

As one, the room behind her clattered to their feet.

Eloise turned back around and looked at them, briefly confused. They stared at her, expectant and waiting.

"Sorry," said Eloise. "Sorry, sorry, sorry. Please be at rest."

Silence. No one moved.

"Right."

Eloise sat.

Everyone else sat.

The cushion still wasn't right.

She'd live with it.

Had her mother endured years of uncomfortable seating to avoid inconveniencing entire rooms full of people? She didn't remember the late queen squirming all the time, but then, that wasn't the kind of thing Eloise would necessarily have noticed.

A few minutes passed with people whispering and looking at her. She assumed they were talking about the disaster in the chapel. Ten minutes later, it occurred to her that everyone seemed to be waiting. Eloise looked from table to table, trying to work it out.

She saw First Advisor Ligurian suddenly lift his index finger. Just a little, but sharp enough and high enough to be noticeable. His wrist rested on the table, his eyes locked on hers, and his index finger was definitely up and wagging slightly, like a pudgy baby cobra paying attention to his music lessons. Eloise furrowed her brow at him. Ligurian crooked his raised finger and pointed at something on the table. His napkin? His goblet?

Eloise gave him a tiny shake of the head.

He pointed toward the table again, then turned his wrist and pointed to the side. To Bënnïë-Änn Thëjëts, maybe? Eloise narrowed her eyes further and shook her head again, just once. Ligurian tilted his chin just a few degrees and shifted his eyes, like he was looking at something in the distance, and pointed again.

Eloise looked in the direction he indicated. There were more tables full of people of all species. Nothing remarkable there. She looked all the way to the wall.

Oh. That was it.

There in the entryway to the kitchens, two columns of servers holding trays stood at attention, awaiting their cue to bring in the meal. Eloise looked back at Ligurian, nodded, and mouthed, "Thank you."

She stood, waited for everyone to do the same, then said, "Let us be grateful to Çalaht for the bounty that is this meal, as well as to the farmers who grew it, and those who prepared it. Bless this food."

"Bless this food," echoed everyone.

"Please be at rest." Eloise sat, allowing everyone to do the same. Then she raised her injured right hand and waved the servants into the room.

Dozens of servers bustled into the Throne Hall, hauling trays laden with a soup that smelled of asparagus and cayenne, dishes of soy ricotta to dollop on top, and baskets of black bread rolls to dunk. The lead server approached the dais carrying her mother's silver tray, but Eloise waved him away. "Please, feed everyone else first."

"I beg your pardon, Your Highness?"

"It's OK. I'm not hungry. I'll wait until after everyone else is served."

"But Protocol insists that the queen—"

"Protocol hasn't had the day that I have had." She looked at the server, a lank man with greased-back black hair, a nose like he'd slammed into a door a few too many times, and a perfectly pressed footman's tunic. "May I ask your name?" said Eloise.

"Nütflüx, Your Highness."

"Lovely to meet you, Master Nütflüx. I appreciate what you're doing, but I'll need to eat later, perhaps once my stomach doesn't feel like a trapeze act."

"Yes, Your Highness. Of course, Your Highness. If Her Highness would let me put the tray on her table, Protocol would be satisfied."

Eloise suppressed a sigh. "Sure. If that's needed."

"Thank you, Your Highness." He put the tray down carefully, but left the meal covered. "Would Her Majesty like something for her royal stomach? Perhaps a drink of slippery elm bark tea? That would be my dear gran's suggestion, although she'd have called it soft elm or moose elm, not slippery elm, although moose don't like the latter name so much. Eldridge the Apothecary would have some, for sure. I could fetch it."

"A slippery elm would be splendid." Eloise held up her fractured wrist. "And if Eldridge the Apothecary has some willow bark or devil's claw, that would be great as well."

"Yes, Your Highness. May I suggest a damp cloth to tidy up..." He trailed off, but waved his open palm subtly to indicate his face. "There are hints of... Of redness."

"Fabulous. I just addressed everyone covered in blood."

"Hints of it."

"A damp towel would be splendid."

"Someone will be back in a moment, Your Highness."

"Thank you, Master Nütflüx."

She watched the server glide back to the kitchen and disappear into its maw. Eloise drew out her father's handkerchief from her sleeve and touched her nose with it again. No fresh blood. Thank Çalaht for small mercies.

Something to settle her stomach had been a good idea. She was grateful to Nütflüx.

Eloise glanced back at First Advisor Ligurian, who slurped soup and dunked rolls with a singular, almost ferocious, determination. Her mother's words about him—some of the last she'd spoken—were burned into Eloise's memory. "The First Advisor is smart and loyal. He knows where the bodies are buried, much better than your father, who doesn't have the mind or temperament for that kind of thing. Most of the bodies will be metaphorical, but not all. I suggest you keep the First Advisor in his role, at least for a while."

Well, it had been kind of him to help her out in his small, finger-pointing way. Perhaps her mother was right, and he'd be someone to rely on. She'd need good, reliable people. Like Jerome. Like Lorch. Like Hector and the Nameless One. Only with a bit of nous for Court.

An approaching servant awkwardly balancing a silver tea tray interrupted her thinking. "Excuse me, mistress— I mean, excuse me, Queen Eloise. Sorry, I'm not used to that yet."

"Läääcy de Aardvark. What a pleasant surprise. And, trust me, I'm not used to it yet, either. Have you started helping in the kitchens?"

"Only a little." The aardvark put the tray on the edge of the table to Eloise's right, sliding the orchid over to make room. She picked up the plant, placed it on a shelf below the tabletop, and slid the tea tray into position. "My sister is a scullery wench, ma'am. Only she has a stomach ague of some sort, and I didn't want to leave them short-staffed on a day like today. So I popped on her apron and took her shift."

"That's very kind of you." There was a damp napkin folded in the shape of a lotus blossom. Eloise patted it across her cheeks, nose, and chin. Her nose was sore, and she feared she'd be badly bruised. The cloth came away tinged red. Eloise showed her face to the aardvark. "Did I get it?"

"Mostly." Läääcy pointed to several spots on her own cheeks and forehead, indicating where Eloise needed to try again.

How had it gotten all over? Eloise tried to remember if she'd smeared it somehow.

She dabbed a second pass. "Now?"

The aardvark shook her head and pointed to her face again. "Still some here, here, and here."

Eloise held the cloth out to Läääcy. "Could you?"

"Oh, mistress!" whispered Läääcy. "I mean, oh my queen! Surely not here in front of everyone."

Eloise let the cloth droop. "It would hardly be the most embarrassing thing that's happened to me today." She proffered the handkerchief again. "Go on."

"Yes, ma'am." Läääcy approached the throne with a curtsy, then took the cloth. Blocking the room's view with her body as best she could, she gave her queen a delicate and discreet face wash. When the aardvark finished, she stepped back, took a careful last look, and gave a nod of approval with her tubular snout. "There you go, Queen Eloise."

"Thank you, Läääcy," said Eloise. "I look forward to seeing a bit more of you as a handmaid, now that I'll have a retinue and not just Odmilla."

Läääcy looked down at her forefeet and said nothing.

"What?" asked Eloise.

"Nothing, Queen Eloise."

"Go ahead."

"Lady Seneschal has not brought me onto the Queen's personal staff of ladies-in-waiting or handmaids."

"No?"

Läääcy shook her head. "It is her domain. We serve at her pleasure."

"Not at mine?"

"With due respect, my queen, it has always been Lady Seneschal who has organized the queen's servants. The queen has much more impor-tant things to do than worry about her maids."

"Is Odmilla on the handmaid staff?"

"No, my queen."

"Really?"

"Not that I know of, my queen."

That was odd. Why wouldn't her handmaid automatically stay in that role, even if it were part of a larger group? Clearly, there was a conver-sation to be had with Lady Seneschal.

Eloise picked up her cup of slippery elm tea and sipped it. The viscous texture was always a bit of a shock, but a generous dollop of rice malt helped the taste. It was like drinking sweetened slime. She sipped, then sipped again.

Eloise set down the cup and looked at Läääcy, She tilted her head slightly, considering, and beckoned the aardvark to come closer.

Läääcy curtsied nervously, took a few steps toward the throne, and curtsied again. "Yes, ma'am?"

Eloise leaned forward and whispered, "Would you like to be one of the queen's handmaids?"

The aardvark looked down, and Eloise guessed the skin beneath her cheek fur was becoming pinker. "Yes, ma'am. It would be my honor, if it would please the queen."

"I'd love to have you," said Eloise. "I can't make any promises, but let me see what's possible."

"Thank you, Queen Eloise." The aardvark curtsied without looking up. "That... That would be wonderful."

Eloise dismissed Läääcy (which felt awkward) and watched the servant bow her way backward off the dais and disappear into the kitchens. At least one person was now happy she was queen.

It was a start.

The reception dinner wore on, but Eloise's appetite did not return. Normally, she might have slipped herself an extra dessert—who could go past a chocolate cupcake with raspberry buttercream? But one nibble reminded her that Chef hadn't been involved in making them, which made her sad all over again. After drinking the slippery elm, she sipped some of the haggleberry tea that Läääcy had brought, using it to wash down a small mountain of willow bark shreds that had been pulverized and pressed into tablets. They'd take a while to kick in. Meanwhile, the throbbing in her wrist persisted.

She sat there, embarrassed, in pain, and overwhelmed, and did something that had eluded her since her mother died—she thought about things. She allowed memories of her mother to bubble up. The easiest ones to remember were the most recent ones. Eloise didn't think she'd ever forget watching her mother die—her pupils too large for the amount of light in the room, the infinite look in her eyes, the backward pressing of her head into her pillow, and the way her hand had tightened in Eloise's, a squeeze Eloise would always hold in her heart, and maybe her nightmares, too.

The difference between "the Queen is in her body" and "the queen is no longer in her body" was profound, pronounced, and immediate. Eloise understood exactly where the phrase "giving up the ghost" came from.

Her mother had died and a chaos of consequences erupted. They were still playing out, and would continue to do so for months. Years. Probably for the rest of her life.

Even though the reception was not supposed to be a meet-and-greet, now and then, someone would approach the dais with a bow or curtsy, an "Honor to the queen," and a parting wish for her longevity and good health. Eloise recognized some of the people, but there were many she didn't know. Court was awash with faces she didn't have names for, and there were also names she knew but couldn't put a face to. But no matter who it was who came before her, Eloise heard a small, insistent voice niggling in the back of her head, silently asking, "Are you the one who had my mother killed? Was it you who organized for two raw haggleberries to be slipped into her pie? Is her death on your hands, your paws, your claws?"

It was a dark thought to go with her darkening mood. An unworthy question for this particular event.

Or was it?

Eloise had put off focusing on that particular problem, but she'd have to face it soon. The "how" of the late queen's death was well established. But the "who" and the "why" remained cloaked in darkness, and had Eloise spooked.

If someone wanted her mother dead so badly that they had her murdered, then surely they'd be planning a similar fate for Eloise as well. Sauce for the pie was sauce for the cake.

This is getting bleak, Eloise thought. *And this reception is getting long.* She wondered how the thing was supposed to end. Eloise needed some alone time, and maybe a decent night's sleep. Now that she was queen, it seemed like that was a reasonable thing to expect. She felt like she'd done her bit at the reception—she'd given everyone time to gawk at her outfit, whisper about her Crown Plonking failings, and murmur in low voices about the ill tidings such a poor performance augured.

How would her mother have dealt with this?

That was easy. She'd have stood up, maybe said a couple of words, and left the room.

Eloise could do the same.

She was queen, after all.

❈ 4 ❈

BO BO AND EVERYTHING

E loise stood, careful to keep her crown balanced.

It took a few heartbeats for someone to notice. The first person who saw her was an elderly mandrill she didn't know, who wore a captain's epaulets and sat at a table to her far right. He stood, then tapped the shoulder of his companion, who quickly did the same. A tide of awareness washed across the room, and over a very long 15 seconds, everyone stood and slowly went quiet.

When all eyes were on Eloise, she said, "My friends." Her voice caught and the words came out with a hint of a squeak.

"Our queen," came the reply.

Eloise swallowed and continued. "Thank you for joining me today to mark this moment. I know that some of you here would have seen my mother at her Crown Plonking, or at least her formal coronation. Perhaps in the coming days, I'll have a chance to speak with you about those times. I'd love to know more about your memories of her from the start of her reign. I..."

To Eloise's horror, she felt tears welling up, uncontrolled and ready to gush. *No!* she thought. *Now is not the time to come across like a blubbering fool.*

She reached up with her right hand to wipe her eye, saw there were still drops of blood staining her cast, and dabbed the corners of her eyes as she fought to control her voice. "I hope you don't mind me saying it, but I miss the late queen, may she stand with Çalaht. I'm sure you do as well. I miss her as a queen, as a role model, and as a mother." Eloise looked around the room. She wasn't the only one with a tear in her eye. "I look forward to gathering with you again in two days for her memorial, when we'll have the bittersweet task of celebrating her life and memory. Until then, thank you again for being here today."

Eloise picked up the Orb of Alleged Omniscience, cradled the Scepter of This is Much Better than the Stick They Used to Use to her middle, hiked the Raiment of the Queens to a safe height above her ankles, and stepped carefully off the dais. Back straight and head high, Eloise strode from the room, determined to exit without making herself look foolish again.

She made it out the door, upright and still holding the two objects. Another minor success. Plus, no one seemed to rush after her to tell her what to do.

Good.

But where to now? More than anything, Eloise wanted to escape to her room, slip out of the awful dress, sit by the fire, have a last haggleberry tea, and then get some sleep. Exhausted and hurting, it palled to think of doing anything more queenlike than saying goodnight to Bo Bo, the stuffed Gila monster that had been her favorite toy when she was a girl, and who still watched over her from her bedside table every night.

She turned and headed down the hall toward her room.

"Queen Eloise?"

Eloise turned and stopped. "Lady Seneschal."

Lady Seneschal Älphonsinä Füüürchtbarkeit Póöòmáäàdéëè was a thin, older woman a head taller than Eloise. She wore a black robe buttoned from her severe collar to her ankles, and her only concession to decoration was a barely perceptible hint of black lace at her neck. Eloise had never seen her wear anything else; it was as if Lady Seneschal spent her whole life in mourning. Her hair was a long, dyed-black braid twisted into a coil at the back of her head like a barnacle, and her face had the warmth of an anvil trapped in a glacier.

For as long as Eloise could remember, she'd been deathly afraid of Lady Seneschal. The woman was uncompromising, stern, and had never been shy about telling Eloise and Johanna what to do, how to do it, and when—with their mother's full backing. "Do as Lady Seneschal says" was a stock phrase of their mother's. It was never "See what you can work out with Lady Seneschal" or "Lady Seneschal, perhaps it might be OK this one time." It was "Lady Seneschal knows what she's talking about," "Lady Seneschal deserves your respect and obedience," and "If you cannot abide what Lady Seneschal says, you may stay in your room until you can."

Lady Seneschal held a scroll in her right hand. She was forever checking it or noting something down on it, and she was not above rapping it on someone's noggin if she felt they'd not heard her adequately. "Queen Eloise, may I ask what you're doing?" She crossed her arms in front of her and tapped the scroll against her bicep.

"I'm tired. It's late enough. I'm calling it a night."

"First Advisor Ligurian has your briefing ready."

"Does he?"

"He does."

"Briefing for what?"

"He is in the habit of briefing the queen on matters of importance daily."

"I see."

"If you'll follow me, I'll—"

"Lady Seneschal, may I ask a question first?"

"Of course, Queen Eloise."

"Is there anything of particular import that First Advisor needs to convey? Any great urgencies? Any matters that need a rapid decision?"

"I don't know. I'm not privy to the contents of his briefings."

"Lady Seneschal, you saw the Crown Plonking, did you not?" asked Eloise.

The dour woman tried to keep her face neutral, but couldn't help pursing her lips. "Yes, I did."

"Then, please, allow me some quiet. Do me the kindness of asking the First Advisor on my behalf if we can pick up the running of the queendom tomorrow morning. If he absolutely must see me, then fine. Otherwise, we'll resume my mother's routine after I've slept."

"Very well, Queen Eloise. I'll speak to him after I've taken you to your room."

"No need. I'll make my own way."

Lady Seneschal ignored that last comment and said, "Please follow."

Which didn't make sense. It wasn't like Eloise was going to get lost. But she was too tired to argue, so she fell in behind the older woman and focused on not falling or dropping anything.

Five minutes later, as they neared Eloise's door, Lady Seneschal continued on past it.

Eloise paused. "Lady Seneschal, where are we going?"

She looked at Eloise, puzzled. "To the Salle de la Famille."

"Why?"

"It contains the queen's bedchamber."

Eloise knitted her brow. "That's where my parents sleep. Well, just my father now."

"It is the queen's room. You are queen now. It is your room."

"What? What are you saying?"

"The dowager king has taken a room further down the hall, more suited to his status as dowager king. The queen's room is now your room."

"Please don't call him the dowager king. He'll hate it. Also, you turfed my father out of his room? Just like that? That's not..."

"Queen Eloise, we followed Protocol. Would you have us do otherwise? The queen sleeps in the queen's bedchamber, which is in the queen's quarters beyond the Salle de la Famille. We have systems and processes set up that rely on that fact. The infrastructure and resources devoted to supporting the queen in her duties are in place with that assumption."

Eloise stopped. "Resources?"

"Yes. The servants, handmaids, chambermaids, keepers of the wardrobe—"

"Did you just refer to people as 'resources?'"

Lady Seneschal gestured for Eloise to keep moving. "Yes, of course. There are human resources and non-human resources, although technically speaking, non-human resources cover both the living and the inanimate. Would you have us disrupt the living resources, both human and non-human, in carrying out their duties?"

"I guess not. But can we not call them 'resources?'"

"Not resources? What then?"

"People."

Lady Seneschal gave her a you-have-so-much-to-learn look. "You can, of course, decree that you'd rather sleep somewhere else in the castle. You could decree that henceforth, you'll be sleeping in a ditch behind the Drunken Baboon Inn and Haberdashery, and I would move heaven and earth to make that happen. But I can't just snap my fingers, just like you can't snap yours. Organizing the resources—sorry, Your Highness—organizing the *people* that would allow you to sleep in a ditch would take some coordination. It's doable, but I'd need half a day."

"I don't intend to sleep in a ditch, Lady Seneschal. Although, it would not be the first time if I did."

"Yes, my queen." There was something in the way Lady Seneschal said it that sounded like a criticism, an unspoken comment about Eloise's months away, and the fact that she hadn't been there when her mother had taken ill.

They reached the doorway to the Salle de la Famille, and Lady Seneschal stopped so that Eloise could enter first.

Eloise walked into the front room. It looked the same.

She stepped through the family room to the queen's bedchamber beyond, stopped, and peered around.

It felt wrong.

The room didn't belong to her, even though she'd spent hours and hours in there with her parents and sister, especially when the twins had been girls. The canopied bed, the furniture, the mirrors—they belonged to her parents.

Plus, the last time she'd been in the room, her mother's lifeless body had still been lying under the covers. Its presence lingered, and Eloise wondered if there was still a whiff of it hanging around. Not comforting.

That thought made her wonder just how many of her ancestors had given up the ghost on that particular mattress. Surely it had been swapped out sometime over the centuries?

The thought made her skin crawl.

Lady Seneschal stepped past Eloise and pointed with her scroll. "We've brought in your things."

It was true. Her parents' personal touches and accoutrements were gone. Her mother's inevitable stack of scrolls, ink, and quills. Her father's dish of polished stones. Their clothes. Her mother's powders, ointments, medicaments, and unctions. Her father's favorite paintings by Alstaria Snotearrow McCcoonnch—one depicting cats wearing period garb playing hockey sacking and one with the cats wearing period garb playing whist. There was a different color to the wall paint where they'd once hung. She guessed they were now in her father's new room, wherever that was.

The chamber had the tidied sparseness of a well-kept inn.

In place of her parents' stuff, Eloise's possessions were now placed around the room. Her combs and hairbrush sat on her mother's vanity. The trunk with her dresses had been hauled in and put in a corner near a wardrobe, and the clothes taken out and hung. Whoever had moved her things in had tried to approximate their placement, which was considerate. But her knickknacks and precious things felt out of context and wrong.

It was disorienting.

And someone (or more than one person) had touched all of it. She didn't like that.

Bo Bo was there, sitting on a shelf like he didn't matter, instead of taking pride of place on her bed. That, and the fact that her robes and dresses weren't hung in strict order of rainbow hue, showed that whoever had done it didn't know her very well. Odmilla had clearly not been involved.

Eloise put down the Scepter and Orb on a side table, nodded to the older woman, and said, "Thank you, Lady Seneschal. All seems in order. Is there anything else you need from me?"

"No, Queen Eloise. Is there anything else you require of me?"

"No, Lady Seneschal. Thank you."

"I'll send in one of the handmaids to help you undress."

"That would be helpful. There are a lot of buttons. Plus..." She lifted her hand with the cast.

"Yes, Queen Eloise. I'll see you in the morning. Please call out or ring that bell if you require anything."

"Thank you. I will."

Lady Seneschal curtsied and took her leave.

Eloise picked up Bo Bo, gave him a little pat and a hug, and placed him on the bed. Then she sat on the stool of her mother's vanity, yearning to be free of the ridiculous dress. She closed her eyes and tried to feel if her mother's spirit was still in the room. Her odor was there—hints of the perfume she sometimes wore—mixed with whiffs of her father.

This was going to be weird.

She reached up and touched the crown on her head. "How did you wear this thing?" she asked the air.

There was no reply

LEAVE IT WITH ME

There was a knock at the door.

Expecting the handmaid, Eloise called, "Come in, please."

The door opened. It was the Crown Jeweler. The red-faced rhesus macaque took a deferential step into the room. "I'm here for the royal regalia, ma'am."

"Which bits did you want?" asked Eloise.

The macaque squinted a little. His deep-set eyes made it look like he was seeing her from very far away. "Why, all of them. We'll collect the Raiment of the Queens from you tomorrow, since you're still wearing it. But tonight, I'll secure the Orb of Alleged Omniscience, the Scepter of This is Much Better than the Stick They Used to Use, the Queen's Robe, and the Gumballic Heraldic Crown."

Something made Eloise hesitate. She hardly felt like she was queen, and now he wanted to take away the only things that made her feel the least bit queenish? And how was she supposed to get used to wearing the crown if she didn't have it on? Surely her mother didn't have the required neck muscles right away. Eloise needed to get used to the thing.

"I'm happy for you to take the scepter, the orb, and the cloak. And, of course, the dress. You can burn the dress for all I care."

The macaque gasped at that, but said nothing.

"However, I'd like you to leave the crown with me."

The Crown Jeweler took a step backward. "I beg your pardon, ma'am?"

Eloise pointed to the GHC. "The crown. This. I'd like you to leave it here. With me."

"My queen, I'm supposed to—"

Eloise held up a finger to stop him, like she'd seen her mother do ten thousand times. The Crown Jeweler closed his mouth. "Crown Jeweler... Sorry, I don't know your name."

"Esteban, ma'am. Esteban de Macaque."

"Crown Jeweler de Macaque, who does the Gumballic Heraldic Crown belong to?"

He swallowed. "Technically, it belongs to you."

"Technically or actually?"

He hesitated. "Both, ma'am."

"May I ask, do you, in your professional opinion, think I present a risk to the crown?"

Eloise knew the correct answer was, "Of course. You flattened the thing just a few hours ago." But the Crown Jeweler knew better than to be truthful. "No, ma'am. Of course not."

"Do you think the crown is at risk here in this room? Or from those who will come into this room between now and tomorrow morning?"

"No, ma'am. Everyone who would be likely to come in here was properly vetted, especially since the, uh, the, uh..."

"Since the problem that killed my mother?"

"Yes, ma'am. Since then." A flush pinked the Crown Jeweler's cheeks. Eloise could just detect it beneath the hair on his face.

"Then, if you could please leave the crown with me, I'd—"

"Ma'am, I'm sorry, but—"

Eloise stood up from the chair, and the Crown Jeweler bowed his head and fell silent. She lowered her voice to a whisper, something else she'd seen her mother do ten thousand times. "I have had a most unusual day, and I'm feeling out of sorts for a million different reasons, not the least of which is that we're still having this conversation. I don't mean to be curt, but will you please just leave my crown with me."

"Queen Eloise, I—"

"Just for now. I understand it is a rare and precious thing. I understand that your responsibility is to get it, and what I'm supposed to do is give it to you so someone can put back in its proper spot. Maybe you'll repair it first. But see it from my point of view. I just need to get used to a few things. So, leave the crown with me. I promise not to drop it a second time."

"Yes, Queen Eloise. I understand."

"Thank you."

The Crown Jeweler moved to the table, picked up the Orb and deliberately did not examine it, although Eloise could see his long fingers feeling for the damage.

"Yeah, sorry about that," said Eloise. "I'm hoping you can fix the metalwork and jewels. I don't know what you'll be able to do about the chip out of the sphere itself."

"Actually, Your Highness, the missing sliver has long not been there. That, uh, change, did not happen today."

"Oh. Good to know. Sorry for the rest of it, then."

"Yes, Your Highness." The Crown Jeweler stowed the Orb of Alleged Omniscience in a bag around his waist, hefted the scepter, and waited while Eloise undid the clasp of the cloak and laid it across his outstretched arms.

"Thank you, Your Highness."

"And again, sorry about the oopsie."

"It was an oopsie, Your Highness. A dramatic oopsie, but an oopsie." Eloise couldn't tell if his tone was forgiving or chastising, so she let it be.

There was another knock as the macaque bowed his way backward toward the door.

"Yes?" called Eloise.

The door cracked open, the Crown Jeweler slipped out, and a hand-maid—a peahen whose name Eloise didn't know—peeked in. "Queen Eloise?"

"You're here to help with this?" Eloise held up her arm and waggled a sleeve.

"Yes, Your Highness."

"Thank Çalaht. Please come in."

The peahen's beak was incredibly dexterous, and she had Eloise unbuttoned and out of the dress in a third of the time that it had taken to put it on. Thirty seconds after that, Eloise was in her nightie, and two minutes later the handmaid excused herself from the room, leaving the new queen with a bedside candle ready for her to blow out when she went to sleep.

Alone at last.

Eloise climbed onto her parents' bed. She picked the crown up off the bedside table and put it on the pillow next to where she'd sleep. She put the box containing the Star of Whatever next to it, then propped Bo Bo against both of them. She climbed under the covers, puffed out the candle, and closed her eyes.

She'd be asleep in moments.

Except she wasn't.

Eloise was what she called "tired-wired," a feeling of exhaustion so profound it left her buzzing and unable to drop off.

Plus, there was too much history in the bed for her to settle. It left her tossing and turning.

Her mother had lain dead on this very spot just days before. *Toss.* The late queen's lifeless expression hung in Eloise's mind and wouldn't go away. *Turn.* Her corpse had first grown cold here. *Toss.* Her parents would have done things in the bed while both of them were alive. *Turn.* In fact, Eloise and Johanna had been born right there. *Toss.* Probably her grandmother had slept there. *Turn.* She'd probably died there, too. *Toss.* When was the last time the bed was swapped out? Or at least the mattress. *Turn.* How many of her Gumball queen ancestors had been born, lived, loved, and died on this very sack stuffed with cotton? *Toss.* Ugh. *Turn.*

Her thoughts chased themselves around and around for hours, long after the banked fire gave up the last of its glowing red light.

I need sleep, thought Eloise. *I can't be exhausted on my first real day as queen.*

After lying on her back staring, wide awake, into the darkness, there seemed just one thing to do. Eloise got out of bed, pulled on her dressing robe, and lit a candle from the fireplace. She grabbed Bo Bo, the box, and the crown, and opened the door as quietly as she could.

She walked down the hall to what had, until that morning, been her room and slipped into it. Her things weren't there, of course, but the furniture was—including, most importantly, her bed with its familiar mattress and bedding.

What was just as important was what wasn't there—the ghosts of her mother and ancestors.

Eloise crept under the covers of her childhood bed, smelled the familiar smell of her pillow, gave Bo Bo a hug, patted the Star of Whatever's box one last time, sending a "G'night, Sparky" to it, and was asleep after half a dozen breaths.

❦ *6* ❦

HELP THE QUEEN BE THE QUEEN

Eloise woke to daylight streaming through the window. She blinked, yawned, and realized she must've slept much later than she'd intended. Her room looked empty without all her things, but at least she'd gotten a few solid hours of shut-eye.

She looked around and sighed. None of her clothes were there. That meant she'd have to walk through the hallway in her nightie and robe to her parents' room. It wouldn't be a mortifying embarrassment. Servants had seen her in her sleepwear often enough. But somehow it felt different to be running around in her jammies now she was queen.

Eloise rubbed the stiff muscles of her neck and looked around for the crown, but it wasn't on the pillow anymore. It had fallen off the side of the bed. She snatched it up and checked for new damage. A couple more jewels had come loose, but it wasn't too bad. She slipped them into a pocket and hoped the Crown Jeweler wouldn't notice.

It hadn't yet been 24 hours since her Crown Plonking, and the new day did not allay her doubt that she deserved to wear the thing. Would she ever feel she did? Or would it always sit like a stranger perched on her head?

She had to get used to it. She had to. So Eloise put the crown on her head and silently vowed to leave it there until it no longer felt like an intruder.

Eloise tied the box with the Star of Whatever back onto her hip, slipped into her dressing robe, smoothed down her nightie, and popped Bo Bo into a pocket. She couldn't check her reflection in the mirror, because it had been moved.

No problem. With any luck, she'd be back in her parents' room before anyone saw her.

"Time to face the day," she said to no one, as she turned the handle and stepped into the hall.

Eloise emerged to full-on pandemonium.

Guards and servants rushed past, their faces scrunched in unseeing worry. Down the hall, she saw Jerome hurrying away from her.

Something horrible must have happened.

"Jerome!" she called. "What's going on?"

Instantly, the chaos clattered to a halt. Everyone looked at her, relief washing across their faces.

"What?" said Eloise.

Jerome's scampered toward her. "Oh, thank Çalaht. You're safe."

"What do you mean, I'm safe?"

Lady Seneschal strode around the corner, past the frozen, staring guards and servants. She stopped in front of Eloise and gave the smallest possible curtsy allowed by Protocol. She looked at her new queen, glanced at the door behind her, stared around at the dozens of people standing in the corridor, and humphed. The old woman crossed her arms and tapped her scroll into the crook of her elbow. "Am I to understand that none of you thought to check the queen's old room?"

Silence.

"Incredible. Simply incredible."

More silence.

"Don't stand there like the Divine One has scooped out your brains." Lady Seneschal's voice was pinched, like she could barely stand to let it out of her throat. "Back to work. Go. Now."

Everyone scattered, and the hall was cleared within seconds.

Except for Jerome. He took a step forward. "I—"

Lady Seneschal pointed her scroll at him. "You, too, Champion Abernatheen de Chipmunk. If the Queen wishes to speak with you, she will let you know. Once she is dressed properly."

"But—"

"Go."

Jerome nodded at Eloise and went.

The old woman turned her severe look on Eloise. "Blessings of the day to you, Queen Eloise," she said in a tone that clearly said, "Good morning, you unthinking, empty-skulled reprobate."

"Blessings of the day to you, too, Lady Seneschal." Eloise's cheeks prickled with embarrassment. She straightened, and held the woman's look. "I trust all is well with you this morning?"

Lady Seneschal arched an eyebrow. "There was a measure of anxiety when the kidnapping was discovered. Other than that, things are fine."

"Kidnapping? Whose?" But she already knew the answer.

"Yours, of course, Queen Eloise." She kept her eyes fixed on Eloise.

The new queen felt her face go the shade of currants and dropped her gaze. "I see."

"The guards who were stationed at either end of the hall have been confined to the dungeons, but have not been tortured for information yet. We've not gone to war with anyone. Nor have we sent search parties beyond the walls of Castle de Brague. No retaliatory assassins have been sent anywhere, nor have we brought in the bloodhounds or consulting psychics."

"You're jesting, surely." Eloise felt her stomach sink.

"No. We probably had another hour before those more drastic measures were initiated. But, as I said, finding the Queen's Chamber empty triggered... concern."

"Right," said Eloise. "Sorry."

"Perhaps Your Majesty will forgive me." Lady Seneschal's expression was far from contrite.

"Forgive you, Lady Seneschal? Why?"

"I thought I'd made myself understood yesterday evening when I described the processes, resources—sorry, the people—and systems in place to support Her Majesty's rule and proper function. It is my error that I thought I had communicated that clearly. For that, I ask your forgiveness."

Eloise felt her cheeks darken from red currants to black currants.

"Apologies, Lady Seneschal. Clearly, the mistake was mine."

"No, Queen Eloise. Protocol tells us that's never the case. Such is Protocol." The old woman's manner betrayed what a fiction that was.

"Such is Protocol," echoed Eloise, feeling even worse.

They stood there, Lady Seneschal silent and Eloise staring down at her slippers, her left hand holding the GHC in place.

Finally, Lady Seneschal said, "I beg you to please remember those who depend on the queen being in the Queen's Chamber to do their work and provide their service. The job of my staff is summed up in a sign we have in the handmaids' gathering room. It says, 'Help the queen be the queen.' But, Your Highness, you have to help us help you. Every moment we spend at cross purposes makes you less efficient and less effective. The queen has to act like the queen for these dedicated servants to enable you. And part of that is, for example, avoiding impromptu apparent kidnappings."

Eloise did not enjoy being scolded like a three-year-old, and she couldn't imagine that Lady Seneschal had ever spoken to her mother that way, but she took it with as much grace as she could. "Thank you, Lady Seneschal, for your..." She swallowed back "feedback," "affront," "brickbat," and "cheek." "Thank you for your candor."

Lady Seneschal nodded once. "Now, if we can get Your Majesty dressed and breakfasted, First Advisor Ligurian would like to give you your briefing." She paused, looked at the Gumballic Heraldic Crown, and said, "Shall I organize the Crown Jeweler to collect the remaining regal vestments?"

"Esteban de Macaque is more than welcome to get the Raiment of the Queens and pack it away for another few decades. I hope for that long anyway." Eloise reached up and touched the side of her crown. "But I'm going to keep this, for now."

"Why?"

"Because I'm queen. I feel I should wear the crown."

"There are other, more practical ones that—"

"This one will do."

Lady Seneschal raised her left eyebrow just a fraction. "Yes, Queen Eloise. As you wish."

VANILLA AND PISTACHIO

The late queen's private office sat next to the Receiving Room, locked, mysterious, and waiting. Eloise had never been in it before, as it was her mother's private sanctum. Not even her father crossed its threshold. There was a small nook where a servant could leave a tray with food, which the queen could access from the inside through a locked, sliding wooden panel, but servants made no direct deliveries. The sole "no visitors" exception was the First Advisor, who was allowed in for briefings and strategy sessions. Other than that, it was the queen's alone. When the door was closed, the castle would have to be on fire, under bombardment, and being attacked by ten thousand rampaging, armored lemurs before someone would be willing to give even the slightest knock.

Eloise found First Advisor Ligurian waiting outside her room, his arms laden with scrolls and standing next to a four-wheeled trolley holding two formidable wooden boxes decorated with the Gumball crest.

"Blessings of the day," said Eloise, careful not to nod too vigorously.

"Blessings of the day, Queen Eloise." First Advisor's eyes flicked to the crown on her head, betraying surprise, but he quickly looked back at her face, saying nothing about it. "Did Lady Seneschal give you the key to the Queen's Study?"

"Yes, First Advisor, she did." Eloise slipped the key from her pocket, slid it in, and opened the heavy wooden door. It swung silently on well-oiled hinges, and she stepped inside.

Given what she knew of her mother, Eloise had expected a tiny, spare, monastic cell lit by a single soy candle. Maybe there'd be an empty desk and a quill and scroll ready for use. Perhaps a single austere tapestry for decoration.

Not at all.

The room was a complete surprise. For one, it was much larger than Eloise had expected—easily 20 lengths deep and 15 lengths wide. Light flowed in from large windows on three sides. Scrolls, paper, hemp parchments, and even a few bound volumes filled the space, packed denser (if that was possible) than the bins in the Bibliotheca de Records and Regrets. A table dominated the middle of the room, covered by a massive, detailed map of the four-and-a-half realms. A piece of purple felt sliced across it, showing the line of the Purple Haze, and a model of the Adequate Wall of the Realms delineated the different borders. To the left, a desk sat against one wall, its hutches, drawers, and cubbies overflowing with scrolls, seals, wax, and knick-knacks. To the right, a fireplace sat in the middle of the one window-less wall. A comfortable-looking chair sat at an angle nearby, flanked by side tables. One was stacked with reading material. The other held a tray with a tea set, including a half-full cup of tea and three ginger snaps, one of which had been nibbled.

Eloise picked up the cup and examined its pattern. It was a strange, if interesting, tangle of pink leaves, small blue flowers, and dark twigs— not a style she'd seen in the castle before. She sniffed the cold liquid. Haggleberry tea with a hint of lemon and anise, the way her mother preferred it. She could imagine her mother sitting in the comfy chair by the fire, having her cup of tea and relishing a quiet moment as she worked through whatever problems she faced.

The room held no other lingering scents of the late queen. From the layer of dust on everything, Eloise suspected it had been some weeks, perhaps months, since her mother had been in there. Whatever odor she might have left behind was long faded.

"Oh, Mother," whispered Eloise. She put the teacup back on its saucer and gently patted the armchair, then sat in it to see if it fit.

Almost. It was a little tight with the Star of Whatever tied to her hip.

Eloise looked up at First Advisor, who stood quietly, letting her take in the room. Leccino Ligurian was an olive-skinned man with a nose like a barroom brawl and hair he kept oiled back in a braided queue. He favored muddy green robes and a matching three-cornered hat that hid the shaved patch of scalp at the front of his head. He also had a strong Eastern Lands accent, which gave extra syllables to certain words: "here," "beer," and "cheer," for example, became "hee-uh," "bee-uh," and "chee-uh"; "yes" transformed into "yay-yes" and "mash" somehow turned into "may-ush."

Eloise found it charming.

She looked at him, not sure what to do. "So, this is the Queen's Study," she said.

"Yes, Your Highness."

"And this is where you give me briefings."

"Yes, ma'am."

Eloise drummed on the chair with the fingers of her good hand. "You know what?"

"What?"

"This is weird."

"I can imagine."

"This is a side of my mother I never saw. The mess. The scrolls. The bound volumes. This chair. That pattern on the teacup. I had no idea."

"She did keep it private."

Eloise waved at all the paperwork. "What's all this?"

"A mix of things. Some of it is records that have not yet been filed. Some of it's research. Any number of the scrolls and all of the bound volumes are reference works—scholarly treatises, learned speculation, that sort of thing. Also, I believe there is a collection of romance scrolls hidden in that corner over there. Behind the cucumber harvest ledger."

"My mother liked romances?"

"Officially, she had no position. Unofficially, I'll leave that for you to decide, but apparently *The Most Torrid Trials and Tribulations of Good-woman Mountebank* is a rather compelling read. Or so I'm led to understand."

"Like I said. Weird." Eloise stood again and walked to the map table. She touched the spot in the middle, where a wooden representation of Castle de Brague sat, much too large for the scale of the map. She walked around the table, considering the realms from different points of view. She ran her finger along the edge of the Adequate Wall and then the purple felt, and wondered what changes were in store now that the spell that had created and sustained the Purple Haze had been broken. "So how do these briefings work?"

"If I may, there are two main flavors. There's business as usual, where matters are routine. And there's not business as usual, where some abnormal circumstances are under consideration, perhaps a diplomatic crisis or a natural disaster."

"So, there are vanilla days and, say, pistachio days."

"I would not have characterized them in that way, but yes. On a business as usual day, I try to bring a spectrum of relevant information and things that need the queen's attention. On a not business as usual day, I try to focus on the essential elements of whatever is going on that makes it unusual."

"Fair enough. So, is today a vanilla day or a pistachio day?"

"It is about as pistachio of a day as pistachio can get, Your Highness."

Eloise furrowed her brow, which First Advisor couldn't see, since it was beneath the crown. "Why is that? Is there a tsunami somewhere I haven't heard about? Are the gossip heralds spreading scandal about me already?"

"The gossip heralds are parasites that we tend to tolerate because they're popular, sometimes useful, and difficult to fully wipe out, although some of your predecessors have tried. And yes, they are spreading scandal. It's what they do. Purvey prurience and rake the royal muck. The, uh, events of the Crown Plonking gave them fodder."

"Sorry."

"There is naught to be done about it now. But no, this pistachioness is not a crisis. It is the first full day for the new queen, and this is her first briefing. When there's a change on the throne, there's always turmoil. More than that, there are all kinds of state secrets, intrigues, and intelligences that the new queen is not privy to. It will take us a while to cover all of those. We must just pray that none of them come to a head before you're across them. In the interest of trying to help you adjust, I've tried to make this briefing as non-pistachio as is practicable."

"So mostly vanilla with a dollop of pistachio, as needed?"

"Yes, Your Highness."

"Then vanilla away, First Advisor Ligurian. Do we sit or stand?"

"As queen, you sit. As befits my role, I stand."

"Isn't that uncomfortable?"

"Protocol is Protocol."

"Of course." Eloise walked to the comfy chair, figuring the briefing might take a while. Ligurian set his armful of scrolls down on the map and shuffled through them until he found a particular one. He then wheeled in the trolley, lifted the two boxes onto the map, unlocked them, and flipped open the lids. "The royal boxes," he said. "The most official of official documents."

Ligurian unfurled the scroll and launched into a blizzard of facts, statistics, details, and speculations relating to all manner of policies, procedures, requests and demands, each supported by a scroll or page from one of the official boxes. There was a lengthy talk about ledgers and budgets, which Eloise took to relate to matters of finance, but she had no idea what he was talking about. She couldn't tell if he was referring to coin being spent, coin coming in, coin being owed, or coin being tossed up in the air for games of chance. She knew that the crown's finances were important, that there were tithes and the "queen's percentage," but it would be a while before she was anywhere close to grasping what it all meant.

"Apparently," Ligurian said as he launched into a new subject, "there are diplomatic tensions between the Eastern Lands and The South, allegedly stemming from Çalahtist theological differences."

"You were born in the Eastern Lands, weren't you, First Advisor?" asked Eloise. "Easties don't give two pitted, wrinkled olives about religion. What has everyone's tunic tied in a knot?"

"Your characterization of the people of my birth realm is true enough. The Southies hold Çalahtism in its many, many forms deeply and fractiously."

"I was just there. All that *Scrolls of Çalaht* thumping they do is deadly serious."

"And they take offense too easily that Eastern Landers don't hold the same devotion. But I fear, Queen Eloise, that the problems only look religious. Commerce is the real culprit."

"Commerce? How so?"

"Across the Eastern Lands, this year's olive harvest was particularly poor. The third bad harvest in as many years. This is a social, culinary, and economic misfortune, and it's shifting the balance of trade toward The South."

"Three years in a row?" said Eloise. "Why?"

"Rain keeps falling at the wrong time and in the wrong amounts. Too little early on, causing small, hard fruits, and then too much late in the season, causing what's there to split and be unusable. Further, there's an olive blight attacking trees that have produced for centuries. Orchards that are dying."

"That's terrible."

"Devastating," said First Advisor. "Eastern Lands olive growers are blaming diseases carried in from The South, even though there's no solid evidence to lay the blame in that direction. Add to this the fact that Southie migrant workers are demanding higher wages to travel to the Eastern Lands as seasonal olive pickers. It is, as your mother might have said, a mess."

"I see. Is there anything I can do?"

"Unless you have a cure for the olive blight or can control the weather, I don't think so."

"I guess we can just keep an eye on it. You said this was a vanilla version of this briefing?"

First Advisor shrugged. "That was one of the more pistachio bits."

Next, Ligurian brought out bundles of paper from one of the boxes.

"Letters?" asked Eloise.

"Yes. All of these have to do with the late queen's passing." There were several tidy bundles tied with string, and he set them on the table. He pointed to the largest pile. "These are from dignitaries who've said they'll attend the late queen's funeral tomorrow." He indicated several smaller bundles. "Those are apologies for not being able to attend. I've taken the liberty of dividing them into groups—those that were expected, those that were unexpected, those that are insults, and those that we're relieved about."

"Any that I particularly need to consider?"

"No, my queen. I don't think so."

"Do I need to reply to them all?" said Eloise. "That would take a while."

"The late queen was comfortable enough with me handling this kind of thing. Simply authorize me to respond on your behalf."

Eloise raised her shoulders. "I should probably look through them first, especially that pile of the people who will be here. I might need to make notes or something in case I have to speak with them at the wake."

"As the grieving monarch, you can be forgiven for avoiding most of them. For that matter, you can choose not to speak to anyone. But it is up to you, and engaging might be advantageous. You can start cementing relationships, that sort of thing."

"If they are there, I'll talk to them. Receive them, at least. It seems only polite, since they've come."

Eloise was starting to feel a little overwhelmed. She wondered how her mother signaled that she wanted a cup of tea. Did she stand at the door and bellow? Was there a bell somewhere? Perhaps a wasp or lady bug servant who hovered just outside, ready to convey her wishes?

She realized that First Advisor was looking at her, waiting. "Sorry. I may have drifted off. Where were we?"

Ligurian put a folder stuffed full of documents on the table. "There's a petition for the queen to resolve a dispute that arose in the weeks before the late queen, uh…"

"Died," finished Eloise. "You can say it. I can handle it. It is the truth."

"Yes, my queen. It is a boundary dispute between three radish farmers from Lower Glenth." Ligurian laid out a convoluted territorial disagreement involving inheritance rights, property sales over time, plot subdivisions, the Lower Glenth public commons, and plain old neighborly dislike. "The argument has been going on for about a decade, and the late Queen told them she would resolve it shortly before the, uh, incident that, uh, proved fatal."

"Is there an urgency? Some sort of radish crisis?"

"No, Your Highness."

"Then why this? Why today? Why this briefing?"

"It struck me as typical of the things that would come before you, Your Highness." First Adviser tapped his finger on the folder and slid it toward Eloise. "Also, the complainants are scheduled to come next week and plead their cases. I thought you might like to prepare."

Eloise flipped through the folder. There were maps, affidavits, statutory declarations, nasty notes, bills of sale, copies of wills, dictated testaments, and at least two previous pronouncements from magistrates. "I'm supposed to decide this?"

"You are the queen."

"I'm not a property magistrate."

"No. But you are the queen. The parties remain dissatisfied, so they are appealing for the queen's justice."

"The queen's justice," mumbled Eloise. She skimmed the top document in the folder—a summary of the matter that repeated a lot of what First Advisor had already said—and waggled it at Ligurian. "Is this accurate?"

"I believe it is, yes."

"All of it?" asked Eloise.

"Yes."

"This is petty and stupid beyond words."

"It would be hard to categorize it as anything other than that. Yet, all three parties are powerful, entrenched landholders. They all consider themselves among your strongest supporters."

"Which means that two of them are going to end up angry with me. How am I supposed to rule? How can I make the right decision in a matter I know nothing about?"

"You are the queen. By definition, the queen always makes the right choice."

"That's ludicrous. Being queen doesn't mean I'll make the *right* right choice."

"Again, by definition, Your Majesty will do exactly that."

"That's absurd." Eloise leafed through the folder again, then closed it. "I shall need some time to ponder this. Can you leave the folder with me?"

"Of course, Your Highness." Ligurian straightened. "Normally I'd finish with your agenda for the day."

"Agenda?"

"A list of planned activities."

"I know what an agenda is. I'm just surprised there's one for the whole day. And every day."

"Your Majesty's time is at a premium, and will get more precious with the passing months and years. You must get the best value you can for it. As such, planning an agenda is paramount for efficiency."

"Right. And you're the one who puts the agenda together?"

"It is one of my duties, yes."

"Do I have any input into it?"

"If you want, yes."

"What's on the agenda today, First Advisor?"

"Your day will be devoted to preparing yourself for the funeral and wake tomorrow, and spending time with your sister and father."

"Right. I see."

Ligurian bowed to Eloise. "My queen, this is all I have for your briefing today."

"Thank you, First Advisor." Eloise stood up from the comfy chair and stretched. She saw a folded piece of hemp parchment at the bottom of one of the boxes. "What's that?"

First Advisor glanced at the box. "Sorry, Queen Eloise. That shouldn't be in there."

Eloise picked it up. It was the roughest hemp parchment she'd ever seen. On the outside, someone with abysmal quillmanship had scrawled "To Her Royal Highness Queen Eloise." She unfolded the page and squinted, trying to make out the words, which looked like they'd been written with a lump of coal. "It is an invitation, I think."

"Yes," said Ligurian. "It is."

"They want me to bless a brunchberry paddock?"

"Not quite. They want you to bless an empty paddock that's going to be planted with brunchberry canes."

"I like brunchberries. Where's Festering Resentment?"

"The village is about a three-hour ride south by southwest. It's just past Ornery Intentions, this side of Splendiferous Disapprobation." First Advisor circled his finger around an area on the map. "Around here, somewhere. I've never been."

"I'll say 'yes.' Please convey to..." Eloise looked back at the invitation. "... Goodman and Goodwoman Rechteckfeld that I'd love to bless their future brunchberry paddock."

"I advise against this, Queen Eloise. It was a mistake that it was in your royal box at all. This invitation is one of, literally, thousands that the queen receives every year. If you accept every invitation that flows into the castle, you will, pardon my directness, do nothing but travel to every podunk village in the realm getting sore of fundament, eating food on a stick that has no business being served that way, remarking on how pretty everything is, and saying how clever it is that so many children can carve daisies from tofu, papaya, celery, or whatever it is that the locals are celebrating."

"That's a bit harsh. I've grown to like local celebrations." She waved the invitation. "I take your point, First Advisor. I won't be accepting every invitation that comes my way. But in this case, it feels churlish not to accept, given how difficult it must have been for Goodman and Goodwoman Rechteckfeld to put this together."

"Your Highness, please understand that it's an invitation in form only. They don't really expect you to show up. And it will be a burden on them if you do."

"Then they shouldn't have sent it in the first place." Eloise was liking the idea of a day trip into the countryside. "Perhaps sometime next week."

"As Her Highness wishes." Only a twitch in Ligurian's left eye revealed his true feelings.

"And since it is a blessing, please ask the Venerable Prelate Herself if she'd like to come along," said Eloise.

First Advisor looked appalled. "Surely not, Queen Eloise. Now? In winter?"

"Why not? I need to get to know the prelate a bit better. Plus, it'll do us both good to get out among regular people. My guess is that it's been years since the prelate has availed herself to worshipers outside the castle gates."

First Advisor swallowed, then said, "I shall organize the trip, and pass on the invitation to the Venerable Prelate Herself. I'm sure she'll be thrilled." Ligurian couldn't quite hide his sarcasm, but Eloise chose to ignore it. "Does Her Highness have anything else, or shall we adjourn?"

"Actually, I do have one last question before we go."

"Yes, Your Highness?"

Eloise looked at him for a full 15 seconds, trying to figure out the best way to ask her question. In the end, she chose directness. "What's being done to apprehend the person who had my mother killed?"

First Advisor Ligurian opened his mouth to say something, then closed it. He'd not been expecting that, and hadn't prepared an answer. "That matter was closed."

"Oh? Then, who had her killed?"

Ligurian paused, looking down. "No one knows."

"Then why was it closed? Surely it's a matter of interest."

"The late queen told me to stop. We investigated, found enough for her to feel we'd gotten what we were going to get, and she didn't want to expend more resources on it."

Eloise wasn't sure what to make of that. "Surely it would have been in character for my mother to pursue the matter to the corners of all the realms, until someone suffered and paid for what they'd done."

First Advisor turned his palms upward. "Would it not also be in character for her to not squander resources on something that would never yield a satisfactory result?"

Eloise considered that. He was right that her mother might have gone either way if prospects were slim. "Were records kept?"

Ligurian seemed to hesitate. "I wouldn't call them records."

"What would you call them?"

"'Notes.' Maybe 'jottings.' Your mother did not want a parchment trail left for something this delicate."

Again, it might have been in her mother's character to clamp a lid of secrecy on the matter. "I'd like to see what you have."

"The late queen really did want the matter to rest. She did not want to upset her family—you, your sister, your father—more than was necessary."

That also sounded more or less like her mother, although feelings hadn't always been high on the list of things she paid much heed to. Maybe she'd had a change of heart over the weeks she'd been unwell.

"I'd like you to bring me the jottings, notes, sketches or whatever it is that's there. Please." Eloise pointed to one of the official boxes. "They needn't go in one of those, if that's a record-keeping issue or something. But I'd like to see them."

First Advisor nodded once. Was that a hesitation? Perhaps a reluctance to dig up a corpse that was already buried. She flinched. Not her best analogy.

"Yes, Your Highness," said Ligurian. "I should be able to have them for your briefing in a few days."

"Sooner, please, First Advisor," said Eloise. "As soon as you can. Like, tomorrow."

"Yes, ma'am."

He nodded again, put the boxes back on the trolley, and bowed his way out the door. It clicked shut and she was alone in the room.

Eloise looked around, sensing the essence of her mother everywhere, at once familiar and strange. She realized she still didn't know how to get someone to bring her a cup of tea.

❦ 8 ❧

FOR ETERNITY

A single, resounding *boom!* echoed from a thousand drums in unison, out through the castle walls and across Brague.

There were ten seconds of silence, and then another single drumming.

After ten more seconds, there came a thunderous, slow, double crash—boom-BOOM—like the heartbeat of a dying giant.

The castle gates juddered open and a thousand drummers—human and non-human alike—marched forward in lockstep, their faces grim. They thumped their double beat in a languid, deliberate, steady pulse. It seemed to take forever for the last drummer to clear the gates and move into the silent, snow-covered, throng-lined streets outside the castle.

Next came a full company of horses. The magnificent Horse Guards, tacked out in full ceremonial military decoration, stepped forward at quarter speed, led by Hector de Pferd. They held their knees high in a stately pose, frozen motionless, faces stoic, moving only to match their forward pace to the forlorn drumbeats.

Then a lone Friesian appeared, moving with the same deliberate slowness. It was Ferdinand de Pferd, the royally appointed leader of the Queen's Stables, high commander of the Horse Guards, and father of Hector. Ferdinand was decorated with a single black sash around his neck as he undertook a final task for the queen he'd served for more than two decades—pulling her casket on a two-wheeled, ebony funeral caisson. His midnight-black tail, mane, and coat showed every speck of falling white. His face was emotionless, but bore the remnants of earlier tears that had frozen in tracks under his eyes.

The full-couch casket was open to the gray sky, and angled so that the mourners jamming the streets could glimpse her snow-flecked body one last time. The late queen was dressed in a favorite jade-green gown, and wore a simple silver band where her crown once had sat. Her arms lay by her sides, a burgundy rose extending from her left hand and a white alstroemeria from her right—both brought from some secret, out-of-season source. Someone had powdered her pale face to emphasize its pallor. Her hair was loose and brushed out, and strands of it wafted gently in a light winter morning breeze that was as cold as she was.

Behind the casket came the longest funeral procession anyone had ever seen. Chafed, as widower and dowager king, walked immediately behind the caisson. He was dressed in a black tunic, breeks, boots, coat, and cape, and he, too, wore a simple silver band where his crown once had sat. Hot tears streamed down his face, but he kept his back straight, his chin level, his jaw clenched, and his eyes fixed on the casket in front of him.

Eloise and Johanna walked behind their father, both in formal dresses, veils, and coats of deepest black. Like their mother, each held a burgundy rose and a white alstroemeria. Protocol insisted that Johanna should walk ten lengths behind her sister, now that Eloise was crown-plonked and officially into her reign, but Eloise wouldn't hear of it. "Stuff Protocol," she'd said. "We were sisters three days ago, we're sisters now. Plus, you're going to be a queen soon enough." So the twins each held two flowers in one hand and walked side-by-side, holding hands.

Behind them waddled the Venerable Prelate Herself. The tapir swung an earthenware censer that belched the smoke of smoldering sage, lavender, eucalyptus, pyre blossom, and mourner grass.

Next came, literally, everyone of any importance. They were arranged by families, attachments, affinities, and houses—all ranked by nobility, wealth, status, class, and how in favor or out of favor they were, although Eloise was unsure who'd made that decision. Perhaps Lady Seneschal. It certainly wasn't Eloise. There were nobles from every species and every district of the realm, merchants rich and middling, representatives of every guild, union, consortium, and quasi-amalgamated collective. There were the heads of every Çalahtic order, sect, schism, and devotional quirk. In short, if one was vaguely in charge of something or could pretend to be, they could be found in the funeral procession somewhere behind the late queen's corpse. At the very back, a coterie of professional funeral wailers screeched, beseeched, rent their clothes and seared the air with their lamentations. Eloise was grateful they were a good distance behind. Closer, their keening would have been unbearable.

The streets of Brague teemed with people paying their respects to the queen they'd affectionately called Two (the late queen's mother having been disparagingly referred to as One). Many cried, wore black, and stood soberly as the caisson trundled past. Many held candles, tapers, and torches despite it being the middle of the day, and many muttered prayers that the deceased queen might stand with Çalaht. But most stood silently, holding up two fingers, a simple gesture representing her nickname.

It made Eloise wonder if she'd ever be thought of as "Three," and if so, if it would be with a smile in the heart like her mother, or with a dismissive scowl like her grandmother. Or maybe she'd just be thought of as "Two's daughter," and never emerge from the late queen's shadow. It wouldn't be the first time that had happened.

With the Crown Plonking disaster as her start, she didn't like her chances.

The slow double drumbeats thumped a dignified pace as the procession wound through Brague. The drummers, horses, caisson, royalty, and other marching mourners made their way from the castle to the town's outer wall, around, and back. People of all species stood at silent attention as they took one last look at their queen. Hers was neither the shortest nor the longest rule in history, but Eloise Hydra Gumball II had clearly found a place in their hearts. Eloise was gratified to see so many people paying tribute to her mother.

They walked for three hours through light flurries of snow. Eloise mostly focused on stepping carefully and keeping the GHC on her head. But over and over, she couldn't help asking herself the one question she had no answer for. Why was her mother killed?

Why?

The procession finished threading through Brague and wound its way back into the castle gates. A cadre of pall bearers lifted the casket from the caisson and carried it into the chapel, the scene of the Crown Plonking just two days before. Eloise sat in the front pew feeling thoroughly numb in both mind and body.

The Venerable Prelate Herself stood on the pulpit and said words that Eloise could not take in about a person who only somewhat resembled the mother she knew. The eulogy swam from "warm," "good-hearted," "Çalaht-fearing," and "capable" to "beloved," "righteous," "chives," "tilde," and "splortle" (or at least that's what the words sounded like when the prelate mumbled them).

Finally, after what seemed a decade, the Çalahtist yammering and praying finished. Chafed stepped up onto the altar and stood by the open lid of the casket. He placed a hand softly on his wife's cold cheek and whispered goodbye. Then he lowered the lid, paused a moment, and then, using a T-shaped tool, twisted screws into the lid to seal her in. The chapel was silent, save for the scritch of metal drilling into oak, as the room full of Court nobility watched his last interaction with his wife.

The dowager king finished and handed the tool to the prelate. The late queen's champion, Sylvia Cloisterfeld, a muscled marvel of a woman in her middle-years, stepped to the far side of the coffin at the front of the chapel. She was joined by four of Court's highest-ranking guards. The six of them hoisted the coffin from its trestles, turned so they faced the side, and rested it on their shoulders.

Using a high-kneed step like Ferdinand de Pferd had used, they moved to a less-used doorway at the back of the chapel. The devotional house minder fumbled keys and unlocked a wrought-iron gate, and the pall bearers conveyed the coffin down into the Gumball family crypt.

Eloise stood and followed with Johanna a step behind. They'd both been into the crypt plenty of times—at least once a year at Afternoon Tea for the Dead. She hated the place, with its dust, its cool dampness, and its proximity to dead bodies. Afternoon Tea for the Dead was supposed to celebrate the lives of those who'd passed and give their spirits a chance to feast on the delicacies brought into the crypt (never eaten by the living). Eloise had never believed that the spirits actually did anything with the food. Still, she couldn't stop herself from imagining long-dead queens clacking their bony jaws and gumless teeth in joyous anticipation of cucumber sandwiches, jam-covered scones, petit fours, pastries, and miniature desserts.

The whole bringing arvo tea to a bunch of corpses thing had always creeped her out. Hauling her mother's body to join them wasn't much better.

They stepped into the crypt and the cool dryness of the vault. Torches lined the walls, casting shadows over stone markers for dozens of dead queens. The oldest, Agnes Delion Frostbite Gumball, was on the right, just at the front near the gate, like she was a sentry for the place. The history of the Gumball line moved forward in time as one stepped toward the back of the space. After hundreds of years and dozens of deceased, they reached the spot where Eloise's mother would go. The tube-like shelf, only slightly bigger than the coffin, was newly carved into the earth, just to the left of where Eloise's grandmother lay interred. She imagined her mother and grandmother standing at

Çalaht's side, reconciling their differences over in the spirit world, and then gossiping about Eloise's reign from beyond the grave. Except her mother hadn't been one to gossip, and Eloise figured it might take the two of them a few years to work out their own mother-daughter issues. Perhaps Eloise was safe from their ghostly chatter for a while.

The pall bearers slid the coffin feet-first into the hole. Chafed patted the box one last time, then nodded to Cloisterfeld. The ex-champion hauled up a heavy stone cover and placed it over the opening, locking away the body forever. The grave marker was chiseled with simple, blocky letters that spelled out the late queen's name, the dates of her birth, ascension to the throne, and death, and the words, "Standing with Çalaht for Eternity." Eloise wondered what her mother might have added if she'd been allowed a line of comment. Maybe, "I Thought That Pie Tasted Funny."

Gallows humor. Clearly, Eloise was trying to compartmentalize her emotions while standing in the crowded crypt.

She thought about the idea of "standing with Çalaht." People said it all the time when referring to the dead. "May she stand with Çalaht." "May he stand at Çalaht's side." But to do it for eternity, like the gravestone said? That seemed like an awfully long time. Would her mother get to speak with anyone while she stood there? Did the Divine One dispense wisdom. Or gossip? Would the dearly departed be able to chat among themselves? Engage in learned discourse? Or would it be more like a frozen tableau, like a tapestry full of dead people sewn into stillness?

She hoped not. Her mother had had a keen mind, and Eloise didn't want her bored in the afterlife.

One by one, everyone touched the grave marker and said, "Farewell, my queen," then turned and walked out of the crypt. Eloise went last, standing a little longer than the others in the flickering light of the torches, looking at the grave.

"If you have any advice, I'd be happy to hear it."

The grave looked back at her, silent.

"Really? Now would be a good time."

Nothing.

"Didn't think so."

Eloise traced the letters of her mother's name on the gravestone with an index finger. One last moment of contact.

"Well, goodbye, Mother. Say hello to Grandmother. I hope you two get along better wherever you are now."

Eloise left the crypt and went to join the wake in the Throne Hall.

9

LIKE STEALING FOOD

The wake was long, sad, and tedious. Eloise, Johanna, and Chafed stood in a line so that hundreds of people could walk, crawl, slither, and creep by to express their condolences, then walk, crawl, slither, and creep to the buffet table for something to nosh. After four solid hours of shaking hands, allowing hugs, and accepting bows and curtsies, Eloise had heard every possible variation of, "I'm sorry for your loss," "She was a great queen," and "May she stand with Çalaht." At some point, her responses became rote recitations. At least she didn't have to smile.

By the time the last person—an ancient, giant slug named Mr Herbert —had slimed past with his condolences, Eloise's neck and shoulders felt like they had been hammered by the court blacksmith. Three days straight of wearing the Gumballic Heraldic Crown had taken their toll. Eventually, the crowd thinned, and she followed her father and sister to the buffet, where the remaining food was down to half a dozen wilted black bean seaweed rolls and an entire plate piled high with what looked like slightly burned apricot strudelettes, but topped with caraway seeds and dollops of something that smelled like a green curry paste. No wonder they were left untouched.

Chafed looked at the ravaged buffet and frowned. "I think I might call it a night. I'll have some dinner brought to my room."

He reached out his arms, inviting the twins into a hug. Eloise guessed it had been a decade since he'd last done that.

"Ëëëlöööïïïsëëë. Jöööhääännäää." Those were his nicknames for them —northernifications of their normal names. "I... I don't know what to say. Maybe just, I love you both." It was a little jarring. They were not a family given to demonstrating affection. Perhaps their mother dying had given their father a little more freedom in that department. Or maybe one just had to cut a grieving widower a little slack.

"Love you, too, Father," whispered Johanna.

"Yeah," said Eloise. "Me, too."

He tightened his arms and the three of them relaxed against each other. Chafed drew a breath like he was about to say something else, but didn't. He let them go, took a hand each, squeezed again, nodded, and said, "G'night."

They watched him walk down the hall toward the private wing of the castle. Eloise didn't even know which room he'd moved into.

"He's in a bad way, isn't he?" said Johanna.

"What's he going to do?"

"I have no idea."

Johanna paused, looking a little chagrined, then did something unexpected—she nodded upward at Eloise's head and in their sign language asked, *What's it like wearing that thing?*

The crown? Eloise signed back. *Tiring. It feels like it weighs ten strong weights.*

That's not quite what I was asking.

Eloise reached up and adjusted the crown so it sat a little better. *Very, very, weird.*

And?

And I feel like a fake. This is Mother's. Not mine.

Johanna nodded. *I get that. I think you'll get used to it.*

I hope so.

Johanna reached up and tapped the crown on one of its metal struts with her fingernail. It made a little *tick* sound. *I hope so, too.*

You want to... Eloise lifted it, ready to let her sister have a go.

"No, no," said Johanna out loud, holding up a palm. "That's quite alright. That one's your burden. If I get my own, I'll make that one mine."

"You sure?"

"Definitely."

"Right, then." Eloise let the crown settle back on her head.

Johanna picked up one of the apricot strudelettes, sniffed it, and set it back down. "Ugh. I think I may do the same as Father—have some dinner brought to me and take an early night. Big day tomorrow." That last sentence was one their mother had often said when they were girls, trying to get them to accept the inevitability of bedtime.

"Every day is a big day," said Eloise. It had been their way of arguing back, of saying that argument held no import. Not that they could have articulated it that way.

"Now more than ever, it seems." said Johanna.

They hugged, and Eloise watched her sister go down the hall.

With nothing better to do, Eloise made her way to her parents' chamber so she could change into something more comfortable, find a bite to eat, and enjoy some solitude.

As soon as she crossed the threshold, a lady in waiting popped up from nowhere to help her out of her dress, and a server she half recognized appeared with a bowl of minestrone that was quite tolerable except for chunks of what she was pretty sure was okra. It was filling enough, but the okra sat wrong, and Eloise, still both exhausted and hyped up from the day, didn't feel like going to bed. Not yet.

On a table to the side, there was a pile of scrolls that hadn't been there before, which she guessed were there for her to read. She unscrolled the top one enough to see its title: "Being a Report on the Spike in the Speculative Trading of Oregano Futures." "Scintillating," mumbled Eloise as she reached for the next. "Being a Report on the Widespread Failure of Olive Cultivars in Eastern Lands Groves."

Had her mother suffered from insomnia? If so, Eloise was sure this reading would have been medicinally appropriate.

She paced a little, unable to settle. She looked out the window, where the rooms of the castle, and the dwellings of Brague beyond, glowed with candles.

Eloise wondered if Johanna might be having trouble falling asleep as well. She tied the Star of Whatever back onto her hip, pulled a dressing gown over her nightie, popped the crown back on her head, and flap-flapped out into the hall in her slippers to see if she could find Johanna.

A knock on Johanna's door went unanswered. Her sister wasn't in the kitchen cadging a snack or in the Bibliotheca de Records and Regrets reading. Eloise turned down a hall to see if Johanna was on the far side of the castle, visiting her private garden, when a voice suddenly spoke behind her.

"Queen Eloise."

It was Lady Seneschal.

Eloise stopped in her tracks, her cheeks flushing pink. She felt like a toddler who'd been caught with her hand in the biscuit jar for the second time in as many days. Eloise wondered how Älphonsinä Füüürchtbarkeit Póöòmáäàdéëè managed to make her feel that way with two words and the tone of her voice. "Yes, Lady Seneschal?" said Eloise.

"Is there something you require?"

"Require? No, not really," said Eloise. "I was just looking for my sister."

Lady Seneschal let a hint of an exasperated huff escape. "May I speak freely, Queen Eloise?"

Absolutely not, thought Eloise. *That's the last thing I feel like.* "Of course. I wish you would."

"You should not be doing what you are doing right now."

"What am I doing? I'm just walking around the castle."

"No, Queen Eloise. You are taking the food from someone's mouth. Or perhaps from the mouths of their children."

Eloise's jaw dropped. "That's outrageous. I'm doing nothing of the sort."

"Respectfully, Queen Eloise, you are."

Eloise narrowed her eyes. This rake of a woman was getting on her nerves. "I find that offensive."

"Do you now." Lady Seneschal folded her arms across her chest and held her ground. "Let me ask a question. How many staff do you think it takes to support the queen and her family?"

"I... I don't know. A few dozen, maybe? Fifty-ish, perhaps?"

Lady Seneschal couldn't contain her snort. "There are 'fifty-ish' in the kitchens alone, everyone from the new Chef down to all the serving wenches and scullery maids." She took a step forward, crowding Eloise just a little. "Scores, Your Majesty. There are scores people awake, working, ready to help you and your rule at any time of day or night. And that's just the household and associated activities on a normal day. The military and guard side of things is a whole different matter, as are special events, like receptions of state or, if I may say it, funerals and wakes."

Lady Seneschal took another step, and Eloise matched her with a step backward.

"What do you think the most precious thing in the castle is?" she asked Eloise.

"Ooh, hard one," said Eloise, trying not to feel harangued. She pointed to her head. "This crown, perhaps?" She looked around, but saw nothing of greater value. "Maybe the piles of coin in the counting house? Maybe that knuckle bone in the devotional house reliquary that supposedly came from the left hand of Çalaht?"

"Wrong." Step.

Step backward. "What then?"

"The queen's time."

"How so? How is my time any more valuable than anyone else's?" Eloise knew it was a stupid thing to say as soon as the words were out of her mouth.

Step. "The queen only has so many minutes in the day, yet she is called on to do ten times as many things as she could possibly hope to complete." Step.

Step back.

Lady Seneschal took another step forward. "The best we can hope for is that the queen will do as much as she can, as best she can. To that end, the queen has her household staff to support her being efficient and effective. But, as I said the other day, you have to let us do that. More than that, if you do not let a page do a page's work, or a serving wench serve, a lady in waiting wait on you or a herald make her pronouncements, then you are, in effect, making them unnecessary, and thereby taking food from their mouths."

"I see." Eloise took another step back.

"Let me give you a demonstration of what you need to do. You wanted to see Princess Johanna?"

"Yes, Lady Seneschal," said Eloise.

The woman turned her head to the side and barked, "Page!"

From nowhere, an antelope jackrabbit scampered into the hall dressed in a page's tunic. "Yes, Lady Seneschal?" Then, seeing who was next to her, he quickly bowed, and said, "My queen."

"The queen has a request for you," said Lady Seneschal.

"Of course." He stood, perfectly balancing himself on two legs as Protocol dictated, long, slender ears twitching like he was making sure he didn't miss anything.

Eloise looked from Lady Seneschal to the page and back. She didn't need someone to do this for her. She was perfectly capable of finding her sister on her own.

But she was queen now. She was going to have to get used to people doing things for her. And she certainly didn't want to be accused of stealing food from anyone. "May I ask your name, please?"

"Rögër, Your Highness. Rögër de Alleni." His voice twitched as much as his ears.

"Rögër de Alleni, I'd be grateful if you could please let my sister know that I'd like to see her, if possible and if she's not busy."

"Here, ma'am? Shall she come here?"

"In the hall?"

"If you wish, ma'am."

"No, I'll meet her..." Eloise had no idea where to meet her. Nowhere particularly public. "Actually, if she could possibly meet me at the Queen's Study, that would be great."

"Yes, ma'am. Of course, ma'am." He tensed like he was ready to sprint off, but asked, "Anything else, Your Highness?"

"If someone happens to be available in the kitchen, then tea and something to nibble for two would be nice, delivered to the Queen's Study."

"Right away, ma'am. Thank you, ma'am."

And he was gone, bounding through the castle hall like he was trying to win a race.

"There you go," said Lady Seneschal. "That wasn't so hard, now was it? And did you see how eager he was to please?"

"Yes. It's true. He seemed happy to have the job. You could see it in his ears."

"Exactly. My staff members pride themselves on doing the best they can. Let them."

"Yes, Lady Seneschal. I'll try."

"Does Her Majesty require anything else?"

"Actually, yes," said Eloise. "I'd like to ask you about the staff of people who are my handmaids and ladies in waiting."

Lady Seneschal's eyes narrowed. "Has there been a problem?"

"No. Not at all. I was wondering how they were selected."

"I choose them," said Lady Seneschal. "They are the best of the best, allowed to serve the queen only after years of training in Protocol, propriety, and proper manners. I identify the best possibilities, groom them myself, and then deploy them in a way that best suits their skills."

"I see."

"Is there an issue?" The way she said the words made it clear there ought not be.

Eloise looked up at her. This was one tough woman. And that made sense. To run a staff of scores, to make sure the household functioned well, and to manage so many individuals, each with their problems and egos, preferences and foibles, all in a way that was invisible to those they served—of course she was a tough nut.

"I would..." Eloise trailed off. "Do I have any say in this?"

"The queen has other, more important concerns. These matters are best left to me."

"Right."

Lady Seneschal waited, unmoving.

"May I ask a question?"

"Of course, Your Highness."

"Why is my handmaid Odmilla de Platypus no longer serving me?"

"Simple. Her service is fit for a princess. But she does not have the skills it takes to serve the queen."

"I... Really?"

"That is my opinion."

This surprised Eloise. For four years, Odmilla had been nothing but kind, patient, and supportive. More than that, Eloise liked and trusted her.

"Lady Seneschal, can you accept that suddenly wearing this..." She pointed to the crown. "That this is unsettling to me?"

"One can imagine that might be the case."

"And that all these things..." She pointed down the hall, indicating the page who'd just run off, and waved a palm at Lady Seneschal to include her. "They're all unfamiliar and strange to me?"

"Yes, again, I can imagine. It was strange for your mother as well, when she assumed the throne. I was a lady in waiting to your grandmother then. I remember the late queen's nerves."

"Right. Then, you understand. I would be grateful if you could make an exception, and include Odmilla as one who serves me. The familiarity will... It will help."

Only a tic in the old woman's eye betrayed any reaction. "As Her Highness wishes."

"And another. Läääcy de Aardvark. If you could please find a place for her in the circle of those around me, I'd be grateful."

"As Her Highness wishes." Lady Seneschal's tone was flat. Eloise could tell she would do as she'd been asked, but disliked the meddling in her realm.

"And a third. RoyLee, the wombat who came back to the castle with me. I need him to have a real role. He'd like to be a warrior. Or maybe a guard?"

"Trainee page, perhaps?"

"Yes, please. That will keep him closer to me. Let's start with that."

"As you wish."

"Also, I'm going to need a new mattress. I'll never get to sleep if I'm thinking of the late queen every time I get under the covers."

"That's doable."

"Good."

There was another long moment, and then Lady Seneschal surprised Eloise.

She smiled. Just a little, but it was a smile—perhaps the first Eloise had ever seen from her.

"That wasn't so hard now, was it? Let us help the queen be the queen."

10

PROMISES

Eloise arrived at the Queen's Study at the same time as her sister.

Johanna wore a scowl. "You had me summoned? Really?" she said.

Eloise took a step back. "What are you talking about? I didn't summon you."

"The page said, and I quote, 'The Queen requires your presence,' end quote. That sounds like I'm being summoned."

"What I actually said was, 'I'd like to see my sister, please, if she's available.' It was supposed to be an invitation. Did the page mention a light supper?"

"No. No mention of food or beverage of any sort."

"Sorry, I didn't mean to be demanding. I'll have to figure out some way to get more nuance into the page-based communications channel." She produced the key from her pocket with a flourish, like a conjurer at a children's birthday party. "I wanted to show you this." She pointed the key at the door to the Queen's Study. "And, more to the point, this."

Eloise slid it into the lock for the second time that day. It clicked and the door eased open. She bowed like a valet and said, "After you, mademoiselle."

Johanna stepped into the dark room and looked around. Moonlight illuminated the crowded jumble with an eerie paleness.

Eloise used her candle to light several others that were scattered randomly around the room. "Have you ever been in here before?"

"Nope. It's strange. It doesn't look like Mother at all."

"I know, right? All the stuff. All the mess."

Johanna walked around the room touching things—a few scrolls, the map on the table, the headrest of the comfy chair. Then she picked up a figurine. It was a clay artwork in an extremely naïve style. It might have been the likeness of a dog. Or maybe a profiterole.

"I made this," said Johanna. "I haven't thought about this thing for years."

"What is it?"

"It was supposed to be Rüüütÿÿÿ, my stuffed toy rutabaga. I loved it so much that I wanted Mother to have one too. But I couldn't sew a toy, so I made her a clay one."

"That's sweet."

"I can't believe she kept it."

Then Johanna did something that Eloise hadn't seen since their mother had died—she cried. "I'm going to miss her."

"Me, too."

Johanna put the figurine back on the shelf and sniffed.

"Keep it, Jo. To remind you of her."

"Really? Thanks." She slipped the clay rutabaga into her pocket.

The two of them spent the next ten minutes examining the room, trying to glean what they could of their mother. They were interrupted by a knock on the sliding hutch door. Eloise stepped to the nook and opened it. There was no one there, but a tray with haggleberry tea and what looked like slices of a fresh-baked sachertorte sat waiting. Eloise picked up the tray and set it on the map table, covering most of the Eastern Lands, a desolate, remote section of The South, and a fair chunk of the Gööödeling Sea. "Tea?" she asked.

"I'd love some."

Eloise poured them a cup each, invited Johanna to take the comfy chair, and pulled over the desk chair so it was near one of the side tables. They each took a sip, and then started in on the slices of cake.

"That's not terrible," said Johanna.

"Not terrible at all," agreed Eloise.

Johanna sighed a little and put down her fork. "It's not Chef."

"No, it's not Chef at all."

"Were you here when she killed herself?"

Johanna shook her head. "No, she was already gone a few weeks before I arrived. It makes this whole thing that much sadder."

Eloise nodded. Food was such an important part of Court life, and she could taste the change with every mouthful. "Do you know who's taken over the kitchen?"

"The new Chef is Chef's son."

"Really? I didn't know she had a son."

"She did. Apparently he's a chip off the old sachertorte."

"But not the whole slice," said Eloise.

Johanna took another forkful, looking wistful. "No, not the whole slice."

They sat there in silence, sipping tea and nibbling cake. They looked around the candlelit room, taking it all in, adding this unexpected place to the picture each had of their mother.

Eloise thought how nice it was to just sit and be a little normal for a while in this most abnormal of situations.

Johanna broke the quiet. "I need to tell you something."

"You want more cake?" said Eloise. "We could go get some. We wouldn't even have to sneak in anymore. We could just waltz in there and say, 'Could we please have another slice?'"

"I'll be heading back to the Half Kingdom the day after tomorrow."

Eloise froze. "What? No." She waved her fork back and forth. "No. No, no, no. You can't go yet. I need you."

"I think I have to." Johanna took another sip of tea, then clicked down the cup on its saucer. "For a bunch of reasons."

"Like what?"

Eloise knew she was being selfish. Of course her sister had to go back. But she didn't want to hear about it. Not yet.

"It's far from certain that I'm going to get the crown," said Johanna. "I know there are plenty who don't think I should. I mean, Father has a more direct claim than I do, being the deceased monarch's brother when there are no children in place as heirs. I've been away from Stained Rock for weeks. I'm not criticizing, but you've only just gotten back. If I'm going to make a real push to get a crown plonked on me, I have to go get it. You know what Courts are like. People, especially nobles, don't tolerate empty thrones for very long. If a spot is open, there will be someone there to step in."

"Father doesn't want it?"

"Not in the least. He was very clear with me about that."

Eloise nodded and—Çalaht curse it—for the billionth time since she got back, she felt her eyes brimming with tears. Maybe she was a crier after all.

She took her sister's hand across the small table. "I understand. I don't like it, but I understand. The Half Kingdom will be lucky to have you. I'm sure you'll do a much better job of the queen thing than I will."

"Don't say that."

"It's true." Eloise lowered her eyes and pointed to the half-mangled crown. "I'm terrible at this."

"I mean it. Don't say that, El." Joanna laid her other hand on top of Eloise's, making a hand sandwich like they'd done ten thousand times when they were girls. "Let me be clear. You are not the person you were half a year ago. You've done some crazy things since you sucked it up, left home, and found me at the Legs Not Arms in For The Love of Çalaht Cut It Out You Two with Uncle Doncaster. Absolutely bonkers. Some of it was crazy stupid, but a lot of it was crazy brave, and all of it was crazy goodhearted. The Western Lands and All That Really Matters could do much worse than have a queen who was crazy good-hearted."

"That's... That's kind of you." Eloise sniffed and wiped her eyes with her cast. "You haven't even left and I miss you already. More than I can tell you."

Johanna gave Eloise's hand a squeeze. "I know. I'm going to miss you, too."

Eloise put her cast on top of the other three hands and pressed, a kind of broken wrist equivalent of a squeeze.

"Can I tell you something?" asked Johanna.

Eloise nodded.

Johanna lowered her voice to a whisper. "I'm scared."

"You are?"

"I'm at least as scared as you are. I just seem to be doing a better job of hiding it."

"Really? Why are you scared?"

"A thousand different reasons. I'm scared they won't make me queen. Or that they will, but I won't be a credit to the realm."

"But that's not really it, is it?"

"No, it's not." Johanna stood up, walked to the desk, and picked up one of their mother's quills from a pot. She ran a finger along the edge of it, then held it in front of her, a symbol of the late queen. "Someone had Mother killed. What if they want to do the same to you? Or me? You have to find out who it was."

"I know."

"And why."

"I know."

"I don't understand why no one seems to know anything." Johanna put the quill back into the pot.

"I agree. There seems to be a strange lack of curiosity about the matter. First Advisor Ligurian told me Mother shut down the search."

Johanna looked at her. "What? She didn't say anything about that to me. Why shut it down?"

"I don't know yet." Eloise thought for a moment. "Mother said something about it when I... before she... in my last conversation with her. She gave me the impression that everything that was going to be found out had been found out. And that was that. She was just done with it."

"Maybe she was too sick to care," said Johanna. "Or maybe they did find out, but whatever they found was better left unfound."

"Even if that left us in the dark and worrying?" Eloise shook her head. "That doesn't sound like her." She paused. "Then again, maybe it does."

Johanna waved a hand to indicate the room. "Clearly we only saw a fraction of what was going on."

"True."

"And maybe they really just didn't work it out."

"Also possible."

Eloise lifted the teapot, offering her sister a refill, but Johanna put up a hand to stop her. "I need to call it a night. There's a big day ahead of getting ready to go. I've got some plants, seeds, and saplings to prepare for the journey."

"This is going to be strange—me being here and you being there."

"Yes."

"We should..." Eloise trailed off, feeling awkward.

"What? Say it."

"We should write. You know. Keep in touch. I know things were weird for a few years, but it feels different now."

Johanna stepped close to Eloise and hugged her. "I'm going to miss you. Yes, let's write. We can send messengers back and forth."

"Messengers. Right," said Eloise. "I don't know if I want messengers reading our notes."

"No, I wouldn't want anyone reading our notes. We could use a wax seal, but that's hardly an insurmountable security measure." They drew back from their hug. "This must be a solved problem," said Johanna. "Mother must have been able to communicate in confidentiality. Maybe trusted couriers or something."

"We could use our code."

Johanna brightened. "Our code! I haven't thought of that in years. The one we had to create for our Weapons and Stratagems lessons."

"What were we, eight, maybe?"

"Nine. We had those matching maroon dresses with the goofy sleeves."

"I hated those dresses. But I remember Spymaster Glönk talking us through a substitution cipher."

"Can you imagine being the spymaster, and being dragged in to teach nine-year-olds?" said Joanna. "Looking back, I almost feel sorry for him."

"At least we paid attention and did what he asked. I remember it being fun."

"I remember arguing if it should be the Eljo Code or the Jo-el Code. You won that one."

"Only because 'Jo-el' looked too much like 'Joel,'" said Eloise.

"No, there was more to it than that. We each picked a number, because the text was double encrypted. You picked 11 and I picked 17, and we had to remember that to encrypt, the text was shifted first by 11, and then by 17. So El, then Jo. Eljo."

"I don't remember that bit. But now that you're saying it, it sounds familiar." Eloise reached out and took Johanna's hand. "So we'll write?"

"We'll write."

"Promise?"

"Promise. But you also have to promise me you'll figure out why she was killed."

"I'll figure it out," said Eloise.

"And that when you do..."

"Yes?"

"You'll do something about it."

"If I can, I will. Promise."

❧ II ❧

TASSEOGRAPHY

Eloise woke the next morning, had a moment's disorientation while she tried to work out where she was, remembered that it was her parents' chambers, felt a pang of grief for her mother, and then began trying not to worry about the day.

As she sat up, Odmilla de Platypus came in through a side door. Her rubbery snout beamed a massive grin. "Blessings of the day, Pri— I mean, my queen. Apologies. I've been saying 'princess' so long, it's taking me time to make the change."

The platypus's grin was infectious, and Eloise smiled back. "Blessings of the day to you, Odmilla. It's lovely to have yours be the first face I see this morning."

"Yes, last night Lady Seneschal found me in the laundry and said I'd been promoted to Probationary Handmaid to the Queen."

"I'm pleased for you." Eloise furrowed her brow. "What were you doing in the laundry?"

Odmilla looked down, but said nothing.

"Odmilla?"

"As there was no more call for my services as a princess's handmaid, I'd been reassigned to the laundry as a Second Assistant Washer Wench, Fourth Class."

"Oh, really? That's... That's terrible," Eloise said. "That's just wrong."

"It's kind of you to say, but that's what it's like here at Court for folks like me. But it's true—if I may be so bold, I'm thrilled to be waking you up this morning. I can't tell you how pleased I am to be a probationary handmaid."

"I'm glad you're happy."

"Oh, I am, I am." Odmilla waddled to the wardrobe. "Do you know what you'd like to wear today?"

"I'd like to try getting in my running this morning. So, my exercise breeks and tunic. I can dress for the work day after that."

"Yes, Pri— Yes, my queen."

"You know that's strange for me, too, right?"

"I can imagine."

Eloise dressed and let Odmilla brush her short-cropped hair. It was still just a fraction of the length she'd had before her journey to get Johanna back. And though it felt like forever, it had only been growing a few weeks since she'd hacked it all off in a panicked frenzy after Melveeta the Elusive's blood had soaked it. Eloise was getting used to how her hair looked, now turned white after her time in the Purple Haze and still short enough to pass for a trainee guard. It was just starting to show the first hints of her unmanageable curls. She didn't look forward to the daily hair wrestling matches that Odmilla had previously had to go through. Maybe she'd keep it short.

Eloise managed 22 loops of the Culpability Courtyard at a very light pace. Her body still ached in places where she'd expected it to—wrist and shoulder, mainly—as well as some that she hadn't (back, legs, arms, neck, and, incredibly, her left earlobe). Back in her parents' room, she had a quick, slightly-too-hot bath and was soon dressed. With the Star of Whatever at her hip, and wearing the GHC, she was ready to break fast.

A serving wench opened the door to the Salle de la Famille and brought in Eloise's tray of food. She saw Jerome standing outside the door, and waved at him.

"Jerome! Blessings of the day to you."

The chipmunk stepped inside the doorway and gave her one of his sarcastic, overly ornate bows, complete with hand and tail waggling. "Blessings of the day, Queen Eloise."

"Will you break fast with me?"

"Thank you, my queen. I might have a little something, if you don't mind."

She patted the chair next to hers and a second place was set. Moments later, they had cups of haggleberry tea steaming in front of them, Jerome was spreading a small hill of brunchberry jam on his toasted half bagel and Eloise was pouring maple syrup on griddle cakes.

"I had the strangest dream about you last night," said Jerome after swallowing his first mouthful.

"Oh, please tell me," said Eloise, setting down her knife and clasping her hands with mock pleading. "Please, please, please tell me about the brain burps you had during the night."

"Look, I know you don't like hearing about my dreams, Eloramus," said the chipmunk. "But this one included you. I thought that might spark your interest. Just for that, I'm going to tell it to you."

"You know I can have you hauled out of here bound and gagged, right?"

"You'd do that to the queen's champion? I don't think so." Jerome took another bite of his bagel. His whiskers sagged and he set it down. "I miss Chef."

"They're not that bad."

"I know, I know. But Chef had a certain whatever-it-was that's just not there anymore. It's not the same."

Eloise went quiet, and focused on cutting her griddle cakes into as close to equal pieces as was possible with a rough circle.

The silence stretched long enough that Jerome noticed. "What?" he asked.

"Nothing."

"Come on, what?"

"What you said about Chef. Or about the new Chef, by inference."

"What about it?"

"That's what people will say about me, if I'm lucky—or worse."

"What? That there's a whatever-it-is that's not there anymore? Oh, El." Jerome reached over and put a paw on the back of her hand. "You're going to be fine."

"'You're going to be fine' is what people say to you when you're not going to be fine, like when you're going to be dead of an ague in a couple of days or when a tax auditor shows up. Just because someone says, 'It's going to be fine,' doesn't mean it will actually be."

Jerome gave the back of her hand a squeeze. "Elimissimo, what's going on?"

Eloise looked down, laced her hands in her lap, and hunched her shoulders. "You sat next to me in all those years of Histories and Hearsay classes. Not every Gumball queen is a Gwendolyn the Irritable or an Agnes Delion Frostbite Gumball. Or even my mother. Some of us end up a Queen Joan the Sadly Befuddled, a Queen Aubrey the Parasitic, a Queen What's-Her-Name the Infinitely Forgettable, or even my grandmother. Have you heard the disdain people have in their voices when they refer to grandmother's memory as 'One?' Compare that to how they say 'Two' when talking about my mother. With 'Two' there's reverence and deep respect."

"You're worried about your legacy? Or about the nickname the histories will give you?" Jerome pointed to her crown. "You've only been wearing that thing a couple of days. Cut yourself some slack."

"It's not about my nickname or my legacy." Eloise sipped her tea and gathered her thoughts. "But what are those things built on? They're built on what one does while one's wearing this ridiculous thing."

"So?"

"So?" Eloise wiped the corners of her eyes with her index fingers, then fished out a handkerchief from a pocket and blew her nose. "So, I don't want to end up Queen Eloise the Good Intentioned But Ineffectual, Queen Eloise the Sadly Misguided, Queen Eloise the She Wasn't As Good A Queen As Her Sister and Why Couldn't The Other One Have Ruled Us, or even Queen Eloise the Thank Çalaht She Died As Soon As She Did And Someone Else Took Over."

"Queen Eloise the She Wasn't As Good As Her Sister?"

"You know what people are like. We're taking over realms at the same time, assuming Johanna works that out. They're going to compare us. It's inevitable."

"Who cares?"

"I care. Not about how good a job Johanna might do. I'm sure she'll be fine. That's the way she is. Very solid, my sister. But I want to do a good job, too, Jer. I really do. And..."

"And?"

"And I have no idea how."

"Surely every Gumball queen thinks the same thing when she takes over. If she has any self-awareness, she'd think that. I reckon your mother might have felt the same when she first wore the crown."

"I wouldn't know."

"What do you mean?"

"She never talked to us about this kind of thing."

"Really?"

"Really."

"Unfortunate."

"Yes."

They sat quietly for a moment. Eloise tilted her teacup forward, but there was just a small hint of liquid above the sediment of haggleberry leaves. She contemplated pouring herself another cup, but before she could, Jerome put up a hand to stop her. "I have an idea," he said. The chipmunk walked to her cup.

"What?"

"Can you let me try something? Please, El?"

"Try what?"

He struck a dramatic pose, arms wide and tail at a jaunty angle. "Tasseography."

"Tasseo... What? Wait. That rings a bell."

"Tasseography is the fine and ancient art of prognostication through the reading of tea leaves."

"Oh, yeah. I remember. We tried that a few times in Oracles and Insights class. If memory serves, you said it was 'Stupid down to the stem' and 'Dumb down to the bone.'"

"Well, I've been trying to do it since we got back. So now it's a fine and ancient art. Can I try to do a reading for you?"

Eloise shrugged. "Sure. Why not."

"May I please have your cup?"

She slid her cup and saucer toward him. "All yours."

"Thanks. Do you want a general reading or something specific?"

Eloise shrugged. "General is fine."

"OK." Jerome peered into her cup. "Have a last sip. Clear your mind and open yourself to the realm of possibility and insight."

Eloise raised an eyebrow at him, but did as he said.

"May I have your napkin?"

"Sure."

Jerome put it on the saucer and poured most of the remaining tea onto it. "Swirl what's left around three times."

Eloise gave the thick mixture a good swish, then handed it back to Jerome, who inverted the cup onto the napkin in the saucer and gave it a moment to let the remaining liquid drain. "Touch the cup to let your energy into it, then rotate it three times widdershins."

Eloise put two fingers on the dome of the inverted cup for a moment, then turned it counter-clockwise.

Jerome turned the cup right-side up, leaving it on the saucer. Concentrating, he started walking around it, his claw idly scratching the fur of his face. "I see you standing in a forest. But it's not a forest, because there is yellow there. Not yellow like autumn foliage. It's like you're standing in a shortish forest-ish kind of place. More than shrubs. Less than trees. They are eye-like things. Big, yellow eye-ish eyes with big, brown pupils, massive like they're dilated. Like bee eyes, but not really. Huge. And single. Not pairs. There are masses of them, slowly looking from one side to the other. There's green, too, with the huge yellow and brown eye-like thingies."

"Huh." Eloise tried to make it a neutral sound.

The chipmunk continued circling the cup, studying every tea sediment's shape and nuance. "Hmmmm..."

"Hmmmm?"

"Hmmmmmm. Very interesting."

"What's interesting?"

"It's very interesting that that's all I got." He looked up at Eloise. "There you go. There's your reading."

Eloise kept her face blank. "Well, thank you then."

Jerome went back to his spot and resumed nibbling on his bagel. "So, what'd you think?"

"Spectacular."

The chipmunk gave Eloise a narrow look. "You're being sarcastic."

"My future is huge, yellow and brown, bee-eye-like thingies. How does that sound to you?"

Jerome cleared his throat. "How about unlikely, inane, and bogus."

"There you go, Jer," said Eloise. "Self-awareness is a good thing. But keep at it. I'm sure you'll get better."

"Like I got better at being your champion?"

"You did get better at that."

Jerome looked at her.

"Really. You did."

"That's very kind of you to say."

"Jer, I *like* having you as my champion."

"It is one's pleasure to serve."

"Did this just get weird?"

Jerome relaxed and bit his bagel. "Nope. No weirder than having a chipmunk as your champion has ever been."

"Hush up and pass the brunchberry jam."

"Of course, Your Highness."

❧   12   ❧

IMPUDENCE

First Advisor Ligurian found Eloise and Jerome just finishing up their breakfast. He wore a plain, burgundy version of his robe of office, matching breeks and tunic in a deeper crimson. His hair was wet as if he'd just bathed, and his eyes were shot through with red, as though he'd been on a crying jag. Perhaps he missed the late queen more than he let on. Or maybe someone had burned his toast. With Ligurian, it was hard to tell.

"First Advisor, blessings of the day to you," said Eloise.

"Blessings of the day, Queen Eloise. And to you, Champion Abernatheen de Chipmunk."

"Blessings of the day," said Jerome through a mouthful of bagel.

"Would you care for a bagel?" asked Eloise.

"No, my queen. Thank you, but no. I had an early meeting, so broke fast in my chambers."

"I see. You're already at work, then."

"'The queendom beckons,' as your mother always said."

"You're right. She did always say that. Well, then." Eloise stood, smoothed down the front of her dress, unconsciously felt for the Star of Whatever's box under her robe at her hip, and clasped her hands in front of her. "The queendom beckons. What's on the agenda?"

Ligurian glanced at his scroll. "This morning you need to formally accept the credentials of the ambassadors and envoys from the other realms. For that, we need to go to the Receiving Room, Queen Eloise."

"To the Receiving Room, then." She and First Advisor headed for the door.

"Hold up," said Jerome, dabbing his mouth with the corner of his napkin. "I'll come with you, eh, Elosaurus?"

First Advisor whirled and stared at the chipmunk. "I beg your pardon, Champion Abernatheen de Chipmunk."

Jerome looked at him, confused. "I said I'd come with. That one's not so difficult, is it?"

"Outrageous!"

"What? I'm her champion," said Jerome, surprised at the strength of First Advisor's response. "I'm supposed to be with her."

"That is not the matter at hand," snapped Ligurian.

Jerome's eyes narrowed. "What then, your First Advisoriness?" He stood on his chair, clasped his paws behind him, and jutted his jaw forward. Eloise could tell from the fluff of his tail that he was winding up, and fast.

"One does not refer to our queen with impudence."

"Impudence? What insect flew up your nose and called you home?" said Jerome. "It's a nickname. A term of affection. I have a thousand of them for her. She has a thousand for me."

"That might have been fine last week. Or last month. But see that thing on her head?"

"What, the Cranium Crusher? What about it?"

"The Gumballic Heraldic Crown—or for that matter, any and all of the crowns she might wear—they are all symbols of who she is and what she represents."

"I know that. So what?"

"So things have changed for her. Things. Have. Changed. And because they have changed for her, they have changed for those around her. And that includes you, even if you are her champion."

"Don't go telling me how to interact with her. I'm more than her champion. I'm her best friend."

Ligurian stepped forward, towering over Jerome. "And she is your queen! You will treat her as such. How you behave toward her sets an example for others."

"Look around! Do you see anyone else? Who am I setting an example for?"

Eloise raised her hand.

By reflex, Ligurian took two steps and lowered his head. Jerome looked like he was about to spit another retort, but she held up a hand and stopped him. "Stop it. Both of you."

She gave them a moment to let the tension dissipate.

"Apologies, Queen Eloise," said Ligurian.

"Apology accepted." Eloise looked at Jerome, and when he didn't say anything, raised an eyebrow at him.

"Apologies, my queen," muttered the chipmunk.

"Accepted. First Advisor has a point, Champion Abernatheen de Chipmunk. People need to see others treating me as queen to help them get used to the idea that that's also what they should do."

"It was just us," said Jerome. "You also need to be a regular person."

"When it really is just you and me, then maybe. But First Advisor was here, too. Plus her." She pointed to a serving wench standing invisibly in the corner. "Sorry, what was your name again?"

"Éëètáää, ma'am," she drawled with a thick Southie accent.

"Thank you," said Eloise. "Plus Éëètáää."

"OK, OK. Point taken." Jerome bowed to Ligurian, Eloise, and the serving wench, managing to keep the snark in his manner to a minimum. "My apologies to both of you. And you," he added with a nod to Éëètáää. "I will henceforth and forthwith be more circumspect in my choice of nomenclature for our beloved monarchal person."

Eloise saw First Advisor's left eye twitch, but he seemed mollified enough.

"Right," she said. "Who else am I seeing this morning? I'm not going to have to pass judgment on anyone or decide anything important, am I? I don't know if I'm quite ready for that."

"Not this morning, Queen Eloise. This session in the Receiving Room is just the ambassadors and envoys. We can discuss the rest of the day's agenda afterward."

"That seems painless enough. Shall we?"

"Yes, Your Highness." Ligurian waved her toward the door with a flourish that looked a little like something Jerome would do, but the gesture lacked any sense of mocking. "After you, of course."

Eloise turned to Jerome. "Champion Abernatheen de Chipmunk, you're still welcome to join me in the Receiving Room. Would you care to come?"

"Thank you, Queen Eloise, I shall."

Eloise led them on a brisk walk toward the Receiving Room. As they went, she thought about the only other time she'd sat on the Listening Throne and received people on behalf of the late queen. There'd been no one at all, until Jerome's mother, Seer Maybelle de Chipmunk, had shown up and tried to persuade Eloise that her prognostications—

inevitable as they always were—seemed to say that she should marry Jerome. Eloise had side-stepped that awkward possibility by naming him her champion. It had been an odd choice, but he was her friend, and it had worked out OK, more or less.

Just shy of the main door of the Receiving Room, Eloise stopped at a small door that led to a side chamber where the queen could be private prior to appearing before the public. It also allowed the crowd to gather first, which made for a more dramatic entrance. Eloise stood on her toes and looked through a peephole into the main room. Perhaps two dozen people were there, from what she could see. She recognized most of them as dignitaries from other realms, heralds from the legitimate heralding services, a gossip herald from one of the more scurrilous outfits, and the ever-present Court scrivener, who sat, quill at the ready, prepared to note every detail of the proceedings, which he would transcribe into the official record.

First Advisor nodded to the row of capes hanging from pegs along the wall. "You'll want to choose one of these, of course."

"Of course," said Eloise, having only remembered when she'd seen them hanging there.

The choice of cape the queen wore while sitting on the Listening Throne spoke volumes. Her mother had always been extremely deliberate in her selection. Eloise looked up and down the row, and recognized many, but not all of them. Most of the capes back here were generally obscure. The more commonly used ones were hung along a wall inside the room itself. She should probably choose one of those. But not necessarily. There really were a lot of them. She'd have to get someone to tell her about them, but wasn't sure who knew all that lore.

Eloise knew she shouldn't choose the Adjudication Cape, since First Advisor had indicated that this session would not be about grievances, justice, or entreaties. Nor should she wear the Tribute Cape, as this was not about tithes or the queen's percentage. It was clear that the Cape of Dashed Hope, the Disavowal Cape, the Jangled Cape, and the Really, You Don't Want To Mess With Me Today Cape would send the wrong message. In the end, she straightened herself, made sure the

Gumballic Heraldic Crown was properly seated, and stepped into the room. She didn't look at anyone as she moved to the wall and put on the familiar Attention Cape, then took her seat on the Listening Throne.

"My friends," she said to people that she knew were not her friends. "Please be at rest."

AMBASSADORS AND ENVOYS

First Advisor Ligurian walked to a waiting herald who stood at the corner of the dais. "Good morning, Harold," he said, and handed him a scroll.

Harold Hairauld the herald unscrolled it, gave it a quick glance through, then began declaiming in a booming, basso voice: "A prrrrrrresentation of official crrrrrrrrredentials by the rrrrrrrrrepresentatives of other rrrrrrrrrealms." He rolled his r's like a boulder careening down a mountainside. The man looked at Eloise. "Is the queen rrrrrrrrready to proceed?"

Eloise gave what she hoped was a lofty nod. "Yes, please."

"Then lllllllllllllet us begin! Will the ambassador from The South please step forrrrrrrrrward."

A squat, beautifully berobed man creaked out of his chair and waddled toward the front. He was pushing six decades and bald on top, but tried to hide it, not by combing a side bit over the top like a normal self-conscious bald person, but by wearing a pair of strategically-placed ferrets on his head, trained to hold very still and look like a toupee. Why he didn't just wear a toupee was beyond Eloise, but to each their own. Perhaps it was some sort of make-work employment opportunity. Or maybe he and the ferrets were friends.

Despite the ferrets and the stunningly bad "hair" arrangement, Eloise recognized him. At Jerome's Naming Ceremony, when the chipmunk had officially been named her champion, this same man (pre-ferrets— Eloise would have remembered those) had given Jerome a small, embroidered, felt-lined pouch with a tenth of a weak weight of prattle-weed in it. It had been a generous and daring gift, since possession of religious herbage by non-humans in The South was strictly against the law—much worse than speaking the Queen's tongue in public, and Eloise had first-hand knowledge of just how bad a breach of that particular edict was.

He Who Wore Two Ferrets made it to the front, handed Ligurian the scroll with his credentials, and then he and the furry beings gave Eloise a well-practiced bow. When he straightened, the ferrets settled back into their former position and resumed their hairlike appearance.

"Ambassador Gléëèngarland Póöòíïntilist, Your Highness," he said. "I bring greetings from Her Majesty, Onomatopoeia Handrail Lúüù-derming. Her Majesty sends her personal condolences on the passing of your mother, and well wishes on the success of your reign. She specifically asked me to say, 'May the little songbird sing glory for her realm.' Which, I might add, I don't quite understand."

Eloise wasn't about to explain that "little songbird" was a reference to her having gotten prattled off her head while sitting next to the Southie queen at a Çalahtic devotional in the Sclerotic Wold. Some embarrassments were best left unremembered. "Thank you, Ambassador Póöòíïntilist. Please convey my thanks to Queen Onomatopoeia."

"I shall, I shall. Her Majesty also asked me to present you with this token of her esteem." Póöòíïntilist looked at the back of the room and waived forward an attendant.

The second man had a similar hair arrangement, but being both junior and probably less rich, he wore a single raccoon instead of two ferrets on his head, with the raccoon clinging to the back of his skull and the tail flopped somewhat hairlike over the top. The effect was remarkably less successful. Raccoon Tail stopped just behind Póöòíiìntilist, dipped a knee, and held forward a pillow with an embroidered linen bag on it. The ambassador took the bag, and with another bow, offered it in Eloise's general direction. Ligurian retrieved it, stepped onto the dais, and gave it to her.

Eloise rubbed the outside of the bag, which gave a linen sliding on linen feel. "Is it…" With a creeping feeling of dread, Eloise opened the drawstring and saw more bags inside. She drew out the smallest one of these, untied its string, and found herself looking at what, for her, would be seven lifetimes' worth of prattleweed seeds. Another bag had stems. A third, root shreds. A fourth, leaves.

What was she supposed to do with this? She'd never, ever use it.

And did it even belong to her, personally, or was it a gift to the greater queendom? Was there a difference? How did all that even work?

"Queen Eloise, I present to you a supply of the highest quality prattleweed that the devotional house suppliers in The South have to offer. This selection was handpicked by none other than…" Here he gave a dramatic pause. "Madam Righteous herself. It comes from her 'special' collection that is not available to usual patrons of her shop, Something Sacred This Way Comes, nor even her more unusual patrons."

"Súüùsáäàn Jóöònéëès chose these herself? Aw, that's sweet."

Póöòíiìntilist's eyebrows went up so far that they slipped under his ferrets. "You know her?"

"We met. Someone must have rushed awfully hard to get it here so quickly after my mother's passing."

"Queen Onomatopoeia did insist on speed."

"That would be her way," said Eloise.

"Each small bag is a different strain of the plant, chosen for maximal efficacy, strength, and all-round *boom*, if you know what I mean. The seeds are Seeker's Succor. The roots are Devotee's Detonation. The stems are the ones Queen Onomatopoeia favors, Undead Monarch. And the leaves are from my personal favorite, *¡¡Whammo!!*"

"Whammo?"

"Close. *'¡¡Whammo!!'*"

"*'¡Whammo!?'*"

"That'll do. That's how most people say it." Póöòíïntilist gave a little "ta-da" motion with his hands. "With this gift, the queen wishes you close communion with the Divine One herself."

"Why, uh, thank you?" Eloise hadn't meant to make it a question, but the last thing she wanted to do was get prattled and seek Çalaht ever again.

"If you need instruction in the application of such religious supplies, I can arrange—"

"That's very generous of you, Ambassador Póöòíïntilist. Very, very generous. I'll let you know if I need help."

He nodded, then stood there, waiting.

Eloise wasn't sure of the proper way to officially accept his credentials, so she faked it by raising her palm toward him and saying something she hoped sounded reasonable. "I recognize you as the ambassador from The South. Thank you for your service at Court."

"Thank you, Your Highness." The ambassador, his ferrets, the assistant, and the raccoon all bowed and backed away.

Harold Hairauld glanced at his scroll and called out, "Will the trrrrrrade rrrrrrrepresentative from the Half Kingdom please step forrrrrrrrward."

A heavyset, dandyish fop stood from a chair at the back and moved forward with a gait that would have been at home on a dance floor. He reached the front, handed Ligurian his scroll, doffed his tricorn hat, and gave Eloise a two-armed swoop of a bow. "Trade Representative Theoplonkilis, at your service, Queen Eloise."

"Master Theoplonkilis," said Eloise. "How pleasant to see you again. You're looking well."

"Thank you, Queen Eloise. May I express condolences for your loss, especially as it comes so close after the loss of your uncle, my late monarch."

"Thank you. My condolences for your loss as well."

"Thank you, Queen Eloise."

"May I ask…" Eloise wasn't quite sure how to word her question.

"Yes?" Theoplonkilis raised an eyebrow, curious.

"Well, don't take this the wrong way, but how is it that you're here presenting credentials as a trade representative," asked Eloise. "Instead of an ambassador or a senior envoy or something?"

"Çalaht must have smiled in my general direction this morning, Your Highness." Theoplonkilis gave a palms-up shrug. "Actually, it's fairly simple. The ambassadors and envoys were all automatically recalled to the Half Kingdom at the king's passing. Matter of course. I happened to be in the neighborhood, and was asked if I might stand in."

"If there's no king, who asked you?"

"Why, your sister, Princess Johanna. She didn't want there to be… How did she put it? Discontinuity. She didn't want discontinuity of representation here at the Western Lands and All That Really Matters Court. But she's not in a position to promote or appoint, so she just sort of asked if I might do it."

"And you said yes."

"And I said yes, exactly." Theoplonkilis smoothed down the front of his tunic, and his hand ran into an embroidered pouch tied to his belt. "Oh!" he said, and he fumbled open the button flap on the pouch. Extracting something from it, he cleared his throat and said, "On behalf of the Half Kingdom, I present this as a small token of the great esteem we hold for you and your queendom."

He held forward a pot, which Ligurian ferried to Eloise. She took it, held it up to see it better, and turned it around in her hands. The ceramic pottery was intricately pattered in shades of purple, and there was a seal of purple wax.

It was a purple that Eloise knew very, very well, and it brought back memories of the extreme discomfort caused by chiggers in a Southie jail, as well as the Purple Haze itself. "A jar of wart cream, Master Theoplonkilis?"

"Exactly, Queen Eloise." Theoplonkilis chortled with delight. "It is grade A, top of the line, best in class, award-winning wart cream, produced and packaged exclusively for the monarch of the Half Kingdom. This is a particularly rare blend, and is known for its extreme warty effectiveness."

"How very considerate," said Eloise. "Thank you, Master Theoplonkilis."

"Do you like it?" He flashed puppy eyes at her.

"Of course. It's... It's delightful. Thank you, again." Then to get past the matter, Eloise raised her palm toward him and said, "I recognize you as the acting representative of the Half Kingdom. Thank you for your service at Court."

"Thank you, Queen Eloise," said Theoplonkilis, pleased. He bowed his dancing steps back to his chair.

Herald Harold Hairauld didn't look at his scroll this time. He simply said, "Will the ambassadorrrrrrr and lead trrrrrrade negotiatorrrrrrrrr from the Eastern Lands please step forrrrrrrrward."

A woman moved from a side wall and strode toward the dais. She was tall, built like a javelin, and dressed in a flowing cotton robe dyed a traditional shade of olive green that was typical of her realm. Her waist-length black hair was plaited into a five-strand braid that hung to her waist. She wore just a hint of make-up, with a dusky smear of eye shadow in a green that matched her dress. Her smile had the warmth and sincerity of an undertaker's second apprentice, and her black eyes practically sucked the light from the room.

She stopped at the front of the dais and gave a curt nod to Eloise. As she handed two scrolls to Ligurian, a python of extraordinary size and color joined her from the opposite wall. The scales on his back were a bright, iridescent blue. They lightened on his sides, then blended to a brilliant white at his underside. Eloise had never seen anyone that color, much less a snake.

But as incredible as his coloration was, what struck Eloise most was his head. The snake had three eyes.

Three working eyes.

Just looking at him gave Eloise the willies.

Two of his eyes were in the expected places, on either side of his head, but an extra one stared out at the world from the middle of his forehead, where his wisdom eye ought to have been. The supernumerary eye worked independently of the others. It flitted around, taking in everything from a different angle.

Eloise tamped down an involuntary shudder as he coiled himself into a formal posture next to the Javelin Woman.

"My name is Picholine Manzanilla," she said. "I am the new Eastern Lands ambassador to your fair queendom, if you'll do me the honor of accepting my credentials, on behalf of Her Majesty, Queen Aglandau Gaeta Cerignola Ponentine. In her place and as her mouth, I bring you greetings from the Eastern Lands, well wishes for your reign and its longevity, and the deep desire for our queendoms to stand side-by-side in friendship, tolerance, and enduring cooperation."

"Thank you," said Eloise. "May it please Çalaht enough to make it so."

"And I am Bosana de Coluber," said the snake. "I am lead trade negotiator." His diction lacked the sibilance that many snakes struggled with due to the split in their tongues. His speech was perfect, but he was unsettling to look at. "Queen Eloise, congratulations on your ascension, and condolences on the passing of the late queen."

"Thank you, Master de Coluber."

An assistant in a kalamata-olive-brown tunic carried forward a jar on a pillow. Manzanilla picked it up and held it out toward First Advisor, who took it. "This is from the personal grove of Queen Aglandau. She offers you this small gift as a token of affection and in recognition of your ascension to the throne of the Western Lands and All That Really Matters."

Ligurian brought the jar to the throne and handed it to Eloise. She looked at the olives. What could she say? They looked like olives. Big olives, but olives.

"These look like very nice olives," said Eloise. "And large. They're big."

"The tree that grew these olives is known through documentation to be at least 2,000 years old, although we suspect it is more like 6,000," said Manzanilla.

"I see."

"The Divine One is said to have sat under its branches and attained her enlightenment," said de Coluber. His third eye winked. Eloise wasn't sure it if was a "just between us, this is funny" kind of wink, or simply a blink, but because it was only from the one eye, it came across as a wink. It was unsettling to watch him speak. Perhaps that's why he was their trade negotiator. The weird eye gave him an edge.

"Oh, we have some of those here in the Western Lands and All That Really Matters as well," said Eloise.

The two them looked at her like she'd spat in their carrot juice.

"I'm just saying, you hear that here, too. Not with olive trees. But, there's an avocado tree somewhere southwest of Lower Glenth where Çalaht is supposed to have had her vision about her hangnail tribulations. There's a live oak by a devotional house at Rockslide where she allegedly had a vague inkling about the whole thumb stretching thing that was coming. I've even heard about a Trident Maple bonsai that she put her big toe beneath, which supposedly triggered a full-on nirvana for seven seconds. The bonsai is passed from one devotional house to another on a fixed rotation that lasts decades, and people come from strong lengths around to put their big toes under it."

The carrot juice spit look remained. Eloise wondered if she was in the process of causing a major diplomatic spat.

The snake broke the awkward silence. He coughed and said, "To be fair, there are at least half a dozen trees in the Eastern Lands that vie to be recognized as the tree of her enlightenment."

The woman shot him a sharp look, but held her silence.

"Well, there you go. Something we have in common," said Eloise, hoping to slide past the moment. "And thank you for this precious gift." She set the jar on her lap and lifted her palm. "I recognize you as the ambassador and lead trade negotiator of the Eastern Lands. Thank you for your service at Court."

"Thank you," they both said and retreated to opposite sides of the room.

Harold Hairauld took another look at his scroll. "Will the envoy from the Central Rrrrrrrranges please step forrrrrrrrward."

A mare entered the Receiving Room from the hallway, striding in with a stately walking gait. Her hair coloring was striking, and a pattern that Eloise had not seen before. Her face, neck and forelegs were midnight black, save for a white circle of a blaze in the middle of her forehead that was smeared with a blotch of ocher. Just past her withers, her body became a blinding white. The line of demarcation was so straight and sudden that it looked like someone had dangled her head first in a vat of ink. She was unadorned, except for a pure white bag draped around her neck like a collar.

The horse stopped where the others had stood and spoke to First Advisor. "My documents are in the pouch. You may remove them, if you wish."

Ligurian opened a flap and took out a small scroll of hemp parchment. When he'd stepped back, the mare looked directly at Eloise and did not bow. "I am Naranbaatar Enkhtuya. I offer my credentials as the representative of His Alacrity Khan Nergüi Unbenannt Nimetuseta and the Us."

"Welcome to Court, Envoy Enkhtuya," said Eloise.

"Thank you."

Eloise waited for her to say something else, but she didn't. No offer of condolences. No gift. That seemed very in line with the ways of the Us. Eloise tried a question. "Are you newly arrived in the realm?"

"Yes."

That was it. No elaboration.

Eloise waited again. The mare stood still, as still as any of the khan's warriors, who Eloise knew could stand for hours without twitching. She wondered if she should stand up and offer Enkhtuya a nose blow greeting. But to do so seemed both out of context and too familiar, and it didn't look like the horse was open to that kind of thing, so Eloise stayed put.

The mare remained silent. Not very diplomatic for a diplomat, but certainly in character for one of the khan's people.

Eloise broke the silence. "Well, if that's it, then..." One last pause for the horse to say something, then Eloise raised her palm. "I recognize you as the envoy from the Central Ranges. Thank—"

"No," interrupted Enkhtuya.

Eloise blinked at her. "I beg your pardon?"

"I am not the envoy from the Central Ranges," said the mare. "I do not represent the Not Us, nor the savages who are tolerated to dwell in the lands of the khan. I represent Nergüi Unbenannt Nimetuseta and the Us." There was no rancor in her voice. She simply stated facts.

This irked Eloise. The Us were insular, but come on. "And if matters arise that concern the Not Us or the other peoples of the Central Ranges?" she asked.

"That is not of concern to me. Nor to the Us."

"I see." Eloise shifted her position on the Listening Throne. "May I ask, what happened to the previous consul from the Central Ranges? I remember he gifted my champion a small knife at his Naming Ceremony."

"He was a savage—not even one of the Not Us—and did not represent the Us. When I arrived yesterday, I relieved him of any pretensions he might have had about speaking for the Us or the khan."

"I see." Eloise looked at First Advisor. "Are her credentials in order?"

Ligurian looked over the scroll. "Yes, Your Highness."

She looked back at Enkhtuya, who stared straight ahead. Eloise swallowed, paused, then said, "No."

There was an audible intake of breath from a few watchers in the room.

Enkhtuya tilted her head, and aimed one eye at Eloise so she could see her better. "No, what?"

"No, I don't accept what you've said."

The horse stood still, not reacting.

"I have met the khan, you know."

"Yes."

"I have a sense of the Us from my time among you. I have shared tea with your khan. I have taken the vision herbs and quested into the unseen with him. I found him very reasonable."

"I know. That is why I am here."

"I have exchanged breath with your people," said Eloise. "It took me half a morning to say goodbye."

"I was there," said Enkhtuya. "You and I have shared breath."

"I see," said Eloise. "I'm sorry. I don't remember that. There were a lot of you."

The mare did not respond. She simply waited.

Eloise stood up and everyone in the room stood or straightened. It gave the moment more import than she'd meant. "The khan is the one ruling force in the Central Ranges. There are not two realms, nor two rulers. There is just Khan Nimetuseta. I know the Us don't think much of the Not Us, and even less of those you call savages. But like it or not, they are people, too, no matter the species. In my court, that matters."

It was the first time Eloise had actually thought of it as her court.

"Naranbaatar Enkhtuya," said Eloise, "I invite you to act as ambassador for the Central Ranges and all her people. Otherwise, I invite you to pack your things, return to your khan, and ask him to please send someone who will."

The mare flinched, but kept her composure. Unconsciously, she licked her lips. Eloise had seen that before—both with Hector and the Nameless One. They did it sometimes when they were thinking, like they were chewing on a thought. Eloise stood still and let the mare think.

After a full minute, the horse nodded. "I shall convey your terms to the khan and let you know what he says. It should take no more than a week."

Then the mare turned and walked out of the Receiving Room.

Eloise gave it a moment, then looked around the room. "Right. Any other business?"

No one said anything.

"First Advisor?"

"No, Queen Eloise. No other business."

"Then thank you all for coming." Eloise turned and walked off the dais. Jerome hesitated a moment, then followed.

"Well, that was strange," he muttered as Eloise hung up the Attention Cape. "But good for you, Queen Eloise."

"Thanks, Jer," she said. "I hope being queen isn't always this odd."

❧ 14 ❧

WHAT KIND OF QUEEN

That afternoon, Eloise went looking for her father to see how he was, as she'd barely seen him since the funeral. She didn't just want to yell, "Page!" and have him sent for. It seemed rude to do that to her dad.

He wasn't in his new room or his study. He wasn't in the corner of the kitchen where he used to grab a cup of tea and pretend he didn't want to sneak a sample of whatever delicacy Chef was working on, perhaps a pumpkin scone fresh from the oven or a slice of mango pie liberated from the cool room.

Eloise eventually found the no-longer king sitting in the chilly stillness of the Square Root Garden, which was laid out in curving swoops of low hedges surrounding beds full of flower bulbs napping in the winter soil and guarded by the leafless, sleeping skeletons of deciduous trees. The garden was named for the mathematical pattern used to plan its bed outlines and plant placement. The name also referred to a set of permanent, hollow, rectangular forms set in the very middle, which were used to shape growing tubers, mainly potatoes and sweet potatoes, into squared-off shapes. Chef had used those particular spuds to create her special Right-Angle Fries, served exclusively at the annual

Mathematicians Guild High Tea. Eloise always wondered why Chef didn't just cut normal potatoes into flat squares, but assumed there was a culinary reason to go to the effort of growing them this way.

But Chef was now gone. Eloise wondered if the new Chef would keep up the tradition of growing rectangular tubers in the Square Root Garden. She hoped so.

But it would never be the same.

Chafed sat near the hollow square forms on a wrought-iron chair with a cushion below him, a blanket across his lap, and a pot of haggleberry tea on the garden table. His eyes were red and his nose was running, a combination of cold air and hot grief.

The dowager king stood as his daughter approached.

"Please, Father, don't do that," said Eloise.

"It's Protocol. I did the same with your mother. Surely you noticed."

"I guess so. But it makes me uncomfortable."

"You'll get used to it." He motioned to a second chair at the table. "Tea?"

"Please."

"Sorry, there were a few almandines and chocolatines earlier, but..." He shrugged, and didn't seem to have the will to finish the sentence.

Eloise sat, leaving her father free to do the same. "Are you OK?"

Chafed shook his head.

"You miss her."

"Yes. More than I can tell you. It's just..." Chafed raised his cuff to his eye and caught a drop of moisture. "It's just I guess I thought we'd have more time together. Years. But we didn't." He sniffed and dabbed his eye again. "It hurts too much to be here, Ëëëlöööïïïsëëë."

"I can imagine." She gave his arm a gentle squeeze.

"She's everywhere. In every corner, in every hall, in every echo."

"At one level, I guess that's nice. Memories to cherish."

"Like you'd cherish a hot fire poker up the…"

"Father. Please."

He sighed, long and deep. Then, remembering the tea, he poured her a cup, then took a sip of his own tea and grimaced. "We've lost enough friends and colleagues for me to know that it won't always feel like this. But right now, it does. Right now, I'm finding the overwhelming sense of her ghost being everywhere a torture." He looked at his daughter. "I guess it might be the same for you?"

Eloise reached for her father's hand and laced her fingers in his. "It can only be different. I lost a mother, but you lost a wife."

The former king gave a small nod. "Yes, I did. But I lost more than that."

"How so?"

"I've lost my place in the world. The crown's on your head now." He tapped the Gumballic Heraldic Crown gently. "Such is Protocol."

"Such is Protocol," echoed Eloise.

"She was the center of my life, the center of Court, the center of every-thing. With her gone, my support role is gone."

"You can support me," said Eloise. "I want you to support me. I need you to support me."

Chafed allowed himself a shrug. "I don't think I can. It's your turn to run the realm. You don't need me hanging around in the background making you second guess things, or making you wonder what your mother would do or decide. And I hate being called the 'dowager king.' That makes me sound like I should be old, crotchety, and wandering around with a hump on my shoulder."

"I keep asking people not to call you that."

"Protocol."

Eloise nodded. "Protocol, yes. But, to the point, I like having you around. I like having your advice."

"You have First Advisor Ligurian. You mother always listened to him more than me. I mean, she sought my opinion often enough, but First Advisor was always much better with strategy and tactics. That's just not how I think. That's part of why I'm going."

Eloise turned on her seat to look at him. "'Going?' What do you mean, 'going?'"

"Johanna has invited me to return with her to the Half Kingdom. I thought I might do that, and stay at least until she's settled in as queen."

"But Father..."

"I need to make it clear that I won't sit on my brother's throne. People need to know that I won't take the crown," said Chafed. "They must know I support Johanna becoming queen. Otherwise, there will be rumblings that I should be the monarch, not her."

"I hadn't thought of that. You don't want to be king of the Half Kingdom? You have a stronger claim than she does, especially now that..." She coughed. "Now that mother and Uncle Doncaster are both..."

"It's OK. I can barely say it either. Now that your mother is standing with Çalaht and my brother... Well, I'm not sure where your uncle's soul is. Your sister filled me in on everything."

"Everything?"

"I think so. There were plenty of unsavory and uncomplimentary things about him and his jester. I assume she didn't hold back, but who knows." Chafed took another sip of his tea and wrinkled his nose. "I let my tea get too cool." He slid the saucer away from him. "No, I don't want to be king. Quite frankly, I couldn't think of anything worse." Still holding Eloise's hand, he used his free one to slide the cup back toward himself, dump the cold tea onto the snow-covered ground, and pour a fresh cup. "I couldn't rule like that without your mother. I'd just find it too painful. Like being here is too painful. Right now, anyway."

"I guess I understand. I don't like it, but I understand." Eloise unlaced her fingers and withdrew her hand, but Chafed took it again and held it between his. He drew it up to his mouth and gave her knuckles a small kiss. "I can leave now that your mother is laid to rest. Johanna feels the need to get back sooner rather than later and make sure there are no shenanigans going on."

"It's a court," said Eloise. "There will be shenanigans. Always."

Chafed grunted a laugh. "And it's the Half Kingdom Court, with no clear successor. Shenanigans will abound. So, we'll depart when Johanna feels ready to go."

"She's talking about tomorrow."

"She told me. There were things she needed to do, but, yes, I suspect I need to be ready to leave tomorrow."

Eloise imagined the two of them leaving, rolling off in one of Lurid Eddie's garish carriages. Johanna favored the more outlandishly decorated one. There'd be an emptiness with them gone. Eloise could feel it already.

"You think she can handle it?" asked Eloise. "Being queen?"

"Yes," said Chafed. "Yes, I do."

Eloise let the unasked question hang, waiting for her father to answer it.

It took Chafed a minute. He turned to face her. "You weren't asking about her."

"I was. And I wasn't."

He reached up and put a hand to her face. It was more contact than she'd had with him in a decade. Perhaps the hands-off approach to parenting was her mother's way. "Yes," he said.

"Yes, what?"

"Yes, I think you can handle it."

Eloise blinked back tears. "Thank you."

"I might not have said it with such certainty a few months ago. But your time away changed you. You're different now that you're back. Less beholden to your, uh..."

"My habits."

"Yes, Your habits. Being queen won't be easy. You'll need allies. You won't be perfect. No one is. But, yes, I think you'll be a fine queen once you find your feet."

"Find my feet."

"It takes a while."

"Not too long, I hope," said Eloise. She squeezed his hand. "If you're going, then you'd better give me any advice you want me to have."

"Advice?"

"On how to be queen. It's not like I'm doing it very well so far."

"There has been the odd..." Chafed looked away. "The odd hiccup."

"If you can call an abject, unmitigated catastrophe of a Crown Plonking an 'odd hiccup,' then sure."

"It wasn't that bad."

Eloise looked at him.

"OK, it was that bad."

"So, help me, Father. Help me do better."

Chafed looked down at the square tuber forms, and scuffed his boot against the nearest one. "Actually, I might have a word of advice, if you'll have it."

"Please."

He drew a deep breath and blew it out. It clouded in the cold air. "At some point, you have to decide what kind of queen you want to be."

"What do you mean?"

"Every queen is different. You'll be one kind of queen, and Johanna will be another. Your mother did things her way, and Onomatopoeia rules The South differently. That's only natural. You're different people. But that's not what I'm talking about."

"Oh?"

"You're going to find that for a while, it will be all you can do to muddle along, getting from one end of the day to the other."

"So far, that's how I'm feeling."

"You know what? That's OK. For a while, just getting to the end of the day will do. It'll be enough. But there will come a time—a moment—when you realize it's no longer sufficient."

"A moment? I..."

"Please, let me finish, Ëëëlöööïïïsëëë." He freed his hand and smoothed the blanket across his lap. Then he leaned forward on his elbows. "Your mother talked to me about this several times. Her moment happened before I met her. She'd been queen a while, maybe a year or two, and things were not going as well as she wanted. She told me how one summer's day she was having haggleberry tea out under that tree right there." He pointed to a linden, starkly bare against the backdrop of winter gray. Eloise could imagine it in full summer foliage, and her mother with a tea service at a table beneath it. "She was there to escape a particularly hot afternoon, but also the problems of Court. She'd been having 'issues' with someone. It was that cane toad who was exchequer for so long."

Eloise snorted a laugh. "I can imagine her having issues with him. My experience is that cane toads are a humorless lot. But him? He's so dour he makes the rest of them look like jesters."

"So you met him."

"He sometimes took our Numerals and Quandaries lessons as a substitute tutor. So, yes, I've met him. He's an acquired taste—a taste I never acquired, I'm afraid."

"So you understand what Elsie—sorry—what your mother might have been dealing with. She and the exchequer were butting heads about priorities and finances and coin and budgets and Çalaht knows what, and it was making her cranky. Very, very cranky, from what she said to me. At some point over her tea, she said to herself, 'Stop grousing and be queen.' And she did. From then on."

"'Be queen.' What did she mean?"

"Like I said, every queen has her own style, her own way with people, her own approach to making decisions, shaped by her innate personality. You've had Histories and Hearsay classes, so you've read about the various queens. Queen Flotsam the Unmoored had a very different style to Queen Adirondack the Mollassonne, or even your grandmother, One, may she stand with Çalaht. I happen to think your mother was very good at being queen, but then, I could easily be accused of bias."

"I saw you two together. It is a well-earned bias."

"Some queens naturally gravitate toward command. Others toward consensus. Some toward indecision. Your mother's point was that how you rule should be conscious. It should be based on one's values and reflect how one wants to move in the world. Take Queen Gwendolyn. She made conscious choices toward revenge and ruled with an iron determination. It wasn't just who she was. It was who she resolved to become."

You don't know the half of it, thought Eloise. She put her hand on the box with the Star of Whatever. It wasn't yet widely known that Gwendolyn had sent her champion Melveeta out to use the Star's magic against the Northern Lands and, in the process, turned the realm into the Half Kingdom. Eloise and Johanna had learned that fact when they met Melveeta in the fog of the Purple Haze, but it was still so recent that no one yet knew that the histories would need to be rewritten.

"So you're saying I should decide what kind of queen I want to be and then try to be that kind of queen."

"Not immediately. But eventually. There will come a moment when you'll work out what kind of queen you're going to be. Your mother, for example, liked a tight ship, but it doesn't have to be that way. While I suspect Johanna will value order, she's learned a lot from being in her garden. From what I've glimpsed, she doesn't mind if the plants go all over the place, so long as they thrive. I suspect her queendom will be the same."

"And me?"

"I'm not sure I know. When you left to go after your sister, your, uh..."

"Just say it."

"Your... Your idiosyncrasies would have made me think that you would be a rigid queen, since everything needed to be just so for you to feel comfortable."

"Was it that bad?"

"Unfortunately, yes. It was." Chafed aligned their cups, saucers, spoons and napkins, deliberately copying one of the behaviors her habits insisted on.

It was true. For years, Eloise had been occupied by these habits. They were little patterns she had, ways of being in the world that helped her get through the day—having all of her clothes arranged by hues of the rainbow, or keeping track of the columns of the Culpability Courtyard as she ran past them to ensure that her exercise runs ended with having gone past a "pleasing" number of them, whatever that was on a given day. It didn't cripple her if things weren't "right," but it helped her to have a certain kind of order that worked for her. And if she couldn't have things the way she wanted them, she could ease the urge with simple counting or, if under more duress, counting in more complex patterns. Her journey to retrieve Johanna had helped her break free of her habits—mostly, anyway, and at least for now. She had an inkling that something that deeply ingrained might be hard to totally escape.

Chafed continued. "The fact that you seem to have shaken off those quirks while you were away is a good thing, in light of what you'll need to do as queen. Flexibility will be important if you want to do a good job."

"Right."

"But you haven't been back long enough for me to get a sense of what kind of queen you'll be now. Time will tell." Chafed leaned his head one way, then the other, stretching his neck muscles. "But like I said, don't feel like you have to make that decision today. Or tomorrow. When the moment comes, you'll know it's there. And maybe you'll remember to think, 'Oh, this is what he was talking about.'"

"Good advice." Eloise suspected that he was talking about things like not accepting an ambassador who wouldn't represent all people in a realm, but she was pretty sure that wasn't the "moment" her father was referring to.

"Oh, and make sure you always have good, comfortable shoes," said Chafed. "You'll be standing a lot."

Eloise nodded. "I'll keep that in mind."

The dowager king's face darkened. "And I suggest you find out who murdered your mother. They might want to do you ill as well."

"I'm working on it. I don't have any answers, but I'm looking. Anything else?"

Chafed took a last sip of tea. "Try to keep a little love in your heart for those who come before you or with whom you must work," he said. "Even if you can't find it in yourself to express that love, even if the person you're dealing with is a disagreeable cane toad who never thinks there's enough coin to fund a paper folding contest, finding a little love for everyone will help."

"I'll try." They stood, and Eloise hugged her father. "I'll try," she repeated.

"I know you will." He gave her a last squeeze. "I know you have it in you to be a great queen. Promise me you'll try to be great, whatever that means to you."

"I promise."

They moved apart and looked at each other.

"So," said Chafed.

"So," said Eloise.

"I'd best go finish packing."

"Yes. I'll say it again tomorrow, boring travels to you, Father."

"Boring queening to you."

"I doubt that."

"So do I," said Chafed. "So do I."

❧ 15 ☙

LURID EDDIE SPECIALS

Eloise and Jerome arrived outside the castle just before dawn to formally farewell Johanna and Chafed. The traveling party of guards, specialist goods transportation equines (both horses and donkeys), and Johanna's handmaid, Nesther de Duck, stood in the pre-breakfast light, ready and waiting.

Jerome pointed to a pair of carriages that were laden and ready to depart. "Whose choice do you think they were?" asked Jerome. "My teeth are getting a sugar ache just looking at them."

The matching carriages were decorated with a theatrical explosion of color, gilt, and asymmetric carving. Scrolling curves, sculpted molding, and trompe l'oeil scenes both inside and out sought to surprise and give a sense of motion and drama, even as the vehicles stood still and waiting. They glared in the morning sun with all the subtlety of a crate of rotted mangos being smashed with a sledgehammer then hurled against a wall with a trebuchet.

"They're Lurid Eddie specials, that's for sure," said Eloise, referring to the most renowned carriage seller in the realm. "From the luminescent green side panels, I'd guess Johanna was the one who chose them. Father tends to prefer luminescent blue."

"At least the decorations aren't overwhelmed with carved, toga-clad woodchucks," said Jerome.

"No. You're right about that." Eloise considered the two carriages. "Instead, they're overwhelmed with carved, toga-clad weasels."

"I'm not sure that's an improvement."

"No."

Jerome pointed at a corner toward the back. There, worked into the nymph scene, was a caricature of Lurid Eddie with an arrow through his head and a razordisc poking out of his skull. "He's put his logo on there. So now the carriage is a traveling advertisement for him."

"Isn't that a bit, I don't know, tacky?"

"This is Lurid Eddie we're talking about. Tacky got left behind a long time ago. This thing aspires to tacky. It wishes that tacky would come and kiss it on the cheek. Tacky runs along a strong length behind the carriage, hoping the axle will break down and it can catch up."

"Are you done?"

Jerome wagged his tail "no" and kept going. "Tacky formed a consortium with Unbecoming, Unstylish, and Unsuitable, and they still got outbid for this job."

"That one was pretty good."

"Tacky asked Ugly to marry it and their babies— And what lovely weather we're having right now, don't you think, Queen Eloise?"

Eloise looked around and realized Johanna and Chafed were emerging through the side door, ready to leave.

She started toward her father, but he held up a hand. "We're supposed to come to you," he said. She stopped and waited for them to walk the dozen steps to where she stood. "Blessings of the day."

"Blessings of the day," echoed Johanna.

"Blessings of the day to you both."

"Well, we're off, eh?" said Chafed.

"That you are." Eloise felt a plum-sized lump forming in her throat.

"Are you going to be OK?" asked Johanna.

"I hope so. But I guess we'll see. I'm going to miss you both."

Chafed stepped forward. "I'll miss you too, my wee Ëëëlöööïïïsëëë." He pulled her into a hug. It was warm and solid, and felt more like "goodbye" than any words he might have said. Then he drew back, and gave her the customary Western Lands and All That Really Matters kisses —right cheek, left cheek, forehead. She returned them. "Boring travels, Father."

"Thank you."

He stepped aside and it was Johanna's turn.

Eloise held her sister by her forearms. "May the road be smooth, the weather pleasant, may Çalaht light your path with her gap-toothed smile, and may you not be accosted by wild, marauding, bloodthirsty, ravenous bandicoots."

"I really don't like that bit about the bandicoots," said Johanna. "Never did. It's so antiquated."

Eloise raised a shoulder. "It wasn't when they wrote it. But such is Protocol."

"Indeed, such is Protocol."

Eloise drew her forward and they exchanged Western Lands kisses. "Boring travels to you," she said.

"Thanks, El."

"Good luck becoming queen. And good luck being queen once you have your Crown Plonking, because I'm sure that's what's going to happen."

"Thanks. Good luck to you, too."

"I'm going to need it."

"You'll be OK."

"I hope you're right."

Johanna gave her a final hug. "Will you come to the Half Kingdom for my coronation?"

"Will you come back home for mine?"

"Of course."

"Of course."

A minute later, Johanna and Chafed were in one of the garish carriages, heading toward the gates surrounding the castle.

Eloise felt her chest go tight and her stomach clench.

What was she going to do without them?

She looked at Jerome. "I need to go for a run before I break fast and have my morning briefing. Care to join me, Champion Abernatheen de Chipmunk?"

"So long as I remain a spectator, I'd be happy to, Queen Eloise."

❧ 16 ❧

JOTTINGS

Eloise got in her run, then took her breakfast alone in the Queen's Study. Sadness and tears at Johanna and Chafed's departure engulfed her, but what could she do besides get on with things? She went through three handkerchiefs and as many blueberry muffins and cups of tea before she finally felt halfway composed.

Eloise stood and said to the room, "Right, then. If you're going to be mine, I'll need a few changes. For now..." She took two items out of her pocket.

The first was a small parcel wrapped in exquisite green rag paper with a lighter green bow that looked like Çalaht herself had woven it. It was a gift her mother had left her. One of the last of the half dozen things she'd said before passing over was, "Oh, by the way. It's a little late, but happy birthday. There's a present for you over there." But when Eloise had reached for it, her mother had stopped her. "Later."

Eloise had picked up the box at some point in the buzz of busy that had followed the queen's death, but she hadn't had a chance to open it. In fact, she didn't want to see what was inside. Eloise wanted to put off that particular mystery so that, at some point in the future, her mother could surprise her one last time.

She set it in one of the cubbies in the desk's hutch.

The second item was a transparent sphere with a flattened bottom, so it sat without rolling. Inside, in a viscous clear liquid, was an incredibly beautiful flower—a crocus from Johanna's garden, presumably raised from a bulb using her weak magic for growing things, and preserved in its perfection forever. Johanna had given it to her before leaving on her trip with Doncaster, and Eloise had carried it for months on the journey with Jerome, Hector, Lorch, and the Nameless One.

She held it so it could catch some of the morning light. The hard, solid, glassy material was clear as spring water. Eloise instinctively started counting the crocus petals, but stopped herself, recognizing the echoes of her habits. She needed to consciously keep them at bay.

She set it next to her mother's gift-wrapped box. The crocus and the box could watch her as she worked, small presences from her family. She'd have to find something from her father to round out the set.

First Advisor Ligurian knocked. "Queen Eloise? Are you ready for your daily briefing?"

Eloise blew her nose one last time and opened the door to wave him and the royal boxes in.

Compared to her first briefing, this one felt a little more like something that could become routine. The reports First Advisor Ligurian presented her were unremarkable. There was something about a spike in olive prices in the Eastern Lands. A delegation of badgers was petitioning her to make a royal decree preventing the use of "badger" as a verb. Ligurian showed her a roster of upcoming adjudications that she was going to have to face sooner rather than later, both civil and criminal matters—things that the magistrates could not resolve on their own. She wasn't really looking forward to that, but the queen's justice now sat on her shoulders.

Ligurian slid a scroll across the desk to Eloise. "The Coopers' Guild is arguing with the Wood Sawyers' Guild over the price of staves."

"Again?" Eloise skimmed the report. "It seems the Wood Sawyers have the Coopers over a barrel." Ligurian didn't register that she'd meant it as a joke.

"They've been squabbling for a couple of centuries. The late queen asked me to keep her informed from time to time, in case things flared up."

"How would we know if things were flaring up?" asked Eloise.

"When the Hoop Makers' Guild picks a side and makes it a three-way bun fight. So far, they're staying neutral."

Eloise couldn't imagine she'd be able to make either side see sense. "Guilds will be guilds, I guess."

"There is, indeed, a traditional intransigence between them."

"Let's hope it doesn't get as nasty as the squabble between the Consolidated Union of Prostheses Purveyors and the Amalgamated Brother- (and Sister-) hood of Artificial Limb Users." The AB-(S-)oALU perpetually pointed fingers (usually wooden) at the Union, accusing them of being in an "unholy alliance" with the Razordisc Craftspersons' Guild and alleging price gouging, profiteering, hoarding, usury, and monopolistic market abuse.

Ligurian nodded. "One can only pray it does not get that bad, Your Highness. As a final matter, there's a letter." He retrieved an envelope from the almost-empty royal box. The wax seal had been broken and the date and time of receipt was neatly written in a corner.

Eloise took it from him. It was a message from Queen Onomatopoeia of the South. "Is all of my correspondence read before it gets to me?"

"Yes, unless instructed otherwise, Your Highness. The volume of material that is received is truly overwhelming. It would take you a week to get through a day's correspondence. And that amount arrives every day. Some sort of filtering is essential."

"And you are that filter."

"With your blessing, yes. Me, with the help of a carefully chosen handful of assistants who date and log everything."

"I see." Eloise felt the edge of the envelope, annoyed. She didn't like the idea of something like a private note from the Southie queen being read, evaluated, and deemed fit for her attention. Or not. This was all so new. Was it fair for her to feel miffed at Ligurian for doing his job?

"What did Queen Onomatopoeia have to say?" asked Eloise.

"Queen Onomatopoeia expressed her condolences and wished you the best of luck with your reign."

"So, essentially what her ambassador said. The one with the…" She pointed to her scalp. "The two ferrets."

"It was the ambassador who delivered the message. I assume he read it as well."

Eloise remained irked. Something wasn't right about this. Shouldn't she get her messages before everyone else, not after? She swallowed. "First Advisor Ligurian, for the next, say, three days, I'd like all correspondence to come directly to me unopened."

Ligurian flinched. "Queen Eloise, if I may speak directly, that is impractical."

Eloise stood and Ligurian straightened. "All memos, reports, missives, messages—everything."

"Your Highness—"

"How can I be expected to get a sense of the full scope of things? How else can I learn to distinguish the trivial from the crucial unless I see both? I get it. You're doing what Lady Seneschal is trying to do. You're trying to free me up to do what's important."

"Yes, exactly. You need to focus. And you need to delegate."

"Sure. But not yet. If being queen generates activity and action, then I need to wallow in the mess of it so I can find my own way to order. Once I've done that, then maybe I can be better at delegating. But for now, I don't need a handmaid choosing my foundation garments and I don't want you or your assistants reading my correspondence. Not before I get to read it, anyway. For a few days, at least."

Ligurian looked like he wanted to argue further, but thought better of it. "As Your Highness wishes."

"Very good. Right. Thank you for understanding." Eloise sat back down. "What's next?"

"I believe that's it." Ligurian reached for the scrolls of parchment Eloise had signed, and put them in one of the official royal boxes. "Will you be staying in here for now? Shall I have some more tea sent to you? You have half an hour before you meet with the sergeant-at-arms for a security briefing."

Eloise folded her arms and looked at him. "Wasn't there a matter I raised last time?"

"Matter?"

"I requested information. How does that stand?"

Ligurian's face pinched. Then he exhaled, looking resigned. "I did as you requested." He reached into a pocket on the inside of his cloak and extracted a document wallet. It had been secured with a small padlock and sealed with wax to prevent tampering. He placed it in front of Eloise, then slipped a key out of another pocket and set it next to the wallet.

She reached to unlock the padlock and found, to her surprise, that her hands were shaking. Eloise wasn't sure she wanted to know more about what happened to her mother. Diving into this exploration of ill intent, of malice toward a reigning queen, would stain Eloise with knowledge that she would never be able to unknow.

Maybe ignorance really was bliss.

Except she didn't feel blissful. She felt fearful and nervous. Her mother's murder was a looming presence. A shadow over every moment of her day.

One of her mother's phrases had been "Knowing is better than not knowing." It was what she always said when she knew bad news was at hand.

Fair enough. It was either get messy with this or spend her life wondering when the equivalent of two stray raw haggleberries would sneak its way into her life.

Eloise took a breath, inserted the key to click open the padlock, broke the wax seal, flipped open the wallet's flap, and extracted pages of hemp parchment. There were fewer than two score pages. More like two dozen. She looked at Ligurian. "This doesn't seem like a lot."

"Like I said before: 'jottings.' Your mother didn't want official records. Not of this particular... research."

Eloise straightened the edges of the pages and began skimming through the notes. Ligurian's quillmanship was scratchy and barely legible—nowhere close to the carefully drawn, calligraphy-like writing on the documents formally prepared for her. The events leading to and following the end of her mother's life were chronicled with a dispassionate tone that sat in Eloise's stomach like an iron scone. There was no cohesive timeline, just a mishmash of dates and the odd arrow or underlining. Phrases like "The queen's internal distress" and "Raw haggleberry suspected" mixed with "Apothecary has no restorative or efficacious remedies," "Server found hanging by the neck," and "Rumors flying; none grounded in fact." It seemed like some of the notes had been made contemporaneously: "I fear we are not far from the end" and "Bells from the devotional house tolled today." Others looked like research notes or comments on an investigation: "No ties to adversaries found" or "Lead on connection to croupier hit dead end."

It was unnerving.

"So, bottom line: why was she killed?"

First Advisor cleared his throat. "We don't know. We truly don't know."

"Who is 'we' in this case?" asked Eloise.

"Everyone."

"Everyone?"

"Everyone. Not the guards. Not the investigators. Not the chirurgeon, the healers, the Çalahtists, nor the apothecary—none who examined your mother in illness, nor who mourn her in her passing."

"Well, that's not good," said Eloise. "That's very not good. We don't know the who of it. We don't know the why of it. It doesn't look like we can make a decent guess."

"No, it isn't a good thing. There's no getting around that."

Eloise clenched her teeth. She wanted to scream, "What's wrong with everyone!? A queen was killed! Don't you care at all?" Instead, she said, "First Advisor, I think I'd like you to talk me through it. All of it, from start to finish."

"If you wish."

"Yes, I wish. But I think I want more than one mind on this. I'd like my champion to hear as well."

"If Your Highness thinks it wise, then of course."

Eloise let that slide. "In fact, I'd like you to set up a separate briefing. While you're letting Jerome know, could you also send for Guard Lorch Lacksneck, Hector de Pferd, and the Nameless One to attend. I want them to hear it."

"I'm sorry, but which nameless one?"

"The Nameless One. The guard horse."

"All of the guard horses are nameless. There are literally dozens of nameless ones."

Of course, he was right. Eloise had learned that months ago. It's just that she had only ever had interactions with the one horse. For her, there was only one Nameless One.

"Right. Of course. I've forgotten. Ask Guard Lacksneck. He'll know who I mean."

"Yes, my queen."

"Can we set it up for tomorrow?"

"Tomorrow you will be traveling."

"Oh?"

"Yes, to Festering Resentment and the paddock blessing. As you requested."

"Right. Of course. Then the day after."

"Yes, Queen Eloise."

❧ 17 ❧

FESTERING RESENTMENT

The ride to Festering Resentment and the brunchberry farm owned by Goodman and Goodwoman Rechteckfeld was misery in its purest form. Icy, slashing, slush-laden rain hammered the party from the moment they stepped out of Castle de Brague, and harangued them the entire way.

Eloise and Jerome rode Hector, and Lorch rode the Nameless One. It was just like on their journey, except it wasn't at all. This time, they traveled with a full company of guards under Lorch's command. Even though Eloise had clearly stated she wanted to ride on Hector, Ligurian had insisted a carriage be brought with them, in case she changed her mind. The Venerable Prelate Herself rode in a second carriage, which kept her out of the rain, but the carriages slowed their procession once they left the Queen's Roadway and headed onto a road that wasn't much better than a dirt trail. Eloise had thought that this might be a quick, fun outing, but that notion was soon overwhelmed by the weight of preparations, the size of the entourage, and the ridiculous weather. She was also giving up on any idea that this would be a way for her to get out among "her" people (which still felt horribly wrong to say—she didn't own anyone). They hadn't stopped anywhere since they'd left.

Eloise tried to keep up a stream of chat and banter with Hector, Jerome, and the Nameless One, but what the skies unleashed was as bad as anything they had ridden through on their journey.

Still, it was nice to be out of the castle and on the road again, even if it was just a day trip. At least that's what Eloise kept telling herself.

She almost believed it.

They reached the village two hours late, stopping at a sign that said, "Welcome to Festering Resentment." Below this was the town motto: "Yes, We Do Still Hold That Grudge."

Beside it was the advance team—a long-haired apple head Chihuahua and a sullen-looking, gray-coated donkey, both of whom were dressed in ruffled collars and sashes indicating their official connection to Court.

"G'late mid-morning, Your Highness," said the Chihuahua as Eloise's procession clattered to a halt. "I'm Nörbert de Lupus and this is Abelardo de Burro, my assistant. I trust your journey was pleasant?"

Eloise tugged her travel cloak around her more tightly. "The weather was perhaps a tad fresher than we expected, but we're here and that's what's important."

"Indeed, indeed, indeed," chittered Nörbert. "The field you'll be blessing is on the other side of the village. If you'll please follow us." The donkey knelt down so the Chihuahua could pop up on his back and the pair led the way through Festering Resentment to the fallow winter field where they would plant brunchberry canes.

A quarter hour later, they were there. A crowd stood at the edge of the paddock, a forlorn patch of bare dirt that looked to have so little tilth that Eloise doubted it would grow weeds, much less brunchberries. There were easily 250 people clustered together—probably a good percentage of those living within a 20 strong length radius. Everyone wore their best clothes, which looked incongruous in a field and in such bad rain. All of them huddled beneath cloaks and blankets, shivering in the icy, wet weather and brushing small snow drifts from their hats and shoulders. As Eloise approached on horseback, they dropped into bows and curtsies—awkward poses from people who almost certainly had never come within a kumquat's throw of a queen before.

Eloise slid off Hector and sloshed forward toward the crowd. Lorch hopped off the Nameless One and took his place four steps to her right, while Jerome positioned himself the same distance to her left. Eloise shouted to make herself heard over the rain. "Please be at rest, everyone. Thank you for coming out today."

The Chihuahua trotted up and waved forward a craggy-faced man and a silver-haired woman. "Allow me to present to Her Highness Goodman and Goodwoman Rechteckfeld, whose paddock you're blessing today." His voice could barely be heard over a sudden, biting wind, but Eloise got the gist.

"Pleased to meet you both," she yelled. "Thank you for your kind invitation."

The woman stepped forward. "You could have knocked me over with a dust mote, you could have, when we got the response," said Good-woman Rechteckfeld. "Finnigan here, that's my husband—37 years we've been married, and in love at least 34 of them—said, 'No need to bother inviting the queen. She'll be busy and won't want to journey out to Festering Resentment. She'll have better things to do with her time.' But I said, 'If we don't invite the queen, the queen won't know that we'd like her to do the blessing. What is she supposed to do, read our minds?' And Finnigan said, 'Her lot are too busy to come to a place like Festering Resentment.' And I said, 'Her lot is just people, isn't it? Maybe she'd fancy a trip to Festering Resentment.' And Finnigan said, 'A hellhole like Festering Resentment? Why would she bother? Surely she'd rather go somewhere nice, like Simpering Futility (which, he's right, is nice this time of year) or Egregious Bodily Harm (which people say is nice, but I have a cousin who went there once, and it wasn't what it's cracked up to be).' And I said, 'Have some pride, man. And draw me an Epsom salt foot bath before I get cranky.' So Finnigan drew me an Epsom salt foot bath, because deep down, he's a lovely man, despite what my mother thinks of him and the fact he could do with a bit more *esprit de village*. Mind you, his mother thinks about the same of me, so it's a bit of a wash. Anyway, while he drew me my Epsom salt foot bath (and who doesn't like a good Epsom salt foot bath? Do you like to soak your feet in an Epsom salt foot bath? I sure do), I jotted down our invitation to our field blessing to you. Well, not you *per se*. To your mother, more like, may she stand with Çalaht. It was before we heard about all the dying that's been going on amongst your lot. Who would have thought that the king of one realm and the queen of another would cark it so close to each other, unless, of course, they'd done it to each other in war or suchlike. Finnigan (that's my husband, here, did I mention him?) said I should bring it up when we saw you, being such a strange coincidence and all, but both my mother and his mother said I shouldn't, so I won't. Anyway, by Çalaht's extensive and blessed nose hairs, you're here, praise be the Divine One. So, uh..." She gave a small, awkward curtsy and her manner changed to that of someone reciting something they'd been told to memorize. "Welcome to the village of Festering Resentment. Thank you for coming and we hope your time here is memorable." With another curtsy, she stepped back next to her husband.

Goodman Rechteckfeld stepped forward next, nodded, raised a palm, and gave a little wave."Howdy," he said. Then he, too, recited something he'd clearly been told to memorize. "Make sure you have fried brunchberries on a stick while you're here." Then he nodded again and stepped back next to his wife.

Eloise smiled as sincerely as she could. "Thank you for your kind welcome."

Ready to get on with the blessing, Eloise looked around and realized that the Venerable Prelate Herself wasn't there yet. The carriage was only just arriving, struggling to make its way on a rutted, muddy track. "Ah, there's Her Holiness. I'm sure she'll be joining us in a moment."

While they waited for the Venerable Prelate Herself to emerge from her carriage, Jerome pulled a pouch from his pocket, opened it, and offered it to Eloise. "Sunflower seed?"

"Thanks, but no thanks."

Jerome nodded, and began poking in the bag.

Eloise frowned. "How can you do that?"

The chipmunk looked at her. "Do what?"

"How can you eat in this weather?"

"What does weather have to do with it?"

Eloise shook her head as Jerome fished out a sunflower seed, held it up to the light to examine it, nodded approval, and cracked the shell between his teeth. He carefully pulled the two halves of the shell apart, detached the seed from the half shell it clung to, dropped the shell fragments at his feet, and began nibbling the seed.

She watched him repeat this process a dozen times. Retrieve, examine, approve, crack, halve, drop, nibble. "Do you know that you do it exactly the same each time?"

"Do I?"

"There's a machine-like precision to your approach."

"Really? I had no idea. I thought I was just snacking."

"Rather fiercely determined snacking."

Eloise's observation of Jerome's nibbling habits was interrupted by a loud grunt from the prelate's carriage, as the door opened and a figure was helped down. The Venerable Prelate Herself was cloaked, rugged, and hooded against the cold from her feet to the end of her short, prehensile trunk. Her expression was hidden, but from the way she plodded over to them, her steps punctuated by frequent sneezes, the trip had been difficult and the blessing itself wasn't going to be a joy for her. Having Nörbert de Lupus, on Abelardo de Burro's back, chattering at her side was surely not helping things.

"Your Grace," said Eloise when the prelate reached them.

"By Çalaht's bleeding bunions, it's bleeping, blessed, blasphemously cold out here," grumbled the tapir. Her voice suggested her nose was stuffed like a pimento green olive.

"It is a might nippy, Your Grace," agreed Goodman Rechteckfeld.

The Venerable Prelate Herself scowled at the man, sneezed three times, snorted back a snoutful of mucus, and stamped her feet into the ground, trying to keep the feeling in them. "Shall we get on with blessing the paddock, so we can—"

"Right, OK, hold on, pardon me," said the Chihuahua. "We do have a bit of an agenda to follow." He handed around pieces of parchment with the list of planned events on them. "Next up is an official portrait of the event. If we could all line up please..."

Jerome stopped his nibbling. "We're having a portrait done? Now? In this weather?"

"That's right," said Nörbert. "Where's my niece?"

"Right here, Uncle Nörbert!" The voice came from an even smaller Chihuahua at the side of the crowd. She had a sketch pad that was bigger than she was strapped to her back, along with a case that held different-sized pencils and sticks of charcoal.

"This is preposterous," grumped the Venerable Prelate Herself, but she allowed Nörbert to position her, along with everyone else, in the middle of the paddock. He had Eloise in front, the prelate next to her, Goodman and Goodwoman Rechteckfeld on either side of them, and then the rest of the traveling party and villagers to the side and behind them.

"Looking good, everyone. Looking good," said the Chihuahua as he paced the donkey back and forth.

A gust of wind slammed them, catching the donkey in mid-stride. He stumbled and almost stepped on Jerome, sending the chipmunk's bag of sunflower seeds flying.

"Watch it!" yelled Jerome. "You almost got me there. And now my seeds are all dirty."

"Oops. Sorry," said Abelardo de Burro. They were the first words he'd spoken that day. "You want me to help you pick up your snack?" The donkey stepped back and forth, trying to see where the seeds had gone, and trampling half of them into the dirt.

"There's no point," huffed Jerome. "Just leave them. It's not important."

"I'm really sorry," drawled the donkey.

"Don't worry about it. Really."

"I'll get you some more sunflower seeds when we get back to Brague," said Abelardo.

Jerome looked at him and spoke with forced politeness. "Thank you. That's most kind of you Master de Burro. But it won't be necessary."

"OK, enough of that," said Nörbert. "Everyone's lined up. Very good. Now smile and say 'pusillanimous!'"

❧ 18 ☙

SOME BLESSING

As almost 15 score people held a frozen smile on their faces and tried to figure out why "pusillanimous" was the right word to say for a portrait. Nörbert's niece frantically sketched, trying to capture a likeness of the moment for all eternity, which is how long it felt like they were standing still trying to let her do her job. Her head bobbed as she looked up and down from person to person, drawing manically on page after page. "Don't move!" she barked. "Hold it... Hold it... Hold it... Keep smiling... Sir! You're not smiling! Those of you with tails need to please keep them still." As Eloise felt her cheeks going as numb as her toes, the tiny Chihuahua finally said, "Aaaaaaaannnnnnnnndddddddd... Done! Thank you everyone. The final portrait will be stored in the Bibliotheca de Records and Regrets at Castle de Brague, where I'm sure no one will ever see it, but welcome to my life. Thank you, Uncle Nörbert."

"You're welcome, petal." Nörbert de Lupus clapped his paws and said, "Let's warm up by singing a hymn, then we'll have the Venerable Prelate Herself do her blessing. Abelardo, over to you."

The donkey cleared his throat, and in a rich, deep voice, crooned out a beautiful rendition of "Wholly Wholly Wholly," which blended seamlessly into "Onward Çalahtist Pacifists."

As he was nearing the end, Eloise whispered to Jerome, "He's got a lovely voice."

"True," said Jerome. "But he's not leading a choir, he's performing a solo. A bit hard to join in. Also, he made me spill my sunflower seeds, so he's not in my good books."

"Let it go, Jer."

Jerome made a fist, then opened his claws like he was letting go of a handful of sand. "It's gone, Queen Eloise, it's gone."

"Good."

Abelardo finished, and Nörbert, still on his back, said, "We'll have the Venerable Prelate Herself lead a blessing, and then perhaps Queen Eloise will say a few words as well." He gave the prelate an elaborate bow and motioned for her to begin. "Your Grace."

The prelate sneezed, then took a few steps toward the villagers. The wind had calmed, so it was not hard to hear her say, "Before I give the blessing, I'd like to take a few minutes to discuss the one mention of brunchberries in the *Scrolls of Çalaht*. It happens in the 'Verses of Her Confused Ramblings,' where the Divine One extols the virtues of a meal between breakfast and lunch. And I quote, 'Nae, verily, there is such divine grace to be had in a meal that sits between breakfast and lunch, and the platters upon which sit the fruits of your labors, such as apples, pomegranates, and even the brunchberry.' Now, what did the Divine One mean by this, with her references to fruits, labor, and the cheeky use of 'verily?'"

At that point, Eloise tuned out, knowing that nothing short of an attacking band of wild bandicoots could interrupt the Venerable Prelate Herself from yammering on once she'd started. She plastered a fascinated expression onto her face and allowed her eyes to wander. The villagers had a midwinter thinness to them, but she could tell that the goodman and goodwoman worked hard and took pride in what they did. They wanted their brunchberries to do well. Otherwise, why would they have bothered to invite the Queen to bless them?

Eloise wondered if there might be something else that she could do that might help them out. Give them an extra allotment of fertilizer, perhaps? Place an order for brunchberries for the castle? Look at how much tithe they had to pay, and maybe adjust it downward? No, none of those were the right thing.

Blimey, it was cold. Eloise crossed her arms and hugged herself beneath her cloak, resting her hand on the Star of Whatever at her hip.

The Star of Whatever.

That gave her an idea. She reached out to the spark of something inside the Star of Whatever. *Hey, Sparky. You there?*

No response. There hadn't been for a while.

Sparky! Wake up! You there?

Eloise felt a sense of alertness awaken inside the Star of Whatever. *Hey, Loulou. That you? How goes it?*

It goes fine. Can I ask you a question? Maybe it's more like a request.

You can ask, sure.

Can you get a sense of where you are?

Sort of. We're outside?

That's right. In a paddock. I was wondering if you could please help me do something here.

She felt a mixed sense of curiosity and haughtiness from the spark. *What sort of something?*

I'm not sure what's possible. Could you maybe help the fertility of the paddock? Please? For the kind people here?

Hmmm... It's not really my decision. I'm just a tool. It's really up to you to ask. Like you've done, really.

Eloise smiled to herself. *So you'll help?*

The Star gave her the magical object equivalent of a shrug.

Thank you. I appreciate it. What do you want me to do? asked Eloise.

Open your eyes. Fix the image of the paddock in your head. The ground. Its borders. Everything. That'll help me understand where you're trying to have an effect. Then close your eyes and make your request.

Eloise did as she was told. She looked around the field, took in the post-and-rail boundary fence and the rock-free bare dirt. She memorized the image of the paddock, then she closed her eyes. Eloise reached out to the spark of something in the Star of Whatever. *Help me help the fertility of this paddock.*

She waited. Nothing. No flash of green light and no sense of anything happening. Eloise cracked open her eyes. There was no visible change in anything. The Venerable Prelate Herself mumbled her way to the end of her makeshift sermon, with the Festering Resentment-ites listening more or less intently. Then she said, "And now a benediction for this field. Heavenly Çalaht. Oh, Divine One of the ages, holiest of all holies. Please shower your blessings on this humble paddock, so that it may..."

Eloise tuned out again. *Sparky? You there?*

Yes.

Uh, did anything happen?

Nope.

Why not?

What did you forget? He (Eloise thought of the spark of something in the Star of Whatever as a "he") gave her the sense of folding his arms and waiting for her to come up with an answer.

Wrong positioning of my arms or body? guessed Eloise.

No.

Wrong expression of intention? Inadequate focus?

No, the intention was there. Your focus was fine.

Then what?

Think about it...

Eloise let her mind drift back to the last time she'd tried to deliberately harness the magic in the Star of Whatever. She'd been stuck in a morass of filth and muck, standing in evil-smelling darkness at the bottom of the Whacking Great Hole, the hugest hole in the realm, doing her best not to break the Whacking Great Hole Greater Park Area's motto, "Please Don't Die While You Are Here."

She'd asked the Star of Whatever for assistance with throwing a rope to help her get out of the hole. She'd gotten that help, at the cost of a broken wrist and a dislocated shoulder.

And then she remembered. *Oh. I forgot to use the magic word.*

In her mind, Sparky nodded. *That's it.*

Let me try again. Eloise opened her eyes, focused on the paddock, pictured the dirt, sensed its boundaries, closed her eyes, and remembered to include the magic word—"please."

Please, Sparky. Please help me help the fertility and tilth of this paddock so that it may grow wondrous plants.

Eloise opened her eyes in time to see a flash of green light extending from her hip in all directions toward the boundary fence. Next came a *fwomp!* sound, followed by a *fweeeeeeeee.* Eloise felt the ground beneath her feet rumble and then right next to her, a single plant screeched upward out of the ground. A stalk pushed skyward, emitting leaves as it grew. It shot upward at the speed of days passing with each heartbeat. It grew until it was as tall as she was, and kept going until it was half her height again. Its leaves spread like spade-shaped dinner plates. A few moments later, a flower bud emerged and within a breath, burst open with a huge yellow blossom straining toward the feeble sun.

It was a golden yellow sunflower. One of Jerome's sunflower seeds had sprouted and grown. But what should have taken two months took a matter of seconds.

Everyone stared at it, confused, no one more so than the Venerable Prelate Herself.

Goodman Rechteckfeld reached out like he wanted to touch the plant. "What in the name of—"

But before the man's bewilderment could fully register, the flower's head dipped and its petals wilted, leaving a seed head with hundreds— no, thousands—of seeds growing and ripening. Seven seconds later, there was an unnatural coughing sound, and the seeds exploded outward in all directions, showering the paddock and people with sunflower seeds.

"That's weird," muttered Jerome. "I've never seen that before."

He'd barely finished his sentence when there was a *fffd-d-d-d-d-d-d-d-d-d-d-d-d-dit* noise. A wave of sunflower plants hurled themselves skyward, growing with the same crazed speed. They pushed up and outward, shoving aside anything and everything in their path. Children and members of smaller species were tossed in the air. Ninety seconds later, the paddock was no longer a barren field populated by Festering Resentment villagers and Eloise's traveling party. Instead, it was crammed, from corner to corner, with the largest, sturdiest, yellowest, sunfloweriest sunflower plants that anyone in the realm had ever seen, each one in full blossom and uniformly facing the wan hint of winter sun that feebly bled through the thick cloud cover. The plants had covered every available square weak length of the turf.

A stunned silence covered the crowd.

Eloise gasped. What had happened? This was insane. She closed her eyes again. *Sparky?*

Loulou?

What exactly did you do? The paddock is ruined!

I didn't do anything. I merely amplified your intention.

My intention? This impenetrable jungle of sunflowers wasn't my intention.

You helped the paddock's fertility and tilth to help wondrous plants grow. The sunflowers are a mere by-product.

Inside, Eloise groaned. *The field is ruined.*

C'mon. Look at the plants around you. You did a great job.

Eloise didn't think so. Not at all. There was no chance this short forest of yellow sunflower eyes ogling at her was a positive result.

She paused her frantic thinking. Short forest? Yellow? Brown eye-like things? This was ringing a very strange bell. A Jerome-shaped bell.

Her train of thought and the general silence were broken by Goodwoman Rechteckfeld. "Well, that was some blessing."

There was a thrashing to Eloise's right. "By Çalaht's gangrenous gall-bladder," swore a deep voice. "This bloody sunflower's grown up my trouser leg and out the top of my tunic. I'm stuck!"

It took more than half an hour for everyone to shove their way out of a paddock that it had taken two minutes to get to the middle of. Clothes were torn, hats were stuck at the tops of stalks, lost children had to be retrieved, and everyone was covered in a thick dust of sunflower pollen.

The Venerable Prelate Herself looked rattled. Eloise overheard the tapir muttering, "I've never seen prayer work quite like that before. Praised be Çalaht, I guess, but what the actual f—"

"Everyone! Everyone!" shouted Nörbert de Lupus. He stood up on his hind legs to get more height. "May I please have everyone's attention!"

The bewildered crowd looked at him.

He waved his bit of parchment. "Next on the agenda is a few words from our queen."

Eloise looked around at the baffled faces. "Uh... Thank you to the Venerable Prelate Herself for such a moving sermon and wonderful blessing. Clearly, the ways of Çalaht are mysterious indeed. I appreciate you having me here and may this paddock, uh, continue to surprise and delight. Praised be Çalaht."

"Praised be Çalaht," mumbled everyone.

The Chihuahua smiled. "Thank you, Queen Eloise, for such rousing words. Next up, refreshments in the devotional house rectory. Please follow me and Master de Burro, and we'll be having onion soup, tea, and brunchberry tarts in no time. Come now. Follow me."

Eloise saw Jerome eyeing her suspiciously.

"Was that... Was that you?" he asked.

Eloise gave him a two-palm "who knows" gesture.

The chipmunk wasn't having it. "Was. That. You?"

"Possibly," she mumbled. "More than possibly. Most probably."

"Most probably."

"Alright, yes it was me, I think. Don't tell anyone."

"Right."

Abelardo de Burro appeared from behind them, carrying a pouch in his teeth. He gave it to Jerome and said, "I collected some sunflower seeds for you. To pay you back for spilling yours."

Jerome wrinkled his brow at the donkey. "Uh, thanks. Much appreciated."

"Abelardo! Abelardo!" called the Chihuahua from somewhere amid the sunflower plants. "Where are you? We need to get everyone back to the village."

"Coming, Nörbert!" the donkey yelled back. Then he bowed to Eloise, turned, and went in the direction of the dog's voice.

"C'mon, Jer. Let's go get warm," said Eloise. She forced her voice to be calmer than she felt. "They'll want me at the front of the line to go in and have the first bowl of onion soup. Do you like onion soup? Yes, of course you do."

"You're prattling," said Jerome. "Are you prattled?"

"Not at all. Just a bit taken aback at the, uh, turn of events."

"OK," said Jerome. "Soup. Then perhaps we can discuss this little mystery of yours on our way home. That was completely out of control."

Eloise nodded. "Completely."

"And scary," said Jerome.

"Very."

PAYING ATTENTION

The cloaked figure stood in a small nook between a closed haberdashery and a permanently shuttered millinery called Numbat Hat, which, according to a weather-faded sign that hung skew-whiff from a single nail, had once upon a time "catered exclusively to the discerning numbat." An overhanging roof provided barely enough shelter for the man to avoid being covered in snow.

Tugging his hood tighter, he stepped as far back into the cramped alcove as he could, trying to remain unobserved. He shoved past disused crates, trying not to snag his cloak, and brooded. He hated the fact that he was there, waiting. He hated that he'd been pressured to come at all.

Moments later, a second figure slid from a nearby corner of darkness, silent as death. "I was wondering if you'd come," he hissed quietly.

"It's not like I was given much choice," grumbled the first one. "Get on with it. It's miserable out tonight. What do you want?"

"And here I thought that people in your position counsel that patience is a virtue. That must be a stereotype." The second one moved closer.

"The world is full of stereotypes, isn't it? Sometimes they're useful, but I guess sometimes they're not."

"I said, get on with it."

The second one sighed languidly and indicated a barrel. "Open that."

The man looked at the thigh-high barrel to his left. At first glance, it didn't look too suspicious, just old. The lid sat on it loosely, so he lifted it off. The smell of pickles wafted up, and he was unexpectedly transported back to his childhood. His mother had sold extra sour dill pickles out of a barrel to the meager customers who stopped by her small grocery shop. That was back when she was still strong enough to have the store attached to their hut. For his entire boyhood, he'd come home in the afternoon after his lessons and helped her out for the rest of the workday. When they were done and she let him flip the sign from Open to Closed, his mother allowed him a choice of treat—a dozen olives from the olive barrel or a pickle from the pickle barrel.

Everyone else he knew would have chosen the olives, but he always chose the pickle. Always.

So, like it or not, the man associated pickles with maternal warmth and comfort.

Even he found that a little odd.

He reached into the barrel's darkness, fearful that he'd find a finger trap or slime. No. Instead, there was a shabby canvas bag about the size of his hand. The bag had a lump of something inside.

"Go ahead," said the second one. "Open it."

The man unknotted the drawstring. Inside were gray strands of something. Thread? No, hair. "It's someone's braid."

"Recognize anything?"

The man looked more closely at it. The hair was clean and gray.

"Look at the band that holds it together," said the second one. "And the style of plait."

The man turned the clump of hair over, and gasped. The clutch of hair was tied with a piece of embroidered linen. He'd recognize his mother's needlework anywhere. "What is this?" he spluttered.

"You know whose hair it is. That's to make sure you're paying attention," said the second one.

The first one stepped forward, threatening. "What have you done with her? Where is she? And why her?"

"None of that matters. She is well. Cared for. Even comfortable. Differently coiffed, perhaps. But safe enough and comfortable."

"If you hurt her, I will end you." He spat the words. "End. You."

"Now, now. I'm the one making the threats here, not you." The second one slid closer. "First question. Has my approach to getting your attention worked? Are you going to hear me when I speak?"

"What do you want?"

"Answer the question."

The first one clenched his teeth and held back any number of curses. "How do I know that she's even alive? How can I trust you?"

The second one tisked. "You can't. That should be obvious. But please, feel free to write some of your neighbors back home and see how recently they've spoken with her. They'll tell you that she writes of the lovely holidays she's having at an unspecified location." He tilted his head. "Clearly, you need something else. How about this: I give you my word."

"That's worth nothing."

"Careful, now. You don't want to hurt my feelings, do you?"

The first one was already thinking through who he could send to investigate. But it would take days for someone he trusted to get there. Days to uncover any information. Days to get back. He wasn't sure how many days, exactly, he had.

"I should've used a finger," the second one said. "Next time, then. It's just that you don't seem to be listening yet."

"I'm listening. What do you want?"

"No, you're not listening. You didn't answer my question."

"Your question?"

"Yes. I asked you if my approach to getting your attention had worked. Are you paying attention?"

"Yes, it worked. You have my full attention."

"I thought that might work."

"What do you want?"

"I'm not expecting much. The odd shading when you describe something. The odd nudge or bump in a deliberation. Nothing too obvious."

"What are you talking about?"

The second one shifted and resettled himself. "Listen to me, and listen good. I'm going to say this exactly once. We want you where you are, active and eager to do a good job—just like you always are. But in the coming days, weeks, and, who knows, perhaps months, there will be opportunities for you to pass on information. You will do so."

"Information? What information?"

"Some of it you will volunteer. You'll know what I'm interested in. Some of it I will request. We'll work all that out. There also might be times where you will need to convey information in the other direction. To disseminate rather than gather."

"I am not going to hand you an open purse. Do you think you can just take what you want?"

The second one shook his head slowly. "Come now. You are not immune to the love of the mother realm. And I know for sure that you're not immune to the love of your mother. You'll do as you're told.

There's no need to create more suffering in the world than there already is. Any suffering that arises from here on out will be on your head."

"On my head? You're the one making threats, remember. It will be on your head."

"Oh, I don't think so." The second one made ready to leave. "Trust me, it will be on yours. Certainly, to you, it will feel that way." The second one nodded once. "You'll be hearing from me. Trust me on that. And feel free to keep my hearing aid as a token of my esteem."

The figure disappeared into the night, leaving the man trembling.

❧ 20 ❧

ON GOLDEN SCONE

Tea at the cafe On Golden Scone was Lady Seneschal Älphonsinä Póöòmáäàdéëè's private indulgence. Some precious alone time. Plus, their haggleberry tea was about as close to perfection as she could get. Maybe not as good as the late Chef's (may she stand with Çalaht), but an order of magnitude better than the thin, weak swill served up by the new Chef. Escaping to On Golden Scone for a quiet tea and a small selection of much-too-rich and way-too-expensive-for-the-size-of-them nibblies gave her a chance to leave the cares and concerns of running the palace behind, even for just a few minutes.

And there had been cares and concerns up to the eyeballs recently, with the ascension of the new queen, such as she was.

Lady Seneschal had her own reserved seat in a secluded corner in the back, well away from the kitchen entrance. The serving wench led her to it, and once she was settled in the cushioned armchair, the young woman said, "The usual, Lady Seneschal?"

"The usual on the tea, yes, thank you, Lücee. But just a bit of your baklava for nibbles. I'm not feeling particularly adventurous today."

"Yes, ma'am. Won't be a moment."

Lady Seneschal watched the serving wench turn for the kitchen, then nestled back into what she thought of as her favorite armchair in all the realms, closed her eyes and, relishing her solitude, gave herself permission to exhale a long, pent-up sigh.

What a week. What a few weeks it had been.

Maybe it *was* time to retire.

But she didn't think of herself as one who walked away from a challenge. Nor did she have any idea what she'd do or where she'd go. Travel and see the realms? Meh. Sit around doing old person things? Double meh. Visit children and grandchildren? There hadn't been any. She hadn't been interested, and then she hadn't been able to. Besides, corralling princesses had always seemed like more than enough child-involved activity.

"Lady Seneschal?"

She opened her eyes to find Lücee and another serving wench standing next to her table with several large trays. "Goodness, what's that?"

Lücee set down an oversized teapot, cup, and saucer on the coffee table, then she and the other serving wench arrayed the trays so they covered the table. "It's an Ultimate Delicacies Selection, ma'am."

"It's not my birthday, Lücee."

"No, ma'am, it's a gift."

"A gift? From whom?"

Lücee lifted her chin and indicated a woman across the room. "The stern-looking woman in the purple chair."

"I see. How kind. An Ultimate, no less. What a treat." She glanced at the woman, who didn't seem familiar. On impulse she tossed out her alone time and said, "This is far too many nibblies for me to enjoy on my own. Perhaps you could ask her if she'd like to join me."

Lücee poured a first cupful of tea for Lady Seneschal. "Yes, ma'am, I'll do that now. Enjoy your treat, ma'am."

"Oh, I most certainly will."

Lady Seneschal dripped exactly three drops of rice malt into her haggleberry tea and plucked a pumpkin mini-pie from the assortment of goodies in front of her. Popping the whole thing in her mouth, she closed her eyes again, this time to focus on the way the mini-pie melted, infusing her tastebuds with a divine combination of spices. It was her little challenge to herself to puzzle out the ingredients by taste. Flour and pumpkin puree, of course. Some sort of milk, probably oat. Baking powder. A sweetener, probably brown sugar. A neutral-tasting oil—she guessed sunflower. Next, the spices. Ginger. Cloves. Nutmeg. Cinnamon. But there was one other thing. Was that a hint of apple sauce? Clever. Very clever.

She chewed, swallowed, and relished the taste for one last moment. Ready for the next morsel, she opened her eyes again.

And found the stern woman from the purple chair standing in front of her. "G'arvo, Lady Seneschal," she said with a voice like a shovel digging up a coffin. Then she stood still, unblinking, waiting.

Lady Seneschal stood, careful not to jostle the laden table. "Good afternoon. You have me at a disadvantage. I'm sorry, I don't recognize you."

"I am Picholine Manzanilla."

"Pleased to meet you. Is that an Eastern Lands lilt I hear in your voice?"

"Yes, that it is. I am the Eastern Lands ambassador."

"Well, then. That explains it." Lady Seneschal waved to the array of treats. "This was most generous of you, but it is much more than I could ever eat. Well, more than I *should* eat, at least. Can I express my thanks by inviting you to join me?"

"That would be lovely."

The two women sat, and in that exact moment, Lücee appeared with another place setting, arranged it in front of her new guest, and asked, "May I pour you a haggleberry tea, ma'am?"

"I prefer olive leaf tea, thank you," said Manzanilla. "It has many health benefits, even if the taste is not for the weak."

"Certainly ma'am. I won't be a moment."

Lady Seneschal waved her hand across the display of goodies. "Please help yourself. I can recommend the lavender lemon shortbread biscuits. They're marvelous."

"I'll have to take your word for it. The sweet things don't agree with me. But I will try one of those."

"Oooh, those are pulled Portobello mushroom barbecue burgeritos. They're quite nice."

"A little mushroom burger. Look how nicely they stack into a pyramid. We don't have those where I'm from." The ambassador took the top sandwich from the pile and ate it. She had the deliberate eating manner of a soldier on campaign, like the goal was to get it in and down to the stomach as efficiently as possible so one's attention could return to avoiding the next arrow. "That was good." She seemed surprised. Manzanilla took another and devoured it.

What a strange woman, thought Lady Seneschal.

Lücee returned with an oversized pot of olive leaf tea, and a second serving wench added a side table to the arrangement so there was room for it. She poured the tea, nodded, and left the women alone.

"So," said Lady Seneschal, plucking up a coffee cake donutette.

"So," echoed the ambassador. She picked a fork, skewered a whole garlic roasted baby new potato, and looked at it like an autopsy specimen. "I've never been here before, but the food is so interesting."

"It's my favorite place to escape to."

"You have very good taste."

"Now you can, too.

Another pause.

"May I ask, to what do I owe the pleasure of your gift?"

"I'm new to your realm and to your court. I don't know anyone yet, and I thought, who's the best person to get to know at a castle? The person responsible for making it tick. A little bird—a sparrow, I think —told me you liked to come here. So I came here, too. This..." She gestured at the spread. "This was just a way of saying hello." She forked another potato, gestured it at Lady Seneschal, and smiled. "Hello."

"Well, hello to you, too. Again, feel free to have as much as you'd like."

The two women noshed away in amiable quiet, each one enjoying the morsels that struck their fancy. A second, then a third, cup of tea washed down the repast. Finally, they both leaned back in their chairs, sated.

"May I ask you a question, Lady Seneschal?"

"Certainly."

"What's the state of things at Court these days?"

"The state of things?"

"Yes. The mood. The sense of how the realm fares."

"Fine. Just fine."

"Really."

"Yes." Lady Seneschal wasn't sure she liked the direction this conversation was taking, but was too polite to say so. "Things are fine."

"I find that surprising."

"Why?"

"Court has gone through a big change, what with the unexpected death of the late queen and the installation of the new one. Surely there are inevitable, how to say it, ructions."

"The late queen's passing was a tragedy," said Lady Seneschal. "I miss her every day. More than I can tell you. She was a fine, competent, and upstanding queen."

"I never met her," said the ambassador. "But what you say comports with what I've heard. Certainly, Queen Aglandau respected her."

"Did she, now? I thought they didn't get along."

"I didn't say they got along. I said there was respect."

"True. There was respect." Lady Seneschal wasn't exactly sure that was true, but it seemed like the politic thing to say.

A few more sips in silence.

"May I ask a question about the new queen?"

"Of course."

"Why does she have a chipmunk as her champion?"

"This isn't The South," said Lady Seneschal. "We're happy to have non-humans as full, active members of society."

"No, no, no." Manzanilla set down her cup and forked another potato. "We're the same in the Eastern Lands. We don't share the Southies' prejudices against non-human people. That's not my question. Why him? Why a chipmunk? It seems..." She wagged the potato like a slow metronome. "How can a chipmunk fill such a role?"

Lady Seneschal lifted one shoulder and let it drop. "I will never say anything against our queen, but, to be honest, you are not the first to raise that question."

"Is it true that he bit the jester at his Naming Ceremony and then ran under the late queen's throne?"

"It was a scratch, not a bite, but yes. Apparently, he has a fear of jesters that no one in charge knew about." She shook her head. "It was quite a sight."

"And yet, he remains her champion. It seems like a failure of judgment."

"Again, I'm not going to speak ill of my queen."

"Of course. And is it true that both princesses were absent during the late queen's infirm period?"

"Well, yes. That's true. Things sort of happened quickly. Princess Johanna left with King Doncaster, then they sent Princess Eloise to bring her back. The two of them were gone for months. Queen Eloise fell ill. Princess Johanna came back, and then Princess Eloise arrived just in time to be at her mother's side when she died. It was all rather tragic."

"It does sound tragic. Very. But, you say they were away for months? That's... odd. For that matter, why would they send one princess to go after another? That hardly makes sense."

"Eyebrows were raised. But as I heard it told, there were political sensitivities that had to be considered with regard to the late King Doncaster. It was thought that the one sister could bring back the other. As for the length of time, it was never supposed to have been more than a couple of days."

"But both of them away for months? Why didn't someone go after them and get them back?"

"I think people were dispatched, but there was some, shall we say, uncertainty about their whereabouts."

"The late queen lost her daughters? Surely not."

Lady Seneschal waved a hand. "No, no, no. I wouldn't put it that way. And it was more the one than the other, from what I can tell."

"So Princess Johanna is the one who went missing?"

"Well, no. It was more Princess, I'm sorry, Queen Eloise."

Manzanilla barked a laugh, an incongruous sound, given how dour she'd been. "This is a story I would love to hear some time, but not now. I don't want you to betray any confidences. Lady Seneschal, will you do me the kindness of meeting me for tea again? I'm finding your acquaintance delightful."

"Well..."

"The Ultimate Delicacies Selection will again be my treat."

"That might well be a temptation that I can't pass up. Perhaps next week? Same place and time?"

"It's a date."

CONCERNS

Jerome sat to Eloise's left and slurped onion soup. "It's good," he said as a serving wench refilled his bowl. "Hearty. And hot, thank Çalaht."

Eloise waved a stick with fried brunchberries on it. "These are a bit strange." She bit off a pair of the crunchy berries. "But surprisingly moreish."

Jerome pointed to a small mound of discarded wooden skewers. "I agree, Your Highness. Do you think you could slide the serving plate back this way?"

The spare village hall was packed, bowls of soup were plentiful, and a thrum of conversation hummed in the air. The unexpected sunflower event was speculated upon, and a thousand different theories were proposed to explain it. Most ascribed what happened to divine intervention, with many of those people laying credit at the hooded toes of the Venerable Prelate Herself. Eloise noticed that the tapir did nothing to dispel that notion. Perhaps she genuinely believed it.

But none of them came anywhere close to the secret truth. Not even the old timers, who might have seen more weak magic than most, guessed what had happened.

That was OK with Eloise.

She turned around and waved the skewered berries at Lorch, who was standing guard behind her, keeping an eye on the crowd, his hand resting lightly on the hilt of his sword. "Would you like one of these?" she asked.

"Thank you, but no thank you, Queen Eloise. I believe the kitchen staff is putting together parcels for each of the guards to take away with them. Gourds of soup, packets of tarts, and berry kebabs. We should all be good."

"That's very kind of them."

The reception banquet wound on, and by mid-afternoon, everyone was feeling sated and drowsy. Nörbert de Lupus wagged his Chihuahua tail and began extricating the travelers so they could depart for the journey home in daylight. Eloise allowed Goodman and Goodwoman Rechteckfeld to say long, grateful goodbyes, which ended with the farmer saying, "I'm sure the sunflowers won't be any problem. We'll start clearing them tomorrow. Thank you again for gracing us with your royal presence and for bringing the Venerable Prelate Herself with you. It's been an amazing day."

"Thank you for your generous hospitality," she said. "The people of Festering Resentment will always have a place in my heart."

Outside, the Venerable Prelate Herself waddled over to her carriage and flopped inside, looking like she was ready to doze all the way home.

Hector waited for Eloise just outside the entrance to the village hall. He stood next to the Nameless One. "I think the weather is going to be even worse on the way home," he said. "There's no shame in availing yourself of the carriage, should you wish."

Eloise considered her options. Taking shelter in the carriage was tempting, but she didn't want them to think that she was going soft (nor did she want to think that of herself). "There are a couple of things I'd like to discuss with the four of you. Hector, if you don't mind, I'll ride with you."

"Of course, Your Highness."

As soon as they had cleared the village limits, Hector and the Nameless One rode in close formation and away from the rest of Eloise's entourage, allowing her, Jerome, Lorch, and the two horses to confer in relative privacy.

Jerome started. "So, Queen Eloise. Care to enlighten us about what happened out in the brunchberry paddock?"

She hesitated, embarrassed.

Eloise hadn't meant to cause a problem, but she had. And she had a sneaking feeling the problem would be worse than anyone thought. Maybe the Rechteckfelds would be able to plant their brunchberry canes, or maybe they'd need to consider going into a business that was a bit more sunflower oriented.

"It's OK, Queen Eloise," said Lorch. "If we are to serve you well, then it is useful that we understand what's going on for you. I'm sure I speak for all of us when I say that you can trust us to keep your confidences, and that you need not reveal anything that you don't want to."

"Absolutely," said Hector. The Nameless One nodded his silent agreement.

"Right. Thank you." Eloise cleared her throat. "It started with wanting to do something nice for Goodman and Goodwoman Rechteckfeld. I hadn't planned on attempting anything. It's not like I came here to test a spell. It was a spur of the moment decision because..." She craned around to see if the Çalahtist carriage was in earshot, but it was well back. "Because the Venerable Prelate Herself was being her usual boring self."

Without going into too much detail, Eloise told them how she had thought it might be a good thing to boost the paddock's fertility with a little of what the Star of Whatever could do.

"So, you used weak magic and it went somewhat awry," said Hector.

"A fair characterization. An oopsie, if you will."

"Queen Eloise, I have concerns," said Lorch.

Eloise looked at him in mock horror. "Why, Guard Lacksneck, it's been at least a week and a half since you last said that."

Lorch didn't react.

Eloise hung her head. "It was stupid. *I* was stupid. I don't know anything about this stuff, and here I was trying to wield magic. Who knows what the consequences of what I've done will be? It was hubris. It was unthinking. And it was dumb beyond words."

They rode in silence for a while, hunching down against the odd wintry blast of wind.

She looked at the others. "No one's going to contradict me on that?"

Jerome cleared his throat. "There are times when it would be prudent not to argue with the queen's pronouncements."

"Your intentions were good," said Lorch.

Eloise shook her head. "I seem to recall something about the paving materials used on the road to hell."

A good ten minutes passed as they thought about what she'd said and done. Then the Nameless One shook his head and snorted.

"What?" asked Hector.

The Nameless One began a series of hoof thumps, coughs, head waggles, and low whinnies. Every now and then, Hector said, "Uh huh" or "OK."

When he finally stopped, Hector tilted his head to the side. "I guess you're right. It is obvious. But sometimes things are only obvious once someone has said them."

"What's obvious?" asked Eloise.

"Your next steps," said Hector.

"Oh?"

"You once said to us that you thought the Star of Whatever was the most dangerous magical object in all the realms," said Hector.

Eloise nodded. "I think it might be, yes. Melveeta the Elusive cast a spell with it that created the Purple Haze. So there's that."

"It's why you have it with you always," said Lorch.

Hector nodded. "Then it is obvious what's next. You need to find out as much as you can about it. Everything."

"He's right, El. I mean, Queen Eloise," said Jerome. "The more you know about it, the less likely it is that there will be another little oopsie in the future."

"Right. I'll just add researching the Star of Whatever to my task list, shall I?"

"I can help," said Jerome. "We could start in the Bibliotheca de Records and Regrets. Surely there's something tucked away in there. Or, if you need, I can do a first search on my own."

"Yes, go ahead. But I'd like to be part of it as well. We'll need to be discreet. We don't necessarily want everyone to know what, exactly, we're looking for."

"Agreed," said Jerome. "We'll need to come at it a bit side-on. That'll take some thinking."

"I'll have to get First Advisor to clear some time for it. But I'll need to be vague with him as well. For now, at least."

"Just call it something stupid, like 'executive time.' That should cover you."

"'Executive time.' That's as dumb as it gets. Perfect," said Eloise. "Speaking of First Advisor Ligurian, I need you four to be part of a briefing."

"Of course," said Lorch. "May I ask, what kind of briefing?"

"Regicide."

The mood sobered, and they all looked at her.

"Regicide," repeated Jerome. He grimaced, like the word tasted bitter.

"I was wondering if that would come up," said Lorch

"I've asked for all the evidence that was gathered. It's slim, but I want First Advisor to take the five of us through it. I need more than one mind thinking about it, and I trust you more than anyone at Court."

"I'll be there," said Hector.

The others nodded agreement.

"Thank you," said Eloise. "Now, let's get home and out of this weather."

❧ 22 ❧

MAILBAGS

The ride home was freezing cold and horribly wet, but otherwise uneventful. The crummy weather gave Eloise plenty of time for mulling, as she spent the journey huddled into herself. Jerome dozed the whole way, snug inside her cloak and sitting on the box holding the Star of Whatever. *Half your luck*, she thought. But at least he wasn't butchering the lyrics to "Three Bags of Groats for My Sweetheart."

A warm, late supper, a halfway decent night's sleep in her parents' bed, then her morning run and a hearty breakfast had Eloise ready for the next day. She made her way to the Queen's Study, where First Advisor and eight large sacks awaited her.

"Blessings of the day, Queen Eloise," said Ligurian

"Blessings of the day, First Advisor. What have we here?"

"What you asked for. All of the correspondence, memos, missives, reports, etc., etc. I had the Security Patrol sniff for dangerous substances, but otherwise, it is untouched, as per your instructions." Ligurian could barely hide his smirk.

"So no royal boxes today."

"The royal boxes are strictly for material that has been prepared or analyzed. Today, royal sacks, as requested."

Eloise unlocked the door, grabbed the closest sack, and tugged. It didn't budge. "Çalaht blasting blasphemous beignets! That sucker weighs a strong weight!"

"It all does rather accumulate. Can I have them moved into the Queen's Study?"

"Of course."

"Page!" called Ligurian.

Moments later, a young wombat skittered around the corner, slid to a stop, and snapped to full attention. He wore a second-hand junior page's tunic that looked like it had previously belonged to a small basset hound. The sleeves needed taking in and the collar wanted mending, but it was clean, pressed, and worn with pride.

"RoyLee!" Eloise leaned down and gave him a hug.

The wombat stiffened and his cheeks went red, but he didn't stop her. "Thank you, Princess—"

Ligurian coughed.

RoyLee looked at him, realized his mistake, and got flustered. "I mean, thank you, Princess, uh, Princess Queen Eloise. Sorry for the mistake, your royaltyness."

Eloise gave his shoulder a gentle squeeze. "It's fine. Really. I'm the same person, despite this thing." She tapped the GHC on her head. "How lovely to see you, and looking so sharp. Junior page, huh? What do you think?"

"Truth be being told, there be a lot less fighting and pillaging than I be used to," said the wombat. "And I no be used to sleeping in a dwelling. I be used to a burrow and all the people in it. But Master Shovelhovel wanted me to have 'opportunities' and Seer Bunkerhunker saw me here at your castle in her visionings. So inevitabilities be at work. That all being said, I be very grateful to you for everything."

"I'm glad you're here."

Ligurian coughed again.

RoyLee snapped back to attention. "Junior Page-In-Training RoyLee Pottagecottage at your service. How may I be of assistance?"

"Could you please find a couple of servants, or maybe guards, who are strong enough to move these sacks into the Queen's Study?" said First Advisor.

"Oh, I can be doing that, your sirness." RoyLee scampered to the closest bag, which was easily five times his size, grabbed it with his clawed forefeet, and hauled on it. The sack slid over onto its side, but barely budged. The wombat ran around to the other side of it and pushed. He managed to slide it almost a full length along the floor.

Undeterred, RoyLee backed up half a dozen paces and flung himself at the sack. It scooted as far as the threshold of the door.

Ligurian shook his head. "Do you think that maybe some help might be in order?"

"No, no," said RoyLee. "It be personal now." He ran forward and rammed it with his head and shoulder. With much grunting and numerous indelicate words, he got it all the way into the room.

"Over by the desk, if you don't mind," said First Advisor.

RoyLee didn't hesitate. He hit the bag like a hockey sacking defensive girder and pummeled and rolled it around the map table until it was next to the desk chair. Then he wrestled it so it was upright and tidy.

"Thank you, RoyLee," said Eloise. "I'll start with this one while you bring in the others. But perhaps in the interest of time, you could—"

"No problem, Princess Queen Eloise," panted the wombat. "I be getting it done. It's just too bad that you no be needing this to be dug into a hole. I be very good at digging holes."

Eloise settled into her chair, opened the sack, and drew out the first item while Ligurian watched. To the extended sounds of RoyLee's struggles, she went through the first two dozen scrolls and pieces of hemp parchment.

After a particularly loud *thump!* and an *oof!* from the wombat, Eloise said, "Are you OK, RoyLee?"

"I be fine. Ow! I be fine, just fine, Princess Queen Eloise." And he went back to wombat-handling the seventh sack of correspondence.

First Advisor leaned over and whispered, "You know, you could just order him to get help."

"I know," murmured Eloise. "But why disempower him? He's new on the job and eager. Let's let him see what he can do."

"As Her Highness sees fit."

By the time she'd gotten through half of the first sack, with Ligurian watching silently, Eloise had begun spreading the items out across the map table. Soon there were stacks everywhere.

Curiosity got the better of Ligurian and he gestured toward the table. "May I ask?"

"Sure," said Eloise. "It's a kind of piling system. Things I understand and know what to do with, I've put on the model of Castle de Brague. Things I don't understand and don't know how to handle, I've banished to the Purple Haze."

First Advisor pointed to the pile on the Gööödeling Sea. "Those?"

"Those I think I understand, but am not sure what to do. This stack on the Eastern Lands are items that strike me as obviously not needing attention, like invoices, receipts, and transcripts from the more scurrilous gossip heralds. Personal notes that I want to read later have gone on the Half Kingdom."

"This rather large stack on the Central Ranges?"

"'Other.' For those, I need more frame of reference."

"I see," said Ligurian. "And here on the Whacking Great Hole, the hugest hole in the realm?"

"Marriage proposals."

"There are rather a lot of them."

"Not interested," said Eloise. "They can go in the hole."

"Hmmm..."

"I'm going to keep going through the sacks. I'd like you to please evaluate my piling and give me feedback. We can catch up after the briefing this afternoon and discuss things that need decisions and talking through. In the meantime, this will take me a while. No need for you to hover."

"What of the date stamping and logging? Will you be doing that as well?"

"No. Your assistants can take over the piles once I'm done."

First Advisor nodded. "That should be workable. I'll leave you to your labors." He bowed his way out the door and closed it.

Eloise opened and sorted. Bill. Invoice. Bill. Invoice. Receipt. Entreaty. Obsequious greeting from a merchant seeking some sort of permission to ignore one of her mother's edicts. Bill. Marriage proposal. Bill.

There really were a lot of bills. She hoped there was enough money in the counting house to cover it all. There was much less mention of the queen's tithe or other forms of income.

Eloise took the next item from the sack. It was a piece of scrawled writing on some of the roughest hemp parchment Eloise had ever seen, like it came from the roughest flop house in the worst corner of the realm. Someone had scrawled "PerInt" at the top, then "Communique from subject intercepted, then allowed on. Subject reports that he/she/it 'made contact, made delivery, sent message.' Actual components (person contacted, message) are unknown. Subject remains unidentified. Handwriting different every time. It's like chasing shadows."

Eloise looked at the back of the page of parchment. That was it. No indication of who had written it—no seal, signature, signet, or initials

—nor who it was intended for. Apparently the intended recipient was supposed to already have some clue about what was going on.

Curious.

Eloise slipped the note into her pocket and reached for the next item. Another bill. Ligurian was right—this really was going to be tedious.

She stood, stretched her back, and opened the door. "RoyLee? Are you still there?"

The wombat came running from around the corner. Once again, he skidded to a stop and snapped to attention. "I be being here, Princess Queen Eloise."

"Do you think you could organize for someone to bring me a pot of haggleberry tea and maybe something to nibble from the kitchens?"

"Of course, Princess Queen Eloise. Right away." And without another word he sprinted off, yelling, "Tea for the Queen! Tea for the Queen!"

23
BRIEFING

Eloise would have had the briefing about her mother's murder in the Queen's Study, except the two horses wouldn't really fit, and having them poke their heads through a window would be both undignified and a security risk. Plus, she was feeling a little possessive about the room. She wanted it to be a private space, at least for now.

Hector suggested they hold it in his father's office, which was as secure and private a horse-sized space as could be found in Castle de Brague.

Eloise, Lorch, and Jerome approached the Royal Stables and saw Hector's father waiting with Hector and the Nameless One. "Equine Master Ferdinand de Pferd," she said. "Thank you for allowing us to use your office."

The Friesian gave a deep, courtly bow and his voice boomed out a rich basso. "G'mid-afternoon, Queen Eloise. We are always grateful to welcome the queen's visit to the Royal Stables. I've had my office swept for bugs. There are no listening creatures present."

"Very prudent, thank you."

Ferdinand took a step backward to clear the way to the door. "If you'd like to go in, I'll let the kitchens know that refreshments can be brought."

"Again, thank you. Has First Advisor Ligurian already arrived?"

"I'm here, I'm here. Apologies, Queen Eloise. My lunch meeting got away from me. G'mid-afternoon, Equine Master de Pferd." The tone of his greeting was frosty, which surprised Eloise. Who didn't like the Equine Master?

"First Advisor. Good to see you." Ferdinand's manner carried the same lack of warmth.

Eloise wondered what that was all about.

Ligurian nodded to the others. "Guard Lacksneck. Champion Abernatheen de Chipmunk. Equine Designate de Pferd. And you are one of the nameless ones. Shall we get on with this?" He motioned for Eloise to go into the office first, then followed. At the doorway, he turned back to Ferdinand. "No need to get anything from the kitchens. I don't think we will be here all that long." With that, he went inside, leaving the others to follow.

Ferdinand's stable office had the simple neatness and meager adornments that reflected a life of discipline and equine military service. The wood of the stall was weathered, polished oak, and there was a manger to the side stocked with four different kinds of hay (lucerne, wheaten, oaten, and meadow), and an ancient, hand-carved trough filled with crystal clear water.

A single overstuffed, comfy chair sat in the middle of the room. It seemed only Eloise was supposed to sit. That made sense enough for the horses, and Jerome could pretty much sit anywhere. But it meant that Lorch and First Advisor would have to stand.

The door closed as she took her spot in front of the chair, but didn't sit. "I assume this discussion will stay in this room. Correct?"

Everyone nodded.

Eloise took the document wallet with the jottings from her cloak, sat, and set it on her lap. She patted the chair's arm, indicating that Jerome was welcome to join her. The chipmunk nodded, and climbed up next her.

"Lorch? Can I have them bring you a seat?"

"Thank you, but I prefer to stand."

"First Advisor?"

"I, too, will stand. As always."

Eloise tapped the document wallet and said, "Then let's start. Over to you, First Advisor."

"Thank you, Your Highness." Ligurian clasped his hands behind his back. "What is it that you'd like to know?"

"What do I want to know? Everything." Eloise had expected him to launch into it, not just field questions. "Perhaps start with a timeline."

First Advisor extended his hand. "May I refer to the notes?"

Eloise handed them over. She was surprised at the reluctance she felt. The folder was a tangible, if perhaps strange, tie to her mother.

Ligurian opened it, leafed through a few pages, then closed it again. "About a week after you left to retrieve your sister, we received a communication from the Adequate Wall of the Realms. By this point, it was clear you had failed to bring your sister back to Brague, as directed by the late queen in response to the visioning of the Court Seer. Further, you had not, as had been presumed, inexplicably continued on with Princess Johanna to the Half Kingdom for a visit with your uncle, the late King Doncaster. You were, instead, apparently intending to make an unauthorized, unexpected, and unprepared-for informal state visit to the Southie queen..."

"I... What?" said Eloise. "That's hardly—"

"Accompanied by your posse of enablers."

The small gathering erupted. Jerome leaped up. "How dare you—"

"That's not—" snapped Lorch.

"Unbelievable," shouted Hector, as the Nameless One pawed the ground.

Eloise held up her hand for silence. She let the quiet hold while she considered just what to say. Finally, she lowered her hand. "Have you had that bottled up inside for long, First Advisor?"

Ligurian's jaw was tight. "I am merely informing you of the circumstances around the matter at hand," he said. "The Queen and King were both relieved and dismayed to receive that communication. Relieved to know you were OK. Dismayed to learn of your trajectory."

"I can't imagine how that had anything to do with my mother swallowing haggleberries."

"You will know that the late queen was not overly inclined toward desserts on days that were not special celebrations, commemorations, or commiserations. I'm not saying you were responsible. I'm saying that as part of the timeline, receiving the communication led to a disquieting of her emotional state, which led her to request pie at an unexpected time, which in turn, gave the unknown actor an opportunity."

"Can I pose a fundamental question?" asked Lorch. "Are we certain that it was raw haggleberries that were responsible?"

Ligurian nodded. "Eldridge the Apothecary diagnosed it almost immediately, and every healer who attended her concurred. Further, the progression of her distress was consistent with damage done by ingesting raw haggleberries. And her late royal highness reported an unexpected crunchiness in her blueberry pie and a bitter taste, but thought nothing of it until after the fact. By then, it was too late to do anything."

"Do we know where they came from or how old they were?" asked Hector. "Don't they lose their potency with time?"

"Yes, they do weaken progressively. The two the late queen ate were considered fairly fresh but not straight off a bush. Otherwise, she would not have lingered as she did. As for their provenance, there are a few possibilities: either they were brought into the castle in one of the controlled shipments, smuggled into the castle as contraband, somehow removed from the apothecary's stores, or were picked locally."

Hector shook his head. "Picked locally? How is that possible? The plants don't grow anywhere near here."

Ligurian looked at Eloise and raised an eyebrow. "Queen Eloise?"

"There's no need to worry about that, First Advisor." She turned to Hector. "My sister has a secluded, walled garden in the castle grounds."

"Of course," said Hector. "It's common knowledge."

"It's more than that. It's legendary," said Jerome. He feigned a scary voice, like he was telling a campfire horror story, and waggled his claws. "None dare enter it. Wooooo."

"That'll do, Jer," said Eloise. "My sister managed to grow and sustain a haggleberry bush."

"I remember that," said the chipmunk. "We saw it that time we snuck in, years ago. You looked at her diary."

"It wasn't her diary. It was her gardening journal. But, yes."

"So the haggleberry could have come from that bush," said Hector.

"No," said Eloise. "I don't think so."

Ligurian looked doubtful. "Queen Eloise, how can you rule out the possibility?"

"Johanna has a weak magic for growing things. Always has. She doesn't talk about it much, but it's there. That haggleberry bush was, perhaps, the first and most conspicuous example of it, but there are many others. She told me herself that she conducted clandestine experiments to prove her weak magic to herself, one of which involve serving up biscuits laced with puke weed she'd grown. I don't remember it, but apparently I was included in the test subjects."

"I don't see how that's relevant to whether or not a berry from that bush can be implicated," said First Advisor.

"Because you can't use magic against blood."

That stopped him. "Ah. I see. I... I hadn't considered that possibility."

"I can say with confidence that the berries that killed my mother came from outside the castle, because the ones from Johanna's haggleberry bush couldn't possibly have hurt her."

"You're positive?" asked Hector.

"I'm so certain I'd walk to her garden now, pluck a berry, and swallow it. No hesitation. None of you could do that, but I could."

"I see," said Ligurian. He glanced down at the pile of jottings, like he wanted to make an annotation but was restraining the impulse. "It's good to be able to remove that possibility from the board." He coughed, then blinked several times. "Very, very good, actually. It was my duty to put forward the possibility that Princess Johanna's haggleberries had been the instrument used against the late queen. But I hadn't liked it." Another cough. "I'd always thought that bush was just a fluke. I didn't realize there was more to it than that."

"I assure you, there was," said Eloise. She let him sit with his feelings for a few moments more, then said, "So we have a means of death and we have an approximate time. What else?"

"To continue the timeline, the queen felt the first stirrings of discomfort almost immediately, and was in acute distress by the end of the meal. As the severity increased, Eldridge the Apothecary was called. He asked a few questions, made his diagnosis, and acted quickly with an emetic to help the late queen expel the ingested toxin. She immediately felt some relief, but if I may say so, I saw the grim look on the apothecary's face. He did not like what he saw, and subsequent events proved his initial assessment correct. The two haggleberries did permanent damage going down, did extensive damage while in her stomach, and then did more permanent damage coming back up. No amount of healing, no matter the modality, could change that."

The room stilled, and the previous rancor faded in the face of Ligurian's cold, somber retelling.

"Immediately after the incident, the guards locked down the castle, strictly controlling all entrance and egress. Every member of Chef's kitchen staff was interrogated, save the server who actually handled the plate between the kitchen and the table. That was Patrinia Tanche, a goanna who'd been in service at the castle for three months and 19 days. She was found hanging by the neck from the rafters of the woodshed outside the kitchen, suspended by a makeshift noose fashioned from a braided length of baling twine."

"A suicide?" asked Lorch.

"No," said Eloise. "My mother said there'd been a struggle, and the goanna's legs had been bound."

"Forelegs, back legs, and snout. From the looks of it, young Patrinia did not go quietly, but the deed had been done swiftly, so we suspect more than one person was involved in her demise."

Hector shook his head. "Why her?"

"I personally did a thorough examination of her burrow. The place had been destroyed. Her possessions—the few there were—were in splinters, and there was a nest with two smashed eggs. It was unclear if these were viable or the by-products of natural processes. A check into her background and references showed them unremarkable to the point of them possibly being faked, but she had no discernible ties to political or advocacy groups. There was no grudge against the queen that could be found. We did find some gambling debts owed by a step-brother, but small coin stuff. A third cousin was being treated for a rare consumptive ague that was expensive to treat, but apparently she was receiving that treatment from a skilled healer.

"Blackmail?" asked Jerome.

"Perhaps she was susceptible to it due to the gambling or the cost of the cousin's healing," said First Advisor. "But the connections are tenuous at best."

"So the goanna is the person who most likely committed the deed," said Eloise. "Do we suspect she was a lone actor or part of a conspiracy?"

"We genuinely can't say. No substantive connections were found. But if I were a betting man, which I'm not, I'd guess that it was a coordinated effort. A person doing this on their own would have wanted the world to know why. They would have died with their revenge, their vindication, their anger, or whatever, flying high and shouted loud for all to see and hear." Ligurian tapped the document wallet. "There's none of that here. Instead, the person slunk in, did the deed, slipped away, and was killed. The silence behind the actions speaks with a clarity of its own. To me, it says conspiracy."

Eloise nodded. "A conspiracy, but with no known conspirators."

Ligurian nodded, but added nothing.

"What else is on the timeline?" asked Jerome.

First Advisor returned to his summary. "The late queen ingested the berries. Pain followed. Treatment began. The castle was locked down. Kitchen staff were questioned. The alleged perpetrator was found hanged. Despite reassurances, Chef took responsibility and experienced deep depression and extreme guilt. A day later, she was found expired."

"Expired," repeated Eloise. "Expired how?" She wasn't sure she really wanted to know.

"Apologies, Your Highness, but it was gruesome. Chef tried to cause herself maximum pain in repentance. She locked herself in her office and..." Ligurian swallowed. "She used one of her knives on herself."

Eloise gaped. "That's... That's horrible."

"It was. Chef was skilled with a blade and, apparently, tolerant of pain."

The rest of the briefing washed over Eloise in a numbing white noise. As she uh-huh'd vaguely at Ligurian's reports from spies and intercepted communications from envoys, she became lost in a sad reverie.

She'd loved Chef, but hadn't realized just how deeply until that moment. Chef had been a constant in her life. Some of Eloise's earliest memories involved her and Johanna begging a nanny to let them go down to the kitchens for a treat. Chef would look up from the pot she was stirring or the bread she was kneading, and would say, "Ah, it's the two smartest, most beautiful, most capable princesses in all the realm."

The twins always replied, "We're the only princesses in the realm."

To which Chef answered, "See, then I know what I'm talking about. Now which of the smart, beautiful, capable princesses would like a..." And then she'd offer some sort of treat—a raspberry tartlet, an apple cinnamon muffin, a bit of peppermint stollen, a slice of chocolate babka, or any of what seemed like ten thousand different delights to emerge from Chef's kitchen. They were uniformly delicious.

The ritual always ended with Chef waving a towel at them and shouting in mock anger, "Now scamper out of my kitchen!" Which they did.

It wasn't the food (at least, not just the food) that made Chef so special to Eloise. It was the unconditional acceptance, which wasn't something the girls found in their mother. Acceptance without judgment was in short supply at Court. To have found it in Chef had been delicious.

And now she was as gone as her mother—more so, since Eloise hadn't had the chance to say goodbye. That Chef had been so distressed to have done to herself what Ligurian had described was simply unthinkable, and didn't jibe with the woman Eloise thought she'd known.

As First Advisor droned on about the reports from spies and merchants, informants at the top of society and those at the bottom, about the endless dead ends that the investigation turned up, Eloise found herself feeling overwhelmed by the sense of loss, in so many different forms. Her mother, Chef, her sister, her father, and quite possibly, her sense of self-worth and capability, were all gone.

She was in for a long, difficult reign. She could feel it in her bones.

That is, if she managed to survive that long.

❧ 24 ❧

ARE YOU OK?

"153. 154. 155. 156." Jerome sat on Eloise's shoulder counting the columns as she ran past them on her loops around the Culpability Courtyard. She was trying to reassert some sort of normality into her no-longer-normal life with regular morning runs. Her splinted wrist nagged and the shoulder that had been dislocated had some complaints, but her head was clear and her lungs drew and blew the crisp winter. Someone had swept her path of snow, so she didn't have to worry too much about slipping.

Usually, Eloise counted them herself, but it was nice to have Jerome up there jouncing along and doing it for her.

Or, it would have been, if not for the way he was counting.

"Is that designed to make me run faster?" Eloise asked.

"Is what designed to make you run faster?" said Jerome.

"You're singing the numbers you're counting to the tune of 'Three Bags of Groats for My Sweetheart.' You're substituting the numbers for the lyrics."

"Am I? Really?" Jerome sounded genuinely surprised. "Sorry, Your Majesterial Most High Highnesssality. My apologies."

Eloise furrowed her brow, still running. "Has that one been bottled up for a while?"

She felt Jerome shrug. "Yeah, ever since First Advisor went after me about nicknames, I keep thinking I have to be careful around you."

"Unfortunately, you do. *I* have to be careful around me. I guess we'll all get used to it eventually, assuming there is an eventually."

"What's that supposed to mean?"

"As my mother proved, there's no guarantee that this queen thing will last a long time."

Jerome humphed. "I guess. I just don't know how it helps you to dwell on that side of it. I mean, eventually, with any luck, we all stand at Çalaht's side. But for now, I don't see how it helps you to think about things that way."

Eloise kept running, the two of them now silent. At least the "Three Bags of Groats for My Sweetheart" thing had finished. For now, anyway. In her head, she ticked off columns 157 through 162.

"Can I ask you a question, El?" said Jerome.

"Fire away."

"Does it feel weird to you, being back?"

"Absolutely. 163." Eloise turned a corner. "But I've had a bit going on. What about you? Also weird?"

"Very. All the Protocol. All the Court stuff. Your becoming queen. I mean, I knew my buddy Elorhino would be made queen one day. But we get back, and, boom, everything's completely changed. Suddenly you're, quite literally, the center of the realm. I wasn't prepared for the enormity of it."

"Yeah. Boom. 164. Neither was I."

Jerome shifted on her shoulder. "Look, I know the world doesn't revolve around me. But my little part of the world does. And it's been strange."

"How so?"

"Well, for one, your mother's champion, Sylvia Cloisterfeld, is out of a job, and there's all this stuff she was doing that I'm supposed to do now."

"Like what?"

"She keeps trying to explain it to me. Security stuff. Personal protection stuff. Weapons stuff. Strategic this and tactics that and, 'Careful with that blade' stuff, as if I could even lift something as big as whatever she was pointing at. It's all a bit daunting."

"165. Are you OK?"

"Yeah, I'm fine. It's just a lot, and I'm sure there are others who would be much better at this kind of thing. Which really has been the problem all along with you naming me champion."

"I thought we'd moved past that discussion."

"We had, El. And it was more or less fine when we were out looking for your sister, and Lorch, Hector, and the Nameless One were all there to fill in the balance of things I can't do. But then we get home and you become queen and things change. Like I said, it's been weird all around."

"Have you been able to start our little research project? 166."

"Only just. There's hardly been any time. I ducked into the Bibliotheca de Records and Regrets for about half an hour yesterday afternoon. The Head Scribe wasn't there. Master Thompkins Lyredog Overbolt was filling in for him, and gave me any number of suspicious looks."

"Master Overbolt? Really? He wasn't asleep?"

"I may have startled him awake. He was sitting in a chair leaned back on two legs against the wall when I got there. When I cleared my throat to get his attention, the front legs of his chair thunked down onto the floor, and he barked, 'Bibble! Erinaceous, gabelle, oxter, ratoon!'"

"167. That sounds about right. He does that when he wakes up. Was he helpful otherwise?"

"'Helpful' might be overstating it. I asked for records pertaining to the reign of Gwendolyn the Irritable, since I didn't want to mention Melveeta the Elusive directly," said Jerome. "He said, 'The public records are over here,' and led me to a far corner of the main hall that had a massive shelf with what looked like several thousand scrolls."

"She did rule for a long time, and was incredibly active as queen. There was that whole ill-fated relationship with King Brüüütus of the Northern Lands."

"Northern Lands?" said Jerome. "Oh, right. I forgot the Half Kingdom used to have a different name."

"Brüüütus got Gwendolyn in the family way, then dumped her. In response, she waged a war against him. I guess it's not too surprising that there's the odd document around."

"I guess."

"168 and 169. I missed one. Did you find anything interesting?"

"Not really," said Jerome. "I mean, I don't know a lot about that time in the realm, so it all seems new. We studied Queen Gwendolyn's reign a little in our Histories and Hearsay lessons."

"I remember that, but it's been a while."

"I've managed to repress most of whatever we learned, although I do recall something about the fling with the Northo king. I hadn't remembered it leading to war."

"Yeah. It's probably why Gwendolyn got so irritable. Melveeta talked about that time when Johanna and I were with her. It was so vivid, the way she described those times. Which makes sense, since she'd lived them."

"So, yeah, I skimmed a few of the tomes there and flicked through some of the scrolls. Nothing in particular jumped out at me. There weren't many mentions of Melveeta, except as her sister and as one of her champions. But nothing particular about magic or the Star of Whatever or anything. Pretty dry stuff. 'Herein be-ith a recounting of the days of Queen Gwendolyn.' That sort of thing."

Eloise ran on in silence for a while, and Jerome resumed counting. Mercifully, he didn't sing this time. At 180, she slowed, stopped, then began her warm-down leg stretches. Without looking at him, she said, "Can I ask you something?"

He nodded. "Sure."

"It's personal."

"Sure-ish."

"Are you OK?"

Jerome's face pinched, and there was a small, irritable twitch in his tail. "I'm not sure I know what you're asking. Of course I'm OK."

"Are you?"

"Why wouldn't I be?"

"I just thought there might be some residual effects from our trip. After all..." Eloise changed from stretching her thighs to leaning against one of the columns and stretching her calves. She continued to avoid his eyes. "After all, you were in jail not once, but twice. There were jail chiggers and taunters. You were snatched by a crazed jester who deliberately clunked you, jumped over a waterfall while holding you by the tail, then stuffed you in a bag for weeks, letting you out only to taunt you into performing for coins."

"That only happened once."

"Shall I keep going?"

"No, thank you," said Jerome. "That will suffice."

Eloise swapped to arm stretches. "So, I'll ask again. Are you OK?"

In her peripheral vision, she saw his whiskers twitching and his jaw clench. "Yes, Queen Eloise. I am."

"Don't go all formal on me."

"It would be my preference—my very strong preference—not to revisit whatever difficulties I experienced in the past. I'm doing my best to put them behind me."

"Have you spoken with anyone about it? Your mother, perhaps? Seer Maybelle always struck me as empathetic and insightful."

"No, Your Highness. I have not."

Eloise stopped, put her hands on her hips, and stared straight at him. "You should find someone you feel you can talk to. I'm happy to talk about it, but if you don't want to talk to me, I won't take it personally. Maybe Lorch. Or the Nameless One. He's a good listener and you can be guaranteed he won't say anything. Or Eldridge the Apothecary. He's ancient, but knows ways of the mind as well as ways of the body."

"Why do you think I need to talk to someone?"

"Because, Jerrific, you've experienced trauma. You've been traumatized, whether you want to acknowledge it or not. You can keep it bottled up for a while, but at some point, it's going to come out. If you can let it out in an appropriate way, it's better than if it bursts out unbidden in an awkward circumstance."

"Are you saying I'm prone to unbidden, awkward outbursts?"

Eloise looked at him, but didn't say anything."

Jerome started to say something, stopped, swallowed, then swallowed again. "I'm fine, El. I really am."

But the bristling in his tail told a different story. Eloise wondered if he was even aware that he was doing it. "OK. If you say so," she said. "You know you better than I do. But think about what I've said. Talk so someone. As your queen, I command it."

Jerome smirked. "You know that's not going to work in this situation, right?"

"I know. But it was worth a try."

"Thanks for being concerned," he said. "I'll let you know if I want to talk."

"You do that. Now, do you want to walk me back to my parents' room? I have to get changed then go deal with some radish growers."

"It would be my pleasure, Your Highnessosity."

GERBIL ORPHANAGE

Eloise listened to the righteous intonations of Goodman Grady Thorstonstone, one of the three disputing radish farmers from Lower Glenth, and focused her entire being on not leaping from her throne and stuffing the Adjudication Cape down the squat, carbuncle of a man's throat. He was 17 minutes into what threatened be a four-hour defense of his claim to the disputed plot of Lower Glenthian radish paddock. It would not have been so bad if she had not already listened to half an hour each from Goodwoman Marlene Wildersteiner and Goodman Stefanio Bolderboulder each stating their own claims to the plot of dirt. In retrospect, it seemed like a bad idea to promise to hear each of them out so she could fully get across their concerns.

She looked at First Advisor Ligurian, who stood to the left of the dais and seemed to be paying rapt attention to the proceedings. Jerome, sitting on a stool to the right, looked in danger of falling off it from boredom. She smoothed the Adjudication Cape against her lap, tried to swallow back her irritation, and sought to channel her mother's demeanor.

Eloise tolerated another twelve excruciating minutes from Thorston-stone, but then could not help herself. She raised her hand to inter-rupt. The farmer glanced up from the scroll he was reading, saw the gesture, and dribbled to the end of his sentence.

"Thank you, Goodman Thorstonstone," Eloise said. "I get the gist of what you're saying. I think between the three of you, we've covered both the essentials and the exquisite details."

"Begging your pardon, ma'am, but you heard out the full statements of Goodwoman Wildersteiner and Goodman Bolderboulder. It would be only fair of you, and I would be most grateful, if you would hear me out in full as well. Now, as I was saying, the radish paddock in question—"

"You're right," cut in Eloise. "That would be fair. However, so far, you have not said anything that either Goodwoman Wildersteiner or Goodman Bolderboulder hasn't already said two or three times at least."

"But Your Highness, the radish paddock in question—"

"May I ask, Goodman Thorstonstone, do you have anything to say that has not already been stated, either in this room today or..." She pointed her elbow toward a stack of scrolls piled as high as a prize-winning courgette. "Or in these?"

Thorstonstone looked down at his scroll, his self-righteousness momentarily subdued, and mumbled as he skimmed his scrawl. His headed bobbed left and right as he rotely ticked off his points with a sing-song voice. "Reputational damage... Unneighborly conduct... Sovereign rights of inheritance... Bad smell... Harpy of a wife... The bloody idiots... Highest justice in all the land... My bloody radish patch... Remove their livers with a blunt spoon..." Thorstonstone looked up at Eloise. "No, Your Highness. I think everything's already been said."

"Well, then." Eloise smiled. "Thank you, Goodman Thorstonstone." She waved to the others. "Could I please have Goodwoman Wildersteiner and Goodman Bolderboulder join Goodman Thorstonstone here before me?"

The two other radish farmers stepped forward and joined their neighbor. Each looked defiant. Surely the new queen would help them prevail over the others.

"This matter has already been considered previously by two property magistrates, is that not correct?" said Eloise, pulling a document from the pile. "Once by a traveling magistrate who visited Lower Glenth, and once by the magistrate at Sonorous Belch."

"Yes, Your Highness," said Wildersteiner. She was a gaunt, bent woman who unconsciously tugged at a stray hair on her chin. "The one at Sonorous Belch was a persnickety old so-and-so, if I may say so myself."

"You're only saying that because you lost that one," said Bolderboulder.

"I'm with her on that one," said Thorstonstone. "He was demonstrably a persnickety old so-and-so."

"I object," said Bolderboulder. "One person's persnickety is another person's careful consideration."

Eloise spoke across them. "I'm correct in understanding that none of you are satisfied with those outcomes, yes?"

"It tweren't just or righteous," muttered Goodman Wildersteiner.

"Untrue!" countered Goodman Bolderboulder. "The property magistrates both clearly stated—"

"The property magistrates were fools," said Thorstonstone.

The three of them fell into bickering, which clearly had been going on for decades. It was rehearsed, vituperative, tired, and reminded Eloise of old, married people who'd long ago forgotten why they'd gotten betrothed.

Eloise held up her hand and the argument trailed into silence. "I've a question for you."

The three farmers looked at her.

"How is the gerbil orphanage doing in Lower Glenth?"

There was a long, puzzled pause.

"I beg your pardon?" said Goodwoman Wildersteiner.

"The gerbil orphanage," said Eloise. "How is it doing?"

"There t'ain't no gerbil orphanage in Lower Glenth, ma'am," muttered Goodman Bolderboulder.

Eloise's eyes went wide. "You're kidding. Really?" She turned to First Advisor Ligurian. "First Advisor, is that correct?"

First Advisor looked at her, expressionless. "As far as I'm aware, there is no gerbil orphanage in Lower Glenth."

"Astonishing. Just astonishing," said Eloise. She looked back at the farmers. "Where do your orphaned gerbils go?"

"You-your H-highness..." stammered Goodman Thorstonstone. "W-we have no place for orphaned gerbils."

Eloise moved her broken arm back and forth, taking in the three of them. "You're telling me that the underprivileged, parentless gerbils of Lower Glenth are homeless?" She looked back at Ligurian. "First Advisor, where is the closest gerbil orphanage to Lower Glenth?"

Ligurian stroked his chin and a faraway look appeared on his face. "Gormless Glades, Queen Eloise, if I'm not mistaken."

Eloise turned back to the farmers. "How far away is Gormless Glades from Lower Glenth?"

The three of them whispered with each other, finally agreeing. "About a half day if you're riding by cart," said Thorstonstone. "Maybe three-quarters of a day. It depending on the weather and whether or not the cart has both wheels working."

"Call it, say, 130 strong lengths?" asked Eloise.

"Mayhaps," said Bolderboulder. "At least. Probably closer to 160."

"So, you three are telling me that a poor newly orphaned gerbil—one who is already traumatized, and who will remain so for the rest of their lives by the sudden, cruel, unexpected loss of his or her parents—must travel at least 160 strong lengths to Gormless Glades to find succor, comfort, and appropriate gerbil-oriented orphan care?"

"I... I never really thought about it," said Goodwoman Wildersteiner. "But that's correct."

Eloise leaned forward, propping her chin in the palm of her unbroken hand. She sat that way for a full five minutes, staring at them, letting the greatest possible awkwardness build. When she thought this had gone on long enough, Eloise stood.

Everyone in the Receiving Room shot to their feet. She stepped forward off the dais and approached the three farmers. Eloise reached out her hands, one to Goodman Thorstonstone and one to Wilder-steiner, and took theirs. With a nod, she indicated they should do the same with each other. When they'd formed a circle, she smiled at them warmly. "I've really enjoyed meeting the three of you," said Eloise. "It has been a singular experience."

"Th-thank you, Qu-queen Eloise," said Bolderboulder.

"With regards to this paddock that has caused you such consternation for so long, here's what we're going to do. I'm going to give the three of you exactly 15 minutes to come to an agreement that you can all live with, and that works to everyone's benefit. In exactly 15 minutes and 10 seconds (or sooner, if you want), you are going to present this arrangement that you've carefully worked out between you, and that you're all happy with, to First Advisor Ligurian." She pointed. "That's him, right there, although you knew that already. You will have exactly 20 seconds to do so. If you don't, or if you present an arrangement that strikes him as unfair in any way, I'm totally OK with that. It's abso-lutely fine with me that you don't suitably resolve the matter. However, at that point, the issue will cease being a matter of concern for you, because the crown will immediately assert eminent domain over the paddock and establish the Lower Glenth Thorstonstone Wildersteiner Bolderboulder Gerbil Orphanage on that very spot, thereby providing a sorely needed community facility that meets the requirements of one of your fair village's disastrously under-served groups."

"But—" started Wildersteiner.

Eloise flashed them her sweetest smile. "Thank you for your time and for the opportunity to consider this matter. I look forward to hearing what you come up with. You have 14 and a half more minutes." She gave their hands a little squeeze. "Good luck."

Then she let go, turned her back, hung up the Adjudication Cape, and walked out of the Receiving Room.

❦ 26 ❦

MESS

First Advisor Ligurian was into his second hour of morning briefing, propounding on how additional rations subsidies had been provided to crofters as an incentive for them to up their wax bean production levels. He was going through wax bean harvest numbers in a ledger, and Eloise was doing her best to both keep up with what he was saying and not to let her mind wander.

Mercifully, RoyLee knocked on the Queen's Study doorway and poked his head in. "Begging your pardon, Princess Queen Eloise, but there be a messenger here for you."

Eloise looked up from the ledger, grateful for the distraction. "A messenger? Come on in."

The wombat turned to someone in the hall. "Go ahead."

The messenger was a capybara dressed in the Half Kingdom messenger's purple road tunic and darker purple breeks, complete with a dust-covered purple fez. The rodent was huge, with a heavy, barrel-shaped body and short head, neatly groomed reddish-brown fur, and the regal bearing of one steeped in the ways of Protocol and comfortable moving in and through a court. He stepped into the room, bowed gracefully and deeply, and with a cultured voice said, "Greetings, Queen Eloise."

Ligurian interrupted, moving in front of him. "Please, Your Highness. These things really should come through me. You cannot be interrupted by every Thomas, Richard, and Harold who stops by the castle with a scroll bearing your name."

"Fair enough," agreed Eloise. "But look at his clothes. He's come a long way to be here."

"The distance he's come doesn't matter. It's process that matters. It's the value of your time that matters." Ligurian waved for the messenger to go out the door. "Whatever it is that you need to deliver, you can wait at my office for me to return and we can discuss the matter then. Now go."

"With respect, I cannot do that," said the capybara. "I bring the queen a letter from her sister. Your Highness, she charged me with delivering it straight into your hands." Then he bowed, straightened, drew a carefully folded, wax-sealed envelope of hemp parchment from his pouch, and offered it to her with both front paws. "From Princess Johanna."

Eloise saw Ligurian reach for it. Perhaps it was reflexive, but Eloise had no desire for him to come anywhere near it. She stood, which froze everyone in place. "Thank you. What a wonderful surprise." She walked forward and took the sealed envelope from the messenger. "I'm most grateful to you."

"Princess Johanna asked me to remain a while in case you wished a return missive delivered."

"Thank you, again. I will. May I ask your name?"

"Ziïimmëëërmäään. But you can call me Ziïimmÿÿÿ."

"Very good. RoyLee, could you please take Master Ziïimmÿÿÿ to the kitchens for something to eat and ask Lady Seneschal to assign him a room." To the capybara, she said, "Did you have a transportation partner who needs food and shelter?"

"Yes, ma'am. Dennis. Dennis de Asinus. My donkey companion has already made his way to the Royal Stables to avail himself of your facilities."

"Good. If either of you needs anything, please ask. And RoyLee will fetch you when I've finished writing back."

Once RoyLee and Ziïïimmÿÿÿ were gone, Eloise found it difficult to return to wax bean subsidies. She was grateful when, half an hour later, Ligurian's explanations finally fizzled out and he took his leave.

Alone at last, Eloise found a sharp knife to use as a letter opener and slit open the envelope instead of breaking the seal. Usually, Johanna wrote with beautiful curlicued quillmanship, but these letters were blocky, disjointed things, the product of labored encoding instead of free-flowing thought.

Eloise grabbed a quill and some scraps of parchment, and set to decoding.

The first part was uncoded plain text.

Dear El,

I hope this finds you well.

The eleventh character (ignoring the spaces) was "I" and the seventeenth was "u." So she had her offsets for the double substitution.

Eloise got to work.

Dear El,

I hope this finds you well.

Father and I made it to the castle at Stained Rock safe and sound, but found the Half Kingdom's Court in a total uproar. It was chaos.

At one level, the problem was obvious: no king, no direct heir, no succession plan. Of course it was chaos. But when you left me here to go home and take Turpy to face the queen's justice, I was already thinking that I'd try to be queen and had started trying to gather support. It hadn't yet solidified in any way, so when news came that I needed to rush back to Brague, I didn't have any authority to say to anyone, "You're in charge while I'm gone. Keep the ship of state afloat until I get back." So I just had to leave.

And when I got back—mess.

I'd forgotten how cumbersome it was to write this way.

Really not that much to say yet. We arrived. We're safe. Father is finding it strange to be back where he grew up, and there's no clear path forward.

Send a message back with Ziïïmmÿÿÿ if you have the time to encode one.

Love,

J

ELOISE READ THE DECODED LETTER TWICE MORE, THEN TUCKED IT away in a locked drawer. A glance out the window showed she probably had enough time before dinner to write back. She reached for a clean sheet of hemp parchment.

DEAR JO,

Winter holds firm, but I look forward to the new budding that will arrive soon.

THEN ELOISE TURNED OVER THE SCRAPS SO SHE COULD WORK OUT the encoding that would follow. She needed to tell Johanna about the very different mess she found herself in.

❦ 27 ❧

HEAD SCRIBE

The Salle de la Famille was both Eloise's favorite and least favorite part of the castle. She loved the antechamber to her parents' quarters because it was filled with family memories. The twins had played for hours on end there as kids. Its fireplace was warm and its stonework walls had always fascinated her with their shapes, colors, and patterns. More meals than not had been had at the old mahogany table. As a girl, Eloise used to imagine all her ancestors eating side-by-side at that table, maybe making the very nicks and stains that were still in the wood.

But now those family memories were bittersweet, a mix of familiarity and loss. Sitting there could send her mind off in a thousand different directions.

Eloise and Jerome sat at the ancient table munching brunchberry muffins spread with raspberry compote. A basket of the fresh muffins sat lightly steaming in the middle of the table, covered by a cloth napkin to help keep them warm.

"These might be the best muffins the new Chef has done yet," said Jerome. "I might just have to have another."

Eloise didn't respond.

"El?"

Nothing.

He cleared his throat and said a little louder, "Queen Eloise?"

Eloise blinked and came back to awareness. She realized she was staring up at a random corner of the stone ceiling, one hand holding the GHC in place on her head. "Sorry. Did you say something?"

"Lost in thought, were you?"

"It would appear so." Eloise dabbed her mouth with her serviette. "I wasn't drooling or anything, was I?"

"No," said Jerome. "Or not much, anyway."

"Hah. Hah." She touched the napkin to the corner of her mouth just to be sure, then spread a bit more compote on the half-eaten muffin.

"What about?" asked Jerome.

"What about what?" Eloise said, taking another bite.

"What were you thinking about?"

"Something you said the other day." Eloise set down the muffin and sipped her haggleberry tea. "Remind me. When you asked Master Overbolt about records pertaining to Gwendolyn the Irritable, how did he answer?"

"He took me over to the public records."

"And you found?"

"Not much that's interesting."

"Exactly." Eloise took a last nibble and slid the plate away from her. She stood, picked up the muffin basket, adjusted the cumbersome bulk of her crown, and said, "Come with me. I have an idea."

"Where are we going?"

"The Bibliotheca de Records and Regrets."

"Head Scribe will have your head if you bring food in there."

"I know."

Eloise led Jerome through a maze of halls and shortcuts, and within fifteen minutes, they'd reached the massive double oak doors that separated the Bibliotheca de Records and Regrets from the rest of the castle.

Eloise looked at the door and shivered. "This thing gives me the willies. Always has."

Jerome nodded. "Me too. When I was a pup, my mother had to drag me to go through them."

The door was carved in exquisite detail, with dozens upon dozens of images, each showing some form of torture, maiming, and death: from someone being dropped in a boiling cauldron or hung by unexpected appendage to someone being whacked with a stick or flailed with a cat o' nine tails (a term offensive to felines). Other carvings showed drownings, impalings, dismemberments, gougings, rakings, rackings, mutilations, lacerations, and strong scoldings. In each case, the perpetrator was a faceless, hooded figure cloaked in a scribe's robes who waved an accusing damaged scroll.

"Not exactly subtle," said Jerome.

"No. The scribes within are definitely protective of their documents."

"True." The chipmunk nodded at the basket she carried. "Is bringing that in here a good idea?"

"Probably not. But we'll see."

Jerome bowed and waved his paw. "After you, Queen Eloise."

"Thank you, Champion Abernatheen de Chipmunk." She pushed her way inside.

The Bibliotheca de Records and Regrets' front room was cavernous and open. Its far-flung walls were lined with packed shelves, and there were several floors of them on each side. High above, filtered skylights let light into the room, directed so that it didn't hit any of the books along the sides at any time of day, but gave plenty to read by.

In the middle of the reading room were dozens of reading tables with hard, wooden chairs. These were occupied by hushed, contemplative scholars scratching notes, their quills dipping into ink pots set a careful distance from any reading matter they studied. Radiating from the open-plan reading room in every direction were hallways and stairways that led to a warren of chambers and rooms, each filled to capacity with bins, cubbies, shelves and nooks holding untold numbers of scrolls, rare bound tomes, and stacks of documents.

At the back of the front room, high on a riser that afforded an unbroken view of the entire space, was the Head Scribe's desk, with places for four Assistant Scribes on either side. Like the entrance, the huge mahogany desk was carved with scenes of pain and punishment, these being somehow even more grotesque and cruel than the door's.

Jerome tugged Eloise's sleeve. "Head Scribe is here. Not Master Over-bolt. Are you sure this is a good idea, whatever it is? He scares me."

"Dunno. Come on."

"He doesn't frighten you?"

"Are you kidding? Of course he does."

Eloise and Jerome made their way to the riser and stepped up.

Head Scribe Bernardo Speculum Twiddle was an ancient, bespectacled raccoon in a dust-gray cloak with wisps of matching gray on his snout and around his eyes. His voice was like a vulture quill scratching the mummified skin of a desiccated mandrill corpse. His posture was a permanent stoop, the result of years hunched over a slanted scribe's table, quill scratching, as it was in that very moment.

Eloise and Jerome stood quietly, and waited for him to stop and see them.

He didn't.

They waited.

And waited.

Eloise decided to interrupt. "Blessings of the day, Head Scribe Twiddle."

"Gaw!" The startled raccoon's quill rucked across the page. He jerked it aside, but his ink pot was too close and clunked onto its side, ink spilling. "Son of a Çalaht-cursed rutabaga-sucking blasphemer!" cried the Head Scribe as he scrambled to protect his source documents.

Eloise gasped, frozen in horror.

Twiddle ducked below the desk and tried to contain the spreading, dripping ink by blotting at it with precious pages of blank hemp parchment.

"Jóöôáäàqúüùîîin! Jóöôáäàqúüùîîin!"

A short, rotund teenager in apprentice scribe robes race-waddled over from a side wall, holding an armload of scrolls. He looked to be the same age as Eloise, but was easily twice her size, and his tonsured head seemed to imply (or perhaps encourage) a religious devotion to scrolls, writing, and documents. "Yes, Head Scribe? Do you need something?"

The raccoon waved the ink-stained pages. "Use your eyes, Jóöôáäàqúüùîîin! Show some initiative!"

"Yes, Head Scribe." The apprentice glanced left and right, looking for a place to put his scrolls. He settled on an empty scribe's table and set them down, but they slid down the slant. He just managed to block them with his belly and scoot them back up. When they rolled down again, he changed their orientation, and finally managed to position them so they stayed.

Jóöôáäàqúüùîîin then stepped behind the desk, picked up Twiddle by his scruff, and plopped him back on his seat. He beamed, proud of his initiative. "There you go, Head Scribe. No one need know you tippled during breakfast and fell off your seat drunk."

"How dare you, you lychee-headed, nonsense-babbling imbecile!"

"It's OK, Head Scribe. My uncle is a breakfast tippler, too. I've had to pick him up off the ground many times."

"I don't drink at breakfast!"

"That's what he says. But if you say so, Head Scribe." Jóöôáäàqúüùíîin looked at Eloise and Jerome and gave a knowing nod and wink. Then his eyes went wide as he realized who was there. "Gorp!" he choked and threw his arms wide in shock. The gesture sent both Head Scribe and the errant ink pot tumbling once more. The raccoon rolled backward into a display case that was filled with a decorative collection of ancient scrolls devoted to matters of tofu lore, and the ink pot splashed everywhere. The apprentice scribe dropped to one knee (which was definitely more than Protocol required), but that meant he was hidden by the high, solid desk. "Y-your H-highness," he stammered, voice sounding small behind the thick layer of wood.

"You incompetent!" snapped Head Scribe. "You're right to grovel before me, you kumquat-snorting, vacant-belfry walking disaster zone."

Eloise heard Jóöôáäàqúüùíîin stage-whisper through clenched teeth. "I'm not groveling for you. I'm groveling for her."

"Her? Who her?"

"*Her* her."

There was the scrape of a chair moving, a rustle of robes climbing, then the raccoon's head appeared once again above the desk. Head Scribe looked at Eloise and Jerome, then turned back to his apprentice. "Çalaht suffering sycophantic sybarites, Jóöôáäàqúüùíîin. It didn't occur to you to mention the queen was here? For the love of cantankerous—"

"Blessings of the day," interrupted Eloise. "I—"

The raccoon glanced her way, smiled, and softened his voice. "Be with you in just a moment, Your Highness." He turned back to Jóöôáäàqúüùíîin. "... cantankerous, cankerous, caustic kissing crabapples, don't you realize that having the queen show up is a Rather Big Deal? Now clean up that mess, care-ful-ly replace the Scrolls of Magisterial Tofuness back in their rightful places in the display, then go recopy your scrolls. And this time, don't use the purple or pink inks."

"But that makes them pretty."

"No purple. No pink. And no hearts for dots above the i's and j's."

"Oh, please, Head Scribe, I—"

"These are royal documents, Jóöôáäàqúüùíîn, not love notes. You have to learn the difference."

"They can be both," whined the apprentice.

"Not if you write them, young man. If she..." He nodded at Eloise. "If Her Highness writes them, then they are royal records, as you just said, and can have all the heart dots she wants. As you're working on recopying the queen's tithe accounts, you're not to use heart dots. Not on accounts, nor royal proclamations, nor Court records. "

"Yes, Head Scribe." The apprentice lowered his head.

"That will do, Jóöôáäàqúüùíîn. You may continue your duties, starting with the tofu scrolls."

"Yes, Head Scribe."

The raccoon flicked a dismissive paw at Jóöôáäàqúüùíîn, then turned his attention to Eloise, starting with a bow that, while being more than what Protocol required, was far less than effusive. "Your Highness. May I please express my condolences on the passing of the late queen."

"Thank you, Head Scribe. That is kind of you."

"She was beloved by many."

That struck Eloise as an odd phrase. Did that "many" include Head Scribe? It might, but it might well not. She stood taller. "Thank you, Head Scribe Twiddle. She always spoke highly of you and your staff." And it was true. Eloise's mother had openly admired and spoken of the scribes' completeness, discretion, accuracy, and overall competence. Eloise had the sense that her mother trusted them, which was something, as she did not give her trust lightly.

"It is kind of you to say so." The raccoon tugged the sleeves of his robe to align its decorative piping. "Now, to what do we owe the honor of your company?"

"My champion and I have some interest in the reign of Queen Gwendolyn the Irritable."

"Certainly. Any particular interest?"

"I'm curious about her fascination with magical objects."

"Was there a fascination?"

"I believe so, yes."

"I was not aware of that. Well, then. I'll have Jóöôáäàqúüùîîin show you to the appropriate public records."

"Public records," said Eloise.

"Yes, public records." The raccoon waved a paw. "They're over there."

"Public records would imply the existence of non-public records, would it not?"

Twiddle said nothing, but Eloise saw his eye twitch.

"Head Scribe?"

"I'm happy for you to see the public records. As I said, Jóöôáäàqúüùîîin can show you to them."

"I'm interested in any non-public records."

Head Scribe shook his head. "I'm sorry, Your Highness. There's restricted access to those. But everyone is welcome to enjoy and learn from the public records."

Jerome raised an eyebrow, while Eloise gave the old raccoon a chance to think about what he'd just said. Or more to the point, to whom he'd said it.

The raccoon stood there, quietly withstanding their looks.

"Head Scribe," started Jerome. "Her Highness is not just any schmoe to walk in the door. Her Highness is Her Highness. One doesn't keep things from the qu—"

"I've got this," interrupted Eloise. "Head Scribe Twiddle, you said access is restricted? From what?"

"Not from what, Your Highness. From whom."

"From whom, then?"

"From those who do not have the proper training to treat the records with the care and respect they deserve. These are exceptionally delicate documents stored in such a way as to ensure that they'll still be around a few hundred years from now. Caring for them, preserving them, is a complex business."

"I—"

"If I may finish, Your Highness. You asked for an explanation. I'd like to give it to you. Now, I see that you carry a breakfast basket." He leaned forward, bracing his paws on his desk, and sniffed, testing the air. "Brunchberry muffins, it seems. My favorites. And those smell like good ones."

"They are." Eloise lifted the basket toward him. "Care for one?"

His whiskers trembled, his nose worked the scent, and if Eloise wasn't mistaken, a small bit of drool formed on the corner of his mouth. "Thank you, but no thank you, my queen." He straightened, leaning away from the temptation. "Were you anyone else in the realm, rest assured that as soon as I'd seen or smelled those delicious muffins, I would have barked at you to remove yourself and your offending muffins from these hallowed halls. I would have, as young Jóöôáäàqúüùíîin can attest, fulfilled every rumor you might ever have heard about me. Do you have any idea how much damage an errant brunchberry can do to a piece of hemp parchment that dates from the time of Gwendolyn the Irritable? Or from the time of your own beloved mother, for that matter?" He stopped and waited. Apparently, he wanted an answer to what seemed like a rhetorical question.

"No, I don't," said Eloise.

"Do you, Champion Abernatheen de Chipmunk?"

"No, I don't either, but—"

"My point exactly," said Head Scribe. "You don't. Neither of you. You don't know what fingers that have touched a brunchberry muffin can do to such precious relics. Without proper training and care, our conservation policies, procedures, and processes may as well be dust in the proverbial breeze. Permanent, incalculable damage can arise from a single errant sneeze. As such, access to them is restricted, limited to those who've done proper training."

"Proper training?"

"Yes. For instance, completing some of the basic scribery courses, like The Care of Really, Really Old Stuff in a Way That Won't Infuriate Head Scribe and Cause Him to Inflict Grievous Bodily Harm, developed by one of my predecessors and still taught today."

"Ugh," piped in Jóöôáäàqúüùíîìn from below the desk. "That course nearly killed me."

"I see," said Eloise. She looked at Jerome. "Have you taken a course like The Care of Really, Really Old Stuff in a Way That Won't Infuriate Head Scribe and Cause Him to Inflict Grievous Bodily Harm?"

"No, Your Highness."

"Me either." Eloise smiled at the raccoon. "Head Scribe, thank you so much for making all that clear to me."

Head Scribe gave a small bow. "My pleasure, Your Highness."

"I think that will do. Jerome? Anything else?"

"No, Your Highness."

"Good. Then there's just one other thing."

Head Scribe tilted his head. "Yes, Your Majesty?"

"I hereby order you to grant me access to any and all records in the Bibliotheca de Records and Regrets, and to make them available to me and/or Champion Abernatheen de Chipmunk at any time, day or night, that I or he requests it."

"Your Highness—"

"Further, I expect that you will provide me and Champion Abernatheen de Chipmunk any and all coaching, teaching, or training that he or I might need in the proper handling of such records so that I might care for them in such a way as to ensure that they'll last another few hundred years."

"But Your Highness, the skill needed to—"

"In return, I will leave any and all foodstuffs here at the desk for your safekeeping. And, if you're so inclined, for your enjoyment."

"Your Highness, that's hardly—"

Eloise raised her index finger and silenced him. "Head Scribe, thank you so much for your cooperation."

"I have no intention of—"

"Yes, you do. Whatever you were going to say no to, it's yes. Now, and from now on. I promise I will be careful. I promise that Jerome will be similarly careful. I promise that we will be respectful to you and the treasure of the Bibliotheca de Records and Regrets. But the simple fact is that we need access to Queen Gwendolyn's private records, and we shall have it."

"Your Highness, I refu—"

She raised her finger again.

His whiskers sagged and he stopped arguing.

Eloise handed him the basket. "Please, put this somewhere for safekeeping. Or for your enjoyment later. Either way is fine with me."

"I—"

"Perhaps you can ask Jóöôáäàqúüùíîìn to tend the front desk."

The raccoon forehead wrinkled. "I beg your pardon, Your Highness?"

Eloise turned to Jerome. "Are you busy? Anything planned?"

"No, my queen."

"Excellent." She turned back to Twiddle. "Head Scribe, I appreciate your time and willingness to share your expertise. Now seems like the perfect time to start our tutoring in The Care of Really, Really Old Stuff in a Way That Won't Infuriate Head Scribe and Cause Him to Inflict Grievous Bodily Harm. It sounds fascinating."

Twiddle sighed. "Yes, Your Highness."

"Then we have some records that need looking through."

✤ 28 ✤

BABIES

Eloise sent a page to let First Advisor know that she would miss her morning briefing, but would catch up with him after lunch. Then Head Scribe took them down a hall behind his desk to a well-lit side room with a table and chairs. Shaking off his initial reluctance, he launched into the first lesson in The Care of Really, Really Old Stuff in a Way That Won't Infuriate Head Scribe and Cause Him to Inflict Grievous Bodily Harm with a question. "What is the first rule of working with the non-public collections of the Bibliotheca de Records and Regrets?" The raccoon crossed his arms across his chest and waited for an answer.

"I don't know, Head Scribe," said Eloise.

"Neither do I," said Jerome.

"That's right. You don't. Listen closely: the first rule of working with the non-public collections is that what's in the Bibliotheca de Records and Regrets stays in the Bibliotheca de Records and Regrets. The public items can be borrowed and returned. The non-public ones? They. Stay. Here."

This riled Jerome's sense of championess. "You can't say that to the queen," said Jerome. "One doesn't say that sort of thing to Her Highness."

Head Scribe fixed Jerome with a fierce look and jabbed a finger in the chipmunk's direction. "I don't care if I'm speaking to Çalaht her divine self. What's here stays here. It's best for the scrolls and documents, and that's what matters."

"It's OK, Jerome," said Eloise. "I'm sure Head Scribe holds the best interests of the Bibliotheca and the greater queendom in his heart when he says what he says. Don't you, Head Scribe?"

"Of course, Your Highness. So, what's the first rule of working with the non-public collections? Say it out loud."

"What's in the Bibliotheca de Records and Regrets stays in the Bibliotheca de Records and Regrets," said Eloise and Jerome in unison.

"Very good."

The things Head Scribe covered after making such a big deal of his first rule struck Eloise as falling somewhere between "Nuh, duh" and "Mildly interesting," on par with learning, as she once did, that it was Queen Audrey the Parasitic who worked out that sponges were a kind of people (very small, not very talkative people, but still people), and not plants.

After two hours, they took a break, and Eloise glanced over the notes she'd made on a spare piece of hemp parchment. "Wash hands to get rid of oils." "Don't use lotion before working with documents." "Wear the cotton gloves, but make sure they're clean." "Gloves available for most species and appendage sizes." "Food and beverages are strictly verboten." "Don't lick your appendage to turn a page." "Don't lick the page." "No sneezing, coughing, oozing, or rupturing pustules in or around documents." "Don't lean on documents while reading." "Unscroll and rescroll scrolls carefully." "If something is stuck together, leave it. If you absolutely must read it, call one of the scribes for help." "If you tear something, expect grievous bodily harm." "If you stain something, expect grievous bodily harm." "If you bend or otherwise crease something, expect grievous bodily harm." "Overall, expect grievous bodily harm, and be glad if it doesn't happen."

Head Scribe may not have developed the lesson, but he delivered it with conviction. At least he was clear about his expectations.

"From now on, I don't want you to use the word 'document' or 'scroll' or 'page,'" said Twiddle. "None of those."

"No?" said Jerome. "What should we call it instead?"

"Baby."

"Baby?" Eloise tried to see if the raccoon was kidding. He wasn't. "Why 'baby?'"

"Because I want you to treat them with the love, tenderness, and care you would lavish on a baby. You wouldn't drop a baby. Or tear, fold, spindle, or mutilate one. You'd treat him, her, or it like the precious thing he, she, or it was."

"I see," said Eloise.

The raccoon continued his lecture. "Babies must always be handled by their edges," said the raccoon as he handed them gloves, blank practice scrolls, and pages of hemp parchment. "Never let them hang off a desk or table, as this increases the likelihood that they will crease or tear. This is particularly the case with these kinds of babies." He pointed to a scroll. "Understood?"

Eloise and Jerome nodded and slid on their gloves.

"Don't hold the babies to read them. You want to flatten them on the table using these." He hefted two stones polished to flat disks and used them to weigh down the top corners. He carefully unfurled the scroll and used two more stones to secure the bottom edge. "See how the baby has a curl on the edges toward the middle? I'll use two more weights to flatten that. The idea is to touch the babies as little as possible. Weighed down like this, you can examine the baby without getting too close, and can remove yourself should you need to sneeze or cough—although if we see you are sick, you'll be asked to leave. Understood?"

More nods.

"Now you try. Pretend this blank baby is the most precious baby in the entire Bibliotheca de Records and Regrets. Who knows, someday, with a bit of ink on it and the right circumstances, it might be."

After a dozen tries, both Eloise and Jerome could unscroll a document, weigh it down, pretend to read it, then scroll it back up again with enough care to earn a grudging grunt of approval.

"Now we'll try the whole process, from opening a drawer or the lid of a bin, transporting the baby to the table, laying it flat, reading it, then putting it back. Queen Eloise, you first, please."

As she opened a document drawer and slowly took out a scroll, Eloise considered how she'd been to the Bibliotheca de Records and Regrets hundreds of times. Maybe thousands. She'd even rummaged in one of the record rooms before, when she was looking for information about her mother's Thorning Ceremony. The location of the scrolls—the babies—stuck in her mind like a popcorn kernel in her molar: sixth level, top floor, bin 185, sub-bin 422, sub-sub-bin A7, sub-sub-sub-bin Mabel. She'd trawled through those scrolls as fast as she could, seeking any morsel that might shed light on what her mother's ceremony had been like. Eloise had had no idea just how much care should have been shown to the items stored there. Thinking back on how reckless she'd been before, she felt mortified. Why had Master Overbolt let her loose in there? Perhaps those babies weren't as treasured, since they were relatively new. But some of them had seemed ancient.

Maybe Master Overbolt had sensed how miserable she was because of the looming Thorning Ceremony, pitied her, and cut her some slack. If so, she owed him a big thank you. And she hoped that Head Scribe hadn't found out and inflicted grievous bodily harm on him because of her.

She vowed to never again be so cavalier with the Bibliotheca de Records and Regrets' babies.

Eventually, Twiddle said, "You've made a good start today. Please remove your gloves and put them in the bin over there so they can be washed."

Jerome tugged the tiny, chipmunk sized gloves off his paws one claw at a time. "So, can we see Queen Gwendolyn's babies now?"

"Absolutely not. There's much more for you to learn first."

"But—"

"No buts. If you want to see those babies, you will be properly prepared."

"Head Scribe," said Eloise. "Would it be possible to just see where Queen Gwendolyn's babies are stored? We don't have to touch them, but maybe we can just get a sense of them, so we can get ourselves there once you're happy with us doing so."

Twiddle looked from her to Jerome and back, slow and hard. "I suppose so," he huffed. "I'll have Jóöôáäàqúüùíîn take you there. Wait here, and I'll send him along." The old raccoon took off his cotton gloves and dropped them in the bin. He walked to the doorway, then stopped, turn back to Eloise, and bowed. "Your Highness, I request your permission to leave the room before you."

"Oh. Yes, of course."

"You will let me know when you'd like your next lesson?"

"After my morning briefing tomorrow. Would that suit?"

"Of course, Your Highness."

"Very good." Eloise dropped her gloves in the bin. "And Head Scribe?"

"Yes, Your Highness?"

"Thank you. I appreciate your help."

"Of course, Your Highness."

"Enjoy the muffins."

The raccoon smiled for the first time in hours. "I will." He bowed and left.

❧ 29 ☙

GCEG 1/27

Jerome walked around the room while they waited. He opened drawers, lifted bin lids, but was careful not to touch any babies. "I wonder how long it's going to take young Jóöôáäàqúüùîîn to—"

"Hi there!" The apprentice scribe effervesced into the room. "Head Scribe said you'd like to see where some of the records are stored? Fantastic. I know all the rooms. Maybe not all the bins, sub-bins, sub-sub-bins, and sub-sub-sub-bins, but I definitely have a handle on all the rooms." Clearly, away from Twiddle the teen was much more comfortable. He lacked the awkwardness that a lot of people had around Eloise now that she was queen. "What are you interested in?"

"Queen Gwendolyn the Irritable," said Jerome.

"Uh-huh, uh-huh, good, good." He nodded. "Was there any aspect of her reign in particular that interests you?"

Eloise and Jerome shared a look. How much should they divulge? Jerome gave a small shake of his head.

"No, nothing particular."

"Right. Right. OK, then. Follow me," said Jóöôáäàqúüùíîin, and he flounced out the door, leaving the others to go after him.

"Not exactly steeped in Protocol, is he?" said Jerome. "Missing a little of the 'Queen goes first' bit."

Eloise waved it off. "Keeps me humble. But if you feel you need to say something to him, you can have a private word later."

"First Advisor would want me to."

"I'll leave that to your discretion."

Jóöôáäàqúüùíîin's voice echoed from down the hall. "Are you coming?"

They followed the apprentice scribe down a series of hallways, up a flight of stairs, along a strange, curving wall that didn't match any external walls Eloise could think of, and up another staircase. They passed dozens of closed doors and the occasional open one, where a scholar in white gloves could be seen hovering over tables with weighted down documents. Eloise wondered if they, too, thought of them as "babies."

Finally, Jóöôáäàqúüùíîin stopped in front of a door, gave a flashy wave, and said, "Ta da!"

The solid oak door stood at the start of a long, dim hallway that had doors facing each other all up and down it. Eloise counted 22, but the far end was dark, so there might have been more.

Jerome read the sign on the door. "GCEG 1/27."

"That's right." The apprentice rapped the door. "That part of the collection starts here."

"What does 'GCEG' stand for?"

Jóöôáäàqúüùíîin looked at the sign, looked at Jerome, looked at Eloise, then looked at the sign again. He folded one arm across his chest, supported with a hand under the elbow, and rested his chin in the crook of his hand. He tapped his cheek with his index finger and made, "Hmmmm, hmmmm" sounds.

Jerome mirrored him, taking the same posture. Eloise clasped her hands behind her back.

A full two minutes went by in silence.

Finally, the apprentice scribe said, "Yep."

"What?" said Eloise.

"Yep. I got nothing."

Jerome stared at him. "You don't know what it means?"

"Nope. But neither do you."

"I'm not the apprentice scribe."

Jóöôáäàqúüùíîìn shrugged. "You've seen me. I'm barely one either. But, I do know what the—"

"Cowpatch," interrupted Eloise.

Jerome turned back to her. "I beg your pardon?"

"Cowpatch. The 'C' stands for Cowpatch."

"Does it now?" The chipmunk's voice dripped disbelief. "And the 'E' stands for what? Exipotic? Essomenic? Epalpebrate?"

"Excelsior."

Jerome threw his forelegs in the air. "How can you possibly deduce that?"

Eloise tapped the sign with her finger. "They are her initials. Gwendolyn Cowpatch Excelsior Gumball."

Jóöôáäàqúüùíîìn beamed and chucked her in the shoulder. "Awesome! That's clever. I never would have come up with that."

Eloise rubbed her shoulder. He'd gotten the one that had been dislocated, and his jocular gesture hurt.

Jerome reached over and gave the teen's robe a sharp tug. "Hey, Scribey. That's your queen. Act like it."

The apprentice's eyes went wide as he realized what he'd done. His hands flew to his mouth, stifling a gasp. He collapsed onto his knees and pressed his head to the stone floor. "Apologies, Your Highness. I'm so, so sorry. Please don't have me banished from the queendom. It'd kill my mother. I really am just a dolt. Head Scribe says so. Every day. My mother says it too. I'm constantly doing stupid stuff like that. Please, Your Highness, I know it's your right to have my head sliced off, but if you could see your way to not doing so, I'll... I'll..." He trailed off into whimpering that quickly progressed to weeping.

"Jóöôáäàqúüùîîìn," said Eloise.

The crying continued.

"Jóöôáäàqúüùîîìn, stop please."

The teen didn't appear to have heard. His weeping progressed to blubbering.

Jerome rolled his eyes and shook his head as he walked to the prone apprentice and stood beside him. He leaned forward and grabbed the apprentice's ear with both paws. "Jóöôáäàqúüùîîìn! That will do. Your queen just ordered you to stop! Get a grip!"

There was a long, wet snort. "Right. Right. Ordered *(sniff)* to *(snuffle)* stop. Getting *(snorffle)* a *(snortle)* grip. Got it." He lifted his head enough to put a hanky to his face and gave a massive, sodden blow. "OK. Grip gotten." His forehead thunked a little when he put it back on the floor.

"Jóöôáäàqúüùîîìn, can you do something for me, please?" said Eloise.

"Of course, Your Majesty. Anything, Your Majesty."

"Could you please answer a question for me?"

"Absolutely."

"It would be a lot easier if you were standing up."

"You're not going to..."

"No. I'm not going to banish you. And I'm not going to relieve your shoulders of your head."

There was an audible sigh of relief and a last soggy sniff. Jóöôáäàqúüùîîn heaved himself to his feet and swiped his sleeve across his nose one more time. "Yes, Your Highness?"

"Why does the sign say one twenty-seventh?"

"Actually, I know this one. It's not 'one twenty-seventh,' it's 'one of 27.'"

"You're saying there are twenty-seven rooms with her non-public records," said Jerome.

"No."

"There aren't? That's good," said Eloise. "Because that would be a lot."

"There are 42." Jóöôáäàqúüùîîn tilted his head, indicating the length of the hall. "The last door on the right says 42/27."

"That doesn't make sense," said Jerome. "How can you have 42 of something that only has 27 bits?"

"I didn't make it up. I'm just telling you how it is."

"It's OK." Eloise tapped a finger on the door. "With any luck the rooms are a reasonable size. Can we have a look?"

"I don't know. Head Scribe said..."

"We promise not to touch anything. We'll just look."

"Of course, Your Highness." Jóöôáäàqúüùîîn turned the door handle and it creaked open. He started to go inside, but Jerome grabbed the hem of his cloak, stopping him so Eloise could enter first. "Right. Sorry. After you, Your Highness." He bowed and let her pass.

She got two steps into the room and stopped.

It was cavernous, easily twice the size of her parents' bedroom plus the Salle de la Famille put together, but with a higher ceiling. The room was lit by a row of windows along one wall, and a dank smell assaulted her. Countless shelves stood arranged like soldiers at attention—tall, imposing, orderly. They overflowed with stacks of scrolls, piles of pages, and endless boxes of who-knew-what.

Jerome gawked at it. "There must be, like, numptibillion babies in here."

"Numptibillion isn't a number," said Eloise.

"I know that. But for this, it ought to be."

"Good point."

She turned to the apprentice scribe and waved him forward into the room. "This is quite something."

"Yes, Your Highness."

"You say there are 42 of these? Are they all this big?"

"More or less, yes. Some are definitely bigger, but there are a few that are, maybe, 4/5 this size."

Eloise walked down the first aisle, hands clasped carefully behind her back to avoid the temptation of touching anything. These records reminded her very much of the dusty scrolls she'd been through three years before. She wouldn't go so far as to call them a jumbled mess. There appeared some sort of order, with cases, boxes, and bins that had cobweb-cloaked labels on them. Every now and then, there'd be something that someone had obviously looked at more recently than some of the others, as the layer of crud was thinner, having been wiped off sometime in the past few decades. But clearly the containers were used to keep time and grime away from the babies within. Researching was going to be dirty business. She'd need to dress appropriately. And maybe wear a mask of some sort.

"Are they all dusty like this?" asked Jerome.

"This is one of the better ones. When people come here, which doesn't happen very often, they tend to start in this room since it's the first. I bet there are some of these rooms that haven't seen paw nor pseudopod for a century."

Eloise wondered if Head Scribe would let her order some servants to do a tidy up, or if that would disturb the babies too much.

Jerome peered at a label. "May I wipe this clean?"

"I'll do it." The apprentice scribe took a small, soft-bristled brush and a hand-sized dust pan from his pocket. With the delicacy of a porcupine's dentist, he brushed the label free of dust and cobwebs, carefully catching all of it in the dust pan. He dumped the mess into a special bag that was tied to his belt and put his tools away. "There you go."

"'Corn harvest yields,'" read Jerome. "Fascinating."

"They can be," said Jóöôáäàqúüùîîn. "All those farms growing all that corn, and how it changes from year to year. Corn production in drought years versus what it was like when the rains fell abundantly. Crops of bounty and crops ruined by marauding bands of locusts or grasshoppers. It was worst when they joined forces with the weevil clans. You can see the yield numbers fluctuate wildly in the years before the Treaty of Grains, which managed to establish a policy and process for the orderly growing, harvesting, and most importantly, sharing out of the fruits of nature among the different species." He looked at the box with longing. "So many stories, just waiting to be discovered."

"You got all that from this box of corn babies?"

"Not this box. There are dozens. I looked at different ones from a different era."

The chipmunk looked at the label on the next box along. "Would you mind?"

The apprentice scribe repeated his cleaning ritual.

Eloise squatted down to read this one. "'Disputations Resolved Between Otters and Seals Relating to Matters of Weeds.' Why is this next to the corn babies? What kind of logic is there?"

Jóöôáäàqúüùîîn chuckled. "Oh, there's no logic. I mean, some of it is loosely arranged by month and year. Sometimes you'll find groups of bins organized by topic. But even that can be misleading." He gestured to the corn records box. "Whatever is in there might have nothing to do with corn at all. It *probably* does, but if someone wants to hide something, it's not that hard to slip it into the wrong box or to purposefully mislabel something. The scribes rectify those things when they're found, but only when the problems are uncovered."

"How are we supposed to find anything in here?" asked Jerome.

"You'll have to rely on the Scroll of Scrolls."

"Of course," said Eloise. "I'd forgotten about that."

"The Scroll of Scrolls?" asked Jerome.

"The Scroll of Scrolls is this massive scroll," said Eloise. "It's the size of one of those overly big decorative copies of the *Livre de Protocol* which you might find in a rich person's house. It's supposed to list everything in the Bibliotheca de Records and Regrets and where it was found."

"Does it?"

"I think so."

"It does," said Jóöôáäàqúüùîîìn.

"I'll take your word on that," said Eloise. "The problem is, like these boxes and bins, there's no order to the Scroll of Scrolls. It simply a more or less chronological-ish, somewhat topically clustered listing of all the scrolls, pages of hemp parchment, and objects that come in."

"So, how does it help you find anything?"

"That's the problem. Given how it's organized, or how it isn't, scanning through it to find any given listing is somewhere between migraine-inducing, challenging, and utterly impossible. Or that's what I remember."

"Who's doing the looking up makes a big difference," said Jóöôáäàqúüùîîìn. "Part of our training is that we're supposed to learn how to find things in the Scroll of Scrolls. The scribes have mnemonics and tricks they use, but it isn't easy. That's how my mother got me this." He indicated his apprentice robes. "I'm good at memorizing. Not so good at other stuff, but I can remember."

"Is the rumor true that Head Scribe knows the whole thing off by heart?" asked Eloise.

"It is. I've never seen him stumped, and I've never actually seen him do more than glance at the Scroll of Scrolls. So asking him is a lot easier than looking it up yourself. But he gets grumpy if you do it too much."

"That raccoon must have a brain the size of a watermelon," said Jerome.

"He's smart, for sure," said the apprentice.

They spent 20 minutes walking up and down the aisles of GCEG 1/27, just taking in the scope of it.

"Jer, I think we have our work cut out for us," said Eloise.

"That we do, Queen Eloise. That we do."

❧ 30 ❧

PURPLE PETALS

Eloise sorted through the growing mountain of correspondence as she waited for First Advisor to arrive and deliver her afternoon briefing. The bags, stacks, and bundles of scrolls and pages were truly out of hand, and it had only been a week. Eloise was getting used to being in her mother's study, but it still felt weird, the way the crown did. So, like insisting to herself that she keep wearing the GHC despite the discomfort, she made sure she spent time in there each day, both with and without First Advisor, to force greater familiarity.

At a knock, she looked up. "G'mid-afternoon, Princess Queen Eloise," said RoyLee as he dragged the first sack of the afternoon's correspondence to the threshold of the Queen's Chamber. "May I be bringing this bag into your lair?"

"G'mid-afternoon, RoyLee. I hadn't thought of this room as a lair before."

"It no be feeling like a burrow. Not enough dirt. Lair be closer."

"I like lair. I might go with that. Come on in."

The wombat wrestled a heavy sack two lengths into the room and stopped. Bags from the previous days filled every available space, save the map table in the middle, which groaned under the weight of the piled items. He looked around, unsure. "Where would you be wanting this?"

"See if you can balance it on top of the ones from this morning."

"They sure be piling up, Princess Queen Eloise," said RoyLee.

"First Advisor warned me this would happen. And you know what?"

"What?"

"He was right." She waved, indicating the sacks. "There's no way I'm going to keep up with all of this. I'll have to let him and his assistants help again."

"Don't be giving up, Princess Queen Eloise," said RoyLee as he heaved and shoved the sack. He managed to wedge it up on top of three others. "I be believing in you. Not that you be needing belief from the likes of me. But it be like what Master Shovelhovel and Gran always be saying to me. 'RoyLee' they both be saying. 'RoyLee, you be a sharp wee tyke.' This being before I be grown up. 'Go clean your room.'"

Eloise waited.

The wombat looked at her like he'd made his point.

"Sorry," she said. "I'm not sure I follow."

"We be living in a burrow, Princess Queen Eloise. There be dirt every-where. It no be possible to clean my room. But I be doing it anyway. Master Shovelhovel and Gran be telling me to clean my room, and I be cleaning my room. When I dared to complain, they be giving me a lecture on persistence. So I be persisting. And you know what?"

"What?"

"Persistence always be making things better."

"Right. Got it. I shall persist. But I do think I'll need to persist with a little more help if I'm not going to drown in hemp parchment here."

"As Your Highnessness thinks best," said RoyLee. "Would Her Highnessness be wanting her haggleberry tea?"

"That would be lovely. And maybe some fruit? I have a craving for fruit."

"Right away, Your Highnessness." RoyLee bowed his way out of the room and closed the door. Eloise could hear his feet thumping down the hall as he ran toward the kitchens, shouting, "Tea for the queen! Tea for the queen!"

Eloise took another look at the letter she held and shook it. "Why would you even think I'm ready to consider getting married?" she said to it. She stood and added it to the stack on the Whacking Great Hole. "All of you. I mean, really," she said to the stack. "I'm going to make a list of your names and make sure you go on the No list right away." She stretched and wandered slowly through her room, stepping around the huge collection of sacks that clogged the Queen's Study. She stopped at a group of sacks RoyLee had dragged in the day before. Or perhaps it was two days previous. Normally, she plowed through the correspondence in chronological order so she could close off one day before starting the next. But every now and then, she let herself dip into one of the newer ones, just to see what was there. Eloise untied the string that held the sack closed and selected a random handful of items. She thought about how one day, some of these, maybe even all of them, would be babies in the Bibliotheca de Records and Regrets, fiercely protected by Head Scribe (or maybe a successor). But for now, they were just drudgery that she needed to get through. Self-imposed drudgery, at that.

She'd enjoyed getting a sense of what it took to run the castle and queendom through the lens provided by the sacks, but it was time to let First Advisor resume his filtering or she'd never get anything else done.

Eloise took the handful of items to her desk and spread them out in a neat line. There were four scrolls, five loose pages, and an envelope. A quick glance at the scrolls showed they were the results of a census for the quad-village area of Higgledy, Piggledy, Smiggledy, and Schmalz, which revealed a strange abundance of jugglers and chalk artists specializing in drawing hors d'oeuvres. The loose pages were two bills of lading, a solicitation to subscribe to one of the more scurrilous gossip heralds, a summary description of an executive meeting held by the Federated Brother-{and Sister-(How Dare You Forget the Sisters Yet Again)}hood of Tie Dye Artisans, and a flyer advertising a concert called The Lyndia Thrind Experience, which promised "All of Lyndia Thrind's most beloved songs performed in a tribute that would make you swear she was in the room with you." Eloise had met Thrind, and had heard her perform when they were both Queen Onomatopoeia's guests in The South. She wondered how close the imitator's look and singing would be, and whether it would be worth attending the performance.

But she wasn't going to go anywhere close to the show. She was queen now. It changed everything. No more sneaking away to hide in the back of a theater. Now, if she wanted to see something, it would be brought to her. Eloise imagined that might be nice, but it changed the nature of everything when it became a Royal Command Performance.

Eloise set the flyer down on the Eastern Lands.

She picked up the envelope. It was by far the most curious item of the lot. The paper was crude rag. It was the kind of thing you might find at a rural craft fair made from a mishmash of old, shredded clothes mixed with twigs, shreds of discarded hemp, and loose bits of cotton. Crude, but interesting. It had no addressee, so no explicit recipient, and no indication of who it was from. A blank envelope closed with a blob of unremarkable wax that hadn't had a seal pressed into it.

She saw a letter opener tucked in a cubby that had been her mother's, which she hadn't noticed before. It had a thin, sharp blade, and a handle carved into the shape of a woman's hand holding an envelope.

And all of a sudden she was crying. That sneaky bastard grief had caught her by surprise. This was her *mother's*. Her mother had sat where she was sitting, held this carved hand in hers, and slit open envelopes just like she was about to. Her mother's heart had pumped, her brain had whirred, and thousands upon thousands of people of all species had spun through their daily lives in her orbit and were touched by the reach of her reign. And now she was nothing more than a shrouded husk in a catacomb niche. Eloise would never see her again. Would never flinch at her stern words or crave her praise or run to the boom of her summons. Her mother had been a force, an absolute manifestation of the power of nature itself.

Now she was dust.

Eloise couldn't believe how much she missed her. She hadn't expected that.

Eloise had very much been one of those people in her mother's orbit. Now, she felt unmoored, missing the gravitational pull of her mother's reign and the way it had tugged Eloise toward the center of Court life, both physically and metaphorically.

Sitting in this room holding this letter opener, nothing felt right. There was a profound wrongness to her mother no longer being there. Eloise kept having the phantom feeling that any day now, life would get back to some version of normal. Except those were the feelings of a child.

Nothing would ever be the same again.

She allowed herself a sigh as she examined the letter opener. The handle was darkest mahogany, and its carvings portrayed a woman's fingers in a delicate grip with uncanny precision. It looked too old to have been modeled on her mother's hand, although she felt there was a resemblance. She wondered how far back one would have to go to find the person who'd sat for the carver. Could it have been as old as Queen Gwendolyn? Older?

Eloise slid the opener under the envelope's flap, and sliced through it with a clean, shushing hiss. She pressed the sides to puff it out so she could see what was inside.

Flowers.

No note. Just dried flowers.

How sweet.

How strange.

Was this a gesture from a random admirer of some sort? She didn't flatter herself that it was, but was hard pressed to come up with an angle that didn't veer toward the romantic, especially given the size of the pile on the Whacking Great Hole.

Eloise poured the petals into her palm. They were dry, but not desiccated. There was a faint odor that vaguely brought to mind roses and sulfur. The purple of the petals had long faded, but she imagined how vibrant they must have once been.

It was a curious thing to have been sent to her. Actually, she only assumed it was sent to her. The envelope hadn't had her name on it. But why would someone send dried flowers to the castle and not make it clear who they were for?

She raised her palm to her face and breathed in the scent again. Yep, definitely rose and sulfur. Plus something else. Copper, maybe? Or the copper tinge of blood? Something like that. Definitely a strange combination for a flower.

Eloise yawned and her ears popped. She hadn't realized just how tired she was. Perhaps she should put her head down and catch a few minutes of sleep before First Advisor showed up to bore her with asparagus statistics or tuber contingency plans. She crossed her arms on the desk, lay her forehead on them, and allowed herself to slip toward oblivion.

She didn't notice the letter opener drop to the ground, the crown roll off her head and clatter onto the floor, nor the stream of blood flowing from her nose.

DARK CHERRY SAUCE

RoyLee was quietly pleased with himself. The wombat had convinced Chef to spice the pot of haggleberry tea with a stick of cinnamon, a dash of ground cardamon, some ginger root shavings, and a pinch of hot chili. He called it the "Ol' Gran," because that's how Seer Bunkerhunker liked hers. She said that particular brew helped open her wisdom eye to the Unseen, but RoyLee reckoned she just liked the taste, and justified the fiddly recipe with spiritual hoo-hah. (Not that he'd ever say anything like that to her face.) He hoped the queen would enjoy the brew.

Also, despite them being out of season, Chef had somehow produced a bowl of fresh fruit—grapes, peeled orange sections, apple wedges, and a mango (a *mango!*) cut in half with its insides sliced and popped out to look like an echidna's back. He liked it when he was able to deliver a surprise to Princess Queen Eloise, and this was definitely going to be a surprise.

RoyLee knocked on the Queen's Study door with a back foot, carefully gripping the tray with his forelegs. He sniffed the tea, and reckoned Chef had gotten it pretty close to right. The wombat had offered to make it himself, but Chef hadn't been Chef very long and seemed somewhat unsure and possessive of his kitchen. Fair enough. RoyLee didn't like strangers in his burrow either.

He waited. There was no "Come in" or "It's open." No "Hold on a tick" or "Be right there."

Odd. Her Highnessness was just about the politest person he knew. She wouldn't leave him waiting outside the door for very long without saying something.

He knocked again, a little firmer.

Perhaps she was deep in thought, or making a plan or something. Or maybe First Advisor was droning on, as he was prone to do. Should RoyLee have brought a cup of Ol' Gran for him as well? Maybe. He didn't know if First Advisor was partial to spiced haggleberry tea. He didn't know much at all about First Advisor, except that he seemed serious and a bit grumpy all the time. But if First Advisor was in there blathering on the way he did, RoyLee would have heard something, even if it was the queen's exasperated sighs.

A third knock. "Princess Queen Eloise? Are you there?"

She *had* asked him to fetch her tea. He hadn't imagined it, had he? No. There was the fresh fruit. She'd definitely asked for that.

RoyLee looked left, then right, and saw the hutch with the window and the sliding door into the room. It was a bit high for him to reach (pretty much everything in the castle was a bit high for him to reach—it had clearly not been designed with wombats in mind), but if he was careful, he could do it.

The wombat stretched up on his back legs and slid the tray into the nook. Once it was safe, he went back to the door and knocked again, this time harder. "Princess Queen Eloise? Hello? Be you in there?"

He tugged on his ruffled collar a couple of times, not sure what to do.

He'd just have a little peek in. Maybe she hadn't heard him.

RoyLee jumped once, twice, and on the third try managed to grab the door handle with his forepaw. Instead of opening, it stayed closed, leaving the wombat dangling by his claws.

He wrinkled his forehead. Now it was getting personal. RoyLee considered the flagstone floor. He'd bet that he could dig through it and tunnel his way into the room, but it would make a mess, and if nothing was going on, he'd probably get chucked out of the castle for destruction of property. No, there had to be a different way.

The hutch! If he could get up onto the hutch, maybe he could open the little sliding door and sneak a peek to check on Her Highnessness. He didn't want to bother her unnecessarily if she was doing something important. Or even sleeping. Sleeping during the day was a fine wombat-like thing to do, and something RoyLee was missing, as there wasn't much of a chance to be nocturnal at Castle de Brague. It was the thing he was finding hardest to adjust to.

RoyLee reached up again, slid the tray back off the shelf of the hutch, and as much as he didn't like doing so, put it on the ground a safe distance away. Then he backed up several paces, squinted to see his target as well as he could, ran forward, and took a flying leap.

Wombats aren't really built for leaping, nor jumping, vaulting, soaring, or clambering. They are more let's-go-through-it or let's-go-under-it types.

As such, RoyLee slammed into the stone wall.

It was a good thing that wombats are incredibly solid. The page-in-training merely bounced off the wall with a *thump*! Not to worry. RoyLee shook himself, checked that he hadn't torn his outfit, and tried again.

Thwumpity-thwump!

RoyLee, RoyLee said to himself. *RoyLee, you be young and determined.*

Yes, RoyLee replied to himself. *I do be young. And determined.*

You once dug through a full length and a half of solid stone.

That I did.

In winter. In the rain. With your bare claws.

RoyLee didn't like to toot his own bombard, even to himself, but it was true. *It be solid stone, except there be cracks in it. But yes, I be getting through it.*

Then you can be delivering Her Highnessness's afternoon tea.

Her Highnessness will have her tea. I be making sure of it.

Having made that agreement with himself, RoyLee backed up all the way against the far wall and rushed forward. He jumped at the last moment and got enough height to sink his claws into the ledge of the hutch. Kicking and scrabbling, he hauled himself up on the shelf, which was just big enough for him to perch there.

He tapped at the sliding door. "Hello? Princess Queen Eloise? Are you still in there?"

Not a sound.

RoyLee really didn't want to impinge on the queen's privacy. The last thing he needed was to see her doing something embarrassing, like drooling in her sleep or dancing around the room in her foundation garments (not that he'd ever seen her do the latter, although he had seen the former when they were traveling together).

There wasn't really a choice. He was going to have to peek. RoyLee slid the hutch door open two weak lengths, just wide enough for him to scrunch around and have a squinty-eyed squiz.

Oh, good. She was in there. And it did look like she was having a wee kip.

Except, something wasn't right. Her face was lying in dark cherry sauce.

Why would Princess Queen Eloise sleep with her face in a puddle of dark cherry sauce? She was messing up her hair, for one. Also, where was the cherry cobbler that you were supposed to eat it with? You didn't eat dark cherry sauce by itself. And she definitely didn't have any cobbler when he left. She'd sent him for tea and fruit, after all.

Suddenly, the pieces in RoyLee's mind clicked into place.

She wasn't snoozing.

There wasn't any dark cherry sauce.

Cobbler was not part of the equation.

RoyLee hit the hutch sliding door with his shoulder, splintering it from its frame. "Help!" he screamed. "Help! The princess! Help!"

TEA INTERRUPTED

oyLee reached her chair. The wombat tried patting her leg, trying to rouse her. "Princess! Princess Eloise!" When she didn't move, he tried again with more force. Still nothing. He froze in place, trying to listen for her breathing. Was she even alive? With his bad eyesight, he couldn't see much above her hip.

"Somebody help!" he yelled. "Somebody be helping the princess!"

RoyLee backed up, ran forward, and gave her leg a solid head-butt.

Nothing.

He hated the thought of what he had to do next. RoyLee was too low. He couldn't really do anything from the ground, and even this close, couldn't see what was going on where the not-dark-cherry-sauce was. That meant he had to get up.

RoyLee flexed his claws and muttered, "I'm sorry, Princess Queen Eloise." Then the wombat climbed up her chair and scrambled into her lap. "I'm so, so sorry, Princess Queen Eloise," he said, and placed a paw on her neck, searching for a pulse.

It was there, thank Çalaht. The queen had a pulse and it was strong.

"Help!" he yelled again. "The queen be needing help!"

RoyLee turned in Eloise's lap and squinted at her face laying in the pool of blood. This close, he could see little blood bubbles forming and popping with every exhale. Another sign of life. Blood had dribbled out her nose and puddled under her face. He had no idea what would cause that. "Princess? Princess!"

No response.

"Help!" he called again.

There was a crashing knock at the door. The person tried the door handle, hammered the door again. "Queen Eloise? Are you in there? I thought I heard someone crying for help."

It was First Advisor.

"That was me," called RoyLee. "The princess—"

"Open the Çalaht-cursed door!" bellowed Ligurian. "Now!"

The wombat leaped from Eloise's lap and sprinted for the door. He jumped for the handle, missed, jumped again, cursed, then failed a third time. "Just a sec!" he called, looking around for something to stand on. RoyLee saw a small ladder leaning against a bookshelf. He ran for it, dragged it over, and propped it up against the door. He grabbed the door handle and pulled, but the ladder was leaning on the door, stopping it from opening inward. He leaned, kicked the ladder aside, then swung out to throw his entire weight against the handle.

No click. No release. RoyLee dangled by his claws.

He looked up and saw the key protruding from the lock. Gripping tighter with his left paw, he attempted to pull himself up so he could grab the key and turn it.

Ligurian rapped the door again. "What's going on?"

"I'm trying to—"

"Do I need the guard to open it?" Ligurian knocked again. "Do I?"

"Just…" *Reach.* "A…" *Swing.*

"Guard!" shouted Ligurian. "Break it open."

"Yes, sir!" snapped a military voice.

"Sec…" *Grab! Twist. Click.* The lock's tumblers fell and the door came free. *Aaaahh!*

Then…

Whump! From the other side, the guard hit the door with the force of a hockey sacking defensive girder tackling a left flutter who'd insulted his mother and gotten fresh with his twin sister. It flew open, flinging RoyLee halfway across the room. The wombat landed on the map table somewhere between the village of Pulchritudinous Expectation and the hamlet of Middle Sanctimonious Prig. RoyLee curled into a ball and rolled across the Eastern Lands coming to a stop, scattering the piles of scrolls and sheets of parchment across all the realms and onto the floor.

The guard who burst into the room called, "Queen Eloise!"

It was Lorch Lacksneck.

Lorch rushed to Eloise, and after a moment's hesitation, muttered, "Apologies, my queen," and put his hand on her wrist to feel for her pulse.

"She be living, Guard Lorch," said RoyLee.

"There's no flutter or irregularity." Lorch let go of her wrist, briefly lifted an eyelid, then peered closely at the puddle of blood by her face. "RoyLee, fetch Eldridge the Apothecary. Quickly."

"Aye," he said, sprinting toward the door.

"And Jerome. The champion should be with her now."

"Got it!" The wombat charged off.

Lorch returned to checking Eloise, touching her as little as possible while still trying to ascertain the extent of her condition.

The First Advisor stepped to Lorch's side and looked more closely at his queen. "You don't seem panicked."

"Panic is not useful. I've sent for help. We do what we can while we wait," said Lorch. "But, she lives. She does not labor with whatever this malady is—there's no struggling for breath, no flailing with palsy, no fire of fever, no retching of the guts, she does not drown in her own blood or humors, and whatever caused the bleeding, it seems to have abated. I'm no healer, but I've seen enough sickness and injury on campaign to get a sense of when a life is threatened and when it is not. I don't get that sense now."

"I hope you're right."

"Indeed. Thank the Divine One." Lorch quickly checked her arms and legs, squeezing them gently through sleeves and skirts, and feeling even more uncomfortable making contact with her person than he'd been when she'd suffered the Soldier's Cold after being swept away by the River Thurmond below Mortimer Falls. He couldn't sense any damage, so he whipped off his cloak, spread it on the carpeted floor, and carefully eased her onto it so she no longer lay crumpled with her face in blood. He took a clean cloth napkin from the tray RoyLee had left behind, dipped it in a pitcher of water he saw on a low table near the fireplace, and began gently wiping the blood from her face.

Eloise did not rouse.

Ligurian leaned over her. "What is it that ails Her Highness? Why is she mind numb?"

Lorch looked at him. There was something flat in his tone. A perfunctoriness. "I don't know, but I suspect those," said the guard. He pointed to the red-tinged envelope and the half-blood-soaked dried petals. "Eldridge the Apothecary will be able to identify those."

First Advisor stepped to where he could see them better, but did not disturb the flowers. "I don't recognize them."

"No, I don't either. Which makes them that much more suspicious. It seems she was handling them, though."

Ligurian picked up the letter opener from the ground, looked it over and used the sharp end to lift the envelope high enough from the blood that he could look at the underside. "No name. No handwriting. No signet in the wax seal."

"So, how is it that the envelope is even in here? Don't you screen the queen's correspondence? Are you not responsible for castle and Court administration?"

Ligurian gestured at the sacks filling the room. "Look around you, Guard Lacksneck. She insists on trying to do all this herself."

"And you allow her unfettered access to unscreened correspondence? That doesn't strike you as a security concern, especially given what happened to the late queen?"

Ligurian frowned. "Have you met Her Highness? Does she strike you as weak-willed? She instructed me to deliver her everything, every day, unopened. I have fulfilled Her Majesty's request."

Lorch humphed but said nothing.

"Tell me, Guard Lacksneck, what would you have me do?"

Lorch was about to reply when Jerome shot into the Queen's Study. "Queen Eloise! Queen Eloise! Where is she?" The chipmunk saw her lying on the ground and scampered to her side. "El! El! Lorch, what's wrong with her?"

"Some sort of mind numbness."

"How long?"

"Not long. RoyLee found her collapsed and called for help."

Jerome didn't have Lorch's hesitation about touching his friend. He grabbed her wrist and checked her pulse, marking seconds with uncon-scious twitches of his tail. He lifted one eyelid, then the other, smelled her breath, and patted her cheek. The chipmunk looked up at Lorch and shook his head. "Should we elevate her feet? Get her humors to flow back toward her head?"

"She bled from the nose. I wouldn't. But RoyLee's getting Eldridge."

"He told me when he ran into me in the hall near the Bibliotheca de Records and Regrets. Shouldn't be long."

Lorch found a blanket and lay it across Eloise. Then he, Ligurian, and Jerome stood looking at their queen and waited.

"Why is it that the wombat found our queen?" asked Ligurian.

"I beg your pardon?" said Jerome.

"Why is it that an apprenticed page raised beyond his appropriate station should be the one to raise the alarm?"

"Who should it have been?"

"Where were you?" asked Ligurian. "Are you not her champion? Should you not be at her side, or at least nearby?"

Jerome straightened and took a step toward First Advisor. "I was where the queen asked me to be—in the Bibliotheca de Records and Regrets doing research. You're *First* Advisor. Perhaps it should have been you who should have been here *first*."

Ligurian dismissed that with a wave. "I'm merely saying that as champion, you—"

"Nobody asked you—"

A creaky ghost of a voice interrupted them from the doorway. "I was summoned?"

❧ 33 ❧

A MESSAGE

Eldridge the Apothecary wore the gray tunic and apron of an herbman, stained like his fingers with decades' worth of splashes from tinctures and decoctions. Long, gray wisps of hair flew in every direction except down, and eyebrows like snowy catkins drew attention to sharp blue eyes that showed the early signs of clouding over. Eldridge clasped the head of his cane with a gnarled hand and limped into the room.

Behind him was a middle-aged woman as thin as Eldridge was old. She wore a similar, if slightly less stained, gray herbwoman's tunic and apron, and her mouse-brown hair was pulled into a frayed, utilitarian braid. Her eyes matched Eldridge's blue, but they twitched with a nervous tic, alternating left, then right. She carried the herbman's healing satchel, and matched the old man's pace two steps behind him.

Eldridge saw Eloise lying on the ground. "Oh. No." He moved closer. "Bërÿl, I'll need you to be my hands and eyes."

"Yes, Father."

The woman ran through a routine similar to what Jerome had done— pulse, eyes, breath. She pinched Eloise's cheeks to examine the tongue, and turned the queen's head from one side to the other to peer into her ears.

Meanwhile, Eldridge leaned in close to the desk, sniffing and peering. He dabbed two fingers into the blood and rubbed them against his thumb. He smelled them, then tasted the tip of his index finger, frowning. When he saw the envelope and flowers he grunted and carefully picked up a single petal. "Bërÿl, my optic, please."

"Yes, Father." The herbwoman fiddled open the bag's clasp and rooted around in it while reciting her report. "Her heart rate is slightly elevated, but not racing. Maybe 120 pulses per minute. That also means it hasn't been suppressed. There are traces of reddening in the sclera, but less than what it would look like if she'd been on a bender. Her breath is somewhat sour, but not alarmingly so. More like she needs a decent meal than she's flooded with toxins. Her tongue, however, looks like the back of a snow ferret. I'd recommend several flasks of water, half a flagon of elderberry syrup taken over two weeks a tablespoon at a time, plus some circulatory herbs. Probably hawthorn, parsley, ginger root, and cayenne pepper. Here you go, Father." She held up his enlarging optic, a two-handled, dinner-plate-sized glass that distorted the stains on her tunic into monster splotches of color.

"So, Her Highness is not in immediate danger?"

"I don't think so, Father."

"Thank you, Bërÿl. Can you help me hold that over the desk?"

"Of course."

They positioned themselves so they did not block the light from the window, and held the glass at an angle that let the apothecary lean over and peer at the puddled blood and the flowers. "Hmmmm," he mumbled. Then he looked up at Lorch. "She bled from the nose?"

"Yes," said Lorch.

"Thank Çalaht," he sighed. "Thank Çalaht and her blessed elongated thumbs."

"What?" said Jerome. "Why is bleeding from the nose a good thing?"

"If she had bled from…" The old man hesitated. "If she had bled from other places, then we'd be calling for the embalmer and funeral wailers. As such, I suspect she'll awaken—"

Eloise gave a soft moan. Another drop of blood came from her nose and trickled down her cheek.

"Right around now, it would appear." The apothecary straightened, let his daughter take the enlarging optic, and moved to stand at Eloise's side. "Bërÿl?"

The herbwoman knelt and took Eloise's wrist. "Heart rate slower. Maybe 90 pulses."

"Good."

Lorch handed Bërÿl the damp cloth and she gave Eloise's face another quick clean.

The new queen reacted by moving her head left and right away from the pressure in a groggy refusal "Strobbit," she slurred. "Reave me arone."

"Again, good," said Eldridge.

"Shall I administer the sal volatile?"

"That might bring her back quicker."

Bërÿl rose and went back to the herbman's healing satchel. She pulled out a series of small glass vials and peered at them in turn, until she found the one she wanted. She tried to hand it to her father, but he shook his head. "Go ahead." She shrugged, knelt by Eloise, and unstoppered the vial under her nose. It belched out a stench like a tomcat's outhouse that hadn't been cleaned since Çalaht's divine feet had sloped across the realms.

Eloise gasped, her eyes flew open, and she shot to a sitting position. "Gah!" She shook her head, caught another whiff, and scrambled blindly backward.

Her head was at just the right height to clunk the edge of the map table. She smacked into it with an unexpected *thwock!*

Jerome, Lorch, and Ligurian winced.

Eloise's eyes rolled up as she slumped to her side, once again mind numb.

"Well, that was unfortunate," said Eldridge. "Bërÿl, do you want to try again?"

"As you wish, Father." The herbwoman stepped toward Eloise's slumped body, holding the stinking vial at arm's length.

"Wait!" cried Jerome and Lorch in unison. "Don't!"

"What?" said Bërÿl.

"If she sits up like she did before, she'll bang her head on the underside of the table again," said Jerome.

"Ah. Right."

Lorch extended his hand. "May I?"

"I... Uh... Uh, sure." She gave him the vial.

The guard squatted a length and a half from Eloise. "My queen!" he said, then blew a waft from the vial in her direction. "Queen Eloise!"

No response.

Lorch moved a dozen weak lengths closer and blew again.

Again, nothing.

Another dozen weak lengths. Another waft.

That seemed to do it.

Eloise's eyes fluttered open and she wrinkled her nose. "That. Is. Vile," she said. "I... I think that's plenty for now."

"Yes, Your Highness." Lorch stood and stepped back. He handed the vial back to Bërÿl, who replaced the stopper and put it back in the satchel.

Eloise began to sit up.

"Hold it!" said Jerome, pointing to the table above her.

"Right. Thanks." Eloise scooted forward and eased herself back to a sitting position.

Lorch stepped forward and offered a hand. "Queen Eloise, if I may assist."

"Thank you, Lorch." She let him help her up and walk her to the chair by the fireplace. "What's happened?"

"You were taken ill, Your Highness," said Ligurian. "Junior Page-In-Training Pottagecottage found you."

"Taken ill? *Taken ill?* She was poisoned," said Jerome.

"Not poisoned," said the apothecary. "It's more a toxin than a poison."

The chipmunk flicked his tail. "Is there really a difference? Either will kill you."

"Eldridge the Apothecary." Eloise gave him a weak wave. "How nice to see you. What are you doing here?"

The old man gave a rickety bow. "I was called to your aid. I'm pleased to see you awake and becoming lucid."

"Toxin. Poison. Difference?" slurred Eloise. She still felt groggy and her mouth tasted like the offspring of the contents of a compost bucket and a soldier's laundress's wash basin. She reached unsteadily for the pitcher of water and almost knocked it over.

"Bërÿl, please pour our queen a mug of water and add a restorative. Also, please enlighten Her Highness on the distinctions between poisons and toxins."

"Yes, Father." The herbwoman began yet another search in the satchel. "A poison is any substance that is harmful to health. It might be natural or something concocted by hand. Toxins, while also harmful substances, are always produced by living things, such as false hellebore or a snake's venom."

"So toxins are a subset of poisons," said Eloise, her diction getting clearer.

"Exactly, Queen Eloise," said Eldridge. "But whether or not something is a poison is sometimes hard to determine. Herbicides, for example. If the substance is damaging to the velvetleaf, waterhemp, and horseweed that are causing havoc in your corn field, but don't do anything to the corn itself, then is it a poison? Certainly to the weeds, but not to the corn."

"I'd never thought about that."

"Excuse me," said Jerome, barely keeping his irritability in check. "Can we hold off on the botany lesson? Our queen was bleeding out through the nose five minutes ago and is probably concussed, too."

Eloise touched the back of her head with one hand and patted her nose with the other. "I was bleeding?"

Jerome pointed at the puddle of now-congealing blood on the desk.

"I see. That looks like rather a lot. And this..." She pointed to the back of her head. "... hurts like I've been in a bar brawl. No wonder I'm woozy."

Bërÿl offered Eloise a mug, which she took and sipped. Her eyebrows shot up and she looked around for somewhere to spit. Motioning frantically, she waved for Lorch to give her a disused chamber pot. When he handed it to her, she spat and spat again. She handed the mug back to the herbwoman and grabbed the pitcher of water. She sluiced, spat, sluiced, spat, sluiced, spat, and wiped her tongue on her sleeve. "Çalaht's cauterized cankers! What was that?"

"You're tasting the restorative. It's made with userer's mushroom, ginseng root, dried beerfruit, a pinch of rancidberry powder, some—"

"That will do, Bërÿl."

"Yes, Father. Sorry, Father."

"Whatever is in it, it tastes like damnation in a cup."

"An excellent description, Your Highness," said the apothecary. "Please do your best to drink it all."

"Of course you'd say that." Eloise ventured another sip and winced. "Ugh. Just, ugh. So what happened?"

"Flower of the beggar's nightshade." The herbman held out his palm and showed her a few of the petals.

"Beggar's nightshade? I don't know it."

"It's not native to our fair realm. It was picked a month too early, if the color of the petals is anything to go by. Overall it's not as deadly as hangman's nightshade, and neither of them are as bad as bishop's nightshade, but definitely more on the nose—oh, sorry, Your Highness —than, say, carpenter's nightshade or maiden's nightshade."

"Is there anything we can tell about this attempt on the queen's life?" asked Lorch.

Eldridge gave a hint of a smile. "Oh, this wasn't an attempt on Her Highness's life."

"How can you say that?" said Jerome. "Look at the blood."

The apothecary shook his head. "They obviously didn't want to kill her."

"How can you possibly say that?"

The old man leaned forward on his cane and looked down at Jerome. "Because beggar's nightshade is an irritant. It's a toxin with a singular effect when breathed in nasally. It's hardly lethal, especially when picked early. This is not an attempted regicide gone belly-to-the-sky. It is not the same as what happened to the late Queen Eloise. Trust me, whoever did this had a particular outcome in mind. They knew this plant and knew what it would do. If they'd wanted our queen dead, that envelope would have contained any number of much more interesting and much deadlier substances. But it didn't. To my old eyes, that means they weren't trying to end her life."

"So why bother?" asked Lorch. "What's their point?"

"It was a message," answered First Advisor.

"A message. A *message!*" Jerome threw his forepaws in the air. "By Çalaht's sweet, sacred, sweaty armpits, man. She bled all over the place."

"I know that."

"I'm still here, you know," said Eloise.

"From her nose!" Jerome tapped his skull. "Right there next to her brain."

"Champion Abernatheen de Chipmunk," said Ligurian. "You're being overly—"

"What if RoyLee hadn't found her?" Jerome was close to yelling. "What if Chef had taken a bit longer to make her tea?"

"You heard what Eldridge the Apothecary said. It wasn't meant to kill."

"I don't care what he said. What, are we just supposed to accept that this was an acceptable level of blood loss from a royal and move on?"

"That will do." Eloise stood, still a little unsteady, and the talking stopped. "I think a better question is, if it was a message, then what exactly did the message say?"

"Isn't that clear?" said Jerome. "It said, 'You ought to be dead.'"

"Jerome, please calm down."

"Actually, I think Champion Abernatheen de Chipmunk is far from wrong," said Lorch. "If what Master Eldridge said is true and the intent was not to kill, then the intent was to disturb. Whoever did this wants you rattled. Looking over your shoulder. Off balance. They're saying, 'I can get to you, and I want you to know it.'"

"Well, you know what?" said Eloise.

"What?"

"It's working. I'm feeling rattled and spooked." She sat back down. "Master Eldridge, do you think I need treatment for the beggar's nightshade?"

"The bleeding has stopped. You seem to have recovered. Before you roused, Bërÿl suggested an increase in water plus some tonics, which I'll organize for you. Otherwise, no, I don't think so. Just let me know if anything unexpected or uncomfortable happens."

"Good. And thank you, Master Eldridge, Mistress Bërÿl. I'm very grateful for your help."

"Of course, Queen Eloise." Bërÿl picked up the healing satchel and offered the old man her arm. Eldridge waved her off, preferring to brace himself with his cane. The two of them bowed and made their way from the Queen's Study.

"Right. First Advisor. I—"

RoyLee burst into the room at full wombat speed and skittered to a stop. "Princess Queen Eloise?" He squinted, looking around and trying to see her.

"Over here, RoyLee. By the fireplace."

"Oh, Princess Queen Eloise!" The wombat flung himself at her and hugged her around the calves. "Thank Çalaht, you be alive!" Tears flowed. "I thought you be dead! There be so much blood."

"I'm, uh, I'm OK, RoyLee. Wow, you're strong. Is it true that you were the one who found me?"

"Yes, Princess Queen Eloise," he sobbed. "That be me."

"Then I have to thank you. If you can let go for a second, I will."

"Yes, Princess Queen Eloise. I just be a moment." The wombat wiped his eyes and blew his nose into her skirt. Eloise wrinkled her nose and clenched her jaw, but didn't say anything. A year before, wombat snot on her clothes might have sent her screaming from the room. Now, it just seemed like an icky part of her day.

Finally, RoyLee controlled himself enough to release her legs, step back, and stand before her on his back legs. "OK, Princess Queen Eloise. I be OK. Please don't be telling Master Shovelhovel or Seer Bunkerhunker that I be crying like that."

"I won't. It's OK. First Advisor, what did you say RoyLee's position was?"

"Junior Page-In-Training Pottagecottage, Your Highness."

"RoyLee, I hereby elevate you from Junior Page-In-Training to Senior Page-In-Training."

"Oh, Princess Queen Eloise!" Overwhelmed, RoyLee flung himself at her again and hugged her lower legs, sobbing once more. "You be so kind to me. Thank you. Thank you. Thank you."

"Uh, that's OK, RoyLee. Senior Page-In-Training Pottagecottage, could I ask you to please do something for me?"

"Of course, Princess Queen Eloise." His voice was muffled by her clothes.

"Could you fetch me a fresh bit of haggleberry tea and maybe something to eat?"

"Of course, Your Highnessness, of course." He wiped his eyes one last time, took a step back, bowed, and ran from the room calling, "Tea for the queen! Tea for the queen!"

Eloise smiled at his receding back.

"I'm glad he's here," said Lorch.

"Me, too," agreed Eloise. "Now, First Advisor, clearly we need to change the process. I would be grateful if you would resume managing the incoming correspondence. You can have your scribes clear out all the bags and help me catch up. My mother trusted you to buffer her from the blizzard of scrollwork. I shall do the same, now that I have a sense of it."

"As Her Highness wishes. Thank you for your confidence, Queen Eloise."

"You're welcome. Was there anything you particularly want to cover?"

"In light of what's just happened, I don't think anything is overwhelmingly pressing."

"Then we'll pick it up tomorrow once your team has been able to start catching up."

"Yes, Your Highness." Ligurian waited, then realized she was done. "I'll take my leave then?"

"Thank you, First Advisor."

He bowed and left.

"Lorch, thank you for your help. Would you mind waiting outside while I have a few words with Jerome?"

"Of course, my queen." He also bowed and left, closing the door behind him.

Jerome sighed. "You OK, El?"

"I think so. It was weird, but apparently short-lived."

"Excellent."

"Jer, I think we need to have a talk."

34

ASSISTANT COURT SEER TO THE COURT SEER

Jerome flicked his tail and looked at Eloise. "'We need to talk' is something one never wants to hear."

Eloise stood. "Champion Abernatheen de Chipmunk, I need you to do something for me."

Jerome flinched at her use of formal address, but he knelt and said, "Yes, Your Highness?"

Eloise sat again and clasped her hands in her lap. "No, that's not how I want to do this. Jeromissimo, I think I need you to..." She swallowed. "I'm not sure how to ask this."

Jerome stood again. "Elloriffic, let me help you out. You need me to stop belching in public."

"No, that's not it."

"You want me to stop sniping at Ligurian. He's an ass, but I can keep it to myself."

"Yes, but no, that's not it either."

"Avoid falling asleep when you're having audiences? Really, that's only happened a couple of times."

"Really? Has it?"

"Uh, well, more than a couple. Five times, at least."

"They can get dull."

"I concur."

"But no, that's not—"

"You want me to stop being late in the morning. That's a hard one for me, but I'll do what I can."

Eloise shook her head. "No, sorry. That's not it."

"I'm running out of ideas here, El."

"Oh, Jer. I'm sorry. But I need to ask you to let me name another champion."

"Oh." Jerome's whiskers drooped and his tail sagged. "Really?"

"I think so. Yes." She reached over and squeezed his shoulder. "I'm sorry."

"I see." Jerome blinked rapidly, holding back tears. "Well, somehow that's managed to take me by surprise. It shouldn't have, but it did."

"I've only just come to the point that I feel it needs to be done. You understand, right?"

Jerome sniffed and wiped his nose. "Let's face it. It was crazy to name me champion in the first place. So, in a sense, this has been coming for forever. Since my Naming Ceremony. No, earlier. Since you named me your Champion Designate. I guess I just didn't realize you were unhappy with the job I was doing. I thought we'd hit our stride."

"I'm not unhappy with the job you're doing. Truly, I'm not. Circum-stances have changed."

"Yes. They have. You're right." Jerome drew a deep breath and allowed himself a deep, long sigh. Then he straightened and bowed with perfect formality. "I serve at the discretion of the monarch. Always have. Always will. I'll miss our breakfasts together."

"We can still have breakfast together. I *want* to keep having breakfast together. It's not like I'm going to turf you out of Court."

"I'll give this back to you." Jerome patted his Champion's Sword. "Çalaht on a sandwich, El. I haven't had a portrait done for the Salon des Champions. Thank, Çalaht you've spared me that. I really do hate the way I look on canvas."

"That'll still happen. You've served as champion. There's no way I'm letting you get out of having a portrait. And I want you to keep the sword. It suits you." Eloise picked at her skirt. She saw there was a stain where RoyLee had been crying before. Too many tears today. "Jer, to be clear, this isn't about whether or not you're doing a good job. And it's not about whether or not I want you around. You have done a good job. And I do want you around. But things have changed since..." Eloise tapped the crown on her head, then pointed at the congealed puddle of blood on her desk. "Since everything."

"I get it. I do."

"Answer me something, Jer. What would you say you are good at?"

"Me? What am I good at?" He wrinkled his nose. "What kind of question is that?"

"I'll tell you what you're good at. You're good at being flippant. You're good at getting under people's skin. You're good at making people laugh, especially if that person is me. But you're also good at getting to the heart of things. You're good at being tenacious and digging into something until you find an answer. You're loyal and funny and quick-thinking and enthusiastic and insightful. I still need all of that from you. But you're not great at taking orders. You don't really have a mind for security. You've conducted yourself admirably in tight spots, but your size is not an advantage in the role of champion. I think that last one's fair to say."

"Of course it's fair to say."

"Now that I'm queen, the security and protection side of things is a lot more important. But there's other important stuff to do, and I need you for that." She tapped on the box that held the Star of Whatever at her hip. "Like this. We need to get to the bottom of this thing, and I can't really have you scouring the Bibliotheca de Records and Regrets when you're supposed to be hanging around near me because you're my champion. I still want you around. I still want you by my side—your mother's prophecy won't be denied. But I do think we can do a better job of letting you do the things you're good at and helping me that way."

Jerome nodded. "I get it. And I'm OK with it. I mean, it'll be weird giving up having a role at Court, but I can get used to that."

"I didn't say you wouldn't have a role at Court. You can't be traipsing around the place unauthorized. I have something in mind, but I don't know what you're going to think about it."

"You have a new role in mind? What?"

"Assistant Court Seer to the Court Seer," said Eloise.

"Assistant Court Seer to the Court Seer?" Jerome clasped his paws behind his back and scrunched his face. "Is that even a role?"

"It is now."

"You want me to be my mother's assistant. Have you spoken with her yet? Is she amenable?"

"Not yet. I thought I'd discuss it with you first."

"But I'm garbage at that stuff. Everyone always laughed at me in our Oracles and Insights lessons. You more than anyone."

"True."

"So why that?"

"You were the one who gave me the idea for it."

"How? What would ever make you think that I'd be suited to be Assistant Court Seer to the Court Seer? I have absolutely no talent for divination or prognostication or any of that vision-y kind of thing. None. Zero. Zilch. Nada. Nothing. Nichts."

"What about all those prognostications you did at Ye Olde Public Inn in the village of Colander? You absolutely saved us doing those."

"That wasn't prognostication. That was desperation. I got lucky."

"You sell yourself short. What about the tasseography reading you did for me?"

"You want to cite that bit of tea-leaf reading?" Jerome began a mincing, high-pitched mockery of himself. "'You're standing in a shortish, forest-ish kind of place. There are eye-like things. Big, yellow eye-ish eyes with big, brown pupils, massive like they're dilated.' That was stupid beyond words."

"Au contraire. You perfectly described the paddock of sunflowers that erupted around us at Festering Resentment when I had my little oopsie while trying to use this." She tapped the Star of Whatever again.

Jerome's eyes flitted as his mind raced. "I hadn't thought of that. Not at all. I guess you could say that the yellow eye-like things were the sunflowers. It was a kind of shortish, forest-ish kind of place. Huh."

"Huh indeed." Eloise stood again. "Jerome Abernatheen de Chipmunk, would you be willing to relinquish the role of champion and take on the heavy and important mantle of Assistant Court Seer to the Court Seer, with all duties, rights and privileges attendant to be conferred upon you?"

"Well, when you put it that way, Queen Eloise." Jerome bowed, adding a ridiculous series of over-the-top hand waves. "It would be a pleasure and an honor to continue serving you." Then he began unbuckling the Champion's Sword from his waist.

"Keep it on, Champion Abernatheen de Chipmunk," said Eloise. "You're still champion until we have a Naming Ceremony for someone else."

"Who are you going to name?"

Eloise lifted her head, indicating the door.

"Lorch?" said Jerome.

Eloise nodded.

"Good choice."

"You're not jealous?"

Jerome started another super-ornate wave, but stopped, relaxed, and shrugged one shoulder. "Lorch was always the logical choice. I said as much when you first named me champion. Even when you convinced me to stay on when we were among the Us, I think we both knew it wouldn't be forever." The chipmunk shrugged his other shoulder and feigned bravado. "Besides, let's see him try to be Assistant Court Seer to the Court Seer. He'd crumple in a heap. There'd be no vague, barely usable yellow, bee-eye prognostications coming out of him. No, you're better off letting him have a role that bespeaks his skills—all that muscle, discipline, and rectitude. He can have the champion's role. A suitable consolation prize."

"Would you..."

"What?"

"Would you be here when I ask him to do it?"

Jerome's whiskers twitched, but only once. "Sure."

"Thanks." Eloise cleared her throat and called, "Lorch?"

The door opened and the guard poked in his head. "Yes, Queen Eloise."

"Could you come in here, please?"

"Of course." Lorch opened the door the rest of the way and stepped through. "Yes, Your Highness?"

Eloise stood. "I have a request of you, if you're willing."

"Certainly."

"Guard Lorch Lacksneck of Lower Glenth, I would ask you to be my champion."

Lorch looked like Eloise had slapped him with a cold slab of tofu. "Your Highness. I'm sorry, but I can't."

Eloise furrowed her brow. "No? Why not?"

Lorch's eyes flicked to Jerome, then back to Eloise. "Because you already have a champion. Because Champion Abernatheen de Chipmunk is my friend, and I could never offend him that way. It would be dishonorable."

Jerome stage-coughed, and Eloise and Lorch looked at him. With his posture straight, he walked forward until he stood at Lorch's feet, looking up at the guard's face. He held his gaze for fifteen long seconds and then, without warning, flung himself at Lorch's leg, hugged his ankle, and began to weep.

"Champion Abernatheen de Chipmunk?" said Lorch. "What's the matter?"

Jerome wiped his nose on Lorch's boot and said, "That's the nicest thing anyone has ever said about me." He squeezed the guard's leg even harder, then let go and stepped back so he was once again at Lorch's feet. Jerome wiped his nose again, this time using his sleeve. "Guard Lorch Lacksneck of Lower Glenth, it would be my honor if you replaced me as champion. Queen Eloise has other tasks in mind for me, and it would serve all of us if you would be her champion."

"Really?" said the guard.

The chipmunk nodded. "Really."

Lorch came to full attention. "Queen Eloise, it would be my greatest honor to succeed Champion Abernatheen de Chipmunk as your champion."

Eloise smiled at him, and then at Jerome. "Good. Thank you, both."

35

"___"

Eloise sat in an armchair in her parents' room, feeling exhausted. She wore a flannel nightgown under a warm robe, and a shawl kept the room's residual chill at bay. The fire in the fireplace cast dancing shadows on the wall, and from a distance, she heard the on-duty horologist cuckoo proclaim, "11:30 PM."

She needed to sleep, but could tell it wouldn't be coming anytime soon.

Thinking, thinking, thinking.

Thinking about the "message" that laid her out and made her bleed. Thinking about Jerome and his willingness to step aside for Lorch to be champion. Thinking how they were no closer to figuring out who had her mother killed.

And for the first time in weeks, she thought about the spark of something in the Star of Whatever. It'd been a while since she'd spoken to Sparky, and it occurred to her that she might have violated the accord the two of them had struck while she was touching the Purity under the influence of the khan's vision herbs. Eloise had agreed, among other things, to take the stone out of its box more often. Sure, she had it with her all day every day. But she hadn't given him an outing.

No time like the present. Eloise stood, got the wooden box from her bedside table, and sat back in the armchair, resting the Star of Whatever on her lap. She took a deep breath and carefully opened the lid with her thumbs.

There it was, an emerald-green stone the size of a hefty grapefruit, nestled safe and snug in padded lining. The faint green glow was dim in the fire-lit room.

"Hey, Sparky," said Eloise.

No response.

She sent her next attempt in a silent mental reaching. "Hey, Sparky."

Again, nothing. Was he ignoring her? Was he "asleep?" Playing hard to get?

Try simpler, she thought, and sent a gentle "?" query.

There was a sluggish "—" in reply.

A response, like he was far, far away (whatever that meant in the case of a bodiless mental device in her head representing a magical force).

Eloise tried another "?", pressing it toward him more firmly.

"__"

"??"

"______"

"???"

"________."

Not exactly chatty.

She closed her eyes and pictured herself going down, down, down into the dark cave where she'd first found a sleeping naked mole-rat—which is what Sparky looked like when she connected with him on the inner planes. His pink, hairless body was surrounded by chewed fragments of an unnamed tuber. "Sparky?"

The naked mole-rat's eyes fluttered open and he yawned, showing his strange, overly long, manipulable front teeth. "Hey, Loulou. Nice to see you."

"You're awake."

"I am now." Another yawn. "Is something going on?"

"Not so much. Or everything. Or both."

"What's up?"

"Oh, you know. The usual. I'm queen. Someone either tried to kill me or send me a very loud message. My search for information about you is going nowhere. I had to fire my champion. And this..." She held up her wrist with the cast on it. "This thing hurts and itches at the same time."

"Right. Another day in paradise, then. Why are you here? With me?"

Eloise shrugged. "I promised I'd give you out of the box time."

"That was, indeed, part of our bargain."

"So was your communicating with me. And teaching me stuff."

The mole-rat sniffed the air in her direction. "Are you in a learning mood?"

"To be honest, not really."

"Whist," said Sparky.

"Whilst?"

"No, whist."

"The card game?"

"The same."

"I'm not very good at it," said Eloise. "Plus, there are only two of us, not four."

"We'll make do. There's a two-player version people sometimes call Southie Whist." From nowhere, Sparky pulled out a deck of cards, slipped them from their case, took out the two jesters, and shuffled. "I'll teach you. You bring any coins to bet with?"

"Uh…"

"I got them." A stack of coins appeared in front of each of them.

Eloise and the spark of something in the Star of Whatever played cards for what felt like half the night, dealing, shuffling, betting, taking tricks, and chatting about nothing. The cards gave her something to focus on that was inconsequential and low stakes, which was nice for a change. Sparky seemed able to chatter almost as well as Jerome, which she hadn't expected. Also like Jerome, he seemed to have a particular interest in food, although she'd only ever seen him eat tubers.

When she regained consciousness as the sun brushed the first hints of dawn onto the sky, Eloise felt like she was waking from one of the most vivid dreams she'd had in a very long time. That is, until she looked down and saw a pile of coins on her lap next to the emerald, softly-glowing stone.

36

NAMING CEREMONY

Eloise had wanted Lorch's Naming Ceremony to be a low-key affair, figuring it was more an administrative move than anything else. But news of the role-change spread and interest in attending the event flooded in.

"Why so much demand for such a small ceremony?" Eloise asked First Advisor when he brought up the topic at her morning briefing. "It's not like it's been that long since we've had one. Jerome's wasn't so many months ago."

"Perhaps that's exactly why," said Ligurian. "The last one was, shall we say, eventful."

"So they want me to repeat my previous disaster? How delightful."

"Think of it this way, Your Highness. Pretty much everything that you've done up until now has been either invisible to most people, like the blessing at Festering Resentment, or prescribed by Protocol, like the late queen's funeral or receiving the envoys."

"I did send one away."

"Exactly. That probably whet the appetite of the various throne-watchers. Now they have a chance to see another choice that they think will help show what kind of queen you're going to be."

"Fine then. Move the Naming Ceremony from the Receiving Room to the Throne Hall and allow more people to be part of it."

"Yes, Your Highness."

"Do I speak with Lady Seneschal about decorations and refreshments?"

"I normally take care of that with her help," said Ligurian. "With your permission?"

"Yes, of course. And thank you."

Two afternoons later, Eloise arrived at the Throne Room to find several score people of all species waiting for her—not quite as many as there had been for Jerome's Naming Ceremony, but certainly more than she'd expected. They ranged from the highest ranking courtiers to court-watchers, hangers-on, and wannabes. To one side, quills at the ready to take notes, were the heralds, including a number of gossip heralds. Eloise hated having the gossip heralds there and had long wondered why her mother had tolerated them. She'd even toyed with the idea of banning them, limiting access to Court goings-on to just the more reputable heralds. But in the end, she'd given up on that idea because she didn't like the thought of squelching everyone's access to information, as tempting as that was. As odious as she found the gossip heralds, so long as they were reasonably accurate, she'd live with them. It was probably one of those keep-your-friends-close-and-your-enemies-closer things.

The Throne Hall was decorated exactly as it had been for Jerome. There was a white canvas canopy stretched above the dais. Wisteria-purple bunting decorated the front, which set off the streamers on the wall in champion's gray. Tasteful. Simple. Enough to say "special" and "not all that special" at the same time.

Eloise had allowed Odmilla to talk her into wearing one of the more ornate day dresses that Seamstress Linttrap had delivered over the previous week. The echidna and her helpers had churned out close to a dozen queen-ready garments in Eloise's exact size, all without bothering her for measurements or asking about her preferences. And they were, without question, the most beautiful clothes she'd ever put on. For Lorch's Naming Ceremony, Odmilla had encouraged her to wear a maroon laced-behind cotehardie with full-length virago sleeves in five segments and silver buttons down the front and sleeves (one of which accommodated the cast on her wrist). Over this was a sleeveless surcoat in a deep blue with white accents. Even Eloise, who usually wasn't all that fussed about what she wore, had to admit it was a spectacular bit of sewing and it made her feel queenlier when she wore it. On her head, Eloise continued to insist on wearing the Gumballic Heraldic Crown over the objections of the Crown Jeweler. Her neck muscles still complained every time she put it on, but not as much as they had when she'd first been crown plonked.

Everyone stood and faced her as she strode toward the middle of the dais, doing her best to ignore the butterfly acrobatics going on in her stomach. Would she ever do this without feeling overwhelmed by nerves? Eloise smiled, drew herself up to full height, and clasped her hands in front of her to dampen their visible shaking. Then she said the words her mother had spoken at the start of hundreds of gatherings like this. "My friends."

"Our queen," came the rote reply.

"Please be at rest."

Eloise sat, and with a rustle of clothing and the scrape of chairs, everyone settled.

So far, so good. She hadn't shed any tears yet, so that was a bonus. (Although thinking about them seemed to bid them forward. *Not now. Not now.*)

Eloise swallowed back the emotion and braced herself to start. Her mother had delivered such a lovely speech for Jerome's Naming Ceremony. But then, she'd needed to, because Eloise's choosing a chipmunk had been so bizarre. This time, the champion was someone of such clear championish material that the curiosity factor should be mitigated. All Eloise needed to do was say a few platitudes, not trip over anything, run through the words set out in the *Livre de Protocol*, dip her pinky into the symbolic oils and wipe them around on the champion's sash, and let Jerome and Silvia Cloisterfeld do what they needed to do to invest Lorch with the Champion's Sword. Last time, her whole family had been there to share in the ceremonial finger dipping and some of the text of the rite. This time, she was up there by herself and would have to carry it off on her own.

So be it.

"It's lovely to see so many of you joining us today to mark the passing of the Champion's Sword from one fine champion to the next. Allow me to say that I have such deep gratitude for Jerome Abernatheen de Chipmunk. He has carried out his duties as champion with vigor, grace, and aplomb. I'm thrilled Jerome will continue to serve me, Court, and all of you in his new role of Assistant Seer to the Court Seer."

There were scattered snickers at this, and Eloise scowled her disapproval, although that didn't seem to make much difference. She snuck a glance at Jerome, but he stood frozen like he hadn't heard a thing. She assumed that meant he'd heard every bit of it, and he was lucky that the fur on his face hid any blushing or anger.

"Let's get started, shall we?" Eloise said to the hall and began the ritual. "I welcome to the Throne Hall the Champion Select."

"Welcome, Champion Select," chorused the crowd.

Lorch appeared in the doorway resplendent in a gray tunic and breeks of champions. He'd cut his hair to a fresh, precise military length. Eloise had spent months with him on the road and considered Lorch a friend, even if he tended toward formality when dealing with her. Looking at him now, she realized just how big he was. If he was any broader in the shoulders, he'd have to step sideways into the room.

Lorch strode in and gave a small nod to Hector de Pferd and the Nameless One, who stood to one side by the entrance. The two horses had been groomed to perfection, and grinned at the guard as he walked past. Lorch reached the dais, stepped up, and knelt.

Eloise consciously looked away from Lorch and out to the Throne Hall. She continued the words from Protocol. "As is our way and the way of those who came before us, it is my privilege as queen to call upon one of us to grace our court as Champion. Do I have your permission to name a Champion?"

"Yes, you have our permission," came the formal reply.

"Who among you will step forth as Champion?"

A small bell rang, signaling the start of 60 seconds of silence, and Eloise looked around the room like she was trying to find someone. When the bell rang again, Lorch spoke up. "My queen, I volunteer!"

"A volunteer!" The people in the hall did a fair approximation of fake astonishment.

"State your name, volunteer," said Eloise.

"I would prefer to be faceless and nameless in service to the House of Gumball. However, since you asked, I am Lorch Lacksneck."

"Who are your mother and father?"

"Lydia and Lorien Lacksneck of Clan Lacksneck from Lower Glenth."

"Are you true, dedicated, and determined?"

"I am."

"Will you be brave, humble, and selfless?"

"I will."

"Then let it be done."

Next came the sash. Eloise held up the emerald and navy Gumball sash she'd worn since her Thorning Ceremony. It had already had a chunk snipped out of it to make a sash that fit Jerome. Seamstress Linttrap had cleverly taken what was left of it, sewn in some extensions so it would fit, gussied it up with a bit of embroidery, and voilà, a sash fit for a new champion.

There were four finger bowls set on a table near her mother's throne, each with a different mix representing four different qualities. Eloise stood behind the table, kissed the sash, dipped her pinky in the first dish, and said, "These are the oils of cananga, yellow swede, haggleberry, and ebony. Together they represent insight, for that is what we wish for the champion." She drew a rough queen's insignia on the sash, then moved to the second dish, kissed the sash again, and did the pinky dip again. "These are the oils of cedar, applewood, ragwort, and olibanum. Together, they represent gallantry, for that is what we wish for the champion."

Eloise glanced up and saw that all eyes were on her. Good. People were paying attention.

She kissed the sash, drew the king's insignia in oil, and moved on to the third. "These are the oils of pantswood, guillotine fruit, vetiver, and sedgeland willow. Together, they represent resourcefulness, for that is what we wish for the champion." She kissed the sash, sketched the Gumball insignia with the oil, and moved to the last dish. "These are the oils of spikewood, dandelion, neem, and hedgehog cactus. Together, they represent humility, for that is what we wish for the champion." One last kiss, then she drew her name in oil. Eloise held the sash up for everyone to see. "I offer this sash to the champion as a token of our esteem." She walked over to Lorch, who still knelt, head bowed, and whispered, "You ready for this?"

Lorch's eyes flicked up and his always-serious face betrayed the slightest grin. "Yes, Your Highness. I am."

"I assume Jerome ran through all the statistics he came up with about the champion's longevity in the job."

"Yes, Queen Eloise. He did."

"And you're still game?"

"Yes, Your Highness."

"I'm glad. I said it before, and I'll say it again, I think you'll be a great champion." Eloise slipped the sash over his head and Lorch threaded an arm through the loop. "Sword next."

"Yes, Your Highness."

The Champion's Sword was a small, basket-hilted broadsword that sported an intricate version of the Gumball crest on both the hilt and scabbard. The Court bladesmith modeled it on the one carried by Townshend Bellicose Shinglehefter, the first champion, who served Agnes Delion Frostbite Gumball, the first Gumball queen, hundreds of years before. The Champion's Sword was supposedly strictly ceremonial, but it was made with full lethality "just in case a need arose," as tradition dictated. Each Champion's Sword was crafted to meet the individual who would carry it. Jerome's, for example, was small and light, weighing about the same as an oak knitting needle. Her mother's champion, Sylvia Cloisterfeld, had a sword that was like a deadly willow switch in broadsword shape. For Lorch, the bladesmith had accounted for the muscles in his arm and the fact that he was ambidextrous, designing a gleaming weapon that was longer, thicker, and heavier than any of its predecessors fashioned in the past century. As was common for a Champion's Sword, the blade was engraved with a pattern of knot work in addition to its words, and Eloise suspected that was so it might channel blood away from the cutting edge, facilitate delivering a poison, or both.

Eloise eased the sword in its scabbard from a second table using both hands and held it horizontally in front of her. To the room, she said, "The Champion's Sword, etched with a prayer seeking blessing from the divine Çalaht."

That was Jerome and Sylvia's cue to step forward from a hidden corner at the edge of the dais. The former queen's champion took it and drew the freshly wrought sword from its scabbard. Together, she and Jerome held it (somewhat awkwardly, due to their size difference) and, speaking in unison, said, "May this sword never be called on to express the purpose of its making, but should it be needed, may it be swift and sure in the hands of the Champion. Honor to the Champion!"

"Honor to the Champion!" repeated the crowd.

Sylvia sheathed the blade, then she and Jerome knelt and presented it to Lorch, saying, "From one champion to the next, may you continue our traditions of service and loyalty."

Lorch bowed. "Thank you, Champion Abernatheen de Chipmunk and Champion Cloisterfeld. May I be worthy of your traditions."

They bowed back. "Congratulations, Champion Lacksneck."

Next, the ambassadors from the other realms (save the representative from the Central Ranges, who hadn't returned yet) presented token gifts—prattleweed from The South, wart cream from the Half Kingdom, and a huge olive from the Eastern Lands.

When the gift-giving finished, Eloise wanted to relax, but knew she couldn't. Jerome's Naming Ceremony had gone off the cart track with the next bit—Lorch had to drink the entire container of water, which had been drawn from the source of the River Thurmond. It was a symbolic thing, a kind of nod toward inter-realm unity that drew on the emblematic fact that the river touched each of the realms. The Champion's Cannikin was brought out by the Court Jester Stoofy Trebuchet McNniister. Stoofy, who was as about old as Çalaht's bunions and could hear about as well as they could, sat on his three-legged stool, slumped against the side wall, snoring. A trickle of drool dripped out of his mouth and puddled on his harlequin-patterned tunic.

Here goes nothing, Eloise thought, and prayed that Lorch didn't happen to share Jerome's phobia of jesters. "Bring forth the Champion's Cannikin," she called, her voice much too loud. Or it would have been too loud, except that if she had any hope of waking Stoofy, she'd need to shout.

The jester didn't move.

Eloise tried again. "Bring forth the Champion's Cannikin!"

Nothing.

She took several steps closer and practically shouted. "Bring forth the Champion's Cannikin!"

Stoofy moved, but only enough to tilt his head from one side to the other. Whispers and titters burbled up from the crowd.

"Oh, Çalaht bearing bushels of broad beans," muttered Eloise. She went to Stoofy, picked up the Champion's Cannikin, and held it up for everyone to see. A small amount of the River Thurmond slopped over the side and dribbled down her sleeve, but it was probably less than Stoofy would have spilled on a good day, and clearly this wasn't one of the jester's better days.

She carried the cannikin to Lorch. Normally, this was all between the jester and the champion, but without Stoofy, Protocol was silent on what Eloise should do. She was winging it (a phrase birds of all types generally found offensive). "Champion Select Lacksneck, I present you with the waters of the River Thurmond."

"Thank you, my queen." Without another word, Lorch took the bucket and downed every drop of the water like he'd been about expire from thirst. He finished with a theatrical lip smack and held up the empty container.

"Honor to the champion!" called Jerome.

"Honor to the champion!" echoed everyone, and then cheers erupted.

The ceremony was done. It had gone off without a hitch. There was a palpable relaxation in the room. At last, something at Court had just felt normal.

What a relief.

✣ 37 ✣

BROWNIE BOW

alf an hour later at the reception, Eloise held a plate of finger food and attempted to let Lorch be the center of attention. She stood at the side of the room and gave all her focus to nibbling at her chili battered cauliflower florets. These were supposed to be dipped in a sriracha sauce, but Eloise found it far too piquant. Plus, the chili-battered cauliflower, and sriracha sauce combination didn't exactly go well with the dessert—a brownie that Eloise swore had been made with black beans (oddly tasty, but definitely strange). The new Chef was clearly trying hard. She had to give him that. But for the ten thousandth time, she missed old Chef.

People kept coming over to her and trying to make small talk, proving that hiding in plain sight wasn't going to work. Now that she was queen, there would be no fading into the woodwork like she'd been able to as a princess. Eloise found herself pinned into conversation with an unremarkable minor noble from Flachberg—a coastal canton that shared a border with the Eastern Lands. He was accompanied by his slightly taller, slightly less unremarkable sister, who'd said she was a seaweed monger with a business called Won't You Please, Please Kelp Me. When Eloise saw Jerome sauntering past looking askance at his black bean brownie, she caught his eye with a nod of the head and gave him a subtle help-me-out-here-for-the-love-of-Çalaht waggle of her eyebrows.

The chipmunk nodded his understanding and joined the three of them. Interrupting, he gave a courtly bow replete with baroque hand-waving, the grace of which was undone by the fact that he still held the brownie. "My queen."

"Jerome, how lovely to see you."

"It's been far too long, Queen Eloise." That didn't make sense, since he'd been on the dais with her less than an hour before, but whatever. The chipmunk gave the barest nod to the man and woman. "I'm Jerome Abernatheen de Chipmunk, former Champion to Her Majesty and now honored to serve her as Assistant Court Seer to the Court Seer. With whom do I have the pleasure of making my acquaintance?"

"I'm Livinia Heterokont," said the woman. "And this is my brother, Skartabel Junker Heterokont, Esquire."

"Pleased to meet you both." He gave each of them a brownie-exaggerated bow. "I'm so sorry to interrupt your conversation." Turning to Eloise, he said, "My queen, may I impose upon your time privately for a moment? There are matters of an..." He paused and slowly wafted the brownie above his head airily. "Matters of an unseen nature that I must raise with you."

"Of course, Assistant Court Seer to the Court Seer." Eloise nodded to the Heterokonts. "Lovely to meet you both, and good luck with the kelp. If you'll excuse us, please."

"Of course." Livinia tugged her brother's elbow, and the two bowed a retreat.

When they were out of earshot, Eloise whispered, "Thanks for that, Jer."

"Any time, Queen Eloise." Jerome took a nibble of the black bean brownie. "You know, this isn't as bad as I'd feared, nor as good as I'd hoped."

"I think you just named our new Chef's style." She imitated the voice of one being interviewed by a gossip herald. "My school of cooking? The School of Low-Grade Yet Inevitable Disappointment."

Jerome took the same tone. "We use the finest ingredients and combine them in a fresh and unique way to make sure that every bite —" he bit the brownie and continued with his mouth full, "—is not as bad as you fear, but never as good as you might hope." He nibbled again. "My, that's certainly adequate. Yum-ish!"

Eloise took a bite of hers. "You're right. This has to be the most tolerable, nay, I say the most acceptable black bean brownie in all the queendom."

They stood eating their brownies, smiling at each other.

"There hasn't been a lot of laughing lately," said Eloise.

"No. It's been somewhat grim. Busy, overwhelming, and grim."

"Indeed." Eloise put down her half-eaten brownie. "Jer, can I say something?"

"You're the queen. Say away."

"I want to thank you for being champion. I was grateful you said yes, and I was grateful for the job you did. And I want to thank you also for being willing to let go of being champion with such grace. You're a true friend, and I value that."

Jerome looked at her, waiting.

"What?" said Eloise.

"Nothing about how good looking I am?"

"Oi."

Jerome reached over and patted her shoe. "Thanks, El. I appreciate it. It was a lot like the brownie."

"Oh? How so?"

"Not as bad as I'd feared. But also maybe not as good as I'd hoped."

"Fair enough."

"But hey—I lasted more than seven months. And I didn't die in the job. So, there's that."

"Definitely, it was an above average performance."

Jerome tilted his head. "Statistically, it was."

"I'm agreeing. You did a good job. Things changed is all. Plus, I'm pretty sure you set a record for smallest champion ever. So, there's that as well. I can't imagine that record being beaten any time soon."

"No. Unlikely."

Eloise and Jerome looked around to see where Lorch was. The newly named champion was talking to Livinia and Skartabel Heterokont. It seemed a somewhat intense conversation.

"Assistant Court Seer to the Court Seer Abernatheen de Chipmunk, I do hope you let your mother train you in some of the seer's arts. I think you'd have more of a knack than you give yourself credit for."

"She's offered."

"Take her up on it."

"I guess."

"No, I mean it. Take her up on it. Court and the queendom can't be relying on just one seer with no backup. Learn everything you can." She raised her palm and faced it toward him. "I command you to do so."

"Well then." Jerome broke his remaining brownie in half, and gave her a ridiculous, obsequious two-brownie bow. "Your command is my wish, Queen Eloise."

Eloise returned the bow, the hand with the cast on her crown, the other waving extravagantly. When she looked up, Lorch was there with the Heterokonts. "Lorch! I mean, Champion Lacksneck. You surprised me."

'My queen. Apologies. I was just speaking with Master and Mistress Heterokont, and I felt you should hear what they have to say."

"We were just speaking," said Eloise. "Is there a problem? You should have brought it up."

"My brother and I didn't want to bother you with our troubles," said Livinia. "Certainly not during your social time."

"We were considering trying to get an audience," said Skartabel.

Eloise took a more careful look at the two of them. Livinia was tall and elegant with an open expression and green eyes that bore a distinct twinkle. She wore her dark hair in a bun on top of her head, with what looked like seaweed woven into it. Her day dress was green—not one of the shades you associated with the Eastern Lands, but not far from it—and embroidered at the hem, neckline, and cuffs with stitching that depicted the same kelp leaves that were in her hair.

Her brother Skartabel could easily have been a twin—almost the same height and green eyes, but his expression was more serious, worried, even. His hair was pulled into a dark topknot that seemed to flare like a black cockatoo's crest when he moved, and his breeks and tunic were maroon, not sea-green.

Skartabel seemed reluctant to speak, so Livinia jumped in. "There have been incursions into our canton from the east."

"Incursions?" said Eloise. "What exactly do you mean by 'incursions?' Raiding parties? Pillaging?"

"Nothing so overt," said Livinia. "More like scouting. Scoping. Skulking."

"Spying," said Skartabel. "They're spies."

"I disagree. They're merchants."

"Spies wearing the clothes of commerce with the physical build of soldiers."

Livinia lifted a shoulder. "Possibly. No question it is suspicious."

"What do you think they're looking for?" asked Eloise.

"I had one of them engage me in conversation," said the woman. "The woman asked me questions about how much happiness I felt being part of the Western Lands and All That Really Matters. And whether or not I felt my heritage sat more with the Eastern Lands."

"Does it?" asked Jerome.

Livinia laughed. "Of course it does. For hundreds of years, Flachberg was in the Eastern Lands. We even have olive groves, for goodness sakes. Look at the color of my dress. Absolutely we have a cultural tie to the Easties."

Skartabel scowled. "Do not speak that way in front of our queen. We are proud, tithe-paying subjects of the Western Lands and All That Really Matters, and have been since Queen Gwendolyn the Irritable added the canton to her realm."

Livinia poked her brother in the arm. "You and your tithe-paying loyalty. No one is questioning that. The former champion asked about our cultural heritage. Didn't you learn your sums by arranging olives on a plate?"

"Of course I did. You were the one who taught me."

"Don't you give your mother-in-law a jar of olives every birthday?"

"Yes—"

"Haven't you wooed each and every one of your paramours with olive branches in blossom?"

"Everyone does that."

"That's not true. Everyone in our canton does that. Everyone in the Eastern Lands does it. But they don't do that here. The Southies don't. The Northos don't. And I'm pretty sure those equine savages rampaging in the Central Ranges would have absolutely no idea what to do with an olive branch in blossom, except maybe eat it."

Eloise didn't want to let this prejudice go unchallenged. "Hold on—"

But Skartabel cut across her, gobsmacked. He spoke to Jerome and Lorch. "You're telling me that you don't get olive branches in blossom for your sweethearts? That you don't use different species and different stages of blossoming, depending on where you are in the courtship, to signal that you'd like to shift the alliance either toward or away from intimacy? You've never been granted a first kiss across a half-opened Nocellara del Belice or had your heart broken by a withered Megaritiki left on your pillow?"

"That's the first I've ever heard of it," said Jerome.

"Me, too," agreed Lorch.

"But..." Skartabel wrinkled his forehead. "How do they know your intentions?"

"What do you mean?" said Jerome. "You just tell them. 'Hey, I like you. Wanna grab a bite to eat sometime?' Like that."

Skartabel's jaw dropped and he looked at his sister. "Surely he jests. You're telling me they don't know the language of olive blossoms?"

"Sorry, Skart," said Livinia. "That's how they do it here. They speak."

"That's..." His face went red. "That's barbaric. I would die of shame."

"One adjusts," said his sister. "Brace yourself, Skart, but I had one gentleman caller address me by my first name on a second date."

"Oh, this is too much. Now you're just creating fictions at my expense. Do you think I'm that gullible?"

"Would it be possible to return to the matter at hand?" said Eloise. "What's going on in Flachberg?"

"So, again, nothing so bold as raiding parties or pillaging," said Livinia. "But it's like Skartabel said, lots of muscular merchants—men and women alike—walking around Flachberg and surrounds, talking up the historic ties to the Eastern Land."

"There's more," said Skartabel. "We keep getting word from people passing between the two realms at the Adequate Wall of the Realms that Queen Aglandau Ponentine's guards and soldiers are conducting training exercises on their side of the wall."

"Getting word?" Livinia snorted. "You can practically hear them sweating and swearing from our side of the Adequate Wall guard house. They don't seem to be making any effort to keep things a secret."

"Are you alarmed?" asked Eloise. "Or is it just one of those things?"

"I'd go with somewhere between 'nervous' and 'concerned.'" Skartabel crossed his arms, and plucked at his sleeves with both hands.

"Lorch," said Eloise. "Remind me, please, to raise the matter with First Advisor Ligurian. Let's see if he knows anything."

"We'd be grateful," said Livinia. "Let's hope it's nothing."

❧ 38 ❧

NEITHER LOUD NOR SHOUTY

The next morning, RoyLee brought morning tea and Lorch stationed himself outside the door of the Queen's Study just as Ligurian arrived for Eloise's morning briefing. The room had been unburdened of its overflowing sacks of correspondence and, as he had done at her first briefing, First Advisor wheeled up a cart with the two royal boxes into the room and closed the door behind him.

"Blessings of the day, First Advisor," said Eloise as she poured out a haggleberry tea. "May I offer you a cuppa?" She knew he'd refuse, but it seemed impolite not to offer. Eloise wondered how many months or years it would take for him to either accept or for her to stop offering.

"Blessings of the day, Your Highness. Thank you, but no thank you. I've just broken fast. With your permission, I'd like to begin."

Eloise blew across her teacup, sipped, then carefully set it down on its saucer. The echoes of her habits were still there—she preferred the cup and saucer to be in the exact middle of the table on a serviette whose edges were equidistant from the table's. And she still liked the spoon on the saucer to line up with the serviette and the table. At least the urging of her habits had been quieter since she'd been home—

more nudges than demands, thank Çalaht. The compulsion to put the spoon across the top of the cup to add to the symmetry was barely a whisper, where once it had been nearly impossible for her to ignore. "First Advisor, may I start with a question?"

"Certainly."

"Do you know Skartabel and Livinia Heterokont?"

Ligurian snorted and shook his head slowly. "Of course," said First Advisor. "They're from Flachberg. Livinia trades in pond scum and Skartabel is a second-rate laird, at best. I saw them briefly at the Naming Ceremony reception, and managed to avoid speaking with them. He's come to Brague with her on a sort of vacation while she delivered wares to the market. What about them? With those two, there's not much 'there' there."

"She sells seaweed, not pond scum," said Eloise.

"Is there a material difference?"

"I'm sure there is, but point taken. So, you don't think highly of them, then."

Ligurian waved her comment away. "They have a history of worry and seeing that which is not there. Did they discuss suspicious activity in the Eastern Lands across the border from their canton?"

"Yes."

Ligurian exhaled a bemused, here-we-go-again sigh. "This is not unfamiliar behavior. They raised similar concerns from time to time with the late queen."

"Did they. Right. And?"

"The first few times, your mother investigated. Each time, it was fruitless. Toward the end of her reign, the late queen became disinclined to expend more resources chasing that which had never been there. They had not endeared themselves to her and while she remained polite, she also kept them at arm's length."

"You're saying there was never any friction or disagreement between the Flachberg canton and the Easties?"

"I wouldn't go that far. It's Flachbergers we're talking about. And Easties, for that matter. It seemed like squabbling across the Adequate Wall of the Realms was a pastime. What I'm saying is that there was never anything that our spies or merchants looking into the matter cared to raise to a level of 'concern.'"

"I see." Eloise looked at him, unsure what to do. "If the Heterokonts are known time-wasters, then they don't merit the expenditure of resources chasing their follies. End of story."

"As Her Highness commands." Ligurian returned to shuffling through the documents in one of the royal boxes.

"Except..." Eloise trailed off.

"Yes, Your Highness?"

"The thing is, they didn't strike me as time-wasters. They didn't bring the matter up with me, but with Champion Lacksneck. Even when he brought them back to me, they had to be pressed to open up about their concerns. They seemed... I don't know... It was like they were embarrassed to ask for my help."

Eloise absently picked up a cookie from the tea tray. It was a soft, chewy thing that seemed to be made with sea salt, lime, cinnamon, and unrealized good intentions. She broke it in half, then quarters, then halved the quarters into eighths. If she used a knife, she could probably get sixteenths, but then they'd be indistinguishable from crumbs.

"Your Majesty, the next item of business—"

Eloise held up a finger and stopped him. She methodically arranged the pieces on a napkin, placing them carefully in their original order and orientation, creating an exploded diagram of cookie-dom that had the same diameter and circumference as the rim of her teacup. "I kind of liked them. Did you know Flachbergers court one another using blossoming olive branches?"

"I know Eastern Landers do that. I wasn't aware the practice had dribbled over onto this side of the Adequate Wall."

"Hmmm." She picked up the eight at the top of the circle and bit it. Reasonable. She hadn't thought sea salt, lime, and cinnamon would necessarily work together, but they sort of did. "First Advisor, if one did want to look into this, how might it be approached?"

Ligurian frowned. "It depends on what kind of message you want to send."

"Message? I'm not trying to send a message. I'm trying to get information."

"With respect, Your Highness, everything you do sends a message to someone—usually lots of someones—in some way."

"Everything?"

"Yes, Your Highness."

Eloise picked up the six o'clock cookie section. "For example?"

Ligurian rubbed a palm against the underside of his chin, like he was testing how much stubble had grown since his last shave. None, that Eloise could see. "For example, Your Highness, take your choice to change your champion."

"What about it?"

"It sent all kinds of messages. To Court and your subjects—"

"I don't like 'subjects.'"

"It's what they are."

"My mother avoided saying 'subjects,' as best I can remember. Let's use 'people.' Nice and neutral."

"Yes, Your Highness. To Court and your *people*, the change of champion said that you wanted a more traditional champion, one with muscle, grit, and fighting skills. It's a move that was generally well-received as a sign of sound judgment and an improvement on your previous choice."

"There was nothing wrong with Jerome."

"And yet you made the change. It was a message. To the person who sent you that envelope with the beggar's nightshade, it was a message as well. It said, 'I hear you and I'm prepared to respond.'"

"This seems awfully complicated." Eloise sipped her haggleberry tea. It was heading toward too cold. "What are my options with the Heterokonts and their problem? Could you give me a range?"

"Certainly. At one extreme, there is doing nothing. But that doesn't achieve your intentions. At the other extreme, you gather an army, head to the border, and start a war."

"Please, First Advisor. Useful suggestions only."

"Begging your pardon, ma'am, but knowing the extremes gives you a chance to sense where along the continuum the options in the middle sit."

"I see. So what sits between *nichts* and all-out war?"

"You could send a trade delegation. That would be open and more or less honest, as well as transparent. I don't know how deep that kind of group can dig."

"Noted."

"You could dispatch spies."

"Surely there are spies there already."

"Certainly. But they would be known to everyone in the area who matters. Sending new spies gives you a greater level of stealth and a higher probability of uncovering something."

"Again, noted."

"You could send some number of military representatives. Not to attack, but you could organize a similar set of exercises on our side of the Adequate Wall."

"Oh?"

"I wouldn't take that option off the board, but I also wouldn't play that particular piece if I could avoid it. It would be seen as incredibly provocative. And it would be. If we are talking messages, then that is a loud, shouty one."

"You're saying we don't want loud or shouty."

Ligurian nodded. "There is a time and place for loud and shouty. We are not then or there at the moment, in my opinion, Your Highness. Another option is to call in the Eastern Lands representatives and grill them. They won't tell you anything useful, but it sends its own kind of message. As would expelling them, which is also possible, but toward the loud and shouty side of things. It would also engender an unnecessary fracas, which would certainly count as an own goal."

"Unfortunately, I've scored too many of those on the hockey sacking field over the years. Best avoided."

"Yes, ma'am."

Eloise picked up three of the remaining eighths and ate them, not really tasting them.

"Your Highness, if I may. I think really what is needed is information gathered in a way that doesn't set off diplomatic alarm bells. Quiet, but effective."

"Is that possible?"

"With the appropriate spies, yes."

"Spies it is, then. When can you arrange it?"

"Consider it done."

"And when should we expect a result?"

"It will take weeks. Possibly months. They have to prepare. They have to get there. They have to do their work. And they have to return and make their report. It all takes time."

"That seems way too long," said Eloise. "We can't be lollygagging around. We need information as soon as possible."

First Advisor folded his arms. "The spies are not miracle workers. Nor do they fly."

"Wait, wait, wait..." Eloise stood, picked up her mother's letter opener, and poked it down into her cast to try to reach an itch. "You're saying that none of our spies can fly? I've been in bugged rooms and rooms that have been cleared of bugs. They're a kind of spy. They fly."

"That's internal to the realm. None of the realms has used flying spies against each other in over two centuries, not since the Treaty of Aerial Eschewment."

"I don't know that one," said Eloise.

"It's one of those treaties that has been there so long that no one even thinks about it anymore, but it still holds sway."

"You were saying that all of the realms eschew the use of aerial surveillance? That seems far-fetched."

"It would be, except the spies themselves enforce it," said Ligurian. "It's a bit like the Great Avian Accord between the Messengers Guild and the Interceptors Guild governing the prohibition against the airborne delivery of messages. No one thinks the bloodshed is worth it, so those most affected by it abide by it, and ensure that others do as well."

"Fine then, First Advisor," said Eloise, standing. "Use the spies that you can use, but please ask them to hurry."

"I'll do what I can, Your Highness."

BRICKS OF BANANAS

Eloise found Jerome in GCEG 14/27, gloves on, head down, and tail up, peering at a properly weighted-down scroll. It was better now that Head Scribe now trusted them enough to work unsupervised. They could examine the babies more freely.

"Hey, Jer."

Jerome looked up. "Hey, El."

"Find anything interesting?"

"Interesting, yes."

"Do tell."

The chipmunk pointed at the scroll with his foot, careful not to touch it. "Toward the end of her reign, Queen Joan the Sadly Befuddled tried to replace the use of metal coins as a medium of exchange with bricks of pressed, dried bananas."

"What? Why?"

"She thought it would make everyone rich, since there are so many bananas everywhere."

"How is that supposed to work?"

"The banana bricks were made in different shapes and sizes. The quality of the bananas varied from one brick to another and was the main determining factor in the value of the brick."

Eloise adjusted the Gumballic Heraldic Crown on her head, settling it a little better. "How does one work out the quality of a brick of dried bananas?"

"The scroll doesn't go into that. Using the flavor, maybe?"

"If you determined the brick's value by taste, presumably you'd devalue the money every time you tested it, since you'd have to eat a little."

"That's not the only problem. It suddenly made banana growers the wealthiest people in the realm and they started lording it over everyone. Everyone tried to plant banana trees, pushing the price of them way up. The bricks themselves were perishable, which meant a leaky roof could literally cost you a fortune. And as there was no obvious, standard way to determine value, the wheels of commerce practically ground to a halt since everyone had to haggle about the value of their medium of exchange, which took time."

"How did it turn out?" asked Eloise.

"Seen anyone try to buy a cup of haggleberry tea with a banana brick fragment lately?"

"That's not what I meant. How did it end?"

"Not long before Queen Joan died, a bunch of merchants got together with a bunch of guilds, and together, they made the largest banana pudding the realm had ever seen, and which I'm sure has never been matched since. Then they dusted off their coins and went back to using them."

"Remind me, why are you telling me this story?"

Jerome flicked his tail. "You asked me if I'd found anything interesting."

"Right. Perhaps I should have asked, have you found anything useful and germane?"

"Useful and germane? No."

"Nothing?"

"*Nada. Nichts.* Zip. Zero."

"OK. Thanks, Jer. Keep looking."

"As Her Highness wishes."

"Jeremiad?"

"Yes, Elltastic?"

"Now I want banana pudding."

"Me, too. So bad."

❦ 40 ❦

SPARE

RoyLee found Eloise and Jerome having breakfast in the Salle de la Famille. "Princess Queen Eloise, that Half Kingdom capybara be being here for you again."

Eloise slid aside her perfectly tolerable barley-malt-sweetened bowl of quinoa and iron-cut oats and stood. "Where?"

Ziïimmÿÿÿ stepped into view and his rich, cultured voice filled the room. "G'mid-morning, Queen Eloise." His bow reminded her of one of Jerome's joking ones, but he pulled it off with such sincerity that it came across as elegant instead of ironic. "I bring you greetings from the Half Kingdom and another missive from Princess Johanna."

"Very good. And thank you. Are you here long?"

"That depends, Your Highness."

"On what?"

"On how long you need to write back, assuming you want to."

"Right. I'm sure I will."

She sent Ziïimmÿÿÿ to get some food, and RoyLee to let Lady Seneschal know that the capybara would be their guest again. She waved the letter at Jerome and said, "I need to go read this. See you in a bit?"

"Of course."

In the Queen's Study, Eloise examined the envelope. The quality of hemp parchment had improved since the last time—there was more heft to it and it was finer—like she'd had time to find a source that was more to her taste. There was also a light rose smell, which was nice.

She slit open the note and found it once again written in her sister's blocky, deliberate hand.

Dear El,

Did you hear the one about the nightingale with the sore throat?

"So 't' and 'b.' Got it," murmured Eloise, reaching for quill and scraps. She set up a grid of letters to make the double decoding faster.

Today, I write in frustration, but it has been a while since our last correspondence, and I didn't want to let too much time go by. Thanks for your letter. It sounds like you're managing to muddle through, which is good. I hope you really find your feet soon.

Muddling through? Is that the impression she'd given? Probably. It's how it felt. No surprise it's what she would have conveyed.

The Half Kingdom Court is driving me spare. So much intrigue! So many machinations. So many egos to assuage or bully or coddle. It's exhausting knowing who is who and whether or not they actually have any influence (and whether that influence is their own or dependent on someone else). It really makes me appreciate how Mother kept everyone at hand. That's not something I ever gave all that much thought. I wish I had. Let me tell you, the way you got your crown was much simpler. I don't say that with rancor or jealousy. I say it as a fact. A clear path simplifies that journey. I can't find a clear path here.

My saving grace is that I know Protocol. As in, I know Protocol. I know what it expects, what it suggests, and what it demands. I know where it is likely to bend, and what might be broken. Half Kingdom Protocol has differences to ours, but they are minor, so all those years I spent studying the Livre de Protocol were not wasted. It has given me a foothold at the Half Kingdom Court that I wouldn't have been able to establish otherwise. Still, it's tricky, and the outcome is far from certain.

You should see Father here. He seems both at home and a complete stranger. I keep coming across him in some corner of the castle staring at things. Sometimes he'll say something like, "I used to sit here and eat stolen blackberries. It occurs to me now that as a prince, I probably didn't need to steal them. I could have just asked for them, and people would have given them to me. I thought I was being clever, but it's quite possible, I was being a complete jerk." When he remembers his brother, he calls him "Donnie," which is both cute and very strange. "Donnie and I used to sword fight with sticks on these stairs." Or "Donnie always insisted on seedless green grapes, and I always had the purple ones with seeds."

And Çalaht on a cinnamon bun, he hates it when people call him the "dowager king."

Mostly, he's still pretty mopey.

Father's trying to be helpful with me and Court, maintaining his stance of not wanting to be king and trying to provide bits of advice here and there. But the simple fact is that I've spent more time here than he has recently, and his information is practically antiquated.

My garden is doing well. It's cooler here than at home...

Goodness. That's a revelatory statement. In that moment, in writing that phrase, I realized I don't think of here as home yet. Something to ponder. I might have to work on that.

Fingers crossed for me wrangling a crown out of these people.

Write when you can.

Love,

J

A pang of loneliness filled Eloise as she realized how much she missed her sister and father. She blinked back tears as she reached for her own page of parchment.

❧ 41 ❧

GOTTEN WIND

A winter rain like a surly snowmelt poured down onto the streets of Brague, providing uncomfortable, but effectively secret cover for the hastily arranged meeting. The cloaked figure was once again waiting, this time next to a shop called Chalice Alice, which claimed to sell the finest goblets in all the realms. He knew that if it had been any good at all it wouldn't have been located in such a disreputable part of town. At least the torn awning provided a small respite from the rain. He stamped his boots and rubbed his hands in a low-key interpretive dance that said, "Holy crud, it's cold out here."

At least there was no barrel nearby where something unpleasant or frightening might lurk.

The second one seemed to appear from nowhere, sliding from one shadow to the next until he, too, was under the awning. There was something different about the way the second one moved. A bit sluggish. Lethargic, even. That must be the way of his kind in cold weather.

"You have news for me?" hissed the second one. "It had better be good to call me out on a night like this."

No point in prevaricating. "She has gotten wind of the stirrings in the border region."

"Really." The second one bobbed his head from side to side, thoughtful. "How is that possible?"

"The Heterokonts spoke to her at the Naming Ceremony reception."

"I thought I tasted them in the air. A disappointment, that is. Those dimwitted scum-suckers actually used their eyes and ears for once, did they? Well, there's a first for everything."

A bead of sweat trickled down inside his collar despite the weather. He clasped his hands in front of himself to decrease their visible shaking.

"What is being done?" The second one's speech was as sluggish as his movements. The slurring made him seem less dangerous, but more mesmerizing.

It was an illusion to think the threat had lessened.

"All I can say is that she has been convinced to step timidly."

"All you can say? You will say what you are told to say." The second one sighed out a frosty breath. "But that will do. She is most certainly not her mother. Back home, they are making book on how many months she'll last."

"She... She is good-hearted."

The second one stuck out a tongue built for blowing raspberries. "*Pfffffftttt!* Because good-heartedness is what one needs to rule a queendom. Please. Tell me another."

The cloaked figure held his tongue.

"Time is of the essence," said the second one. "Therefore, you must work to ensure that a significant measure of hers is wasted."

"How—"

"Not my problem."

"I—"

"I said, Not. My. Problem."

"I..." The cloaked one trailed off. What was the point? "I've heard you. Your desire is clear."

"Good." The second one straightened and prepared to leave. "This has been a productive meeting. Your mother would be proud of you. That is, if she's ever in any position to hear about it."

The cloaked one gritted his teeth and said nothing.

"You were right to reach out. But let's try to make it a less odious journey next time." Then he slithered into the darkness and was gone, leaving the first one to contemplate what it must be like to have a third eye like that.

❧ 42 ☙

BETTER HALF OF THE DEAL

Lady Seneschal spread a schmear of jalapeño spinach dip across a parchment-thin slice of sourdough bread, being careful not to rip it. It was her sixth slice, but who was counting? She'd decided to go through the various savory choices first, and had already enjoyed half a dozen finger-sized strips of a black bean, mushroom, and corn quesadilla, followed by about the same number of squares of baked tofu and lentil rigatoni. She knew she had to pace herself, because she still had sweet potato biscuits, a zucchini crêpe she'd never had before, and grilled veggie skewers—all before turning attention to the sweets. If she kept meeting the Eastie ambassador like this, she was going to find herself a hundred strong weights heavier and in need of a new wardrobe.

Picholine Manzanilla, on the other hand, ate like a distance runner and didn't seem under threat of anything more complicated than emptying her plate.

"Madame Ambassador, may I ask, how do you keep such a slim physique?"

"Worry," she said. "And constant movement."

"What are you worried about?"

"I'm an ambassador. I worry about everything."

"The other ambassadors I've met don't seem to share your concerns."

"Did any of them serve Her Majesty, Queen Aglandau?"

"No, I can't say that they did."

Manzanilla waved a forkful of cooked dandelion greens. "There you go. My queen is not what one might call low maintenance. She is one tough pavlova."

"I wouldn't call mine low maintenance either."

"No? How so?"

"It wouldn't do for me to say."

"Come on. It's just us girls. This will stay between you, me, and the zucchini crêpes."

Lady Seneschal paused, nibbled a little pesto pizza roll, then said, "Let me put it this way. She's young. She's still new at being queen. So, one could cut her some slack for that. It takes time to adjust, and the staff, like the rest of the realm, takes some time to get used to a new monarch. Especially when the last one was beloved, and this one..."

"This one isn't?"

"I didn't say that. Nor would I."

"Of course you wouldn't. Nor should you."

"There's something in the new queen's manner that I don't care for. I don't know... It's like she's hiding something, or she knows something you don't and doesn't want you to think she knows something you don't. Truth, be told, I find it irksome."

"It must be difficult to be so supportive of someone like that."

"I do my duty and play my role." Lady Seneschal pinched the corners of her mouth to wipe away any stray flecks of pastry. "It's possible I might not be relishing it as much as I once did."

"It helps to love one's queen when one is in service to her."

"Love." Lady Seneschal sighed. "I'd say I loved the late queen. But not her mother. And, sadly, not her daughter." Lady Seneschal sipped her tea in thought. "I've known her since she was born. There's definitely always been a tension between us. Especially now."

"You've known both of the princesses since they were born. How different are they?"

"Very different. Princess Johanna could be a thunderstorm, for sure. There'd be crashing and lightning, and then it would pass. Queen Eloise was quieter. More compliant on the surface, but underneath, she was stubborn and insubordinate." She picked up a profiterole. "But you know what?"

"What?"

Lady Seneschal's face sagged into sadness. "I think it's possible the Half Kingdom might have got the better half of the princess-going-on-queen deal."

"I'd never say anything against your queen. But if I did, I'd say you were probably right." Manzanilla leaned over the laden table. "I might try one of the sweet treats this time, and see if my system can tolerate it."

43

A MIRACLE OR A MIRACULOUS EVENT

Three weeks later, Eloise was well into her morning briefing when First Advisor Ligurian interrupted a discussion about the need to expand the realm's ability to store seed potatoes more reliably. "Queen Eloise, may I ask you a question?"

"Certainly, First Advisor. Ask away."

"Can you tell me what happened in Festering Resentment?"

"Festering Resentment? What do you mean?" Eloise knew exactly what he meant.

Ligurian clasped his hands behind his back. "I've had reports that your visit there was, shall we say, unusual."

"Unusual? In what way?"

"Your Highness, as you probably know, I tend to get reports from time to time about various things that happen around your royal personage. Lady Seneschal, for example, keeps me informed about household matters. In this case, Nörbert de Lupus and Abelardo de Burro fulfilled their reporting duties with information that was, how should I put it..."

"Unusual. That's the word you used. So again, I ask, unusual in what way?"

"Apparently, there was a bona fide miraculous event." His expression showed that he doubted anything extraordinary had actually happened. "They're calling it the Rampaging of the Holy Sunflowers."

"A miracle. A sunflower miracle."

"'A miraculous event.' That's the phrase they used."

"Is there a difference between a miracle and a miraculous event?" Eloise did not like the direction this was going in. *No, it wasn't a miracle. It was me misusing a magical object. Sorry for the damage to the paddock, by the way.* Not exactly something she could say out loud to him.

"Well, Your Highness," Ligurian began. He unclasped his hands behind him and one by one, started squeezing the individual fingers of his left hand with his right. In the past month-plus of these daily briefings, Eloise had learned this was a tell of his. He unconsciously twisted his fingers this way, sometimes getting them to pop, when he was saying things that he thought stupid, repetitive, or that she should already know. It was one of two tells that she'd worked out. The other was when he clasped his hands in front of him. When he did that he was either prevaricating, bending the truth, or outright lying. So it seemed what he was about to say was in the "She's being stupid" category. Eloise could live with that.

"Your Highness, I'm no theologian, but I would think that a miraculous event would be something that appears to be, or could possibly actually be, a manifestation of divine intervention in the affairs of people."

Eloise gave him an open-palm shrug. "Which do you think it is more likely to be, First Advisor? An actual divine intervention or something that could possibly be construed as a divine intervention?"

"The latter, of course."

"And yet, the Venerable Prelate Herself was there leading the prayers. She is one very holy tapir, is she not? Surely whatever happened can be ascribed to her particular grace." Eloise took a sip of her tea. "If I may say so, she seemed rather pleased with herself. May I ask, who is calling it the Rampaging of the Holy Sunflowers?"

"Gossip heralds, mostly. The word has spread that something happened there. Caravans of pilgrims have begun making their way to the village. Festering Resentment appears to be experiencing a miraculous sunflower-based economic boomlet. The brunchberry crofters, Goodman and Goodman Rechteckfeld, sent this." Ligurian took a handwritten note from one of the two royal boxes.

Eloise read the half-literate scrawl out loud: "Thank you ever so ever so ever much, Queen Eloise. And please thank the Venerable Prelate Herself. We are grateful for the Miraculous Sunflower Manifestation. We've been able to leave brunchberries behind, instead focusing on sunflower snack bars, sunflower salads, sunflower tahini bites, sunflower cheesecake-like cheesecake, sunflower pesto, tamari sunflowers, sunflower burgers, sunflower crispy treats, spicy sunflower nibbles, sunflower crackers, sunflower oil, sunflower and yam fries, and just straight sunflowers sold by the half-weight. Maybe next year we can invite youse again and we can get you to bless a tomato patch. Thanking you kindly, the Rechteckfelds."

Eloise set the letter down. "That seems nice. I'm glad they're benefiting from the Venerable Prelate Herself's little miracle. The ways of Çalaht are strange and wondrous," said Eloise. "I don't think we'll ever really know what went on that day. Say, you don't think that puts her in line for canonization, do you?"

"No, Your Highness. A single miracle is usually not enough for sainthood."

"Pity. I'm rather fond of the old tapir. She deserves that kind of thing."

"So, you don't have anything to add to the analysis of the goings on?"

"No, First Advisor, I don't. I admit it was strange. Unusual, as you said. But, no, I have nothing to add." Not wanting to say anything else, Eloise thought it was time to change the subject. "While we're asking questions, what of your inquiries with regard to the Heterokonts' concerns? Any news?"

Ligurian clasped his hands in front of him.

Eloise blinked a few extra times, but kept her face neutral.

"Not yet, Your Highness. The wheels of progress turn slowly sometimes."

"When do you anticipate a result? Have you had any interim communications?"

"I expect to have something once they have arrived and established themselves. A few more days, maybe a little more, depending on circumstances on the ground."

"You'll let me know as soon as you have something?"

"Certainly."

Eloise wondered just how certain "certainly" was.

❧ 44 ❧

MAMMALERS

Over the two weeks that followed, a kind of routine settled across Eloise's days. Not a monotony, as she'd feared, but definitely a predictability. Up early. Run (usually with Lorch accompanying her, which was an interesting change—he was fast!). If she felt like she had the time, then a few hammer throws (which Lorch was also very good at). Then a bath and getting dressed for the day (which always took longer than she thought it should, even with two handmaids helping). She'd next break fast with Jerome (Lorch politely declined to eat with them, citing vague champion duties). This gave her former champion the clear signal that he was still included. It also gave her a chance to hear the results of the research he was doing (so far, nothing to report), as well as what was going on in the world of Court gossip.

"You know, I really don't like listening to the gossip heralds," said Jerome. He picked up a mini-croissant, sniffed it, decided it was OK, then broke it open and smeared an enormous glob of kiwi jam onto it.

"Even if listening to them serves the purpose of helping me stay on top of things?"

"It makes me feel dirty."

Once upon a time, being a herald in the Western Lands and All That Really Matters was a noble profession earning high standing in the community and a reasonable amount of coin. Heralds in Brague plied their trade for centuries with dignity and seriousness, informing their fellow citizens of the important goings-on around the queendom and promulgating decrees, edicts, directives, and announcements. If one had a stentorious voice, a stout demeanor, a good memory, the ability to read, and a box to stand on, it was a good way to go.

Then came the gossip heralds.

They ruined everything.

Gossip heralds piddled on everything the serious heralds valued. They couldn't give a fig jam jar about the serious issues of the realm. Their domain was scandal, tittle-tattle, hearsay, chitchat, blather, and buzz. It didn't matter if you had a voice like muskrat belch, and it didn't even particularly matter if what you said was true. If you could stoke the flames of chatter or rake the muck, you could gather a following who'd toss coin in your direction.

Coin that thus didn't get tossed in the direction of the serious heralds.

Still, commerce is commerce, and the heralds and gossip heralds found themselves uneasily co-existing. Court found there was reason to give both an ear, since it was better to be informed by the serious heralds, but you could get a better sense of the realm from the gossip heralds.

Eloise plucked a boysenberry from her fruit plate and held it up. "So what are the gossip heralds saying?"

"The usual. Apparently some noble snogged someone they shouldn't have and everyone is atwitter. Court is apparently overrun by the mendacious and the avaricious. Nothing new there. A professional hockey sacking player on some team I don't care about revealed part of his anatomy in a time and place that was inappropriate, and someone decked him for it. Deservedly so."

"That's not what I'm asking. What are they saying about me?"

"Nothing."

"Jerome."

"Really, nothing." Jerome sighed. "The word 'flibbertigibbet' is getting a lot of use at the moment."

"Flibbertigibbet?"

"Flibbertigibbet."

"Huh." Eloise ripped a mini-croissant in half with a bit more vigor than needed. She stabbed a splotch of elderberry compote onto it and shoved it in her mouth.

"El, if you're going to let every little thing from the gossip heralds get under your skin, you're going to have a lot of things poking under a lot of places."

"Flibbertigibbet? Why that? Do I strike you as particularly chatty or air-headed?"

"No. They're just being mean. That's their job. It's their business model. How many people would stand around a gossip herald chucking coins if the herald stepped up on their box and said, 'Relax everyone. Our queen is doing a rocking job,' and then stepped down again?"

"I suppose. But it irks me. I'm trying to do a good job here. I know more about military deployments, castle ledgers, diplomatic niceties, queen's tithes, and making pronouncements than I would ever have guessed."

"You're doing fine. It's still all new."

"Can you imagine someone calling my mother a flibbertigibbet?"

"No, not if they wanted to keep their appendages attached."

"So is that the solution? Rip off a few arms and legs? Show everyone how terrifying I can be?"

"It worked for your mother."

"Yeah, I guess it did. She certainly had my number."

"Our beloved late queen had everyone's number. It was one of the things she did well."

"I don't think I'm the get-everyone's-number type."

Jerome raised his palms and shrugged. "You might not be. From what I know, you're not. But you don't necessarily have to be a number gatherer to be a good queen."

"What's a good queen, anyway?"

"That one's easy," said Jerome. "Someone who cares about her people. Someone who makes the best decisions she can using the imperfect information available with heart, compassion, and in a way that's to the benefit of those she's supposed to serve. Someone who will pass the boysenberry compote to her breakfast companion even without being asked."

"I guess." Eloise slid the pot of compote in his direction. "Hey, can I ask you something else?"

"Of course, Your Highness."

"Do you know many birds?"

"Lots."

"Lots?"

"Yeah, I belong to a mammal watching club," said Jerome. "We have a huge number of birds in our group. They're really good at it."

"Mammal watching? What's that?"

"We mammalers go to places where mammals are likely to be found and try to spot them in their native habitats. Most of us keep lists of the kinds we've seen and where."

"Mammal watching."

"It's a lot of fun, and it takes you to places you wouldn't necessarily go."

"What kinds of mammals?"

"All kinds. Some people like to specialize, like noble mammals, mammals dressed in purple, mammals in hats, mammals with tails, mammals carrying pointy objects—that kind of thing."

"I see. And birds are good at it because..."

"Well, that's kind of obvious. They can fly up into a tree or onto a rooftop and scope out where the mammals might be at the moment, and direct the group to where they should go next. Plus, some of them have really excellent eyesight. Auks, cormorants, kingfishers—some of those can tell a cravat-wearing, sulfer-babushka'd banker from an ascot-throated, lemon-hatted pawnbroker from a strong length away. It's amazing. It also makes them popular in mammaler groups."

"Jerome, you know you're a mammal, right?"

"I'm not stupid, El. Yes, I'm a mammal. But one doesn't count one's home species on one's own list. But you're right, someone could spot me and tick off 'incredibly smart, verbally acute, forthrightly handsome, pleasant-smelling chipmunk' from their life list."

"I see."

"Why do you ask?"

Eloise looked down at her napkin. "I need someone to have a look at something."

"So just ask. Or get First Advisor to get it looked at."

"First Advisor is looking into it. But it seems to be going awfully slowly. So, I need a bird to take on a task. And it isn't, uh, strictly by the rules."

"Oh. I see." Jerome swallowed the last of his mini-croissant and licked a stray bit of boysenberry compote from his claw. "I have just the bird for you. Göööber. A nightjar. He's a sort of friend of mine."

"Who's Goober?"

"No, it's 'Göööber.' He's fussy about the way people say his name. Actually, he's fussy about a lot of things—how ripe a banana is supposed to be before you can eat it, never washing whites with colors, even in cold water, and that you should only ever buy even numbers of things when shopping. Never odd. And Çalaht help you if you suggest that the dramas of Leonard the Quill aren't the pinnacle of artistic creation in all the realms."

"Leonard the Quill? Never heard of him."

"For Çalaht's sake, don't tell him that. He'll launch into reciting lines from 'Tragic Was the Milkmaid's Bucket,' 'Camel Lot,' or 'The Curious Incident of the Spork in the Day-Time.'"

"So why are you suggesting him?"

"Because, my fair queen, he's my friend, he can fly like no one's business, and his memory is encyclopedic. For example, he can recite every mammal on his life list—and there are hundreds—including subculture, size, shape, colorization, when and where he spotted them, and what they had for lunch that day. Plus, he's the kind of person who might not mind doing something that isn't strictly in the boundaries of the rules. Also, he's a nightjar. They're nocturnal, which might help if what you want done is clandestine."

"Can you discreetly bring him in and let me meet him?"

"Nope."

"No?"

"No. He's a bit of an anti-royalist. Don't take it personally. It isn't you. It's the idea of you. If you want him to do something for you, you're better off going to him. And bring your coin purse. That is a language he'll be happy to speak with you."

"Fine. Where do we find him?"

"At the Tilted Perch."

"A public inn?"

"A public inn that caters to birds. Did I mention he likes a bit of the old liquid consolation?"

Eloise squinted at her friend. "Are you sure this is the bird for the job?"

"Yep. Trust me. You'll think so, too, once you get to know him. Plus, it sounds like you're trying to do an end run around a certain First Advisor. So an off-site meeting might be better."

"Set it up, then."

"As Her Highness commands. And I'll talk to El Lorcho about how we might get you there without raising eyebrows."

❧   45   ❧

THE TILTED PERCH

The Tilted Perch was an absolutely primo dump. A dump's dump. A dumpy perfection. The *ne plus ultra* of dumps. A dumpissimo. The kind of dump that dumps put up paintings of and sigh at before they go to sleep.

Eloise hated it on sight.

It wasn't just the grime-encrusted walls, the soiled sawdust that caked the floor, or the mass of winged miscreants who sat, wobbly, on elevations around the room, imbibing who knew what from chipped and cracked mugs. It wasn't the surly half-eared ocelot behind the bar or the bird regurgitations littering every flat surface.

No, it was the stench.

A noxious, nose-searing cocktail of fermented grains, over-ripe fruits, and guano assaulted her even before she stepped into the place. "Ugh," she said. "Just ugh."

"Yeah," said Jerome. "It's definitely an acquired enjoyment."

"You get used to this?"

"Not so much. But it's known to not get a lot of scrutiny, so this lot likes it."

With Jerome in the lead and Lorch bringing up the rear, the three of them picked their way through the Tilted Perch toward a roost at the back. Hector and the Nameless One had wanted to join them on this task, but Lorch was concerned it would be too visible, and Jerome pointed out that they wouldn't be able to come inside the Tilted Perch anyway, and would just end up standing around waiting outside the inn.

Eloise had left her crown and fancy outfits at home and worn her travel outfit as a kind of disguise. She was grateful for sturdy boots, and as she *sklitched* and skidded her way through the mess, was already sorry for Odmilla, who'd be the one to tidy them on her return. With her cloak hood up, she hoped she wouldn't be recognized, which seemed pretty likely given how snockered everyone appeared.

Jerome stopped at a secluded perch in a dark corner where a nightjar sat, eyes closed, either asleep, pickled, or both. The bird had long, speckled wings in shades of brown, short legs, and a bill that looked like someone had replaced his real one with a tiny, novelty beak. He had a skull like someone had taken to it with the flat part of a shovel during an argument, and his feathers looked like he'd started molting, decided not to, and ended up with some weird halfway result.

"Göööber?" said Jerome softly, not wanting to disturb his friend. When there was no response, he tried again, a little louder.

The bird opened one eye and swiveled it left and right, then up and down until it pointed at Jerome. This raised sufficient interest for the nightjar to open a second eye. "Jerome! My good fellow." His voice was incongruous to both his size and his looks. It was deep, melodic, and trained like an actor's. Its thespian richness rumbled up from his throat like a boulder dipped in rice malt, and crashed out of him with the resonance and verve of an avalanche.

"Göööber, my avian hero," said Jerome theatrically, mocking the bird's intonation. The chipmunk then began a head-ducking, arm-flapping, birdlike ritual posturing, saying, "Who's the bird? Who's the bird? Who's the bird?" over and over and over.

Göööber responded with his own stylized strut, holding one taloned foot like it was a chipmunk's forepaw, hunching over, and thrusting his rear end up and splaying his feathers in rough approximation of a fluffed chipmunk tail. To this, he added head bobbing and a chant of "Who's the chipmunk? Who's the chipmunk? Who's the chipmunk?"

"What in the name of Çalaht's tumid tonsils?" murmured Eloise. She rolled her eyes and looked at Lorch, whispering, "Are you going to join in this male bonding ritual?"

"If the qu—, uh, if Her High—, I mean… Sorry. If you'll allow, I might sit this one out."

"Are you sure? It seems important."

"Quite sure, thank you."

During a full 45 seconds of testosterone-inflected swagger, Jerome climbed up to where the nightjar stood. The bird and chipmunk ducked and wove around each other, until the grandstanding ended with several solid chest bumps between them, a mutual "Hoooahhh!" and a hug.

When they'd finally finished, Jerome turned to Eloise. "Your H—. Oh, sorry. You, who we're not naming, allow me to introduce Göööber de Caprimulgidae, my mammaler buddy. Göööber, this is, um, I present you the person that you and I were discussing previously."

"Well stuff a pimento in my ear and call me an olive," said the nightjar. "It's none other than the oppressor of all hard-working people everywhere. Your Maj—, I mean, you who we are not referring to by name or title at this particular time, welcome to my office."

Oppressor? Why would he call her that? Eloise decided to let it slide. "Pleased to meet you, Master de Caprimulgidae," she said.

"Please, call me Göööber. What can I order you by way of fine libation? The grog is very groggy, the booze is most certainly boozy, and the hooch will put down feathers on your chest."

"Do they do tea here?"

"They say they do," said Jerome. "But it's about as close to real tea as broccoli is to a sequoia."

"Water?"

"Only if you're fond of digestive distress, my lady," said the nightjar. "Sadly, I speak to that from personal experience."

"Cordial?"

"Cordial. Cordial. Cor-di-al." He said the word like it was a tantalizing mirage from a foreign land.

"It's a non-alcoholic concentrated syrup used in beverage making," said Jerome.

"Oh, well, there's your problem. The syllable 'non' in front of the word 'alcoholic' has thrown me for a loop. I do not like your chances of finding this supposed elixir of here in the Tilted Perch."

"Very amusing, Master de—. Sorry, Göööber," said Eloise. "Jerome, what do you have when you're in here?"

"Just the company. And the veggie tempura. That's OK."

"Ah, the ve-ge-ta-ble tem-pur-a. It is not OK. It is spectacular," said the nightjar.

"Wait, you won't drink the water but you'll eat fried vegetables? How can that make sense?"

Jerome shrugged. "Welcome to the Tilted Perch. Abandon logic at the door." Then he remembered something and waved his forepaw excitedly. "Oh, oh, oh. I meant to tell you. I saw a red-coated orange monger the other day."

"A red-coated orange monger?" said Göööber. "At this time of year? In this part of the world? How unlikely."

"I thought so too."

"But you saw him. Citrus, cart, coin purse, stupid hat, and all?"

"Sure did."

"Where?"

"At the markets."

"Well, of course," said the bird. "That's their natural habitat. But not in this season. Not in winter."

Jerome nodded. "I know. Maybe he got blown off course in a storm."

"With his oranges? Possible. But not probable."

Once again, Lorch cleared his throat.

"We shall have to table this discussion, my mammaler friend," Göööber said to Jerome. Then he opened his mouth and let out an eardrum-bursting nightjar screech.

No one in the room swiveled an eye or tilted their head, save a harried teenage girl wearing a serving wench's uniform. She looked up, nodded, and threaded her way over to them. The girl pulled a slate and chalk from her apron and said, "Whaddalyousehave?"

"Veronika, my lovely, we'd like four servings of your finest vegetable tempura."

"K." She made a single scratch on the slate. "Yawanasometintadrink?"

The bird fluffed his feathers in a birdish sort of shrug. "My friends are going to pass on that opportunity. I, however, would be grateful for a bottle of Barbarian Bucolic Bastardry. No, make that two bottles."

"K." The teenager held out her hand toward the bird, palm flat, and waited.

The nightjar looked at her like he didn't understand what she meant. Then he lifted his left wing, looked under it, lifted his right wing, looked under it as well, and gave a theatrical humph of exasperation. "I seem to have mislaid my coin purse."

Veronika stayed where she was, palm out, waiting. "No coin, no bottle, no cups."

"I'm afraid..."

"We'll take care of that," said Lorch. He removed a coin purse from his belt and handed over a jingle of coins. "Please keep any excess for yourself. Oh, and one bottle of Barbarian Bucolic Bastardry will be plenty, I'm sure."

The girl looked at him, closed-faced. "K." She shuffled her hand, feeling the weight of the coins and registering just how much clink there was. "Backinnamo."

"In a moment then, Mistress Veronika," said Göööber. When the serving wench was gone, the nightjar indicated a table and chairs behind him hidden in the further darkness of the bird's chosen corner. "Shall we?"

Eloise let Lorch pick the chair that meant he would have his back to the wall and could watch for anyone coming toward them. Eloise chose the one next to him. She looked at the chair, saw it was caked with filth, but ultimately decided it was only marginally worse than a lot of the places she'd sat during their journey. She tucked her travel cloak beneath her, made sure the Star of Whatever remained concealed, and settled along with the others at the table. "Shall we get down to it?" she asked.

"Yes, let's," said Göööber. "What does the people's oppressor need from a humble late-middle-aged, chronically underachieving bird like me?"

There was that oppressor thing again. The bird certainly had a strange way about him. "Jerome here has vouched for you, your flying prowess, your eyesight."

The nightjar swiveled his head so he could see the chipmunk. "Very kind of you."

"I need some unofficial reconnaissance done."

"'Unofficial reconnaissance.' I see." Göööber closed one eye, tilted his head, and looked at her. "What could I possibly help you with, a humble bird such as I? Surely you have people at your disposal who can fly around and have a bit of a squiz at something."

"Of course. There are plenty of people at Court who can fly. And lots of them serve the crown. But they're subject to certain... restrictions."

"Ah, our old friend the Great Avian Accord."

"Not exactly," said Eloise.

The bird tilted his head a little more. "No?"

"No."

Göööber closed his one open eye in thought, then opened them both and straightened. "Oh."

"Exactly. Oh."

"You're talking about the Treaty of Eschewment. It's *that* kind of job." The nightjar turned to Jerome. "You brought them here to talk about that kind of thing?"

Jerome looked down. "I thought—"

"Never mind." The bird stepped backward. "Thank you so much. It's been lovely meeting you. Please tell Veronika to hold my Barbarian Bucolic Bastardry for my next visit to her fine establishment." He turned his back to them and looked like he was going to fly off.

There was a loud, thunking *clink!* sound.

Göööber froze, and slowly turned back around.

There in the middle of the table sat Lorch's coin purse.

"Good sir, if you think that a mere bag of coins is enough to—"

Thunk-clink! A second purse landed next to the first one. It was larger. Louder. Clinkier.

The nightjar looked at it, then up at Lorch, disgust marring his face. "How dare you—"

Thunk-clink! Thunk-clink!

Two more bags landed next to the first two.

Göööber looked at them, looked up at Lorch, looked at Eloise, glanced at Jerome, and then went back to the bags. He spread his wings wide. "I don't know about you, but I'm feeling rather in the mood for doing something that will put my life in danger." He looked out toward the room and screeched again.

Moments later, Veronika was back. "Whayawan?"

"Could you please use those lovely opposable thumbs of yours and put those four items in your father's safe?"

"K." She snapped up the bags, tucked them in her apron pocket behind the slate, and nodded. "Backinnaminwidyergrubngrog."

"Thank you, Veronika." Göööber moved back to his spot at the table and fixed his gaze on Eloise. "So, oppressor of hard-working people who carries an adequate amount of coin, what did you have in mind?"

46
PLANNING FOR A SQUIZ

"To start with," said Eloise, "I recognize that the items taken for safekeeping by young Veronika were merely a way to get your attention. If you render the requested service to the crown, Lorch will organize a suitable—and discreet—further contribution to your coffers."

"Good," said the bird. "It's best to be upfront with one's expectations. I would have brought the matter round to subsequent payment soon enough. I trust that your guard and I will be able to reach a meeting of minds."

"Second, if you're caught, or, Çalaht forbid, permanently, um, removed from the realm of the living, it will be as if we'd never met."

"Fair enough. I've no encumbrances of the familial kind. Nonissue. Moving on, let's get to what you'd like me to do."

"I have concerns about what might be going on to our east. I'd like you to take a vacation to the garden canton of Flachberg and do some sightseeing at an altitude that might reveal information about what's happening on the other side of the Adequate Wall."

"First of all, Flachberg is a hole. Maybe not a hellhole, but to call it a garden canton is not just to gild the lily, but to take a whole bucket of gold paint, dump it on the lily, let it dry, buff it shiny, then add some glitter," said Göööber. "The chief lure of going to Flachberg is that eventually you get to leave."

"If you say so," said Eloise. "I haven't had the pleasure."

"Second of all, this doesn't make sense. You have spies. You have diplomats. You have trade representatives. You have envoys. You have bipedal and quadrupedal tourists of all shapes and sizes. Surely if a squiz needs to happen, one of them can do it."

"To organize that kind of squiz, certain people would have to be involved. I'm trying to get a sort of second opinion. It can act as a countervailing take on whatever those more usual channels might reveal."

"You know that the Eastie border guards include winged sentries, right?"

"Uh, no. I didn't."

"They don't like people flying into their realm without having the opportunity to chat with the Eastie customs agents at the Adequate Wall."

"You can't just fly over the wall?"

"Nope. Not if you don't want to be taken down by a squadron of attack hummingbirds."

"Attack hummingbirds?" said Lorch. "How would that even work? They're so small and delicate."

"Trust me. They're vicious blighters. Your typical trained attack hummingbird can hover for hours at a time, fly in precision formation, and wield his armored beak like a needle from hell. If you get one of those up the tail feathers, you won't be sitting on a nest any time soon. Plus, if their military are up to something in the region, they'll have a no-fly zone enforced for strong lengths around. If they don't want something snooped on, the winged elements of their military will be out in force."

Eloise turned to Lorch. "Do we do that? Or do they do that in The South? I don't remember seeing that kind of defense when we went through the Adequate Wall of the Realms before."

"We do have some degree of air capability," said the guard. "But your predecessors did not place much emphasis on it."

"Why not?"

"I can't say for sure. It's not what I know. Maybe First Advisor can give you insight on that."

"It's simple," grouched Göööber. "All that takes coin. And a plan, and determination, and actions taken to reach an objective. But what's the point of all that time and effort when there are treaties are in place and peace between the realms?"

The conversation paused as Veronika served their food from a tray, then waggled a bottle and cup in front of Göööber. "Yawan-metapouryasome?"

"That would be lovely, thank you." The bird's eyes lit up as he watched her decant a viscous green liquid into the cup. It smelled of mint, juniper, magnolia blossoms, and tidal swamp, and Eloise could have sworn there was some sort of steam or mist rising off the filled mug. The nightjar nodded at the bottle. "Anyone else care for a beakful of the finest slime-like beverage produced within a thousand strong lengths?"

Jerome shook his head and addressed the others. "Don't. I had some once. Maybe a quarter of a thimble full. I was hammered speechless for two days."

"Thank you for offering to share," said Eloise. "But I think I'll pass."

"Suit yourself. More for me then." Göööber poked his beak in the cup, took a long glug of the green glop, smacked his beak, belched miraculously loudly, and sighed. "I swear, this would have straightened

Çalaht's hair, at least, during those few months of her divine life when non-believers were doing their best to pull it out."

"Blessed be her memory," said Eloise. "So, tell me, if you can't just fly into the Eastern Lands, what are you going to do?"

"I'm going to just fly into the Eastern Lands."

"Oh? How?"

"At night. Under the cover of a new moon's darkness. While the attack hummingbird squadron are having their midnight tea break. Wearing black camouflage. Gliding, so there's no wing noise. And maybe while having lit an explosive diversion somewhere else to draw away attention. That bit I'll have to think through once I'm at Flachberg."

"Really?"

"Yep."

"This sounds like you've done it before."

"Of course I have. It's a number 27 from the nightjar stealth menu."

Eloise looked at him. "You're kidding."

Göööber glanced left and right, like he was making sure they weren't being overheard, then leaned forward and whispered, "Yes, oppressor of hard-working people everywhere. I'm kidding." He leaned about. "I'm kidding about the menu thing, but not about how I intend to cross the border."

"Right." Distracted, Eloise ignored once again how he'd referred to her, and stabbed a piece of tempura cauliflower and bit it. "Oh, my! That's unexpected. Wow."

"Good, eh?" said Jerome.

"Mhmmm," said Eloise, spearing a chunk of broccoli. "Amazing. I wonder if we could send the new Chef here for some pointers."

"Good idea."

They focused on eating for a full ten minutes, enjoying a few moments of unexpected pleasure in the midst of such unmitigated dumpitude.

When the last battered veggie chunk was gone, Göööber asked, "So, what exactly are you trying to find out? Am I going to be able to see it at night, or am I going to have to rethink my approach?"

"I'm not sure," said Eloise. "Something that looks off. Militarily."

"If I may, Your H—, ma'am, I think specificity is important here," said Lorch. "What we're looking for are signs of military build-up, unusual training patterns or deployments, obvious efforts to hide people or materiel, or movements of unusual scope or scale."

"Is that sort of thing supposed to be going on?" asked the bird.

"Officially, no. Unofficially, we don't know," said Eloise. "Which is where we hope you can bring enlightenment. Do you have any military in your background? Will you be able to recognize what we're looking for?"

The nightjar rustled his wing feathers. "I'm not a spy. I don't have tradecraft. The closest I ever got to the military was a short, unsuccessful stint as a Bird Scout. They threw me out because I didn't like standing in lines. But I get what you're talking about. If it's there, I'd be surprised if I couldn't see it."

"So, Master de Caprimulgidae. You'll help me out?" said Eloise.

"Yes. I will."

"Good. Thank you. You'll have my gratitude."

"And your coin."

"Yes, there's that as well. Please speak with Lorch, and only Lorch, for any arrangements you might need to make. We need to keep this close."

"As you wish." The bird slurped a little more sludge from his cup.

"One last thing," said Eloise.

"Yes?"

"Have I ever oppressed you personally?"

"What?" Göööber took a step back. "No. Not you personally, but—"

"Have I personally ever oppressed anyone that you know?"

"Um, no, but—"

Eloise stood, and the others did the same. "Then please do me the kindness of not referring to me as the oppressor of hardworking people, either to my face or behind my back. It's annoying. I've now allowed you your full quota of that particular annoyance. No more. Understood?"

Göööber looked at her and smiled as much as his beak would allow. "Yes, Your Highness. Understood."

"Good. Then boring travels to you, Master de Caprimulgidae."

47

OBJECT OF HER IRE

Eloise declared "executive time" again so that she could spend a few hours in the Bibliotheca de Records and Regrets looking at Queen Gwendolyn's documents with Jerome. Having left a basket of rhubarb and custard tarts at the Head Scribe's desk, they'd made their way to room GCEG 19/27, where they'd been examining babies for several hours.

"What do you have there?" she asked when she heard Jerome grunt. She'd noticed that Jerome had several distinct grunts that he used with almost cyclic regularity. There was his grunt of, "This is the stupidest document I have ever seen in my life." There was the grunt that meant, "Why didn't this jester get remedial quillmanship when they were young so people could read their ink scratchings a hundred years later?" There was one kind of grunt that meant Jerome was starting to think about lunch, another signified he'd nodded off and had just snapped back awake, while another was, "Oh crud, I may have damaged a baby."

Then there was the grunt of, "Actually, this is kind of interesting, even if I can't quite articulate it yet." That's what Eloise had heard, which prompted her question.

"Sorry, what?" said Jerome vaguely.

"What did you find?"

Jerome looked up at her, down at the scroll, and back. "Oh, nothing in particular. The last few documents that I've looked at are about Queen Gwendolyn's preparations for going to war with the Northern Lands."

"What about them?"

"There's all this talk about readiness, retribution, and Çalaht-derived destiny. The underlying sense of her rage is everywhere. But there's no mention of King Brüüütus himself. The actual person that she's furious with is never mentioned by name, and only once or twice by title."

"So?"

"So why? Given how angry she was—and let's remember that she was pregnant, and, with respect, therefore likely extremely hormonal—this omission of the object of her ire strikes me as a strange absence. There's so much effort and so much applied force of will going into war preparations, but the person it's directed at is missing."

"Interesting," said Eloise. "From everything we know of Queen Gwendolyn, you really didn't want to get on her bad side. Her vitriol was personal. And sustained."

"True," said Jerome. "I remember a story about her forcing someone who ticked her off to spend the next month eating nothing but durian and drinking only kale juice."

"Really? Ugh."

"I know. Cruel and unusual punishment."

Eloise scrunched her face. "That's not the kind of queen I want to be."

"I don't think you have to worry about that. It doesn't seem like your approach to anything. I mean, can you imagine sitting on the throne in the Throne Hall and decreeing, 'You, knave! Durian only! Kale juice only!"

"No. No, I can't."

"That's right. You can't."

"Nor can I imagine calling anyone 'knave.' Too antiquated." Eloise tugged on the fingers of her cotton gloves. "Are you sure that you have the right period in history?"

"It's Gwendolyn. No doubt about that."

"That's not what I mean. I'm wondering if you have the wrong part of Gwendolyn's story. Maybe the babies you've been reading are part of the conflict in the time before Queen Gwendolyn and King Brüüütus met up, parlayed, and had their days of romantic bliss. Maybe you're looking at the war preparations from before she got in the family way —before the rejection, the hormones, and the personal rage against the Northo king. Not the war she waged in response to him dropping her after their dalliance."

"I hadn't thought of that."

"It would explain Brüüütus' absence. It wasn't personal at that point."

"I guess that explanation could work."

"It's still the same era, just earlier. But we know Melveeta was there, loyally serving her sister the queen. She told Johanna and me about it. Melveeta and her command of the Star of Whatever were used as a weapon in that war. Just not in the earlier part of it. It's possible you're looking at babies from weeks or months before the Purple Haze was created. I doubt it'd be more than 18 months out."

"Then I'll keep looking."

"Any sign of Melveeta or the Star of Whatever at all in there?"

"Nope."

"She has to be here somewhere. All we can do is keep looking."

"Yep."

❧ 48 ❧

KITES. SONGS. JAMBOREE

he second one had picked another odious, out-of-the-way meeting place—the alley behind a public inn that catered to maggots and flies—and the cloaked figure's patience, which had been fraying for weeks, was on the verge of snapping. He'd never been very good at duplicity, and it worried him that he'd let something slip that he shouldn't. So what if keeping secrets was two-fifths of what he did every day. With his mother at stake, his nerves were getting the better of him, which he feared would make him sloppy.

The second one slithered around the corner, tasting the air with his tongue, searching for unexpected observers. The first one shivered when the third eye locked onto him, held his attention, and seemed fixed in space as the curled blue body pushed its way forward. "G'late evening to you." Ever polite. Ever with the sincerity of an ink-squirting boutonnière.

"What do you want this time?"

"What, no small talk? No inquiries as to one's health? No questions about the well-being of one's captives?"

"We are not friends, associates, or colleagues. Your desire for small talk can bite my fundament."

The snake closed his two normal eyes in mock exasperation. "We're not friends? And here I thought we were getting along so well."

The cloaked one was not to be diverted. "Again, I ask, what do you want this time?"

The snake coiled himself in a neat pile at the cloaked one's feet. Not so close that he was likely to get kicked or stepped on and crushed, but close enough to get in a good bite, if the situation dictated it. Not that he was a biter. His kind were more constrictors. And that's what he was doing to this human—squeezing him, in part to see how much tightness he could stand. "What have the spies revealed?"

"I don't know what you're talking about."

"Spies were sent. Spies report back. I'm asking what they reported."

"They observed massing of troops in the strong lengths around the border crossing at Flachberg. What did you think they would find?"

"A fun, if large, training exercise aimed at improving troop morale and readiness. Lots of songs. Good food. Some marching. But nothing to worry about."

"That's not what the spies reported."

"Of course not. But it's what you'll report. I give you my assurance that what your spies think they saw was not what they saw. Yes, it happened to be near the border. Yes, there were a lot of them. But it's more in the nature of a jamboree. Feel free to use that word. It's a happy word. A fun word. 'Jamboree.' Makes me want to build a kite and fly it. Oh, that's good. Kites. Put some kites into your report."

"Kites."

"Kites."

The cloaked one stared hard at the snake, who left his normal eyes closed and bored in with the third one. The cloaked one gritted his teeth, choking back innumerable, anatomically improbable suggestions as to what the snake could do with his kites. But he broke eye contact first.

As he always did.

"Kites. Songs. Jamboree." The snake slowly blinked his strange eye. "Got it?"

"Got it."

"Say it."

"Say what?"

"Say what it is that you've got."

"Kites, songs, jamboree. I said I got it."

"I'll let your mother know what a good boy you've been."

Anger flared, and without thinking, the first one struck forward with a hard step that would have broken a spine had it landed.

But it didn't land. It slapped the cobblestones weak lengths away.

By Çalaht's scabies and buboes, he hated humans. The snake was slower than he should have been due to the cold, but he didn't care. He flung himself not away, but forward, wrapping himself around the cloaked one's leg, then climbing up his body, ignoring the hands that tried to snatch him away. He reached the first one's neck and encircled it using a move he'd learned when he was a grunt in the first week of boot camp. He constricted his coils, choking off air and causing drastic flailing. The first one fell backward onto the ground, kicking and thrashing. The second one held on and tightened. "That was anti-social. Ill-advised. Stupid."

"Stop," choked out the first one, barely audible.

The snake tightened even more. He knew how much it took to break a human neck or crush a windpipe. But this buffoon just needed some severe bruising to make sure he had something to contemplate when he looked in the mirror. Clearly, he didn't have a sufficient level of fear.

"You really don't value your mother's fingers. Or maybe it's her tongue you don't value. Perhaps a kidney. Did you know that one can remove a kidney, and if infection doesn't set in, one can survive? I found that fascinating when first I learned of it. Even more fascinating when I was able to independently verify it."

The first one's ability to fight off the blackness of unconsciousness waned, and his kicking lessened. If he hadn't felt like he was dying, he would have cried. Knelt, cried, and begged for forgiveness.

The snake tightened just a little more. "Kites. Songs. Jamboree," he hissed, his mouth right at the other one's ear. "It remains to be seen if the price of that stunt was a finger, a tongue, or a kidney. Your ability to convey the sense of kites, songs, and jamboree to that child with a crown will come into that decision. The greater your success, the less damage will be inflicted. Slap the ground with your palm if you understand."

The first one hit the ground with a weak palm.

"Pathetic, but that will have to do." He loosened his coils and released the first one, who rolled onto his side gasping for breath. "I'm watching," said the snake. "In more ways than you can imagine. Now go do what you've been told, you rancid excuse for a person." With that, he left the cloaked one rubbing his neck and doing his best to draw in the frigid winter's night air.

❦   49   ❧

PRECISE, VERY STRAIGHT ROWS

Unlike the stark black tunics and dresses that Lady Seneschal Älphonsinä Póöòmáäàdéëè always wore, her office was a floral explosion. From the upholstery to the wallpaper to the tchotchkes, it was a riot of rhododendrons, a pandemonium of pansies, an anarchy of agapanthus, a turmoil of tulips, a ruckus of roses. It was her private sanctuary away from the storms of castle and Court, and the overwhelming floral theme gave her a chance to retreat into what she thought of as beauty.

She rarely had people in there, and when she did, it was usually staff there for a scolding or to be relieved of their position. Social visits were out.

Which made the Eastern Lands' ambassador's visit there so out of the ordinary.

"Thank you for having me," said Picholine Manzanilla. "It is an honor to visit you here."

"I thought it would be a nice change to the cafe."

"It is, it is." Picholine Manzanilla moved around the lushly decorated room with an approving nod. "I like what you've done with your office.

Mine leans more toward an olive tree motif, but the use of flowers works very well for you."

"Thank you."

There was a knock at the door.

"Come on in," said Lady Seneschal.

Läääcy de Aardvark eased herself into the room, balancing an over-sized tray. "Your tea, Lady Seneschal." She set down the tea service on a coffee table. "Haggleberry tea for you, ma'am, and olive leaf tea for the Mistress Ambassador."

"Thank you, Läääcy."

"I'll mention that Chef said he'd never made olive leaf tea before, so if it isn't suitable, please, let me know, and I'll bring something else."

"I'm sure it will be fine," said Manzanilla.

The aardvark turned back toward the door. "Stäääcy, come on in." A second, almost identical aardvark stepped in, placed a silver tray next to the tea set, then stepped back with a bow. "The snack tray you requested, ma'am."

"Thank you."

"It looks very nice, ma'am."

"Good to hear."

"May I pour your tea, ma'am?" asked Läääcy.

"I'll get it. That will be all."

"Yes, ma'am."

Lady Seneschal hefted the teapot with the olive leaf tea and poured the ambassador her cup. "I hope you don't mind meeting here rather than at the cafe."

"It's a nice change. And I get to see where you work, which is nice." Manzanilla lifted her teacup, blew across it, sipped, and nodded. "And that's a perfectly adequate cup of tea."

"Good." Lady Seneschal lifted her cup. "Cheers, then."

"We say, 'May your life be full like the olives fruiting in your orchards.'"

"Well, then, may your life be full like the olives fruiting in your orchards."

"Cheers," said the ambassador.

Lady Seneschal picked up the snack tray. "Can I interest you in a potato knish? They're not fancy, but to me, they're comfort food. As you don't care for sweets, I thought you might enjoy them."

"My mother made these before she went to stand with Çalaht," said Manzanilla. "Of course, she added chopped olives. But, I too, think of knishes as comfort food."

The two women talked of nothings, comfortable in the friendship that had formed between them. Eventually discussion turned, inevitably, to Court. "So, how are things?" asked Manzanilla.

"I'd say about the same, more or less. There's a sense of normality returning."

"That must be comforting."

Lady Seneschal nibbled a knish. "You know, I never think to ask, how are things for you at home? How fares the Eastern Lands court?"

"I'm glad to be away from it," said the ambassador. "Intrigues are not my thing. I do get dispatches and updates from Her Majesty, but to be honest, I'm happy to be away when this sort of thing goes on."

"What sort of thing?"

Manzanilla waved off the question. "It's nothing."

"Go ahead. You can tell me."

"It's silly, really."

Lady Seneschal gave her the space to decide whether to say anything. She found that sometimes if she just let the silence be, people will often fill it. After a solid twenty seconds, the ambassador puffed her cheeks and blew out a stream of air. "OK, I'll tell you. But you'll keep it to yourself.

"Of course."

"Her Majesty likes parades."

"Parades? What kind of parades?"

"Parades with soldiers. Lots of soldiers and guards wearing fancy clothes and marching around in precise, very straight rows. She has one coming up soon." The ambassador rolled her eyes. "She's very particular about the rows and how far apart everyone is spaced, and how they hold their swords or pikes or whatever they're carrying."

"Why?"

"It's the way she is. And Çalaht forbid if you get something wrong. At one parade, a regiment of guards let their line get all squiggly and she forbade them from having olives for two months."

"That seems awfully severe."

Manzanilla tilted her head and nodded. "It gutted them."

"So what do people do?"

"They practice. Practice, practice, practice and then they practice some more. My reports tell me that a few battalions have found an out-of-the way spot on the western border—near some hole called Flachberg, I think—and they're marching day and night, making sure everything is perfect."

"That sounds very dedicated."

"It sounds incredibly tedious, if you ask me. Soldiers and guards marching around making sure their lines are straight? Please, give me a break." Manzanilla looked around to make sure they weren't being overheard. "It's exactly the reason I tried to get a diplomatic role."

"Oh?"

"Yes. For a while there, Her Majesty had me in charge of parades."

"Parades. You were in charge of parades. That seems so unlike you."

"I was pretty good at it," said Manzanilla. "But it wasn't my thing. So here I am, enjoying knishes with my new friend." She reached across the coffee table and gave Lady Seneschal's knee a little pat, then she snagged another knish from the tray and popped the whole thing in her mouth. "So, Älphonsinä. If you happen to hear about anything going on near Flachberg, just think of me, and how grateful I am not to be on the parade ground there barking orders at soldiers."

"I'll do that."

$$\clubsuit \quad 50 \quad \clubsuit$$

CROCHET HERESY

The late Queen Eloise (Two, not One) held regular audiences in the Receiving Room as far back as Eloise could remember, normally three or four times a week. Every now and then, she'd tell Eloise and Johanna to watch the proceedings from the side, commanding them to remain still and not make any noise. Usually, the twins had found it all as dull as dirt, and being forced to observe felt like a penance. But every now and then, there was a matter that struck the young girls' fancy, and they'd watch carefully.

For example, there was a rival pair of quinoa farmers, one who had a missing leg and the other a missing arm. Each complained that the other's crop variety was invading theirs, spoiling the purity (one grew white, the other red). The argument got so heated that the one-legged man had his wooden prosthesis stolen by the one-armed neighbor, who had it graffitied with uncomplimentary sayings before returning it. The one-legged farmer retaliated by stealing the other man's fake arm, then having the carved wooden hand recut so it looked like it was constantly making a rude gesture. The entire village was forced to take one side or the other, and everyone cascaded into recrimination and acrimony. Eventually they'd appealed to the queen to settle the matter.

Then there was the time a querulous noble tried to force everyone in his principality to speak only in iambic pentameter.

Or the merchant who sold "wondrous tonics" that promised to "transform anyone who drank them in the dark of night by a full moon's light." And it was true—anyone who drank his potions had their teeth permanently stained purple—but he timed his sales in a way that ensured he was long gone by the designated night.

As Eloise sat on the Listening Throne wearing the Keep It Quick I Have Stuff To Do Cape, it occurred to her that nothing she was hearing now was anywhere near as novel as those cases. These sessions made her uncomfortable. Those seeking justice made her feel like she didn't know nearly enough about the rules and laws of the land, nor how magistrates work, or any of that legal-ish stuff. Those who sought trade concessions made her realize just how little she knew about commerce. Those who made diplomatic representations usually spoke with such cagey obfuscation that she could barely understand what they were saying.

Over and over she leaned on First Advisor to intercede on her behalf, but this also made her feel bad. She was torn between fearing that she'd appear weak for consulting with him at all, and not wanting to make a bad decision.

Plus, between her research in the Bibliotheca de Records and Regrets, the futile efforts to find out more about who had her mother killed, and the briefings and behind-the-scenes decisions she had to make, Eloise was doing well to receive people twice a week.

Which meant things were piling up.

Which meant that each session seemed to go on longer and longer.

Which meant that sometimes, Eloise wished that someone, *anyone*, would do her the kindness of standing up, speaking up, keeping it simple, not arguing, and going away with an answer or outcome they accepted, and, where necessary, actually implemented.

"Your Highness?"

A matronly woman stood in front of Eloise. She realized she'd wafted off while this woman was speaking to her. "Sorry, can you say that again?"

"I said, as Head Knitter of the Brague Circle of Knitting Enthusiasts, on their behalf, I'd like to present you this token of our regard." She gestured toward a large, rolled, knitted item being held by six boys.

"What is it?"

"It is the largest mitten in all the realms. Our Circle has spent half a year knitting it for you. Boys, now, show her."

In a carefully rehearsed motion, the half dozen carefully stepped backward, revealing what was certainly the largest mitten Eloise had ever seen. A giant's mitten. A multi-colored feat of knitting that could house a village of mice with space for a honeymooning pair of slow lorises.

"Um, OK. Thank you? Yes, thank you for this, uh, marvelous gesture." Eloise tugged an ear, unsure what she should say, or what she was supposed to do with such a massive mitten. She said the first thing that came to mind. "Where's the other one?"

"Other one what?" asked the woman.

"The other mitten."

The knitter looked puzzled. "What other mitten?"

"Don't... Don't mittens usually come in pairs? I just assumed there'd be two, that's all."

The woman's face flushed and her eyes widened. She looked down at her feet, over at the mitten, and then back at her feet.

One of the boys muttered, "I told you."

"Shh!" snapped Head Knitter. "Good point, Your Highness. Our Circle did, in fact, think of that. We decided that, as it was taking so very long, a single mitten was—"

"One mitten is fine. Really. I shouldn't have said anything."

"No, you're right, Your Highness. Mittens come in pairs," she said. "Perhaps we can spend the coming half year—"

"One mitten is fine. Really," said Eloise. "It's a gesture, right? Symbolic. It's not like you're expecting anything to come of the mitten? It's simply a grand expression of mitten-ness. For which I'm duly grateful."

The woman looked down at her feet again, and said nothing.

"It *is* a gesture, isn't it?"

Again, no response.

"Oh, by Çalaht's repetitious ramblings. It isn't just a gesture. You have an agenda." Eloise forced a smile. "Right. Please, go ahead."

Head Knitter seemed too embarrassed to speak.

"It's those blasted crocheters." It was the boy again. "They're harassing us. We need you to make them stop."

"Crocheters? Harassing? Why would crocheters have cause to harass knitters?"

"They're evil," said the boy. "The Militant Cadre of Crochet Activists. Evil, spiteful, and self-righteous."

"Evan, shush," said Head Knitter.

"I won't hush, and it's true."

"I see," Eloise said, although she didn't. "Evan, is it? Can you step forward?"

The boy let go his part of the huge mitten, causing the thumb to droop unceremoniously. As the other five scrambled to de-droop the mitten thumb, the boy stepped forward to stand next to Head Knitter.

"Why, exactly, do you say they're evil, spiteful, and self-righteous?"

"It's obvious, isn't it? They come around to our weekly craft gatherings and try to lord it over us." He mimicked a sarcastic, taunting tone. "'Our yarn art only requires one hook. Knitting takes two needles. That makes us more efficient.' Which is hooey. 'We complete each stitch one at a time, whereas knitting keeps all those stitches open while you work.' Which, truth be told, is true. But it doesn't make knitting less. It's just different."

Head Knitter piped in. "Evan's right. Those old crochet biddies go on and on and on about how crocheting is so blinking wonderful, so blinking perfect with their completed stitches and simpler tools. But the openness of knitted stitching is the point! Openness! Flexibility! Open stitches, open mind. That's what we say."

"They think they're so clever with their skullcaps, their socks, and their arboreal stunts," said Evan.

"Arboreal stunts?" asked Eloise. "Oh, wait. Are they the ones who do the tree cozies?"

"The same," spat the boy.

"Those are cute." Eloise looked at First Advisor. "Have you seen them? They're tea cozies, but for trees."

"Sounds fun," said Ligurian in a tone that indicated "fun" wasn't high on his list of priorities.

"Fun? To desecrate a tree that way?" said Head Knitter. "It's just showing off. It's disrespectful to the trees and to the spirit of yarn."

"I thought the tree cozies showed whimsy and a sense of playfulness," said Eloise.

"Sense of playfulness? Yarn is serious stuff. One does not crack jokes with yarn, whether you're knitting or, Çalaht forbid, crocheting. It's unseemly."

"Right. I see." What Eloise saw was that the people before her seemed devoid of humor. "And what, exactly, are you asking me to do?" She smoothed the cape over her lap, which gave her hands something to do that didn't involve throwing objects in frustration.

"You, Your Highness." The boy pointed his index finger at Eloise. "You should ban them. Ban crocheting. All of it. Ban their petty little hooks and their swaggering stitching. Ban their 'Knitting is so last century' and their 'We can crochet circles around you pathetic knitters.' We're not pathetic, and you should tell them that. We want you to ban the Militant Canker of Crochet Activists and their ilk, once and for all."

"'Cadre,' not 'canker,' Evan," said Head Knitter.

"Whatever. The point is that those heathens refuse to acknowledge knitting as the One True Form of yarn craft."

"One true form?" said Eloise. "You're saying no one should ever crochet?"

"That's right," said Head Knitter. "Knitting is the One True Form. Çalaht herself was known to knit booties and mittens. In this, we follow her divine path, Through knitting, we achieve a closeness to her holy ways. In our circle, we say, 'Knit one, purl two, pray three.'"

"That seems like it might be limiting. Like you are closing yourself off to other forms of yarn-based expression."

"Exactly," said Evan.

"What about something like macramé?"

The boy's eyes flew wide. "Heresy!"

"Broomstick lace?" asked Eloise. "It uses a crochet hook and something thin and straight like a knitting needle. Plus, it uses an open stitch, like knitting does."

"An excellent question, Your Highness," said Head Knitter. "We think of people who commit acts of broomstick lace as misguided souls, but not damned, since they're halfway to the salvation of proper knitting. They might still make it to glory and paradise."

"I see." And in a twisted way, she sort of did. It was known that Çalaht had knitted, although Eloise wasn't sure she never picked up a crochet hook. Still, people had all sorts of notions. It was clear to her, however, that not all of them needed to be taken seriously.

Eloise looked at Leccino Ligurian, standing respectfully at the edge of the dais, face blank. She waved him over.

He stepped up and came near. "Yes, Your Highness?"

Eloise lowered her voice so only he could hear. "Were you aware that there was anything behind the giant mitten?"

"To be honest, no. I thought it was a gesture of esteem. Apologies. They were not screened as well as they should have been."

"Any suggestions on a graceful way of getting out of this?"

"Your mother was fond of saying, 'I shall take the matter under advisement and give it full consideration.'"

"That doesn't actually mean anything."

"Precisely."

Ligurian stepped away again and Eloise addressed the knitters. "Thank you again for this glorious mitten. The queendom shall cherish it with all the respect it deserves." Given that they were talking about a lone, massive mitten, it was not clear how much that would be.

"Thank you, Queen Eloise," said Head Knitter, obviously pleased.

"As for the other issue, thank you for bringing your concerns to my attention. I shall take the matter under advisement and give it my full consideration. That will suffice?" Although the last sentence was phrased as a question, Eloise spoke it as a statement. From Head Knitter's and the boy's smiles, it looked like the prevarication had worked. The knitters rolled up the mitten, handed it to half a dozen pages, and Head Knitter, Evan, and the rest of them bowed their way from the hall.

"What's next?" Eloise asked Ligurian.

"I am next," said a haughty voice. A mare came in from the hallway. Eloise recognized the stately gait, the unusual, sharply divided, black and white coloring and the smear of ocher in the white blaze on her forehead. She came to the dais, bowed perfunctorily, and said, "I have returned from the Central Ranges."

"Welcome back, Naranbaatar Enkhtuya," said Eloise, surprising herself by remembering the name. She'd wondered what had happened to the mare. "I hope your journey was pleasant."

"It was a journey," said the mare in a tone that said every one was the same and not worth noting. "To business. I conferred with His Alacrity Khan Nergüi Unbenannt Nimetuseta and conveyed your utterances to him."

Utterances? That was a bit dismissive. "I see. And?"

"His Alacrity does not accede to your demand."

"No?"

"No. His instruction to me is as it was before. I am to present my credentials to you as envoy from the Us."

"I find that disappointing."

"His Alacrity anticipated that response."

"Did he now."

"He did. His suggestion is that the Central Ranges be represented by two envoys. Me, on behalf of the Us. And another, on behalf of the Not Us and the savages."

"I'm not sure I like the precedent that sets," said Eloise. "Court can't accommodate representatives for every different species. We'd be over-run. Just as we have to aggregate representation by geography, so must we aggregate across peoples."

"If Her Highness would prefer that there not be representation from the Us, little sleep would be lost. You are well within your right." Enkhtuya stood with that unnerving stillness as she spoke.

Eloise believed her. The Us were so insular, so completely self-contained, that if she chose not to accept the mare as envoy, she'd lose contact with the horse tribe. That was a connection she'd rather not break, if for no other reason than that it had cost so much to establish it.

"Did your khan have someone in mind to act as representative?"

"He did not care," said Enkhtuya. "He left that to me."

That rankled. Did the khan value Eloise so little?

Probably. As far as she could tell, what happened in the Western Lands and All That Really Matters had little bearing on the life of the Us. "And did you find someone to take on the position?"

"I did. In my pouch, you'll find my credentials documents. Next to them is a container and a smaller scroll. You may remove them, if you like."

As he had weeks before, First Advisor opened the pouch's flap and reached inside. He removed a hemp parchment scroll, a second, much smaller scroll, and a stoppered, black pottery jar. He set the jar on the dais and passed the documents to Eloise.

"I am Naranbaatar Enkhtuya. I offer my credentials as the representative of His Alacrity Khan Nergüi Unbenannt Nimetuseta and the Us."

"Welcome to Court, Naranbaatar Enkhtuya," said Eloise.

"First Advisor," said the mare. "If you could open the jar, please."

Ligurian removed the cork from the jar, pulling it out with an echoing, liquid *pop!* The tang of something alcoholic wafted out.

Enkhtuya nodded at the open jar. "Your Highness, may I introduce Silvestre de Gusano-Rojo."

Everyone looked at the open jar and waited.

And waited.

And waited.

Nothing happened.

"Excuse me," said the mare. She stepped forward so that she could lean over the mouth of the jar and shout. "I said, may I introduce Silvestre de Gusano-Rojo."

Again, nothing.

"Apologies, Your Highness." The mare slapped her hoof on the wooden dais next to the jar, hard enough to make a loud *bang!*, bounce the vessel into the air several weak lengths and have it thunk back down. "Silvestre, you worm! You missed your cue. Get out here!"

"Spork me," slurred a voice from inside. "I'm sporking coming. No need to scare the spork out of me like that, you sporking..." The voice trailed off as Silvestre struggled to emerge from the mouth of the jar.

Flopping himself upward, Sylvester managed to stay on the edge.

It was an actual worm. Eloise had thought Enkhtuya was being metaphoric. Apparently not. His reddish, segmented body, with a black tip at one end, swayed unsteadily on the lip of the jar.

"I'm..." The worm belched. "Sorry. I'm Silvestre de Gusano-Rojo. Pleased..." Another burp. "Sorry. Pleased to make your acquaintance." He bowed.

"Other direction," said the mare.

"Right. Sorry." The worm rotated and bowed in Eloise's general direction. "Your High—" *Hic!* "Your Highness. Sorry, I don't see too well."

Eloise looked down at the worm, then back at the mare. "You chose a worm to represent the Not Us and the ones you call savages."

"Technically, I'm not a worm," said Silvestre. "I'm actually..." He hiccuped. "I'm actually a larva."

Eloise frowned at Enkhtuya. "You selected a juvenile moth to represent all the non-equine peoples of the Central Ranges. Is he qualified at all? Does he have any experience?"

"I have no idea. It matters not to me." The mare flicked her mane. "I consider that an issue between you and him."

"Whoa!" The larva flopped out of the jar and splashed onto the dais. "Sorry. Sorry, sorry, sorry."

"Is he... Is he drunk?"

The mare shifted a shoulder upward, as close to a shrug as horses got. "He does live in a bottle of mezcal."

"Mezcal. He lives in a bottle of mezcal." Eloise shook her head in disbelief. "Is he ever anywhere close to sober?"

"Not from what I can tell. But then, I've only known him a day or two. We met at a public inn near the border between our two realms. I was about to cross the boundary when I realized I had not fulfilled my khan's desire for me to choose another envoy. Silvestre was conveniently located, pliable, amenable, and easily transported. All good qualities. So here we are."

"Here we are, indeed." Eloise glanced at Ligurian, who kept his face steadily blank. "First Advisor, could you please read Master de Gusano-Rojo's qualifications out loud?"

"Of course, Your Highness." Carefully, he unscrolled the smaller document. "It says, 'Brap.'"

"Brap?"

"Brap. It's in italic, if that helps."

"Master de Gusano-Rojo," said Eloise. "What does 'Br—'"

"*Brrrrrrraaaaaaapppppp!*" It was the longest, loudest larva belch Eloise had ever heard, impressive for the scope of its endeavor. The smell of mezcal filled the room.

Silence followed. A long, awkward silence.

The mezcal worm righted himself, stood as best he could on his back sets of legs, gave a passable bow roughly in Eloise's direction, and said, "I'm Silvestre de Gusano-Rojo, and I shall be the envoy to your fair queendom on behalf of the Not Us and so-called savages of the Central Ranges, if you'll be so kind as to accept her credentials on behalf of... Uh... Actually, leave that bit out. No one really sent me. She just picked me up at the pub and said she had a job for me. I said, 'Do I need to do anything?' And she said, 'Probably not.' And I said, 'Perfect!' So she picked up my mezcal bottle, and voilà! Here we are. I'll be an ambassador, for sure!"

Then the larva keeled over and began to snore.

Eloise raised an eyebrow at the mare.

"I can't say that went exactly as expected," said Enkhtuya. "But, given what we now know of him, perhaps it's also not completely unexpected."

"No," said Eloise.

"I shall endeavor to find a more suitable representative of the Not Us and the savages. Perhaps one a little less..."

"Snockered?"

"Yes."

"That would be good."

❧ 51 ❧

NOPE

Eloise poked her head into yet another dust-caked, records-filled room. She was pretty sure it was 4,000,000,000/27. Jerome was hunched over a baby at the table. "Anything yet?" she asked.

"Nope."

"It's been days. Weeks."

"Yep."

"Well, keep going. I'll join you when I can."

"Absolutely."

52

AFOOT

Another miserable, snowy night. Another dark, hidden corner.

"Report," said the second one.

"No suspicions, from what I can tell," said the first one.

"Good. Keep it that way. Things are afoot, but slowly, so as to not be obvious."

"When will something happen?"

"When it happens."

53

UNMITIGATED CATASTROPHIC DISAPPOINTMENT

Eloise and Jerome were elbow-deep in documents from room GCEG 33/27. By now, the routine was familiar: Eloise declared executive time, they'd trundle over to the Bibliotheca de Records and Regrets, say hello to the Head Scribe or Master Overbolt, whoever was on duty, leave a basket of baked goods for "safe keeping" so they might be enjoyed later by one or the other of them, pull on their cotton gloves, arm themselves with a brush, dust pan, and bag, don a mask against the dust, and spend as many hours as they could removing the residue of decades from crates, bins, boxes, and cartons, then digging into ancient scrolls, hoping against hope they'd actually find something useful.

It was in a box labeled "Travels" that Eloise found something that scratched at her awareness just the tiniest bit. She humphed softly, but it was loud enough that Jerome looked up from the scroll he was reading, A Proposal to Consolidate the Table Grape Vineyards of Upper Slalom. "You find something?" he asked.

"It's a list."

"Ooooh. Those are always exciting. What's on the list?"

"Stuff."

"Stuff? What kind of stuff?"

"Stuff with annotations." Eloise pointed to a random item on the list and read. "'A needle, found near the village of Splink that, when threaded with blue thread, will magically sew stitches of even length, no matter what the skill of the sewer. Efficacy: dubious.' I could have used something like that when Seamstress Linttrap was teaching Johanna and me to sew. I was terrible."

"Yes, you were," said Jerome. "You still are. Fortunately, neat stitching is not required in your current role."

"Thank goodness for small blessings. Here's another. 'Brunchberry diviner, purchased from an elderly numbat on the Elysium Road. The branched twig supposedly could magically assist in the finding of ripe brunchberry bushes. Efficacy: very high if standing in a bunchberry patch. Otherwise, unproven.' Huh."

"Huh," agreed Jerome.

"It's just that, it's... I dunno. It's familiar somehow. Come have a look. Does it look familiar to you? Or does anything strike you?"

Jerome walked across the table to where Eloise worked. Careful not to disturb the scroll, he leaned over and read the title: "'Acquisitions During Collections.' OK, I'm looking." He hummed a little, walking around the open scroll and looking at it from different angles. "Still looking. And nope."

"Nope?"

"Nope. Nothing's really making me think, 'Oh, wow.' Or even, 'Huh.'"

The two of them stared at it. Eloise imitated Jerome and walked around the table so she could look at it from different angles. "Hold it."

Jerome reached to pick up the scroll.

"Not that way," said Eloise. "Wait, I have an idea. Have a good last look at it."

Jerome looked. "OK."

"Now come with me. We'll be right back, so I'm going to leave this here."

"OK. I just hope Head Scribe doesn't happen by and find it unattended."

"What's he going to do? Yell at me?"

"I wouldn't put it past him."

"Come on."

They walked from GCEG 33/27 out into the hall and into GCEG 12/27. Eloise moved to the third aisle, found a bin labeled "Championings," opened it, and retrieved a scroll. As carefully as ever, she spread the scroll out on the reading table.

Jerome read the title. "'Queen's Tithes.' Another fascinating document."

"Notice anything about this one that reminds you of the other?"

"Uh, they're both dull?"

"Look at it carefully."

"I'm looking. I'm looking." Jerome peered at it. "OK, I've looked."

"The quillmanship," said Eloise. "I think the same person wrote both."

"Yeah, I can see that."

"This one was definitely written by Melveeta the Elusive. See, each line where she records the tithes collected is initialed 'MG,' for Melveeta Gumball. And here..." She pointed to the bottom. "Here she's signed it."

"Right. OK. I see where you're heading with this. That thing with the brunchberry diviner and the sewing needle. They're magical objects."

"They're *allegedly* magical objects. Come on. Let's go back." Eloise rescrolled the record of tithes just like Head Scribe had instructed, and they walked back toward GCEG 33/27. "Melveeta talked about this when Johanna and I were with her."

"She spoke of tithes?"

"Sort of. She was Queen Gwendolyn's sister and champion, right?"

"You mentioned that before, yes."

"She told us about how she traveled with Gwendolyn, and how the queen had a fascination with magic. Melveeta was always on the lookout for things that might be magical. That Acquisitions During Collection baby might be her list of purchases."

Eloise opened the door to GCEG 33/27 and went back to the table where the scroll lay waiting. She and Jerome peered at it.

"I agree," said the chipmunk. "The quillmanship is very similar. But the loops of the loopy letters look alike, and see, there's that strange squiggle on her descenders. Is it signed?"

"Not that I can see. Let's look at the back."

Carefully, they removed the weights, turned the scroll over, and put the stones back.

"No signature. No initials," said Jerome. "We'll have to trust our eyes."

"Agree." Eloise went back to the Travels box and took out all of the scrolls, breaking Head Scribe's one-at-a-time rule. "Come help. Let's see if there are any more scrolls like that one."

They found three. After putting the rest of the babies back in their bin, they laid out all three, one next to the other.

Jerome read out a random item. "The Helm of Awwww. Cost: a backscratcher made from elm with a hand modeled on the queen's. When worn, supposedly casts a charm of cuteness, such that all who view the wearer cannot help but say, 'Awwwww...' Efficacy: total bunkum."

Eloise took a turn. "The Bag of Ordure. Seized in lieu of tithes from a peasant sharecropper near Open Soar. Allegedly yields up all manner of foulness when anything is withdrawn from it. Efficacy: Absolute. Was full of all manner of nastiness. However, no apparent magical qualities, for example, it didn't replenish itself. Basically, a sack full of dreck."

Jerome's whiskers flattened. "Ugh."

"I don't get the sense that she was particularly discerning in her purchases."

They spent several minutes looking at the lists. Melveeta's notes were generally dismissive. "Ineffectual." "Stubbornly inert." "Waste of coin." "Note: seek restitution from and retribution on purveyor." "Vile smell. Worse taste." "Junk."

"Doesn't look like she came up with much that was useful," said Jerome.

"No," agreed Eloise. "Looks like a lot of coin for a lot of nothing."

"She says as much herself."

"Come on, Jer. Let's flip them over."

The opposite sides had more of the same.

"It's disheartening to read," said Eloise. "Each of these things must have raised hopes in some way, and there was one disappointment after another. Oh!"

"What?"

"Hold on," Eloise said. "I... I've got this niggle." She looked up and down the scrolls. "Unmitigated Catastrophic Disappointment."

Jerome twitched his whiskers. "That's certainly how I feel about this search. I wouldn't have put it that way, though."

"Melveeta mentioned it. It's a village somewhere."

"Charming name. 'Hi there. I'm Harold Failure. I hail from Unmitigated Catastrophic Disappointment.'"

"Jerome. Focus."

"Sorry. What did she say about Unmitigated Catastrophic Disappointment?"

Eloise tapped the table with her knuckles, thinking. "She said it was not far from Blisteringly Overwhelming Defeat. I remember the names because they were so peculiar."

"Wait, wait, wait—I recognize that name."

"Blisteringly Overwhelming Defeat?"

"No. The other one. Unmitigated Catastrophic Disappointment."

"Really? Where from?"

"When we crossed from the Central Ranges back into the Western Lands and All That Really Matters at the Sometimes-Occupied, Royally Designated Border Xrossing Checkpoint. There was that log book that Lorch flipped through."

"The Queen's Royally Authorized Xrossing Logbook. I remember."

"He read out entries. An herbwoman declared her pukeweed. There was something about a gravedigger whose business was called No Bits Left Behind. And there was a tinker from Unmitigated Catastrophic Disappointment with a box of oddments."

"A tinker. Good memory, Jerome." Eloise paused. "Wait. A tinker? Melveeta said it was a tinker from Unmitigated Catastrophic Disappointment that she bought the box from. The box that had the Star of Whatever in it."

"What's on the acquisitions list for Unmitigated Catastrophic Disappointment?"

Eloise looked over the list. "There's just the one entry. 'Smallish wooden box allegedly containing a 'treasure trove' of magical items. Purchased from a tinker at Unmitigated...' Yada yada. 'Contents: nose ring. Blank for striking a coin. Bagel crust. Stone with a faint glow. Efficacy: Items useless, although a glowing stone could be helpful at night."' Eloise sat back on her stool. "There it is. That's where she got the Star of Whatever. That glowing stone is Sparky."

Jerome smiled. "That's kind of amazing."

Eloise nodded. "Yeah. It is."

They sat staring at the lines of writing for several minutes. Eloise tried to picture Melveeta, not as the broken, shriveled old crone she'd met at Transporters of Not Necessarily Registered, Approved, or Properly Taxed Goods Cove, but as a much younger, stronger, and capable companion to her sister the queen. She imagined Gwendolyn's champion riding from village to hovel, from town to outpost, sometimes at the queen's side, sometimes on her own on the queen's business, but always on the lookout for objects that would feed her sister's curiosity —her yearning—for a connection to the magical world. The quillmanship on Melveeta's ledger was inconsistent. Some of the notes were scrawled in thin ink with a worn quill, while others were composed neatly, with fine, dark ink drawn with a razor-sharp feather. Eloise could sense the different circumstances of their writing. Melveeta would have jotted down some while traveling, notes made in inclement weather or in a room at the top of a shabby public inn. Others, like the lines that described the box that contained the Star of Whatever, would have been written once she was back, safe and comfortable, in the embrace of Castle de Brague. It was like what Jóöôáäàqúüùíîìn had said about the corn harvest ledgers—there were so many stories to be had by just looking behind the lines even a little bit.

"History," said Jerome, breaking their reverie.

"Yes. History." Eloise patted the Star of Whatever in the box at her hip, then pointed at the line scroll. "For this little thing, history started right here."

"So now what do we do?"

"We keep looking. We found the first thread in the cloth. We have to see if there are more. Melveeta told me she conducted experiments and got better at controlling the Star. I didn't get the sense she was exactly hiding it. She also struck me as someone prone to keeping records. Maybe she kept a journal or experimental diary."

"That would be helpful," said Jerome.

"It's what I would do. It's what Johanna would do. It's what my mother would have done. Maybe Melveeta was the same."

Jerome looked around at the stacks of cartons and bins around them. "Best get to it."

"Agreed."

"What are you going to do with this list?"

Eloise very carefully removed the weights and rescrolled Melveeta's list. She removed the Gumballic Heraldic Crown from her head, put the scroll inside the dome of it, beneath a flap of fabric so it would be protected from her hair, and put it back on.

"You're stealing a baby!" Jerome gasped. "Head Scribe will have a fit!"

"Only if he finds out."

"He will! You know he will. It's like he has a weak magic for baby location. You think he won't notice your baby pilfering?"

"I guess we'll find out."

"If Head Scribe comes at me with those beady, little raccoon eyes of his, I won't be able to lie for you, Queen Eloise."

"Sure you will."

"You're asking me to lie now? Oh, Çalaht stifling stupendous sturgeons, he'll know just by looking at me! He'll read it on my face, in the quiver of my tail. I am *not* baby lying for you, El."

"Yes, you are."

Jerome's tail fluffed. "He scares me."

"Good thing you're my champion and are predisposed to protect me from such things."

"Ex-champion. And wow. Just wow."

"Come on, Jer, we have work to do."

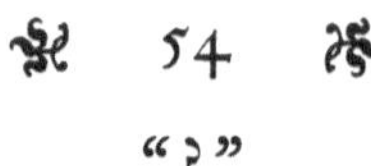

"?"

Eloise once again sat in her comfy armchair late at night holding the Star of Whatever on her lap with the lid open. She closed her eyes and sent it a silent "?".

"…" came back.

So, establishing a connection was easier this time. Interesting. She waited as the "…" seemed to suggest she should. Then…

"."

She sent a "?"

"." Then "??"

Eloise again imagined herself going down into the darkness where she found the naked mole-rat form of Sparky.

He was munching, as usual. "Loulou! Welcome back."

"Hey, Sparky."

He set down the quill and slid the parchment to the side. "You sound down. What's up?"

"Nothing," said Eloise. "Everything."

The mole-rat scrunched his nose and studied her face. "Trust issues."

Eloise looked at him. "How do you do that?"

"How do I do what?"

"That. How do you know what's going on for me?"

"I'm not sure. I just do."

"Come on, Sparky. Tell me. How do you know? You spend all your time in the box. How do you have enough awareness of the world outside to make a pronouncement like that?"

He wafted both front paws in the air with mock mysteriousness. "It's maaaaaaaaaaaaaagic."

"Stop it."

"No. Really. Something something something magic something."

Eloise waited.

"That's it, that's what I got."

"That tells me nothing."

The naked mole-rat took a nibble of his tuber. "It's the nature of things. We have this magical bond now, so I can sense your thoughts and feelings. Can't you sense what's going on for me?"

"I think I can," said Eloise. "I get a sense of you being alert or sleepy or preoccupied. I can tell when you're interested in communicating with me, or not."

"There you go," said Sparky. "Something something something magic something."

"I guess."

"So what trust thing is up for you?"

"An advisor I inherited from my mother. *She* trusted him. And I trusted her. But, I dunno. There's something I'm not sure of."

"OK."

"OK? That's what you got?"

"No, I got more."

"Go ahead."

"Trust yer guts."

Eloise looked at him. He was being serious. "Right. Good advice." She sat quietly for a full five minutes thinking about it all while he chomped his tuber. Then a thought occurred to her. "Hey! I found something today. We came across the scroll where Melveeta noted down acquiring you."

"Really."

"I thought you'd be impressed. You were in a box with a nose ring, a bagel crust, and a blank you'd use for striking a coin. She wrote that the glowing stone might be useful at night. Little did she know what was ahead for her."

"I don't remember being in a box with a bagel crust. I'll take your word for it. Whist?"

"Sure." Eloise sat down on the ground across from him while he produced the pack of cards and started shuffling. "Can I ask you something?"

"Of course."

"Can you teach me how to use magic better?"

"That's a bit like asking a hammer if it can teach you to drive a nail." The naked mole-rat dealt the cards.

"That's a 'no' then?"

"Not a strict 'no.' Presumably the hammer knows something of the driving of nails—matters of velocity, direction, force, and impact.

Some of that could be useful and informative. But it couldn't tell you about holding the handle or how to form a proper swing."

Eloise fanned out her cards and considered them. "Makes sense. So you could possibly tell me something about your perspective of what's going on, but not necessarily how to make it happen."

"Something like that, yes."

"So, tell me something." She plucked the seven of hearts from her hand and played it.

Sparky took the trick, then folded his hand. "Intention."

"Intention."

"Right. Intention."

"What about it?"

"It's fundamental to the process," said Sparky. "Without intention, nothing happens. It's why simple wishes don't work. Intention is the force that gives drive to a spell, gives it oomph. You have to gather it, focus it, and apply it. If Melveeta did anything right with the spell that she created, it was that. Her intention was there—in spades." He played a spade and took the trick to make his point.

"Intention. Got it."

"Just remember, it's simple, but it isn't necessarily easy. You can't just say, 'Now I'm applying intention' and think that's enough. The focusing of intention normally takes practice and time if you want to learn to use it with subtlety."

"Why subtlety? Why would that matter?"

"Maybe 'subtlety' is the wrong word. Maybe 'finesse' would be better. And why would you want to use it? Because if you don't, if you just brute force your way, then you end up with, say, a field full of sunflowers that won't let anything else grow there. Or a broken wrist and a dislocated shoulder."

"Right." Eloise couldn't help but rotate the shoulder Lorch had put back in its socket. There wasn't that much residual soreness. Her wrist, however, was another story. "Thank you for that. Intention. I'll keep that in mind."

Eloise turned her attention to figuring out the next card to play and lost herself in the game.

❧ 55 ☙

NEW FOREHEAD DENT

RoyLee found Eloise stretching, having just finished a late-morning run around the Culpability Courtyard. "G'mid-morning, Princess Queen Eloise."

"G'mid-morning, RoyLee."

The wombat wrinkled his snout at her. "Is there being something wrong?"

"Why?"

"Your expression be looking akin to what Gran Bunkerhunker be looking like when she finds someone in the wisdom who has mange. She be resembling a thunderstorm about two minutes before the lightning lets loose."

"I've got a bit going on, is all."

"Well, don't ever be letting Gran Bunkerhunker find you with mange. It no be pleasant."

"I promise. I won't."

"The messenger from the Half Kingdom—"

"G'late arvo," said Ziïimmÿÿÿ, arriving through an archway accompanied by a castle guard. "I hope you don't mind me coming directly, but I thought you'd want to see me as soon as possible."

"Why? What's wrong? Is my sister dead? My father?"

"No, no. Nothing like that." There was a particular sparkle in the capybara's eye and he bowed with an exquisite flourish. "Queen Eloise." He paused, letting a moment's tension build. "I bring you greetings from the Northern Lands and Queen Johanna."

"Oh! Oh, oh, oh!" Eloise rushed over to him. "Really? *Queen* Johanna? Wow. Just wow."

The messenger's smile lit his face. "Indeed. Truly, I now have the honor of serving the recently crown-plonked Queen Johanna. I bring you her letter, as well as a formal letter of introduction for me, and ambassadorial credentials to present to you at your convenience. With your permission, I will represent the Northern Lands as ambassador."

"Oh, Master Ziïimmÿÿÿ. That's excellent news. On both counts."

"It is an honor to have been entrusted so. Master Theoplonkilis will remain in his role of trade envoy. But, all that can wait." He reached into his pouch and took out a sealed envelope. "Your missive from Queen Johanna. If you wish to reply, I can arrange your letter's safe passage."

"Very good. Of course I'll want to send my congratulations." She nodded to RoyLee and Ziïimmÿÿÿ. "If you'll excuse me." She jogged to the Queen's Study, not even bothering to change out of her sweaty exercise clothes.

The first thing Eloise noticed was the letter's wax seal was different—a royal insignia. When she opened it, she saw that it wasn't encoded. Johanna's loopy, curlicued quillmanship was back on full display. Apparently Ziïimmÿÿÿ was now considered a safe and trusted courier.

That was a good sign.

Dear El,

I did it! I am now also crown-plonked. I'm so relieved that's over. I'm so sorry you couldn't be here. It all happened so fast that barely anyone was there. Really, just the core people from Court.

You might not expect it, but Father was the hero of the day. I was the one who came up with the solution that everyone found acceptable, but he agreed to it and sold it to the people who mattered.

What did we do?

I got Father to say, "Fine, I'll be king."

That stopped all the yammering."

People said, "Really?"

He said, "Yup. That'll clear up the succession problem, right?"

People said, "Yep."

He said, "OK. Let's do this."

People said, "Yep. Let's do this."

So they crowned him.

He served a quarter hour, then abdicated, which cleared the path for me to succeed him.

So in one morning, we had a Crown Plonking for Father, a small, formal coronation for him, an abdication ceremony, and a Crown Plonking for me. It was quite a whirlwind, but it resolved everything very neatly and seems to have appeased a few people with procedural issues.

Which means I have the honor of writing you as the newest queen in all the realms. I hope you're happy for me.

Eloise was. And she was amazed at how the situation had been so deftly handled. Good on their father. Eloise didn't think of him as being clever at maneuvering at court, but clearly he'd been around their mother long enough to figure out a thing or two. She went back to the letter.

El, I need your help with something. One of the first things I did was put out a proclamation that henceforth, the use of the name the "Half Kingdom" was to be banned, and that all references to the realm, both official and unofficial, would refer to the "Northern Lands," like it had been before King Brüüütus diddled Gwendolyn the Irritable and brought on two centuries of consequences. Ever since we were little girls, I always thought that "Half Kingdom" sounded diminishing. Which it was and is. But now that the Purple Haze spell is broken (thanks to you!), things are changing. The fog itself is still there, thick as ever, but initial explorations are proving that it is safe to go in there. I also officially ended the punishment of fogging. I mean, it had stopped working, but symbolically, it sends a message that there's a new head wearing the crown and change is afoot. My feeling is that people are starting to be less afraid overall.

So I want to reclaim the name the Northern Lands to help build everyone back up. If you could support me in this by using that name in any official business or in any speeches you give, that would be great. It'll help normalize the idea. I know it's a smallish change, but I think it is an important one.

Eloise put down the letter for a moment and felt herself sag. Johanna had been on her throne barely a week or so, and already she was thinking about her people, making proclamations, and reforming the judicial system. What had Eloise done? Just felt overwhelmed and afraid. She'd spent her time trying to cope and find out what she could about the Star of Whatever. Had she given any thought at all to what changes she might be able to make that might benefit those in her realm? Not once. Johanna was going to be Queen Johanna the Getter of Stuff Done and she'd be Queen Eloise the Bibliotheca Lurker.

Still, Eloise was happy for her sister. Truly happy. It's what Johanna had wanted. But for the first time, she realized at a bone level that people would compare the two of them. For that matter, *she* was already comparing herself to her sister, and Johanna barely had a dent in her forehead from the newly plonked crown.

Eloise was really going to have to lift her game here.

Somehow.

She reached for a blank piece of hemp parchment and a quill.

*Dear Johanna, or should I say, *Queen* Johanna,*

That's fantastic. Truly amazing. I'm so very happy for you. You've wanted something like this for years, and now you've done it. I think you're going to be a great queen.

And Eloise meant it. Really, she did.

She just wasn't sure at all if she felt the same about herself.

Or if anyone, anywhere, ever would.

Things are a little weird here at the moment...

❧ 56 ❧

THAT ROOM WE DON'T TALK
ABOUT

Eloise and Jerome arrived at the Bibliotheca de Records and Regrets with a napkin-covered basket of still-steaming slices of cinnamon banana bread. Neither of them was feeling particularly enthusiastic as they trudged in. The more hours they spent going through the trove of Queen Gwendolyn the Irritable's historical records, the less they thought they'd ever find anything else useful. The one ray of sunshine had been Melveeta's list from Unmitigated Catastrophic Disappointment. Since then, nothing else even remotely useful had come up. Sure, plenty of it was interesting, if hard to read and often obtuse. Eloise was getting to know Queen Gwendolyn almost better than she knew her own mother. But the ratio of "this is interesting" to "this is useful" was completely unfavorable.

They were greeted by the apprentice, Jóöôáäàqúüùíîìn, who sat by himself at the Head Scribe's desk. The teen beamed with happiness. "Blessings of the day to you both," he stage-whispered.

"Blessings of the day to you as well, Apprentice Scribe Jóöôáäàqúüùíîìn," said Eloise. "Are you in charge of the Head Scribe's desk today?"

"Oh, you noticed I'm here on my own. Very observant. Very, very observant. No, I'm not in charge of Head Scribe's desk today. But I am for now! For the very first time. My mother will be so proud when I tell her. But it's just for a few moments while Head Scribe avails himself of the facilities, although he told me not to mention that to anyone. Apparently, last night's black bean tacos with cabbage, garlic, and onion have had quite severe digestive repercussions. Of course, he didn't actually say that, but there has been ample unseen evidence testifying to the state of his gastrointestinal tract." The apprentice scribe wafted his hand in front of his nose to drive the point home. "Now, quick, before he gets back and sends me off to copy scrolls, what can I do to help you this fine morning?"

"You should probably start by insisting that we don't take this basket of cinnamon banana bread into the Bibliotheca," said Jerome.

"Of course, of course." He straightened, cleared his throat and whispered in a way that was extremely reminiscent of Head Scribe, "I'm sorry, but you won't be able to take that basket of cinnamon banana bread into the Bibliotheca de Records and Regrets. Would you like me to keep that for you here at the desk?" His delivery was sincere and fresh, and not at all like this ritual had happened several dozen times already. "How was that?"

"Very convincing, Jóöôáäàqúüùîîn," said Eloise as she handed over the basket.

"Thank you so much. Now, please, before he gets back, ask me something Head Scribe-ish."

"I'm not sure what to ask," said Eloise. "We've been doing pretty much the same thing for weeks now."

"Surely there must be something you can ask me. I've been waiting for this for a long time. Please?"

He was so eager, Eloise couldn't help but want to make his day by asking a question. So she accidentally asked the thing she really wanted to know. "Is there some sort of documentation about various magical objects in the realm?"

Jóöôáäàqúüùíîïn lit up like a cathedral full of votive candles. "I know this one! I know this one!" He clapped his hands in childlike happiness. "You want That Room We Don't Talk About Because We Don't Want People to Know About It."

"That Room We Don't Talk About Because We Don't Want People to Know About It," repeated Jerome. "That's the name of the room?"

"Yes. A very utilitarian name. Not so elegant. Not like 'The Majesterial Scrollarium,' which sounds regal. Or 'The Reading Room of Righteous Writings,' which has a nice alliteration. But 'That Room We Don't Talk About Because We Don't Want People to Know About It' is a serviceable name."

"Where is it?" asked Eloise.

"Sixth floor. Toward the back. I can show you where it is, if you like. I love it in there. It's full of interesting stuff. Don't tell Head Scribe Twiddle, but I've been known to have my lunch in there."

"No!" said Jerome. "What about all the babies?"

"I don't handle the babies when I'm eating. I just like the room. You'll see."

Head Scribe Twiddle appeared from a side door, adjusting his robes. The raccoon looked both chagrined and relieved, and was wiping dampness from his hands. He moved behind the desk, and Jóöôáäàqúüùíîïn stepped aside and helped him up onto his stool. "Blessings of the day, Your Highness. Blessings of the day, Assistant Court Seer to the Court Seer."

"Blessings of the day, Head Scribe," they both said.

"I was just telling them about That Room We Don't Talk About Because We Don't Want People to Know About It," said Jóöôáäàqúüùíîïn. "I think they'd find it very interesting."

Head Scribe looked at him, eyes wide. "You told them about That Room We Don't Talk About Because We Don't Want People to Know About It?"

"Yes. I did."

"Why?"

"Because they asked."

"Even though we don't talk about it."

Jóöôáäàqúüùíîìn tilted his head. "I beg your pardon?"

"The room," said Twiddle. "We don't talk about it."

"What do you mean?"

"Jóöôáäàqúüùíîìn, I want you to say the name slowly, and think about it as you're saying it."

"Of course, Head Scribe. I'm happy to." The apprentice closed his eyes and mumbled. "That. Roooom. We. Don't. Taaaaaaalk. Ab-out Because. We. Don't. Waaaant. Peo-ple to Knoooooow Ab-out It." Jóöôáäàqúüùíîìn's eyes snapped open and he gasped. "Oh! Oh, oh, oh! By Çalaht's bellicose bursitis, it's right there in the name!"

Head Scribe nodded slowly.

"We don't talk about That Room We Don't Talk About Because We Don't Want People to Know About It because we don't want people to know about the room! I get it! Wow. That's actually a very clever name. Much better than stupid old 'The Scrollarium' or 'The Reading Room of Righteous Writings.' Those absolutely suck when compared to 'That Room We Don't Talk About Because We Don't Want People to Know About It.' Thank you, Head Scribe. A most excellent name. And a most excellent lesson." He clapped the raccoon on the back in appreciation, then turned to Eloise and Jerome. "Since Head Scribe's back, I can show you to the That Room We Don't Talk About Because We Don't Want People to Know About It, if you'd like."

"We'd be most grateful, thank you," said Eloise.

"Let's go then. I'll be back in a bit, Head Scribe." Then he stepped off the dais and headed for a hallway.

"I'm sure you will be, Jóöôáäàqúüùíîìn," sighed Twiddle. "I'm sure you will."

"Enjoy the cinnamon bread, Head Scribe," said Jerome as he and Eloise followed the apprentice.

57

ORGANIZING PRINCIPLES

That Room We Don't Talk About Because We Don't Want People to Know About It had a sign on the door that, in large letters, read, "That Room We Don't Talk About Because We Don't Want People to Know About It."

"This must be it," said Jerome.

"Good eye," said Jóöôáäàqúüùîïin. "Well spotted."

The chipmunk looked at him for signs of mocking, but the apprentice seemed sincere.

Jóöôáäàqúüùîïin took a ring of keys from his robe pocket, a jangling tangle the size of a dessert plate, and began slowly going through them, examining each carefully. He'd flip to one, squint at it, say, "Nope," and flip to the next. Key flip. Squint. "Nope." Key flip. Squint. "Nope."

Two dozen "nopes" into it, he glanced up at the top of the door frame, "Hey, Dale. Hey, Branwen."

Eloise and Jerome looked at each other, but didn't say anything.

Key flip. Squint. "Nope." Key flip. Squint. "Nope."

The apprentice paused and studied the door. "Beautiful work, you two."

Jerome coughed lightly. "Excuse me? Are you talking to us?"

Jóöôáäàqúüùíîìn giggled. "Are you named Dale or Branwen?"

He pointed at the top left corner of the door, then the top right. "That's Dale. That's Branwen."

"Are they..." Eloise leaned forward to look more closely. "They're spiders? I don't see them."

"Yes," said the apprentice scribe. "Dale and Branwen are in the Security detail on the Obfuscation team. See their spider webs? They're responsible for obscuring the use of the door through the careful placement of spider webs. And look at what a great job they do! Really splendid work."

"It's beautiful," said Eloise. "And very effective. It looks like it's been a thousand years since anyone was in here."

"I know. And I was in here last week." He went back to searching the key ring. Flip. Squint. "Nope." Flip. Squint. "Nope." Flip. Squint. "Ah!" Jóöôáäàqúüùíîìn held up an ancient-looking key that was the biggest one on the ring by far. It also had a large, dangling metal tag with the words "That Room We Don't Talk About Because We Don't Want People to Know About It" stamped into it. "Here we go." Jóöôáäàqúüùíîìn fit the key into the lock and turned it until there was an audible click. He looked at the top of the door said, "Sorry to mess this one up. It was a beaut," and pushed it open.

Jerome shook his head and followed him in. Eloise nodded to the two corners where she assumed the spiders were, and said, "Thank you for your service to Court and the crown. And I apologize that we're disturbing your work." If the spiders replied, she didn't hear it (which was usually the case with arachnids).

That Room We Don't Talk About Because We Don't Want People to Know About It was six times the size of the Queen's Study, but much smaller than any of the GCEG rooms. It was full of the now-familiar boxes, binders, cubbies, and nooks. Angled light from side windows washed a glow across everything and revealed much more dust than normal. Despite Jóöôáäàqúüùíîin's fondness for the room, it obviously didn't get much attention or maintenance. The smell was mustier than the other archives, reflecting contents that were deliberately obscured from the vast flow of time's awareness.

The three of them pulled on cotton gloves and each walked down a different aisle. Eloise looked at the cryptic labels, trying to puzzle out how she'd tell what might be worth the time of looking into. There was a bin labeled "Materia Obscura." A box that apparently held "Records for Debunked Relics." A series of scrolls were tied together with a ribbon and a note that said, "Nadia, give me back my heart." Eloise wondered exactly how literal that was.

Jóöôáäàqúüùíîin's voice came from two aisles away. "I'm sorry. What exactly are we looking for?"

Eloise rounded the end of her aisle, caught Jerome's eye, and raised a do-we-tell-him-or-not eyebrow. The chipmunk gave her a he-seems-harmless-enough-and-also-goodhearted whisker twitch. She replied with do-we-say-everything-or-keep-it-simple puffed cheeks. Jerome responded with a no-not-everything-we-can-always-tell-him-more-if-we-need-to tail twitch. Eloise replied with a left nostril flare of agreement. "Jóöôáäàqúüùíîin, can you come here?" she said.

The apprentice scribe joined them. "Late afternoon is better in here," he said. "The light is more favorable for reading. So, what are we looking for?"

"Information about magical objects that were found during the reign of Queen Gwendolyn the Irritable."

"That makes sense, given you've been combing through Queen Gwendolyn's archive. Anything in particular?"

"Hard to say," said Eloise. "But we know she had an interest in them, and the other rooms seemed awfully light on the topic."

"Right. Well, the problem is that the babies in here aren't stored by chronology. I mean, they do go very roughly from older to newer from over there to over there." He swept his arm from one side to the other to give a rough progression of time. "But there are other, more prominent organizing principles, from what I can tell."

"Organizing principles?" said Jerome. "Like what?"

"Type of object. Location of origin. Alleged magical efficacy. Color. Material. That kind of thing," said the apprentice. "The problem is, if you put enough of those categories together, you end with a jumbled hodgepodge of individual items. That's sort of what's going on in here."

"Then I guess all we can do is dig in and see what we turn up," said Eloise. "Jóöôáäàqúüùíîìn, could you please do something for me?"

"Your wish is my command, Queen Eloise!" The teen gave a shy smile. "I always wanted to say that."

"Could you please have a page sent to First Advisor Ligurian to let him know I won't have my afternoon briefing. I'll see him tomorrow morning."

"Yes, ma'am."

"And please, no mention of That Room We Don't Talk About Because We Don't Want People to Know About It."

"Yes ma'am," chirped Jóöôáäàqúüùíîìn. "We don't talk about That Room We Don't Talk About Because We Don't Want People to Know About It. It's right there in the name."

"Exactly."

"Do you want me to come back and help with the search?"

"Only if Head Scribe can spare you. And only after you've had some of the cinnamon banana bread."

"Yes, ma'am. If I don't return, you'll know Head Scribe decided that copying ancient ledgers was more important than helping you. No offense, ma'am." And with a bow that threatened to clunk his forehead on the flagstones, he was gone.

"I like him," said Jerome.

"Me, too. I like his enthusiasm." Eloise opened her arms wide. "Let's dive in."

58

THE PROBLEM WITH THE
BRASS PICKLE

The documents were definitely more interesting, since they dealt with the attempted verification, and inevitable debunking, of allegedly magical items. Some of the items themselves were there, stored along with their descriptions, tests, and evaluations. Others were who knew where, labeled by obscure text and referencing indecipherable storage locations. As Eloise went from one document to the next, she could feel the rise and fall of emotions from people long past, oscillating between hope and disappointment as object after object fell short of what had been rumored.

For example, the Mighty Staff of Perpetual Strength turned out to be an ordinary balsa wood stick that only gave a vague impression of increased power. The related scroll indicated that whoever held it above their head looked more dorky than mighty.

Similarly, the Chalice of Infinite Potage didn't provide an unending flow of stew, thick soup, or porridge. It was just a big, decorated tureen that you had to pour soup into to get exactly the same amount of soup out.

The room was full of magical promises made and magical promises broken.

Eloise and Jerome worked through the day, carefully examining item after item, baby after baby. Somewhere toward late afternoon, Jerome sat down, exasperated. "You know what I don't get?"

"What?"

"I don't understand why all these things were duds."

"Duds. That seems harsh."

"No, it isn't. Everything I've seen and read about in here was a complete and utter washout."

"I guess. Your point?"

"We know that weak magic exists. You have it for throwing, even if you don't like talking about it. My mother has it for Seeing. Your sister has it for growing things. And we know that there used to be strong magic. The Purple Haze. Melveeta." He pointed to the Star of Whatever hidden at her hip. "Not to mention that thing."

"So?"

"So we've been looking through all this stuff for a few hours now. How is it that none of them worked? How can they all be junk when we know that a) there's at least some magic in the world, b) we have an example of one working magical object, and c) the further back you go..." Jerome waved vaguely in the direction of the older records. "... the closer to Back When you get?"

"I see. You'd think that the closer to Back When our research gets, the higher the likelihood that some sort of real, magical object would have been found. Good point."

Jerome looked around. "Maybe there's another room they don't talk about because they don't want anyone to know about it, which has all the good stuff in it."

"Maybe." Eloise rescrolled the baby she'd just been reading, something about the ineffectiveness of the Kerchief of Ultimate Coiffure, which when worn over the head was supposed to give the wearer a stupendous hairdo. The unnamed researcher commented that the hairstyle was never seen since the kerchief inevitably hid it. Even if it had worked, it would have been, at best, cute, but useless. "Maybe," said Eloise again.

"Yeah, maybe," said Jerome.

Eloise went to the next baby in the bin. "Or maybe not."

"What do you mean?" Jerome moved the weights so she had a place to unscroll her hemp parchment. "From the Helmet of Jittery Generosity to the Brass Pickle of Perpetual Dillness, we've found nothing that anyone ever found of genuine magical value."

Eloise thought a moment. "Maybe the problem wasn't that they had no magical capability."

"What then?"

"Maybe the problem was that the people trying to use or test them lacked sufficient magical skill to deploy them properly."

Jerome looked at the new scroll without seeing it. "Huh."

"Yeah. Huh."

Jerome scratched his cheek. "You're saying if a hack uses hack-level skills to examine something that's far beyond them, they wouldn't see the magical forest for the magical trees."

"Yes."

"Does that remind you of someone?"

Eloise looked at him. "Of course it reminds me of me. I know I'm, at best, a hack with hacky skills. That's why you and I have breathed more dust in the past weeks than most scholars will in a lifetime." She tapped the hidden box at her hip. "This thing scares the holy heck out of me. Every. Single. Day. There's part of me that can't stand to have the Star of Whatever with me because I know better than anyone what it's capable of. But I also can't stand not to have it there because I know better than anyone what it's capable of. I can't use it safely and there's no one to turn to for advice, because no one has ever dealt with something like this for over two centuries, except for Melveeta the Elusive, and she's dead. None of the mage scholars, healers, academicians, or the supposedly learned ones—none of them have the faintest clue about anything even vaguely related to the Star. So I'm left trying to find notes that a long-dead educated amateur—which is what Melveeta really was—left behind."

Jerome patted her hand. "I get it, El. We'll find something. This can't be all on you."

"By Çalaht's toxic tonsillitis, I hope not. Because if it is all on me, we're all sunk."

"Don't say that."

"It's true."

"Again, please don't say that."

"Fine. But that's what it feels like."

They turned their attention to the baby laying on the table, and Jerome began speed-reading it out loud. "'Herewith, the investigative undertakings into the unknown capabilities of Spheroid 7276B. The exact origins of 7276B are lost, however it can be accurately traced to the time of the Court of Queen Agnes Delion Frostbite Gumball, when it was purchased from a beetroot monger.'" Jerome looked up from the scroll. "Queen Agnes? That's old."

"Yeah, and weird. What's a record from the first Gumball queen doing in this particular bin? Keep reading. What's it supposed to do?"

Jerome skipped down the scroll. "Here we go. 'The beetroot monger swore that the spheroid granted one the ability to, quote, 'know stuff,' end quote."

"Know stuff? What kind of stuff?" Eloise leaned over the scroll and took over the reading. "'The beetroot monger claimed that, 'When wielding this object, that which can be known, shall be known. Known from the past, the present, the future. Not hinted at nor guessed—known.' Then there's a note that adds, 'Likely this is malarky.'"

"That's quite a claim," said Jerome. "Is it in the bin where the scroll was?"

Eloise stepped back to the bin and looked around inside. "No. There's no obvious spheroid in here. How is it described?"

"Let me see… It's apparently the size of the third-place winning beetroot from that year's Beetroot Bash, Blowout, and Banquet at Bobbin's Bridge. Ooh, and it's fancy. 'A pearlescent color. Gold filigree. Gems.'" Jerome broke off, laughing.

"What?"

"There's a list of possible names for the thing. Oh, this is rich."

"Melveeta said the names were always important to people. They spent a lot of time working on them."

"Well, apparently they didn't spend quite enough time on this one. Get a load of these." Jerome straightened and intoned like a herald. "The Ball of Insight."

"Dull."

"The Globe of Discernment."

"Better, but not catchy," said Eloise. "Like, there's no alliteration or anything."

"'The Globule of Gloaming.'"

"Alliterative, but weird?"

"The Egg of Wisdom. The Pellet of Pansophy. The Ovoid of Observation."

"Those really are bad. Let me have a look." Eloise found where he'd left off. "The Droplet of Learningosity. The Oblong of Obligation. The Knob of Knowingness."

"The Knob of Knowingness?" Jerome let his tail droop sarcastically. "That's shocking. Just shocking."

"Oh. Hold it." Eloise stopped and took a step backward. "Oh, goodness."

"What? What's the matter?"

"The last name on the list."

"What is it?"

"The Orb of Omniscience."

"No. You're kidding. Like, your Orb? The one you dropped and dented at your Crown Plonking Ceremony?"

"Size of a large beetroot. Pearlescent. Gold filigree. Gems," said Eloise. "Sounds like the Orb of Alleged Omniscience to me."

"It does a bit, yeah."

Eloise put her forehead in her hand. "Oh, Çalaht sipping seaweed soup, that just makes my Crown Plonking worse. I fumbled and mangled a bona fide magical object."

"A bona fide *alleged* magical object," said Jerome. "I'm pretty sure that if the other items in this room are anything to go by, that 'alleged' is richly deserved."

"I guess. It didn't feel very magical. It just seemed like an old, tarted up heavy ball that I had a hard time holding onto."

"That's probably all it is."

"Yeah, probably." Eloise straightened. "Come on. Let's see what else we can find."

59

BIRTHDAY PRESENT

The day had started out great. Jerome rode on her shoulder as she and Lorch ticked off 211 columns around the Culpability Courtyard—a nice prime number, and more than she usually ran. It was done in companionable silence, save for Jerome's counting.

But from the moment she stepped out of her post-run bath, things started going downhill. The sleeve of the maroon dress she'd chosen tore as she put it on over her cast, and Odmilla had to take it away for Seamstress Linttrap to fix. It left her with a pale blue one, which she didn't fancy as much. Then the new Chef had prepared scrambled tofu, which Eloise liked, but he'd made it with preserved asparagus, which had rendered it barely edible. The two together just didn't work for her, and the combination repeated on her for the next several hours. Then she had to cancel her hour of time in the Bibliotheca de Records and Regrets when she happened on Läääcy de Aardvark crying quietly in an alcove, having been reprimanded by Lady Seneschal for spilling beet juice on a white handwoven carpet.

By the time First Advisor was boring her with a report of crops that farmers were expecting to plant on the slopes of the Neckline Hills (apparently snowberry shrubs were all the rage at the moment), Eloise was having trouble focusing. "Sorry," interrupted Eloise. "Do I really need to know this?"

Ligurian frowned. "Is there something the matter?"

"Do I really need to know that there's a snowberry fad in the Neckline Hills? Wouldn't aggregating the various berry concerns make things go faster?"

First Advisor unhooked his hands from behind his back and started squeezing his fingers. "Your Highness, my intention is to give you a full sense of what constitutes your queendom. Perhaps the species trends in the Neckline Hills seem a trivial matter. And maybe they are. But my goal is to equip you with the means of ruling, down to the minutia."

Eloise tried not to watch him scrunching his fingers, but realized he thought she was being obtuse. So be it. "First Advisor, what have your sources reported from Flachberg? Is there news?"

"Actually, Your Highness, there is." He clasped his hands in front of himself. "It would appear that whatever might have been going on is no longer going on. Apparently, there had been some kind of training jamboree."

"A jamboree? What kind of jamboree?"

"One that involved kites. Lots and lots of kites. Skies full of kites. Plus singing."

"Songs about kites, presumably." Eloise shook her head. "My champion... Sorry, my Assistant Court Seer to the Court Seer likes that kind of thing. I'll mention it to him. I bet Jerome knows about it. He probably even knows the kite songs they sing."

"If he likes that kind of thing, then it'd be perfect for him. Although, he'll need to catch it next year. My sources say it has finished."

She doubted it. Whatever was going on, his clasped hands had revealed the mendacity of what he said. "Thank you, First Advisor."

Ligurian left the Queen's Study soon after, rolling away the trolley with the two royal boxes on it. Eloise asked RoyLee for a fresh pot of tea, and he scurried off toward the kitchen trilling his usual "Tea for the queen!"

Eloise began pacing the room, nervy. She shook her hands, trying to fling off some of her tension, but it didn't help, and it made her broken hand throb in its cast. *I'm nowhere*, Eloise thought. *Absolutely nowhere. Nowhere close to knowing who killed my mother. No idea what's going on in the border region. No clue as to who got to me with that nosebleed letter. Nowhere close to unlocking the secrets of the Star of Whatever.* Eloise strode around the room, circling the map table in the middle. She found Flachberg's canton and put her finger on a dot labeled "Fl'brg." Someone had thought it worth saving the three characters. How hard would it have been to replace the apostrophe with the "a" and then add in the "ch" and the "e"? What sort of economy was that? Or was it that Flachberg was so unimportant that it didn't merit all the letters?

Who knew?

More pacing.

RoyLee arrived with the pot. Having sensed her mood, he left it on the hutch outside. "Tea, Your Highnessness."

"Thank you, RoyLee." She opened the little sliding door, pulled in the tray, closed the door, poured herself a cuppa, left it to cool, and resumed pacing the perimeter. What she needed was advice. Preferably from someone a little more experienced than Jerome or Lorch. Someone more like First Advisor, except without what she now saw as Ligurian's deception, even if she didn't know exactly what the lie was. Certainly not Lady Seneschal, who seemed to be running things smoothly enough, if sternly. Seer Maybelle, maybe? Possibly. But what Eloise really needed was clarity on the present, not a glimpse into the future. Maybe the Other Places Advocate, Bërnädïce-Ändrëä Thëjëts. She might have insights into what was going on with the Eastern Lands. Eloise would have to set up a meeting with her soon.

Really, what she needed was someone like her mother. Someone who'd give it to her straight, and had the experience to provide insight.

Except there wasn't anyone like her mother anymore. Maybe Queen Onomatopoeia would be open to having that kind of conversation with her, but it wasn't like Eloise could just pop back down to The South and meet up with the Southie queen for a quick kaffeeklatsch.

Eloise picked up the teacup and saucer, carried it to her mother's desk, and sat down in the chair. She picked up her mother's letter opener, tracing the carved lines of the woman's hand holding an envelope. Had her mother sat there holding the letter opener, worrying about the complexity of the life ahead of her or wondering what she should do?

Probably.

Had it helped her figure out what to do?

Probably not.

She ran her finger along the half-sharp edge, dull enough not to be a danger, but sharp enough to open an envelope or pry off a blotch of sealing wax. Yeah, a dose of her mother was what she needed.

Eloise sipped her tea. Still too hot. And nothing to dunk into it.

Whatever.

She tapped the side of the letter opener on the desk. Put it down. Picked it up. Put it down again. Rotated it in a circle with her finger, once, twice.

That's when she saw it. A small parcel wrapped in an elegant rag paper dyed the green of dried nori flakes and secured with a carefully woven ribbon that was attached in the most meticulous bow Eloise had ever seen. It was the birthday present her mother had given her moments before she'd died.

It didn't hurt as much to see it this time. Time was apparently doing its thing to heal the wound in her heart.

Eloise slid the cup and saucer aside and plucked the gift from its spot in the desk hutch cubby next to Joanna's preserved crocus. The paper had a pleasing roughness to it, and the bow looked like it had been tied by a nun after a decade of silent contemplation and meditation. She doubted the late queen had wrapped the gift herself, but the odds were very good she'd chosen the paper and ribbon, then handed it off to someone else to complete the process.

She balanced it on her palm, feeling the heft of it. Eloise wondered how she could unwrap it without destroying the beauty. She hadn't wanted to see inside it before. Now, it was what she wanted more than anything.

Splurgle it, thought Eloise. That was one of the fake curse words her mother had permitted the twins to say, along with "flimpt," "klort," and, when they were particularly mad, "guffintilldlonch." She took the letter opener and sliced through the underside of the parcel, freeing the ribbon and loosening the paper. She peeled it back, revealing what was inside.

A box.

It was a rectangular box that looked large enough to hold a decent-sized blood orange. The wood was dark, like ebony, and the lid was artfully carved with the weasel, onions, otter, and fire poker of the Gumball coat of arms. But it wasn't an exact replica of the crest. It was slightly exaggerated, like the gentlest caricature possible. Unless her mother's eyesight had been failing, she'd chosen this small wrongness for a reason. But what was it?

Eloise lifted the gilded lid, which hinged upward with well-lubricated ease. The inside was padded velvet, and there lay several small items, which Eloise took out one at a time. There was a folded piece of hemp parchment, a brown, dried pod with five seeds peeping out, a sliver or chip of a pearl-colored crystal, and a miniature serpent—not the species, but the instrument made from wood with a brass mouthpiece and side holes, sort of like a flute. Usually the instruments were the size of an overgrown anaconda, but this one was tiny. She sat the items next to each other on the desk and lightly ran her fingers over each, trying to glean a sense of her mother from them.

They were cold.

Her mother was gone.

Carefully, she unfolded the parchment. It was a letter, written in her mother's terse, precise quillmanship, but shakier and much sloppier than usual. She'd not been well when she'd written it.

Eloise read.

❧ 60 ☙

STING IN THE QUILL

T he letter began:

My daughter,

If you are reading this, then I am dead and you are, or are about to be, queen. Sorry about that. Trust me when I say that I wasn't nearly ready to put down the crown. Probably as unready as you are (or were) to pick it up.

If we've spoken between when I wrote this note and when you read it, then I probably called the box that this note was in your birthday present. It isn't. Sorry about that also. I needed a subterfuge to try to keep the parcel protected for you, and to encourage you to open it sooner rather than later.

The parcel had been on her desk for weeks. Months. Curiosity had not gotten the better of her.

Ouch.

How does one write a final letter to one's daughter? For that's almost certainly what this is. It is painful to contemplate and difficult to execute. I can't, given how I am. As such, I won't.

Instead, this is my outgoing note to the incoming queen. There's a tradition of writing notes like this. My mother didn't leave me one—she died with too much bitterness clouding her brain. Queen Gwendolyn the Irritable wouldn't have been caught dead leaving anything approaching guidance to her daughter Queen Aubrey the Parasitic. Queen Joan the Sadly Befuddled was too far off in the La La Realms to pass on anything. But if you dig in the Bibliotheca de Records and Regrets, which I know you're prone to doing, you can find examples of these kinds of missives. Queen Beauregard the Hirsute, Queen Lorielle the Waffler, and Queen Xantheen the Only One Whose Name Starts With X all had enough warning about their impending demises that they left behind a note in a box for their successors. By the way, Queen Xantheen wasn't the only one whose name started with X. Queen XXXionara preceded her by a few decades, but no one remembered her for anything, so it was an understandable oversight.

I'm waffling here. Dying does that to you. You find it hard to concentrate. I resent my body failing. Yesterday, I ruled a queendom. Today, I am bested by a bowl of oatmeal. If there's anything I'm not going to miss when I'm gone, it will be the vicissitudes of the body.

Let's start with the obvious. You're not ready for this. No one is ever ready to assume the crown, but you in particular aren't. It's something I regret and apologize for. I thought there'd be more time. To be honest, I was trying to give you space to get over your quirks and habits. I know you don't like to talk about them, but their control over you is disproportionate. I worry that someone will be able to use them against you and affect your reign and your queendom.

But like I said, you're queen now, or almost so. You'll need to factor these parts of your personality into your decision-making. I can't say that I think it's a good thing. You'll have to see what you can do about controlling them. Çalaht knows I'm out of ideas on that front. So many of your decisions will be instinctive and intuitive. Make sure your instincts and intuitions aren't unduly guided by your quirks.

Eloise set down the letter, clasped her hands in her lap, and rocked a little as blood rushed to her cheeks. She'd been criticized by her mother from beyond the grave. Even dead, the woman could still hammer at her heart and self-esteem.

The thing was, her mother was, of course, right. Her habits had dominated her life for years, itching at her with compulsions to align her cutlery, count her steps, to avoid dirt, to wash herself, to order her clothes—all were the little crutches that had helped her get through the day.

Yes, her mother's criticism stung.

Because she was right.

But her mother was also wrong. Her perspective failed to take into account the changes caused by the experience of journeying across four and a half realms. Yes, she'd practically vomited when horse sweat had first soaked into her riding breeks. And yes, she'd cut off her own hair in a panic after Melveeta the Elusive's blood had soaked it. Yes, being in a chigger-ridden jail cell had sent her spare.

But the ongoing discomforts of the travel, the inability to order her life, the strange food and, worst of all, the trauma of falling into the filth of the Whacking Great Hole, had, of necessity, forced her to reset her relationship with her habits. Today, back home in the familiarity of Castle de Brague, they still niggled at her. But she'd gained control over them. Yes, she still counted columns as she ran around the Culpability Courtyard, but she no longer felt rising dread when faced with disorder and dirt. Plus, it helped that she was overwhelmingly busy from "Blessings of the day" to "Goodnight. Don't let the bedbugs bite" (which bedbugs found nothing less than slanderous, but their voices were so quiet that no one heard their complaints).

So her mother's concerns (because that was what it was—concern, not criticism) were well-placed and founded on fact. But somewhat out of date. That took some of the sting out of the lines from her quill.

Eloise resumed reading the letter.

As for the advice, one queen to the next, there are some obvious things to consider and they bear saying out loud.

If you can avoid it, don't put yourself in a position where you have to go to war. The logic is simple. War is bad. Peace is good. Staying out of war can be an incredibly tricky business. I managed it. Your grandmother did, too, somehow. So have many queens before you. But not all of them. Diplomacy should always be your preference, short of needing to face down a madman.

The opposite of this is simple. If your back is against the wall and fighting is what it comes to, go at it with gusto. With rage and vinegar. With spleen and blood and cunning and steel. Queen Gwendolyn is a good model here. She was fierce, determined, ruthless, and most of all, successful. Crush your enemies, because doing less than that is to invite disaster.

This also sounded like her mother. Practical. Direct. Driven.

Next, don't be in a rush to marry. There's going to be pressure for you to choose a mate as soon as possible. Lots and lots and lots of pressure. I'm certain you've already received marriage proposals from all manner of unsuitable people. Resist. This is your queendom to run. You've got plenty to learn and master. There's time for the inevitable, unavoidable courting later on. Leave it for then.

When you do choose, eschew what my mother did. What they always called One's Grand Mistake was an epic disaster. She should have seen calamity coming, but she was dazzled by my father's blue eyes, blond hair, and the land he brought to the bargain. She should have taken heed of the smell of alcohol on his breath and the slurring of his words.

Instead, if you can, find someone like your father. He is loyal, loving, and he makes me laugh, even now, when doing so literally hurts. Plus, he's smart and often sees things from an angle that I don't. I treasure his mind and I cherish all that we are and have been to each other. I wish the same for you.

Now for non-obvious things.

Wear comfortable shoes. Always. You'll spend much of your life on your feet. Don't make that a misery. You can extrapolate that rule to the rest of your wardrobe. Don't let vanity crowd out practicality, no matter what your handmaids may encourage. You want to look good, but not suffer.

This made Eloise both smile and feel sad. "Make sure you always have good, comfortable shoes" was one of the things her father had suggested when she had her last talk with him before he'd left with Johanna for the Half Kingdom. The similarity of this advice just showed how in sync her parents had been. It made her feel her mother's loss that much more.

Set a good example for your people. Remember Çalaht's silver dictum: "If you don't want it said to you, don't say it to anyone else. If you don't want it said about you, don't say it of anyone else. If you'd like it done, be willing to do it."

The Divine One (or whoever did her public relations heralding) had true wisdom.

"Or whoever did her public relations heralding?" Did her mother doubt the provenance of *The Scrolls of Çalaht?* How unexpected.

Keep the household staff happy, even if you have to cross Lady Seneschal to do it. They're the difference between comfort and woe.

Don't meddle with magic. The weakening of magic is one of the blessings of our age.

That one caught Eloise by surprise. She quickly skimmed the rest of the letter. That was the only mention of magic in the whole thing. "C'mon, Mother. You can't just drop a sentence like that and not elaborate."

But apparently, she could.

How disappointing.

She went back to reading.

Take care of your teeth. When they fail, you'll regret not having done so. I tell you that from personal experience.

Just because you can have anything you want prepared and served to you doesn't mean you should.

Related: you don't have to eat all of it. Whatever it is, leave some. You're an example to everyone. Act like it, so you can be proud when they initiate you, as they will.

Rely on those who are reliable. You already know who they are, or you'll know soon enough.

It appears that's all the aphorisms that come to mind. I hope that's enough. I doubt they'll make much difference to you, but it is more than zero.

Oh, one last thing: be kind.

You already know that acts of kindness foster more of the same. Kindness engenders kindness. You've heard me say that since you were gumming teething biscuits, but it is one to live by. And to rule by.

You should also show kindness to yourself. Being queen is hard enough as it is without flogging yourself to the bone. Don't get sucked into the false belief that working yourself until you're an empty husk is some sort of virtue. It isn't. Don't burn your candle to the nub. That which can't be finished in 16 hours can also not be finished in 14 hours. Or 12. But if you care for yourself, you might get more done in the hours you have.

That's it. That's what I have for you.

A mug of viscous slime has arrived for me. I'll need to slug it down or receive a reprimand from the healers, who are doing what little they can for me, but who are now fully ineffective and tiresome.

Good luck, my daughter. You're going to need it. All of us do.

Love,

Mother

P.S. I know we've never been a family who says, "I love you." It wasn't my mother's way, and I took that on from her. I see now it was a flaw, although up until all this happened, I would have said I was toughening you up and preparing you for the world. That was stupid of me. As I drift closer to standing with Çalaht (I hope she'll have me), I realize I can't make up for words not spoken over the years. So, I'll have to make do with saying them now. I love you. I love your sister. I love you both equally and with full heart. And I'm proud of you.

Eloise gasped. Her mother was right. They'd never been in the habit of saying "I love you." She knew that others passed those words around like sweets at High Yule, but not her mother or father. Tears swam, and she wiped them away with the heel of her uninjured hand. Eloise sighed, and whispered, "I love you too, Mother." The words felt odd in her mouth.

But it was good to have said them.

She swallowed back the lump in her throat, and kept reading.

P.P.S. Find out who killed me. They're probably already working on how to kill you as well.

P.P.P.S. Don't let them.

Eloise felt her pulse flutter and the icy touch of premonition drag a finger down her back. Her skin erupted in goose pimples (a description geese truly hated, since it had nothing to do with either geese or pimples), and her arm hairs stood up. Her mother hadn't needed to warn her about finding her killer, but if Eloise was being honest, she hadn't pushed as hard as she might on the topic. She'd given all her spare mental space to finding out about the Star of Whatever and worrying about what might be going on in the east.

She promised herself that she'd double down on the figuring-out-who-ended-her-mother's-life thing.

Eloise was fascinated by the letter. She read it again.

And again.

And again.

She scrutinized every sentence, every word, every letter, every stray blotch, every variation in her mother's compressed looping scrawl. She sniffed the pages for her mother's scent—there might have been a hint of it, but Eloise suspected it was more likely her desire for contact with the late queen that she was projecting onto the hemp parchment.

Sliding the box toward her, Eloise looked in and saw there was another, shorter note.

I forgot to explain the items in the box.

The seed pod contains ironwood seeds. It's my wish that you plant one some-where prominent. I'd like to be remembered with a living thing. Maybe you can fashion a memorial plaque. The five seeds should give you four to spare, in case you need to try again, given you don't have your sister's gifts in the garden.

That seemed a simple enough request. Maybe she could find a spot to the side of the Culpability Courtyard, somewhere where the tree wouldn't interfere with hockey sacking games.

The serpent is a reminder that disappointment can shape you. I always wanted to learn to play a musical instrument, and in particular, the serpent. My mother thought it was a stupid and unladylike instrument (it's possible she was right). Still, I argued for it, but she refused to budge, forcing me to learn the harp instead. Ugh. Can you imagine? Me with a harp?

I was heartbroken. I let resentment simmer for years, flinging this disappointment at her as a failing whenever it seemed useful. Or hurtful.

You know what? At some point (after One was gone a year or two), I realized that I'd spent a lot of time and energy blaming her, and there had been other options. For example, I could have just picked up a serpent and gotten some lessons. Certainly by the time she was down in the family crypt and I was queen, I had enough agency to learn the damn thing on my own terms. But I had chosen not to. So I forgave her. And I forgave myself. It was a relief to get rid of that cloud of animosity.

I had the miniature serpent made as a reminder—a reminder of the resentment, and of letting go of the resentment.

The sliver of pearl-colored crystal is a chip that supposedly came off the Orb of Alleged Omniscience. I don't know if it is or isn't, and I never bothered to check. My mother gave it to me when I was a little girl, and at the time she said it was off the Orb. At first, I simply believed her. Later, I wanted it to be true, so I didn't question it. This all happened before things really went off the rails between her and my father, and she still had the capacity to do the odd mother-like thing.

When she gave it to me, she told me to put it under my pillow, promising it would help me gain wisdom while I slept. (She was drawing on the alleged omniscience angle, I think.) She said it would help me dream with clarity and perspective. She said that my dreams could show me truth, and how everyday events fit into the wider pattern of the unfolding of Her Divine World. My dreams could help me understand the synchronicities in the web of all things.

I barely understood the words when she said them, but it sounded grand, so I tried it. I don't remember it making me any wiser, but I remember my dreams being wild, rambling things that made it hard to sleep.

So I give this "genuine" piece of the Orb to you to connect you to your grand-mother. Even if it didn't bring me insights into the world or reveal deep truths, I liked the idea of maybe being able to tune into the synchronicities of life and see the larger pattern of things. It strikes me as important that a queen be able to do that, so I pass this stone on to you so you might find it inspiring as well. Try the under-the-pillow thing. Maybe you'll have a different result.

Good luck to you, my Eloise. Think of me from time to time.

Love,

Mother

Eloise picked up each of the items. The ironwood seed pod felt rough and weathered. If Johanna had been there, there'd be no question that the tree would flourish and grow. But she wasn't, so it would be up to Eloise to make sure that it sprouted properly and had as much of a chance at life as she could give it. She could imagine running past it every day and thinking of her mother watching over her.

The stone was cool and smooth, and Eloise could practically feel her mother's hand holding it, probing its polished smoothness with her thumb for hints of an edge or the roughness of a seam. The sliver of crystal didn't have anything near the presence that the Star of What-ever had, but Eloise thought that maybe she could feel a hint of some-thing buried inside it, an echo akin to Sparky in the Star.

Or maybe she was projecting again.

The small gold musical serpent was whimsical. Eloise wondered if her mother had commissioned a working replica. The keys moved like they were functional, and it was hollow enough to blow through. But the brass mouthpiece would require buzzing lips to make a sound. Maybe a titmouse could play it, but not a human. She would have to see if they had one in the Musiquarium and see if it spoke to her the way it had spoken to her mother.

She doubted it. Music was not Eloise's forte.

She put down the serpent and picked up the letter again. "Oh, Mother," she whispered. "Thank you for this. I'm going to miss you. I'm going to miss you forever. I wish I could—"

A loud knocking interrupted her. "Princess! I mean, Queen Eloise!"

"El! Sorry... Queen Eloise!"

It was Lorch and Jerome, speaking over each other.

She swept the letter and her mother's gifts into a pocket in her dress and then opened the door. The two of them stood there panting, faces ashen and taut. Lorch held a roll of muslin.

"What's the matter?"

"We'd better show you," said Lorch.

"Then, please, come in."

61

GÖÖÖBER'S MESSAGE

Lorch stepped into the room, followed by Jerome. "I need an open, flat surface."

"The map table?" said Eloise.

"If you don't mind."

Lorch unrolled the muslin wrap across the eastern half of the Western Lands and All That Really Matters and the western part of the Eastern Lands. Inside was a mess of fluff in the colors of bark and twig, with flecks of crusted red. Bits of the fluff drifted onto the table from the open wrap.

"Bird feathers?" asked Eloise.

Lorch and Jerome both nodded.

She looked more closely, then gasped. "Nightjar feathers."

"Yes, Your Highness."

"Is it... Is it Göööber?"

"We have to assume so," said Lorch. "There's no specific identification."

"This... This is just awful." Eloise felt sadness gathering. "Who? Who did this to him?"

"We can't tell," said Jerome. The chipmunk's tail drooped and he looked like he was barely holding back tears.

"How did the parcel arrive?"

"It was waiting for me on my bed," said Jerome. I found it less than an hour ago. Lorch confirmed my suspicions and we came here at once."

Eloise began pacing in a circle around the table, pressing her palms to her head. Göööber had undertaken the task at her request. And now he was dead, and horribly so. He wasn't a soldier or a guard. He was just someone Jerome knew who could fly fast, far, and with stealth—someone she'd known for barely an hour and who was now dead on her errand. It made her feel nauseous. How did queens send troops into war? How could she ever ask anyone again to put themselves in harm's way, knowing they might return a pile of blood-spattered feathers?

Panic rose. Her breathing accelerated. She walked faster, bumping into things as she made circles in the room.

"El. You need to calm down," said Jerome. When she ignored him, he yelled, "El! Stop!"

She stopped, and looked at him, eyes wide. "I... I... This means..."

"My queen," said Lorch. "Can I suggest that you please sit down. I'll get you some water, and we can think through what this means."

"It means someone knew exactly what was going on," said Eloise. She let Lorch lead her to the armchair. "And who sent him on his mission."

"Yes. But there must be more that we can work out." The guard handed her a mug of water, and she sipped it. "For example, it probably means someone knew to expect him and took action when he arrived. Or they knew to intercept him early, before he got airborne. Perhaps someone figured out what he was doing from his preparations."

"I guess," said Eloise.

"It's very likely that someone overheard us at the Tilted Perch," said Jerome.

"Possibly." Eloise took another sip of water, trying to force herself to calm. "Or maybe the information came from inside the castle."

Jerome shook his head. "Surely not. We barely spoke of it outside the three of us. I don't think even Hector or the Nameless One were aware of the plan."

"They wouldn't have heard it from me," said Lorch. "It was a strictly need-to-know operation, and they didn't need to know."

"Still, we know how hard it is to keep secrets at Court," said Eloise. "Gossip moves faster than a juvenile tiger beetle running for a birthday cake. The odds of someone working something out are high enough."

"The pub remains the most likely source. Should one of us—not you, El—go back over there and dig around? See if we can uncover the source of the leak?"

"It can't hurt. Jerome, you're known there best. Perhaps you can take that on."

"Of course."

"But, please. Be careful. I don't want you ending up in a muslin roll too."

Lorch leaned over the table, staring closely at the feathers, his hands clasped behind his back, cautious not to touch them. Jerome also peered at them, looking for a clue. "Feathers. A few blood drops. But that's it. It's like he was plucked by someone being very careful."

"I don't think that's a whole bird's worth of feathers," said Jerome. "Not for someone the size of Göööber."

"One thing is clear. My little nosebleed incident wasn't a one-off." Eloise set down the mug. "This is another message. It's someone saying, 'I know what you're doing, and I can get to you.'" The thought made her stomach tighten again.

"Unfortunately, I have to agree," said Lorch.

Jerome nodded.

"We need help understanding what's going on here," said Eloise. "I think I need some advice."

Jerome tapped a foot, nervous and arhythmic, and stroked his whiskers, thinking. "Maybe First Advisor can—"

"No."

Jerome raised an eyebrow at her. "What do you mean, no?"

"I'm not sure about him." Eloise quickly sketched her concerns about how she suspected Ligurian was prevaricating.

"Are you sure?" asked Lorch.

"No, I'm not sure. There's been some sort of change since I first became queen. Nothing overt. Nothing obvious. But there's been a shift in his manner. Something subtle. I've asked obliquely if anything was wrong, but he waves those sorts of questions off."

"Your mother trusted him," said Jerome. "That must count for something."

"She did. She said that to me herself. And maybe it's all nothing, and maybe it isn't. Either way, I feel the need to speak to someone else."

"If not First Advisor, then who?"

Eloise thought for a few moments. "What about Bërnädïce-Ändrëä Thëjëts?"

"The Other Places Advocate," said Jerome. "Interesting."

"I don't know her," said Lorch. "What's she like?"

"I don't know her either. But, like Ligurian, my mother trusted her. Maybe I can too," said Eloise. "And maybe, just maybe, she can give me some insights into what in the name of Çalaht's fungus-cracked toes is going on in the east."

62

GONNA GET BEANED

The sight of Göööber's mangled remains haunted Eloise's thoughts as Odmilla helped her get ready for bed that night. "I don't think I'm going to be able to sleep."

"I can imagine," said the platypus. "Do you want to talk about anything?"

"No. Thank you, but no. I'll read for a while. Maybe I'll go through some of First Advisor's ledgers. That usually puts me to sleep."

"Yes, Your Highness." Odmilla brushed Eloise's hair—still a much simpler task than it had been when it was long. "How does your wrist feel?"

"It's not too bad. But often enough, it hurts like Çalaht's own tortured thumbs."

"That's no good. I would have thought it might have healed by now."

"I didn't do it any favors when I fell at my Crown Plonking."

"I can imagine not."

Eloise rotated her shoulder. "At least my dislocation only says 'hello' every now and then. For the most part, I don't think about it much anymore."

"That's something, Your Highness."

Minutes later, Odmilla bowed and left her alone, and Eloise crawled into bed. The new mattress was firm, just as she liked it, and she'd been sleeping the sleep of the exhausted dead recently, despite everything that had been going on.

Not tonight, she feared.

She didn't really feel like reading, and she wanted to avoid ledgers if she could. Instead, Eloise retrieved her mother's letter and the small gifts. Back under the covers, she leaned toward the candle so she could read the note again, as she fiddled with the serpent and the piece of crystal. (She didn't want to mess with the seed pod because she didn't want to hurt it.)

She re-read the bit about the crystal shard. Was it truly part of the Orb of Alleged Omniscience? It didn't really matter. What mattered was that her mother thought enough of it to pass it along to her.

On a whim, she put it under her pillow. Maybe she'd dream something interesting. She could use a bit of, what had her mother said? Wisdom, truth, and clarity. Eloise put the serpent, the letter, and the seed pod next to the box with Sparky in it, blew out the candle, and tried to fall asleep.

No go. Göööber's feathers kept looming in her mind, along with everything else. Inspired by the letter, Eloise tried to focus her mind on remembering nice memories of her mother.

The first thing that came to mind was the family trip to the dervish elder forest in the Kestrel Mountains, when they got to see the rain of winged dervish elder spinners twirling like airborne tops toward the ground. That had been pretty spectacular. One of her fondest memories was standing with Johanna and their mother beneath parasols under the dark, whirling cloud of seeds, all of them fascinated by nature's display of acrobatics.

After that memory... Nothing much. "Nice" memories, it turned out, was too restrictive a category.

So she just let memories float by, just thinking about her mother.

Sleep took her.

✿

HER MOTHER AND FATHER SAT TOGETHER IN THE SALLE DE LA Famille sharing a plate of funnel cakes. They both wore bedtime clothes, and hot mugs of conk-out tea steamed at their elbows. Chafed picked up a funnel cake and nibbled it, then gently wiped away a stray blotch of powdered sugar with his thumb.

The queen bit into her own. "The best," she said.

There was a jump in the scene.

The two of them in the Queen's Chamber leaning back on pillows, reading scrolls. The queen grunted.

"What?" said Chafed.

"It's Eloise," said the queen.

"What about her?"

"She threw a grape at me today."

He furrowed his brow. "My wee Ëёëlöööïïïsёёё threw a grape at you? Are you sure?"

"Very. It was surreptitious, but it was her."

"That doesn't sound like her. What happened?"

"It flew wide."

Her father's eyebrows went in the opposite direction. "She threw something and missed? That most definitely doesn't sound like her."

"No, not at all."

"If our daughter wants to bean you with a grape, you're gonna get beaned."

"I would have thought so, too."

"How very odd. This is right up there with Johanna baking those funny-tasting biscuits."

The queen nodded. "I agree. Those were decidedly odd."

"What did you do about the grape?"

"What do you think I did? I ignored it and pretended I didn't see it happen. As far as I could tell, it was just the one. If I see it happen again, I'll deal with her then."

"Grape-throwing at the queen is not an acceptable pastime for a princess," said Chafed.

"No. Not acceptable at all."

There was another jump.

Eloise's mother was walking into a side room near the Hall of Bald Opulence, followed by a duck and a platypus. A herald announced her and she entered to find her daughters with thorns poking out of them, resembling not-very-convincing porcupines. The twins had just finished their Thorning Ceremony, and Eloise, by some miracle, had overcome her inclinations, finished the ritual in a most unusual way, and been named Future Ruler and Heir to the Western Lands and All That Really Matters. The queen looked at both girls with pride, grateful the wretched thing was over.

She thanked and dismissed the Thorning Master, saying something vague about hoping to be around to need her services for her grand-daughters. Then she stood silently for a few moments and considered her twins. They had acquitted themselves admirably. She knew Johanna would be fine, but also crushed. Protocol didn't cut her much slack as a second born of twins.

But Eloise's achievement had been far from certain. The new Thorning Master (and the old one, her predecessor, who'd just died on the job) had reported how much difficulty Eloise was having with her training. That Eloise had conquered those problems and completed the ceremony was certainly a pleasant surprise.

Now the two of them sat there looking porcupine-ish. The queen still hadn't exactly made up her mind which daughter would get the duck handmaid, and which would get the platypus.

It didn't really matter.

The queen waved the servants forward and made a snap decision. "I would like to introduce you to your designated handmaids. Eloise, I give you Odmilla de Platypus. Johanna, I present you Nesther de Duck. They have been chosen for you based on their skill, loyalty, compatibility, and trustworthiness." This was more or less true. "They will come to know everything about you." This was definitely true. "I assure you, they are worthy of your confidences, and I encourage you to trust them, as I trust mine." This was far from true. The queen didn't trust most of her handmaids further than she could throw them. But Odmilla and Nesther might help her keep tabs on what her daughters were doing.

"Odmilla, Nesther, thank you for caring for the princesses. I ask you to treat them with the same care, consideration, and love that has been shown to me by my handmaids."

"Yes, my Queen," quacked Nesther.

"Yes, my Queen," said Odmilla.

ELOISE JERKED AWAKE, PANTING, SWEATING, AND WITH A FAINT BUZZ in her ear. She fumbled for a mug of water and drank it down. Her mother's words about her dreams being wild, rambling things that made it hard to sleep had certainly proven prophetic. She hadn't dreamed about her Thorning Ceremony for a while, and it felt weird to see the aftermath from her mother's point of view. And did Odmilla report back to her mother? Surely not. She trusted Odmilla like no one else. The thought that the platypus might betray her confidences rocked her.

And her mother had known about her throwing the grape? Surely not. But maybe? And for that matter, when had her parents ever expressed a liking for funnel cakes? That had always struck her as being more of a kid thing. But maybe her parents had liked them. It was a particularly interesting detail to appear in a dream.

It was hard to know if these were true dreams, normal nocturnal brain belches, or something in between. Maybe they could be verified—she could ask her father if he remembered that conversation, and she could ask Odmilla about what her mother had expected of the platypus.

The thing was, the dreams *felt* true, whether they were or weren't.

Most of all, the thought that the crystal shard under her pillow might affect her dreams like that creeped her out.

Whether the chip had caused the dreams or not, she'd had enough for one night. Eloise reached under her pillow and retrieved it. She looked around, trying to decide what to do with it. How far away did it need to be? Did it need to be shielded somehow?

I know where it can go. She took the box with the Star of Whatever in it, focused her attention so she could lift the lid, popped it open, and put the chip into the box with Sparky. "You two can keep each other company."

Then she closed her eyes and went back to sleep.

63

OTHER PLACES ADVOCATE

Bënnïë-Änn Thëjëts was a mountain of a woman. Her bright-and-early, three-rap knock on the door of the Queen's Study was loud, sharp, and self-assured. Eloise had barely said, "Please, come in," before she'd bowled into the room, unwrapped a scarf that could have doubled as a mainsail for a band of colorblind pirates, and dropped into a curtsy that would have bounced a dozen ballerinas off their stage. Her hair dazzled in an artificial shade of azure so bold she'd be visible from three villages away, and it frizzed like she had a binding contract with humidity. Her bloodshot eyes betrayed not a fondness for liquid consolation, but high-strung emotion. "Your Highness," she boomed. "How may I be of service?"

"Arise, please," said Eloise. "May I offer you haggleberry tea and what promises to be passable scones with either a rose petal or a spicy carrot almond jam, neither of which inspire me with much confidence?"

Bënnïë-Änn sprang up, narrowly avoiding clobbering the map table. "De-flopping-lightful, I'd flopping *love* to." She flounced into an over-sized armchair that had been brought in just for her. "I've been in meetings all morning and I'm flopping *starving*." She looked around the room. "No serving wench?"

"Not in the Queen's Study, no."

"Then, may I act as serving wench?"

"Why, um, sure."

"Out-flopping-standing!" Bënnïë-Änn tried to pick up the teapot, but her hand was too big to fit through its handle. Instead, she pinched it between index finger and thumb, pouring tea into the cups with only minor spillage. Next, she grasped the tongs like they were tweezers and she was about to attack a chin hair. "How many scones, Your Highness?"

"I'm hungry as well. Two, perhaps?"

"Very good." The Other Places Advocate placed two scones on a plate, crushing them only a little. "There you go." She took a second plate and served herself half a dozen, along with generous globs of both jams. Bënnïë-Änn sliced open all six scones, and smeared each bottom half with the rose petal jam and each top half with the spicy carrot almond. With single-minded intent, she then chowed through all twelve scone halves, catching crumbs with an upturned palm beneath her chin, and then plucking them out of her hand and eating them. All this in the time it took Eloise to have three sips of tea and half of one of her own scones. It was a gastronomical performance unlike anything Eloise had ever seen, a strange combination of dainty and voracious.

When she was done, Bënnïë-Änn suppressed a belch and said, "That's better. Thank you, Your Highness. Now, how can I be of service?"

"I have some questions about the Eastern Lands."

"I thought that might be the case."

"Oh? Why would you say that?"

The Other Places Advocate picked up the teapot again. "Top up?"

"Not yet, thank you."

Bënnïë-Änn refilled her own cup and said, "Rumblings, Queen Eloise. I've heard rumblings."

"What sort of rumblings?"

"Have you ever met Queen Aglandau in person?" Eloise didn't quite understand that conversational jump, but Thëjëts didn't wait for a response. "No, you wouldn't have. You weren't alive when our beloved late queen had her first and only summit with the Eastie monarch. It did not go well."

"How so?"

"Aglandau Gaeta Cerignola Ponentine is a stereotypical Eastern Lander, to the point of caricature."

"You mean she's a bit obsessive about olives?" asked Eloise.

"That's a given. No, I mean she's thrifty, avaricious, thin-skinned, ambitious, quick-tempered, and prone to bullying behaviors. Mentally, she's as sharp as an executioner's machete."

"How is that a problem?"

"She has the purse of an entire realm to draw on to fund the expression those inclinations."

"I see." Eloise pushed her remaining scone to the exact middle of her plate. "So what happened between her and my mother?"

The Other Places Advocate leaned forward and lowered her voice like she was sharing a confidence. "No one knows. Not even the dowager king. I asked him once, and he said that it was 'before my time' and the late queen absolutely refused to be drawn on the subject, even by him."

Eloise frowned. "That's odd. I thought they had no secrets between them."

Thëjëts shook her head. "In this matter, apparently they did. But what we do know is that your late mother and Queen Aglandau met in a parlay tent on top of the Adequate Wall of the Realms at the Flachberg Gate twenty-plus years ago. As is always the case, it was just the two of them parlaying."

"Just like Gwendolyn the Irritable and King Brüüütus did two centuries before, up north."

"Yes, like that. Except, maybe with a bit less frisson and unintended biological consequences."

"You mean Gwendolyn and Brüüütus's child."

"Yes, the child. Anyway, the discussion between Queen Eloise and Queen Aglandau lasted five days, seven hours, and thirty-seven minutes exactly. We know that because a horological cuckoo timed it. No notes were kept. No advisor's recollections were recorded, because no advisors were there. Neither of them made a statement afterward, either individually or jointly. There are reports that the late queen was emotional when she emerged from the parlay, but those are unsubstantiated and unreliable. I asked the late queen about it once. All she said was, 'Matters were discussed. Decisions were made. You've seen the results. End of the matter.' It was clear that it was not going to be a topic of discussion."

"Results," said Eloise. "What results?"

"Pre-flopping-cise-flopping-ly. That's exactly what I wondered. What results, indeed?"

"Well, there has been peace and trade between the two realms. Olives flow outward from the Eastern Lands. Non-olive foods and all manner of crafts and raw minerals flow back into it. Bills get paid. Envoys and trade delegates come and go. The relationship between the two realms seems to work reasonably well."

"And yet, there are tensions," said Thëjëts.

"Rumblings, you said."

"Rumblings."

"So again, I ask, what rumblings?"

"Discontents. Are you aware that there's a blight affecting an increasing number of trees in the Eastern Lands olive groves?"

"Actually, that rings a definite bell," said Eloise. "I saw a report on the failure of olive cultivars a few weeks back."

"That would have been my report." The huge woman let out a kind of choking noise, which Eloise slowly realized was something like a chortle. "It was called 'Being a Report on the Widespread Failure of Olive Cultivars in Eastern Lands Groves.'"

"That's right. It was next to a report on the spike in speculative trading of oregano futures."

"So, you actually saw it? Really? I didn't know Ligurian had it in him to pass it on to you. 'Don't bother the queen with this soporific dullishness.' I don't know how good First Advisor's inter-realm thinking is."

"To be honest, I can't say I absorbed every detail."

"Still, it made it to your desk. What a pleasant surprise. One works on things and never knows if anyone will ever see them, or appreciate them. I can't tell you how it has made my day that my humble report made it past Ligurian and into your in-tray."

Eloise remembered thinking of that particular scroll as the perfect antidote for insomnia, but kept that to herself. "What of this failure? Just how bad is it?"

"Very bad. Probably worse than I depicted in my report. For the Eastern Landers, this blight is striking tree after tree, rendering them unproductive, and then killing them. It's not a fast thing. It takes some years to go from first detection to dead tree. But it has moved relentlessly."

"That must be horrible, given how important olives are to them."

"Exactly. They've tried all kinds of remedies, from applying fungicides to individual leaves to burning whole infected groves. Nothing has arrested the spread."

"Is there anything that we can do to help them?"

That stopped Thëjëts. "What a generous question to ask."

Eloise lifted a shoulder and let it drop. "They're having a problem. If we have an answer, we should offer to help."

"I don't know that your counterparts in the other three-and-a-half realms would send their thinking in that direction. They'd be more likely to see if there was some advantage they could take. I certainly wouldn't expect it from Queen Aglandau."

"Why not?"

The Other Places Advocate plucked another scone and put it on her plate. "I said that she's a stereotypical Eastern Lander. Well, the Easties always see themselves as aggrieved. They act like bullies, but, typical of the way bullies are, feel they're the oppressed party. They're never content with what they have, they take offense at the least slight, real or imagined, and use that feeling of being wronged to justify any action that retaliates for the affront. They hold their grievances close to their hearts."

"I didn't know that. I'll try not to offend Aglandau."

"I don't know how much good that will do you. They pass their grudges through the generations."

"Really?"

"Of course. They still hold a grudge at having lost land to Queen Gwendolyn, may Her Irritableness stand with Çalaht."

"That's two centuries ago."

"Welcome to the put-upon world of the Easties."

Eloise picked up her teacup and sipped. The haggleberry tea had gone tepid. She put it back down and added some from the pot. "How current is your information?"

"I'm the Other Places Advocate. It's my job to be up-to-date."

"Do you know what's going on near Flachberg?"

"What do you mean?"

"I had a conversation with Livinia Heterokont and her brother Skartabel."

"Liv and Skart. They managed to get to you, did they? I suggested they try."

"Oh?"

"They, too, seem to be perceiving rumblings. Skart is a lunkhead, but I trust Livinia. If she's smelling smoke, then it's quite likely there's fire somewhere."

"It's not just them. I also—"

A loud knocking interrupted her. Eloise looked at the door, but didn't say anything.

Another knock, this one more insistent. Eloise recognized the pattern being used, a distinct set of raps with his knuckles followed by a couple with the back of a curled hand. "Apologies, but I think our discussion is about to end. Thank you for your time." There was another of the strange knocks. "Come in, First Advisor."

Ligurian seemed out of breath, like he'd been running, and his face was tight. "Your Highness."

"Is there a problem, First Advisor?"

"I didn't realize we were having a meeting. Apologies if I'm late." He gave a curt bow to the Other Places Advocate. "Bërnädïce-Ändrëä. Lovely to see you. And you're sitting and having scones. How very comfortable. I hope I haven't missed much."

"I was just—" started Thëjëts.

"The Other Places Advocate was kindly reminiscing on her time with my mother. She's been sharing kind words and comforting musings. Please join us, First Advisor. Pull up a pew and grab a scone with some mostly edible jam. The tea in the pot is still hot."

"I... I..." He swallowed. "I'd love to, if you can spare one."

Eloise smiled, and invited him to bring over a chair from the map table. He'd never, ever accepted food from her, and he looked incredibly uncomfortable serving himself a scone. He added a dab of jam, looking like he'd never done it before in his life.

What was going on that he felt the need to crash this meeting? And stick around?

The three of them passed another quarter hour with meaningless talk that orbited vaguely around the memory of her mother. The whole time, Eloise watched small beads of sweat form on Ligurian's brow.

❦ 64 ❦

A QUEEN'S DEMAND

Once again, Eloise sat on the Listening Throne in the Receiving Room, this time wearing the Keep It Quick Cape and the Gumballic Heraldic Crown, which she was still trying to get used to. At least her neck wasn't aching like a tree stump with a migraine anymore. She reached up a hand and adjusted it slightly.

Lorch stood to one side of the dais at parade rest, the picture of champion-like perfection. Near him, Jerome sat on a chair surreptitiously nibbling a muscat raisin he'd plucked from a stem hidden in a pouch at his waist. On the other side of the dais, First Advisor Ligurian scratched notes on a scroll, and made the occasional comment to the scribe in charge of capturing the goings on for posterity.

Fortunately, the issues on the agenda hadn't been too vexing—the worst being a dispute between two Çalahtist sects who both claimed the right to fill a vacancy at a far-flung bishopric. As the notional head of the faith, the argument's resolution somehow landed in Eloise's lap. She suspected that the Venerable Prelate Herself had fobbed off the matter deliberately so the tapir wouldn't have to disappoint either sect. Let Eloise be the bad guy.

The candidate from the Holy Order of Her Divine Osteoporosis was a bent, smiling, unassuming man who looked like he'd devoted decades to his sect. He seemed pious enough at first glance. Eloise waved him forward. "You're Brother Mááàÿnáäàrd?"

"Yes, Your Highness," he croaked.

"And why do you believe you should become bishop?"

He pointed to his hunched back. "This hump. Pure osteoporosis. I've devoted my life to that aspect of her divinity and have emulated it to its fullest. Also, it's our turn."

"You say it's your turn, but it's not," interrupted an annoyed squirrel. "Your order has received the last two bishopric appointments to this role, which we are supposed to be sharing . You need to let someone else have a turn."

"Your sect has had six of the last ten occupants of the role," quavered Mááàÿnáäàrd. "We are far from achieving anything close to parity."

"How our distant predecessors made their decisions is hardly germane. What's relevant is what's in front of us. And that's that you have had 37 straight years in the role. It's our turn."

Eloise waved the squirrel forward. "You are Sister Katydidn't of the Sisterhood of Her Heavenly Unending Misery?"

She curtsied. "Yes, Your Highness. At your spiritual service."

"What is your sect's approach to devotion?"

"We believe in expressing the deep anguish that the Holy One experienced in her life. Lamentations are our specialty, along with elegies, jeremiads, keening, dirges, threnodies, ululations, piteous moaning, and generalized unhappy wailing to fit all occasions."

"I see." Eloise drummed her fingers on the arm of the Listening Throne and resisted the urge to stand up and swap to the Now You've Really Hacked Me Off cloak.

Eloise didn't really care who took the bishop's role. In fact, she wondered why Ligurian had let this one come before her. Was he just trying to keep her busy? Eloise thought back to her gerbil orphanage threat with the disputing radish farmers, and thought it might be a suitable precedent for this one. She also liked the message it sent—don't take up my time with things you should be able to work out on your own. "I see two options," she said.

"That's right," agreed Brother Máääÿnääàrd. "Her or me."

"That's not what I meant. What I meant was I see two options for me. Option one: the two of you work it out in a manner acceptable to you both."

Sister Katydidn't scrunched her nose. "And the other option?"

"A Rock Scroll Cleaver tournament between the two of you."

"Rock Scroll Cleaver? You mean the..." He curled his right fist, lightly bounced the pinky side into his other palm, then came down the third time like a chopping cleaver. "The children's game."

"Good, you know it. Say, whoever gets the best of eleven games gets the role."

The old man looked puzzled. "That... With respect, Your Highness, that hardly seems a fair basis for choosing a bishop."

Eloise gave an over-acted shrug. "Nor is it fair to force me to choose between two equally qualified candidates based on my particular whim. Do I pick the hump sect or the wailing sect? I don't know." She leaned closer to them and lowered her voice. "To be honest, I'm not sure I actually care. I'm sure you'd both do a splendid job." She looked at Ligurian. "First Advisor?"

"Yes, Your Highness?"

"These two will tell you what they're going to do. Please convey their choice to me by the end of the day."

"Of course, Your Highness.

"And if they go with the Rock Scroll Cleaver option, have Assistant Court Seer to the Court Seer Abernatheen de Chipmunk referee. He'd be very good at it."

"Yes, Your Highness."

She turned back to the two Çalahtists. "Good luck to both of you. First Advisor, what's next?"

"We're next," said a woman's voice from the back.

It was Picholine Manzanilla, the Eastern Lands ambassador. She strode forward with the good cheer of an embalmer. Next to her slithered Bosana de Coluber with his strange three eyes. A chill ran down Eloise's back at the mere thought of having to look him in the face. She glanced down at the hemp parchment in her lap. "I don't see you on the agenda. Have you spoken with First Advisor?" She looked at Ligurian, who seemed to be taking excessive interest in his boot laces at that very moment. "Apparently. Please approach."

A voice rang out. "The ambassadorrrrrrr and lead trrrrrrtade negotiatorrrrrrrr frrrrrrom the Eastern La—"

"Thank you Herald Hairauld," said Eloise. "That will do. "

"Yes, Yourrrrrrrr Highness."

Manzanilla and de Coluber stopped in front of the dais. The snake arranged himself in a formal pose, coils exact, head high, and all three of his eyes fixed on her, unblinking. Next to him, Manzanilla stood tall and still, eyes boring into Eloise with the same snake-like intensity. In unison, they bobbed the precise minimum allowed by Protocol, then resumed their pose, saying nothing.

They waited, letting the silence stretch.

Were they trying to fluster her? This struck Eloise as childish. Did ambassadors always act with such haughtiness and disdain? She adjusted the GHC on her head, scooted back in her throne and stared right back.

Five very long minutes passed. Finally, Manzanilla gave a small, scoffing snort and spoke. "We have a document to present."

Eloise tried to mimic the scoffing snort, but couldn't quite capture the same degree of derision. "Go ahead."

"It's a petition." Manzanilla proffered the scroll she carried toward Ligurian, but Eloise raised a hand, and stopped him from taking it.

"Ambassador Manzanilla, what is the nature of the petition?"

"It's a petition from the people of Canton Flachberg, presented to Her Majesty Queen Aglandau Gaeta Cerignola Ponentine, and forwarded with her endorsement on their behalf to you, with a comment."

"How lovely." Eloise clenched her teeth, not liking the direction this was taking. "What does it say?"

The ambassador unfurled the scroll she held and began quoting in a flat monotone.

Whereas the people of Flachberg and its canton are a peaceful, olive-loving sort.

And whereas in the reign of Gwendolyn the Irritable, the people of Flachberg were subjugated and forced unwillingly under the control of the Western Lands and All That Really Matters.

And whereas the people of Flachberg and its canton remain culturally, and in mind and heart, subjects of the realm of the Eastern Lands.

We petition you to right the wrong that was perpetrated by Gwendolyn the Irritable and bring the Canton of Flachberg and all her people back into the bosom of its rightful queen and annex the canton back into the Eastern Lands.

The ambassador lowered the scroll slightly and looked at Eloise. "Her Majesty has added a note at the bottom that reads, 'To Queen Eloise Hydra Gumball III of the Western Lands and All That Really Matters, on behalf of the good, true, and loyal subjects of Flachberg and in the spirit of peace and cooperation that existed between our two realms for these many decades, I do hereby insist that this request, indeed this demand, be fulfilled.' That is all."

Eloise blinked, jaw still tight. She gripped the arms of the throne and fought to keep both screams and tears from her voice. "Let me see if I understand what all those whereas's mean. You want Flachberg."

"Yes."

"Just, here you go. Have Flachberg."

"Yes."

"In the spirit of peace and cooperation."

"Yes."

Eloise felt blood rise in her face. The sheer cheek of it. Such bald, direct affront. "You do not just gavotte in here and demand I hand over a chunk of my realm."

"We just did," said the snake.

Eloise sat a full two minutes, wondering what she could possibly say in response. Jump up and yell at them? Come up with some sort of cutting remark? Leave without saying anything? Snark? Bile? A simple "no" to these jesters?

What would her mother have done? Have them arrested? Laugh at them? No, because there's no way these two would have done this to her mother. Which meant they thought Eloise was weak. Stuff that.

Still, a proper response would need more time—time to work through implications and get some sort of appropriate strategy together and make sure she didn't create a situation she couldn't handle.

She mastered herself and stood. "Leave the document with First Advisor. I shall take the matter under advisement and give it full consideration." Eloise spat the words with as much ice as she could muster. "You're dismissed. You're very dismissed." Then she headed for the door.

❦ 65 ❦

TING-THWUP!

Eloise stormed away from the Receiving Room, not bothering to hang the Keep It Quick Cape back on its peg. She needed some time alone. Some time to think. Despite the cold of the late winter afternoon, she headed to the Culpability Courtyard to walk its perimeter and clear her head.

She strode around the courtyard, stopping only long enough to grab a hockey sack that had been left in the way and giving it a solid throw across the field to vent some of her frustration.

The demand from Queen Aglandau rattled her. More than that, it angered her. What was she supposed to do? Just shrug her shoulders and say, "Sure, whatever you say. Have Flachberg" and then sign a proclamation decreeing it be so? Was Eloise supposed to be that dim? That malleable? How did it matter that Flachberg was culturally aligned with the Eastern Lands? So what? That's not how borders worked.

She stopped, panting. There was a winter rose planted in a corner, its white buds just emerging into blossoms. Mind racing, she crossed her arms and stared at it.

Flachberg—both the town and the canton—had been part of the Western Lands and All That Really Matters since the earliest days of Queen Gwendolyn the Irritable's reign, back before the whole King Brüüütus debacle. Didn't that much time—more than two centuries of time that included entire decades of relative peace—alter the cultural equation somehow?

Actually, no. That's not how things worked. The duration of culture was stronger than that. Otherwise, Flachbergian kids wouldn't still be learning to count with olives stuck onto the ends of their fingers.

Even so, she wasn't going to just hand over a chunk of land because some out-of-date Eastie wannabes had whined to Aglandau. For that matter, who was to say the petition was even real? And if they had such an issue with being in her queendom, why hadn't someone said something earlier?

Calm yourself, Eloise told herself. *You have to deal with this with clarity. Smell some roses or something.*

Roses? she said back.

Yeah, roses. It'll do you some good.

Fine. I'll smell some blinking roses if it'll make you leave me alone.

Good. Do it.

I will.

Stop talking to yourself and smell a rose.

Stop telling me what to do.

Eloise looked for the most open blossom on the rosebush and tilted herself toward it to inhale its scent.

There was a sudden *ting-thwup!* She felt the Gumballic Heraldic Crown jerk forward on her head and slide over her eyes. The weight of it unbalanced her and she fell into the rose bush. Thorns scratched her hands and face, and she cried out.

She tried to push herself back up and out, but her clothes snagged and she only managed to flop onto her side in more of the thorny branches. There was another *thwup!* and a sharp agony shot through her bicep.

A detached part of her mind was calm enough to think, *Someone's trying to outright kill me.*

The rest of her mind had more immediate things to worry about. "Aaaaaaaahhhhhhhhhhh!" she screamed.

"Princess!" cried Lorch, flinging himself over her. His body shielded her from further harm, but it also shoved her further into the rose-bush. Dozens of thorns poked into her skin, but it was nothing compared to the pain in her arm. "Stop him! Stop him!" yelled Lorch, pointing to a high point near a chimney overlooking the courtyard. "Jerome! Up there!"

The chipmunk leaped onto a nearby vine and scampered toward the roof. Moments later, he flung himself onto the roof tiles at full run and disappeared from view.

There was another *thwup!* and Lorch suppressed a grunt.

Jerome's voice echoed across the courtyard. "You there! Stop! Stop! I said st—"

Eloise looked past Lorch's shoulder and a dark motion caught her eye. A human figure, masked and dressed completely in black, launched himself in her direction from the roof, light glinting off a drawn blade.

The calm part of her thought, *Yep, someone's trying to kill me. This guy.*

The rest of her started thrashing to get out from under Lorch.

The assassin landed badly, one foot coming down on the hockey sack she'd thrown earlier. He tucked into a roll to keep from splatting face-first, and sprang neatly to his feet.

Then he stopped and looked down—at the knife hilt protruding from his diaphragm. He shook his head slowly with an expression that seemed more disappointed than anything else, then he grabbed the handle, held it firmly, and fell face-forward, shoving the blade as high and hard as it would go. He was dead within three heartbeats.

"Are we clear?" yelled Lorch.

"No one else visible from here," shouted Jerome. This was echoed by other guards who had rushed to the scene.

"Apologies, Queen Eloise, for..." Lorch eased himself off her, reached out a hand, and helped her to her feet. "I—Your arm!"

"Whuh?" slurred Eloise, shock starting to set in. She looked at her right arm. "Seems OK."

Lorch's eyes darted to her left arm.

Eloise turned her head the other way. "Oh. Owww!"

A crossbow bolt protruded from her upper arm. Gritting her teeth, she lifted her arm just enough to see that the arrow had pierced right through. "That's not good."

She felt wooziness trying to crowd out her waking mind. *Don't faint. Don't faint. Don't faint. Don't faint.*

Eloise didn't faint.

Instead, she overbalanced and fell backward into the rose bushes again, jarring the arrow and torquing it in her arm.

She heard someone using a lot of words that one did not normally hear in the polite company of Court.

It took her a moment to realize that person was her.

FOR SOME VALUES OF LUCKY

Eloise woke in her parents' bed (no—it was her bed now, she needed to accept that) with no memory of how she'd gotten there. She blinked into awareness to find Eldridge the Apothecary winding a bandage around her left bicep. Her arm throbbed with a sharp ache, a new pain to go with the dull one that still haunted the wrist in its cast. On the bedside table, a crossbow bolt lay in two pieces, cut neatly across like a snipped rose stem. Next to the bolt stood vials of unguents, pots of ointments, bags of herbs, strips of clean, bleached linen like the one Eldridge was wrapping her with, and far too many wads of blood-soaked cloth.

"Eldridge," said Eloise.

"Queen Eloise."

Her mouth tasted like road base. "How long was I out?"

"Long enough for me to do all of this." He waved his hand toward the soiled dressings, bandages, and healing supplies. "But not much longer."

"What happened?"

He pointed to the crossbow bolt. "You were shot with that. It went all the way through. I had to cut it in half and pull the shaft through."

"It hurt. A lot."

"Yes, it would have. You're lucky that you were unconscious while I cleaned it. Otherwise, I'd have had to ask the guards to hold you down while I examined the wound, washed it, packed it with herbs, and wrapped it in a poultice."

"I think I'm glad I wasn't there for that. The thing hurts like Çalaht's stretched thumbs."

"It would. Parts of you saw the light of day that never should have." He tied off the bandage with gnarled hands. "You were lucky."

Eloise moved her arm and winced. "I'm not sure I share that opinion."

"Lucky, for some values of luck, then. The arrow pierced you in a most fortuitous place. It missed the bone and the main blood vessels. Believe me, there are much worse places you could've been struck."

"How very mug-half-full of you. Is everyone else alright? Were there any other injuries?"

"Champion Lacksneck—"

"Lorch!" Eloise tried to sit up, but it hurt too much. "What happened to Lorch?"

"Champion Lacksneck put himself in harm's way to protect you, as a champion should. He earned a crossbow bolt in his posterior for his troubles."

"No. No-no-no. How bad is it?"

"Champion Lacksneck is less injured than you. He is remarkably muscular in that part of his anatomy and his padded riding breeks served him well. Still, even after the healer finishes tending him, he'll prefer standing to sitting for a while."

"I should go see him."

Again, Eloise tried to sit up. Eldridge helped her with a gentle hand under her shoulder, then he popped pillows behind her and leaned her back into them. "My queen, you should let me finish. Champion Lack-sneck will be here as soon as he can, along with Ex-Champion Aber-natheen de Chipmunk." As he spoke, Eldridge moved away a bowl of bloody water and brought over a clean one. He decanted water from a ewer, added several drops of illegibly-labeled tinctures from brown bottles, and dipped a clean linen into the mix. He dabbed her face and it came away tinged with red. One by one, he cleaned her wounds, applying a sweet-smelling salve to each.

"I'm a mess," said Eloise. "I've been a mess for months."

"Çalaht has watched over you, though. This could all have been much worse." The apothecary moved to the top of her head and wiped a particularly raw spot.

"Ouch. What's that?"

"More luck."

"What do you mean?"

Eldridge set down the damp cloth and picked up the Gumballic Heraldic Crown from a dresser. He rotated it so the back of the crown was up, then handed it to her.

"Oh," said Eloise.

"Oh, indeed, Your Highness."

One of the thin steel structural arches was severely bent and several of the jewels and precious stones appeared to have been lost. Eloise poked a finger into a bolt-sized hole in the maroon velvet that covered the arches. She turned it around and poked another finger through the matching one on the other side. "The Crown Jeweler isn't going to be happy. I promised him I'd take care of this."

"With respect, Your Highness, the Crown Jeweler is never happy."

"True."

"So, you see why I say you've been lucky. Just a little lower, and we'd be having a very different conversation."

"Or no conversation at all."

"Indeed, Your Highness."

She'd come a weak length or two from having a crossbow bolt embed itself in her skull instead of grazing it. If she hadn't leaned over to smell the winter rose, she wouldn't be here to be thinking about it. The nearness of it chilled her.

"I think this wound needs stitching. Apologies, but I need to snip away some of your hair to clean it properly. I'm just worried that I'll—"

"It's OK. My hair is part of the disaster story. Do what you need to do."

"Yes, Your Highness." Eldridge picked up a delicate pair of scissors shaped and engraved like a swan. "It won't be too much."

There was a knock at the door. Eloise looked at Eldridge. "Can I admit them?"

"I don't think your modesty will be compromised by me sewing up your scalp while you have an audience. So long as you don't mind." He held a needle in the flame of a lit candle.

"It'll give me something to think about other than being a pin cushion." She adjusted her blankets to cover herself and noticed that her clothes were bloody, too. "Enter!"

The door swung open and four faces peered in—Jerome, Lorch, Hector, and the Nameless One. She waved them forward and they crowded into the room. Jerome climbed onto the bed, Lorch stood awkwardly to the side, wincing noticeably when he moved, and the two horses tried not to bump anything.

"It's terrible what happened," said Hector. "Thank Çalaht you are OK."

"We have Lorch to thank for that," said Eloise. "Along with the dumb luck of smelling a rose."

"I... I'm not sure I deserve any credit." Lorch looked at his feet. "I would like to offer my resig—"

"Stop! I don't want to hear it. Please, Lorch, you didn't know the assassin was there, and you put your life on the line, not to mention your fundament. If the culprit had managed to kill either me or you, then we could have considered your resignation, although there would have been much less need to do so."

"Thank you, Queen Eloise. I'll double down on keeping you protected."

"That I can accept. Thank you, Champion Lacksneck. Now, what do we know about the assassin? Ow!"

"Sorry, Queen Eloise. I should have warned you. The calendula, onion, and witch hazel mix might sting a bit. I'll use some clove oil to reduce the pain. May I begin the..." Eldridge held a threaded needle with gnarled fingers.

Eloise took a breath and steadied herself. "Go ahead. Jerome, you might want to look away."

"Why would I need to—"

The apothecary poked the needle into one of the skin flaps on Eloise's head.

There was a *thump!* as Jerome fainted and fell onto the floor.

"Not good with needles," said Eloise. "Never was."

"So I remember. Ever since he was a pup," said Eldridge. "I have some sal ammoniac. Shall I waft it under his nose to rouse him?"

"Muhmuhfuhfuh," muttered Jerome, slowly waking up.

"Ah, no need then." The apothecary returned to his sewing.

"Ow! Once again—Ow!" Eloise winced but tried not to move her head. "What do we—Ow! Know about the assassin?"

"Not much, Queen Eloise," said Lorch. "No identification, of course. He wore indeterminate clothes reminiscent of the Central Ranges but sewn from local cloth. The crossbow was in the Southie style, but the bolts themselves were made from wood indigenous to the Half Kingdom. What was strangest was his face."

"How so? Ow! He had on a mask."

"His face had been cut and sewn into a grotesque shape. Sort of..." Lorch stretched and folded parts of his face in imitation. "The wounds were fresh. Maybe a day or two at most."

"Why?" asked Eloise. "What's the point?"

The Nameless One snorted.

Hector nodded agreement. "I've heard of this, too. It's a form of identity obscurement for people undertaking a suicide mission."

"Ow! That's disgusting. Who does that?"

"No one knows," said the horse. "It's just one of those things you hear around a stable. No one actually believes it."

"They will now," said Lorch.

They fell into silence, while the apothecary worked.

"Master Eldridge, can my friends and I speak freely in front of you, and count on your discretion?"

"My hearing's gone, Queen Eloise. I haven't heard a word you've said since I got here. Plus, I'm just about done sewing, so I can leave you to it soon."

"Thank you."

"What?" said Eldridge.

"Thank y— Oh, I get it. Ow! Now, can someone—Ow!—answer a question for me?"

"What?" asked Jerome. "And sorry about the..." He waved at the spot on the floor where he'd fainted.

Eloise gave a palms-up gesture, vaguely encompassing everything—them, the room, the queendom, the realm. "What in the name of Çalaht's festering, fungus-riddled fistula is going on?"

"What do you mean?" said Hector.

"Another attempt on my life. A demand for land from the Easties. No clues about who killed my mother or who tried to kill me. The sunflower thing. All that time searching for babies in the Bibliotheca de Records and Regrets and mostly zilch to show for it. All of it. What is going on?"

"I don't know, my queen," said Lorch.

"Me either," said Jerome.

Hector shook his head. "I have nothing." The Nameless One pawed the ground in agreement.

Her worries hung heavy in the room as they all thought about it.

"With First Advisor acting so odd, I don't think I can turn to him for advice. I really don't know what to do. Without him, I feel like I'm blind to the realm."

Jerome's whiskers drooped at the thought. "And what you really need is the opposite. You need to be able to see everything in the realm."

The comment tickled something in the back of Eloise's mind. "Say that again, Jer."

"I said, you need to be able to see everything in the realm."

"Huh."

"Huh?" said Jerome.

"Huh."

Lorch looked at Hector and the Nameless One. "Huh?"

The two horses shrugged.

"Uh-huh," said Eloise as an idea took shape. "Hector, Nameless One, can you be in charge of keeping a close eye on First Advisor Ligurian?"

"What are we looking for?"

"I don't know. But I'm guessing you'll know when you see it."

"We're on it."

"Jerome, can you please get the Crown Jeweler?"

"The Crown Jeweler?" The chipmunk curled his tail into a question mark. "Whatever for?"

"Because I need to step this up. I'm not going to sit here with a target painted on my backside." Lorch's face twitched as he suppressed a grimace. "Sorry. Bad choice of words."

"It's OK, Your Highness. I'm aware that the location of my injury is... was... is... awkward."

"I've been trying to get everyone to call him 'Pincushion Tuchus,'" said Jerome. "But it hasn't caught on yet. Too many syllables, I think."

Lorch scowled at him. "I asked you not to—"

"'Porcupine Butt' seems to be getting more traction."

"Please don't—"

"'Echidna Ass' is almost alliterative, but not quite."

"Jer!" said Eloise. "Cut it out. We have stuff to do."

"Right. Sorry, Queen Eloise."

"Don't apologize to me."

Jerome had the good grace to look chagrined. "Sorry, Champion Lacksneck."

"Apology accepted." Lorch turned back to Eloise. "Why the Crown Jeweler? How's he going to help?"

"I have an idea, but I'm still working it out."

"I'll fetch him," said Jerome.

"And maybe hide the GHC so it's not the first thing he sees when he gets here."

❦   67   ❦

A SMALL FAVOR

The Crown Jeweler arrived in the Salle de la Famille wearing his maroon robes and a suspicious look. As the rhesus macaque bowed, his deep-set eyes flicked around the room. They landed on the Gumballic Heraldic Crown, which sat on a sideboard occluded by a silver tea service. He gasped and rushed to it. "What happened? What happened to my baby?"

Eloise watched him, reminded of Head Scribe, and wondered what it was that made adults refer to their precious objects as babies.

He picked up the crown with long bony fingers, held it a few weak lengths from his face, and turned it around and around, examining every jewel, strut, and scrap of fabric. Every now and then, he looked up and fixed Eloise with a hateful, accusing look. "I trusted you."

"Yes, you did. I'm really sorry about what's happened to it."

He poked his fingers through the damaged velvet. "I can't imagine the circumstances that would lead to such damage. Truly, Queen Eloise, these are ancient, delicate items. They deserve your respect."

"Someone shot at me with a crossbow. The GHC probably saved my life. Surely that must count for something."

"A crossbow bolt?" The macaque's mouth gaped. "I'm so sorry. I hadn't heard. Are you alright?"

"I'm fine. And really? You hadn't heard?"

"No, Your Highness."

"I would have thought it would have reached every corner of the castle by now." Eloise waved him toward her. "Please, come sit for a moment."

Holding on to the crown, he did as she requested.

"Tea?"

"No, thank you ma'am."

"It's haggleberry."

"You'll have to excuse me, I don't care for hot beverages, Your Highness."

Eloise poured herself a cup with the arm that had not been shot and set down the pot. The injured arm throbbed, and Eloise did her best not to move it. "Crown Jeweler, I'm truly sorry about the crown. Do you think you can fix it?"

"It will never be the same."

"None of us are ever the same once we have holes shot in us. But that's not what I asked."

He considered the damage. "Yes, I can fix it. The changes will be visible to anyone who looks closely."

"Not many people will have that chance, though, will they?"

"No, Your Highness."

"Then we'll be OK?"

The Crown Jeweler frowned. "I suppose so."

"Good." Eloise blew across the lip of her cup and sipped. "I need a small favor from you."

His frown deepened and he clutched the crown closer. "What kind of favor?"

"I need you to please bring me the Orb of Alleged Omniscience."

The macaque's eyebrows shot up and he leaned backward. "It... It hasn't been fixed yet. It still has damage from last time. I'm still working out how to even approach restoring it to some resemblance of what it used to be."

"I understand. I still need you to let me have it for a while."

"It's dented. It's not suitable for presentation."

"No presentation. Just me and the Orb."

The Crown Jeweler's face darkened, but he tried to hide it from her. "I... I can't imagine what you might need it for that can't wait until it is whole again."

"And yet, here I am asking for it."

The macaque held the crown tight and said nothing, but the way he rocked back and forth in his chair told her everything she needed to know.

Eloise took another sip, put her cup back down, and held out a serving plate. "Petit four?"

"No thank you, ma'am. I don't care for sweets."

"I see." She took one of the small chocolate-coated cakes and put it on her dessert plate. "You don't trust me. I get that. I haven't earned it."

"Your Highness, I—"

"It's OK. I get it." She took a delicate bite of the petit four. Not terrible, but not spectacular, so ultimately, vaguely disappointing. "So will you help me out?"

"I..." The Crown Jeweler trailed off.

"You know that thing you're holding?"

"The Gumballic Heraldic Crown? Yes."

"You know it represents all kinds of things I'm allowed to do, right?"

"Yes."

"I could, for example, send Champion Lacksneck to just go get the Orb. But I don't want to do that. I want you to work with me."

"I see."

And from his sour look, she could tell he did.

"I'll let you have the GHC back. You could give me a different crown, a more workaday one, when you bring me the Orb. Would that make a difference to you?"

The Crown Jeweler's eyes brightened. "You'd let me have it back? Really?"

"Absolutely. And you know what else? I'm happy for you to make any changes that you want while you're fixing it. Make it as splendid as you can."

The macaque gasped again, but this time it was with delight. He stood and gave her an elaborate bow. "I'll be right back, Your Highness." He dashed from the room in a simian rush.

Thirteen minutes later, the Crown Jeweler stood, panting, in front of Eloise, holding two felt bags and giving another enthusiastic bow. "Your Highness."

From the first bag, the rhesus macaque drew a silver band and held it up for her to see. "Would this work for you?" It was mostly a simple, flattened ring engraved with knot work. At the front, it flared into a disk with an older version of the Gumball crest etched into it (the weasel was on a bunch of shallots, not a bushel of onions, and the one-eyed otter had the fire poker jutting out from his eye).

Eloise took it from him and looked at it from different angles. "The artistry is lovely. And it's certainly lighter than the GHC. May I try it on?"

"Of course, Your Highness."

Eloise settled the crown on her head. "Oh! It fits like it was made for me. Who wore it before me? Did my mother? I don't remember her using this one."

"No, Your Highness, the late Queen Eloise preferred more ornate crowns, which is why you never saw her in it. But, if I may say so, it seemed to me that your tastes might have run in a less-cluttered direction. The last one to wear it was..." The Crown Jeweler consulted a scroll he pulled from a pocket in his robe. "Actually, the only one to wear it was Queen Gladys Plectrum Sprocket Gumball, known as Queen Gladys the Leafstalk Loser."

"I vaguely remember from Histories and Hearsay class. She didn't reign for long?"

He looked at his notes. "Twenty-three minutes."

"Twenty-three minutes? How is that possible?"

"Choked on the crudités at her Crown Plonking reception. She succumbed to celery sticks. Hence the name."

"That's terrible. Do you think the crown is jinxed?"

"No, Your Highness. I think her celery was jinxed."

Eloise tilted her head in different directions to see how well the crown stayed on. "Snug, but not too tight. It doesn't feel like it's going to slip off any second. I think I like it."

"Very good, Your Highness. And next..." He didn't open the second felt bag, just handed it to her. "As Her Highness requested, the Orb of Alleged Omniscience. All the bits and pieces are in the bag, so if you could please keep them together, that would be helpful."

"I'll do that." Eloise felt the Orb through the material. Her thumb came to rest on the dent, and her cheeks flushed with remembered embarrassment. She prayed that she hadn't damaged the inherent whatever-it-was that she hoped lurked behind its name. "Thank you for this."

"Does Her Highness require anything else? I'm eager to see to the Gumballic Heraldic Crown."

"No, that will do. If you could please just send in the page on your way out."

"Yes, ma'am."

The Crown Jeweler left, and RoyLee immediately poked his head across the threshold. "Yes, Princess Your Highness Queen Eloise?"

"Could you please let Jerome know that I'd like him to meet me in the Queen's Study at the quarter hour?"

"Will you be requiring tea?"

"Yes, please."

RoyLee bowed and bolted down the hall, yelling, "Tea for the queen!"

As his voice echoed away, Eloise eased herself from her chair and slowly headed for the Queen's Study, careful not to jar her crossbow-bolted arm.

❦ 68 ❦

DRASTIC

"**A**re you sure this is a good idea, El?" Jerome paced back and forth in front of Eloise as she sat in the comfy armchair in the Queen's Study, with the Orb of Alleged Omniscience on her lap, still in its bag.

"I have no idea, Jer. But I have to do something to get on top of everything."

"But this... This is crazy."

"Which is why you're here. To mitigate the crazy and make sure I'm OK."

He stopped in front of her. "I don't know about this. I really don't. We don't know what the Orb can do. We don't know if the Orb actually does anything at all."

Eloise tried not affirm his hesitation with her grave doubts. "Look, how complicated can it be? I'll just try to tap into it. It'll work or it won't. But it must have originally been called the Orb of Omniscience for a reason."

"It wasn't. It was the Globule of Gloaming. The Ovoid of Observation. The Pellet of Pandemonium."

"It was 'pansophy.' The Pellet of Pansophy."

"Whatever. But what if its actual first name should have been The Brain Eating Sphere of For the Love of Çalaht Don't Touch This With a Barge Pole Run Run Away As Fast As You Can?"

"Not a very catchy name."

Jerome flicked his tail. "You get my point."

"And you get mine. Like you said, I need to be able to see what's going on. I need visibility into the realm. I don't know how else to do it."

"You could find out who in the intelligence apparatus is loyal to you?"

"How would I tell who they are?"

"I don't know. OK, then send out more information gatherers who you know and trust."

"We saw how well that worked for Göööber. Besides, who do I know who I'd trust like that? Am I supposed to send out Odmilla? Läääcy de Aardvark? You? Lorch? The first two are unsuited, and I need you and Lorch here."

"Hector and the Nameless One?"

"Hector stands out like a swollen nose. Perhaps the Nameless One, but I'm loath to separate him from Lorch."

"Look, we can do a better job of information gathering. We just need to work out how."

"I don't have that much time. It feels like things are bubbling over. You know what they say about drastic times needing drastic measures. Well, right now, things feel drastic to me. I have to try *something*." Eloise took the Orb from its bag and turned it around in her hand. "Look, Jer, I'm going to try. Are you going to watch over me or not?"

Another tail flick. "Of course. But I don't have to like it."

"Then let's get on with it. Find a spot to sit, and I'll start."

"Your wish is my command."

"Stop it."

Jerome gave her an exaggerated smirk, and climbed up so he could sit on the side table. He parked himself next to a plate of cream puffs made from almond milk and maple syrup, snagged one from the plate, and started quietly nibbling. "Go on. Orb away."

Eloise cupped the bejeweled sphere between her hands, settled back in her chair, closed her eyes, and tried to sense if there was a magical force in it.

Not at first feel.

She reached her mind toward it, trying to engage it by sending, "Hello? Anybody home?"

Eloise felt a rhythmic pulsing, and drew in a breath. But when she relaxed her hands, she realized it was her own pulse she felt.

What followed was a long, increasingly boring hour as Eloise kept at the Orb. She sent it messages. She probed it with her will. She tried to engage it in conversation. She commanded, cajoled, wheedled, needled, poked, squeezed, beseeched, screeched, whispered, enticed, lured, importuned, implored, prayed, invoked, decreed, entreated, and plain old asked.

Nothing.

At last, Eloise opened her eyes and found Jerome, mouth open, head back, emitting little snores that blew remnants of cream puff from his whiskers. She set the Orb down next to him with a small *clunk!*

Jerome sprang awake, looked around wildly, then found her eyes. He had the grace to look abashed. "Sorry. There's only so much staring at your internal struggles before I doze off."

"You're supposed to be watching over me."

"I was! I was! Well, except for the sleeping bit."

"This isn't working. I'm not getting anything at all from it." Eloise picked up a cream puff and shoved it in her mouth.

"Maybe there's no 'there,' there."

"And maybe there's no 'there,' here." She pointed to herself. "Maybe it's me, not it."

"How would you ever know?"

"That's the tricky bit, isn't it?" She poured herself a lukewarm tea and drank it in one long gulp. "Maybe I need to set it up differently."

"What do you mean? And yes, thanks, I'd love a cuppa."

"No, you wouldn't. It's barely above body temperature."

"Yuck. Pass."

Eloise picked up the Orb again, looking at it. "What I mean is that when we did the questing with the khan in the Central Ranges, there was that whole elaborate ceremony."

"I doubt it was the ceremony that made a difference. It was the vision herbs that the dream wife gave us."

"Right. The vision herbs. Of course. I wonder what it would take to get some."

"A trip back to the Central Ranges, probably. We don't know what was in them. And I think we promised not to try and replicate them."

"True. But we know there was prattleweed in them." Eloise scratched the top of her head, feeling unexpected surprise that the GHC was no longer up there. "And we know I'm susceptible to its influences. How hard would it be to get some of that?"

"You're asking me? How would I know?"

"I certainly don't. You know things I don't know."

"That's not one of them. Ask Lorch. Or Eldridge the Apothecary. Or maybe one of the Southie-flavored Çalahtist devotional houses. Oh, wait!" Jerome opened the pouch at his waist and pulled out a much smaller pouch. "What about this? The Southie envoy gave it to me at my Naming Ceremony."

"No, no, no. I don't want to take that. That was a gift to you, that's special. Also, it's probably not enough."

"It was enough for you when you zoomed off to the La La Realms at the devotion you attended with Queen Onomatopoeia."

"Those were seeds, not leaves." Eloise shook her head. "Listen to me. I sound like a prattle head."

There was a polite knock at the door, and RoyLee poked his nose in. "Apologies, Princess Queen Eloise? Be you be needing anything? I'll be heading on a break soon."

"No, RoyLee. Not unless you can get me some prattleweed," she joked.

RoyLee bowed and sprinted from the door, yelling, "Prattleweed for the queen! Prattleweed for the queen!"

"I like his enthusiasm," said Jerome.

"We might have to work on his discernment and discretion," said Eloise. "I hate to think what everyone in the castle is going to think of me now."

Eloise thought for a moment. "Actually, the Southie ambassador gave me some when I accepted his ambassadorial credentials. I wonder what happened to that?"

"I have no idea."

"Maybe Lady Seneschal would know."

But in no more time than it would have taken the wombat to fetch a tray of tea and scones, RoyLee was back, panting, and carrying a small, round wooden box. "Here you go, Princess Queen Eloise."

"Thank you, RoyLee." She took the box and set it on the map table on top of The South (which seemed appropriate). Lifting the lid revealed five triangular sections separated by wooden dividers that radiated out from the middle, each with a different part of the prattleweed plant.

One had the leathery leaves, whole instead of split down the mid-vein as she'd seen before. Another was half-full of faded bits of the pink and purple flowers. A third was practically overflowing with shreds of brown, stringy bark. The fourth had a tiny amount of seeds, little black specks that were almost invisible against the dark wood. The fifth held downer down, a matted wad of fluff from the seed head of the sober flower. They'd used this to snap Johanna out of a prattled state when she was under the influence of the plant and their Uncle Doncaster's control. "Goodness, RoyLee. This is like a perfect collection of this stuff. Where did you get this?"

"From the kitchens."

"The... The kitchens," said Eloise. "Why the kitchens?"

"Why not? It seems to be having everything else. I just be going in there and saying, 'Prattleweed for the queen.'"

"And?"

"And Chef be saying..." RoyLee lowered his voice an octave, "'Uh, OK.' Then he be saying, 'Uh, hold on.' Then he be going into an office and coming out with that wee box there."

"I see. How very resourceful of you. And how very kind of the new Chef. Please thank him for me."

The wombat ducked his head, abashed but pleased. "Thank you, Princess Queen Eloise. I'll be doing that. If there be nothing else you be needing, I'll be going."

Eloise thanked him again and RoyLee bowed his way out of the door. She turned to Jerome. "OK, let's try this."

"What are you going to take?"

"I don't know."

"You're just going to wing it? That seems a bit dodgy."

"How hard can this be?"

"Shall I remind you of your performance of 'Three Bags of Groats for My Sweetheart' and 'The Baleful Sorrows of Jedd the Sea Urchin' in a Southie devotional house in front of Her Maj Ono and a full congregation? 'How hard can this be?' indeed." Jerome climbed down from the side table. "Be right back."

"Where are you going?"

"To get Lorch. If you're determined to do this, then I want him here. His unfortunate family history with prattleweed means he probably knows more than any one of us about it. He was the one who knew to get the downer down for Princess Johanna. He also knew that you should have only taken one seed, not a whole pinch when you were with the Southie queen."

"You know what?"

"What?"

"That's a good idea."

"Don't take anything until we're back."

"I won't."

69

" ! "

Lorch stood looking down at the open box. "Hmmm…"

"What?" said Eloise.

"Someone's done you a great personal favor, whether you know it or not."

"How so?"

"This is a prayer star. The 'star' comes from the starlike shape of the wooden dividers inside. But these are extremely personal. The tending of the materials inside is performed with meticulous care. Someone lending you this is about the same as someone lending you their toothbrush, if less unhygienic."

"I didn't know that."

"No, you wouldn't have. These are not so common outside The South. I had an aunt who had one, but she was just a prattler. She didn't have the religious connection, but she knew enough about it to know what she happened to have in her possession."

Eloise ran a finger along the inside of box. "Should I send it back? Should I not use it?"

"It has been freely offered, so you should use it. Otherwise you would give offense."

"Wait," said Eloise. "Didn't the Southie ambassador give you some at your Naming Ceremony? Could we use a little of that instead?"

Lorch frowned. "Sorry, Your Highness, no."

"Why not?"

"I disposed of it."

"You got rid of it?" said Jerome. "Why?"

"My family is prone to becoming reliant on it. Addicted. I didn't want to risk it, so I burned it."

"Burned it? All of it?"

"All of it," said Lorch. He nodded at the prayer star. "That's your best bet, if you're in a hurry."

"Then that's what I'll do. So what do you suggest?"

"We know you're not used to it, so I suggest using the flowers. The seeds hit the hardest, the leaves are long-acting, the bark is unpredictable, but the flowers provide the mildest experience, and can be added in with greater precision."

"Flowers it is." Eloise carried the box to the table by her chair, sat down, settled the Orb on her lap, and said, "Ready. Start with one blossom?"

"Maybe a half," said Lorch. "It is easier to have a little more than wait for a too-high quantity to wane."

She picked a blossom from the prayer star, pinched it in half, and ate it. The dried, crumbling petals disintegrated on her tongue, coating it with an unpleasant, grainy bitterness. She spent the next 15 minutes with her eyes closed, trying to focus on connecting with the Orb and waiting to feel anything from the flower.

A couple times she cracked open her eyes to see both Jerome and Lorch completely focused on her.

After another ten minutes, she opened her eyes again. "Nothing."

"You're not feeling anything from the prattleweed bud?" asked Lorch.

"No. Nor anything from the Orb."

"And you're not speaking in repeated synonyms either," said Jerome. "You're definitely not prattled."

"Good point. It's probably safe to try another half bud."

"OK. Also, I need you both to find chairs and face the other direction. I can feel you watching me. It's making me self-conscious."

"Of course, Your Highness," said Lorch, pulling a chair from the map table. Sat backward on it, avoiding any weight on his injury, and faced away from Eloise. Jerome stayed on the Eastern Lands, but reoriented himself from a southerly aspect to a northerly one.

Eloise ate the other half of the first bud. Then, because neither Jerome nor Lorch was watching, she had a second dried flower, just to make sure. Settling back into her chair, she gathered all her focus and tried to connect with the Orb.

Nothing. Nothing, nothing, and more nothing. She may as well have been trying to sense the magic in a pressed dung brick. Nor did the prattleweed seem to be affecting her at all. The stuff really was useless.

She wondered if maybe having a seed would help. Glancing to make sure Lorch and Jerome were still looking the other way, Eloise moistened her index finger and quietly poked it into the prayer star. Not one, but two tiny black specks clung to it. Lorch had said one was enough, but she'd had way more than that in The South and had survived well enough.

She popped them in her mouth, swallowed, leaned forward, and bored into the Orb with everything she had.

Nothing... Nothing... Nothing...

Something.

It was the tiniest hint of a something, delicate as a grain of sand dropped in the waveless calm of a glassy winter lake, as gentle as the idea of a breeze tickling the pollen on a bee's belly, as ephemeral as the ghost harmonics of a harp plucked centuries ago.

But there was definitely a something there.

She took a moment to stare at Jerome and Lorch. They seemed awfully still, motionless, unmoving. Eloise squinted and focused on one of Jerome's whiskers. No, they were moving, just really, really slowly.

That was weird. Peculiar. Strange.

Had Jerome eaten some of the prattleweed while she wasn't looking? That wouldn't be very like him.

Eloise narrowed her attention, trying to get a sense of that something. But no matter how firmly or lightly, how widely or tightly she went at it, whatever it was remained spectral, shadowy, apparitional and out of reach.

After trying for what felt like a full two hours, Eloise flung herself back in her armchair, slumping down and grunting with prattled frustration. Her hand flopped against the box at her hip, and her cast made a muffled *thock!*

She looked down at her cast and thought about the box, container, case beneath her robe. It was a nice box. She'd worn it there for so long now that often she didn't think about it. Just put it on and wore it. All day and night. A great box, all dark and smooth and with a super comfortable sash. That sash was a great, fabulous, fantastic sash, all smooth and purple and easy to tie around her hip. Yep, a great, marvelous, phenomenal sash.

The Star of Whatever inside the box was pretty great, superb, awesome too. Just great. Such a cute emerald glow. She never said it to anyone, but she thought the green color set off her eyes nicely. Not that anyone ever got to see the glow. She should show the Star to

Jerome and Lorch sometime. Jerome would appreciate the color. He was clever, astute, cluey like that.

Thinking of the Star of Whatever made her think about the spark of something inside it. Sparky.

Sparky. Spark. Sparkosity. Sparkaroony. I need something.

Now *there* was a magical object, item, thing. So powerful, strong, mighty. She bet Sparky could do anything that he put his little metaphorical naked mole-rat mind to. He'd helped her with the paddock in Festering Resentment. Heck, he'd created the Purple Haze for Melveeta the Elusive. It didn't get much bigger, larger, grander than that. She bet he could help her do something with the Orb of Alleged Omniscience. Heck, he'd had that alleged chip off the thing in the box with him for a while now. Maybe they'd gotten to know each other, or something. Did magical objects get to know allegedly magical objects in that way? "Hello, I'm Sparky." "Hello, I'm Chip."

Hold it, Eloise thought. *That's an idea. Get Sparky to help with this.*

Fighting through her prattled fuzziness, Eloise stood and checked that Lorch and Jerome were still looking the other way. Turning her back to them, she hiked her robe, untied the sash that held the Star of Whatever to her hip, and resettled her clothes. Eloise popped open the lid, took the stone from its padded nest, set the box on the table next her, and nestled the Star and Orb next to each other on her lap.

She closed her eyes and sent the Star a simple "?".

And got a "..." in return.

Eloise waited.

Another "...".

She started humming to pass the time, until she realized the song was "Three Bags of Groats For My Sweetheart," and stopped.

Another "...".

Eloise sent an impatient "!".

Another "..."

"!!!"

"?"

Finally, thought Eloise. "!"

".?.—.,"

What the...? Eloise had no idea what that meant. She'd never seen Sparky use a broken dash like that before, nor that combination of symbols. It felt, however, like assent, or permission. So Eloise traveled once again down into the darkened hollow that was the home of the naked mole-rat version of the Star of Whatever. She found him neatly stacking tubers in a corner of his lair. The sense of him was sharp, clear, and cogent.

"Hey, Sparky, Sparkler, Sporky."

"Hey, Loulou. Nice to see you again. How long has it been?"

"Not so long."

He picked up a tuber and waved it at her. "Care for one?"

"I might pass, but thanks."

"More for me." He took a delicate nibble, biting with his strange, moving teeth. "You OK?"

"Sort of. I've got a bit going on. You?"

"Oh, I'm fine. Hangin' out. Nibblin' tubers. The usual." He waggled good teeth at her. It was a disconcerting look.

"Sparky, I was wondering if you might please help me with something."

"What do you have in mind?"

"Do you know the Orb of Alleged Omniscience?"

"Not personally. Only what I can gather from your thoughts. Nice dent, by the way."

"Yeah, not my finest hour." Eloise sat down on the dirt floor and smoothed her robe over her crossed legs. She noticed that there was no cast on her right wrist. Eloise flexed it to feel how much movement it had, and was surprised to find it was like nothing had ever happened to it. What an odd detail. "So, I want to try to use it. I think its omni-science might be maybe less alleged than the name suggests."

"Really."

"I need information. I need insight. I need *something*."

"And you're sure you want to do this?"

"Why not?"

Sparky gestured at her with his tuber. "Your experiences with what you call strong magic have had mixed results."

"What am I supposed to do? My First Advisor is untrustworthy. I can't get the information I need to make proper decisions. I've had another threat on my life, and I can't tell who's behind it. I need to see what's going on. This is the only approach I can think of to get it done and get it done quickly."

"Whatever you say, LouLou. This is your gig." Sparky waggled the tuber vaguely in the air. "Do you know if the Orb actually has any magical capability?"

"No. I don't. Can't you tell?"

"Nope. Not from here. Nor from what I can perceive from your memories. You seem to think something is going on there, but it's not clear to me you're right."

"But it is possible."

"Of course. It's also possible that you'll find a magical kumquat in your fruit salad capable of conjuring a mountain of tapioca. But it's not likely."

"Is there any way to be certain?"

"Sure." The naked mole-rat stood and moved his tuber like he was a third-rate community theater actor portraying a quarter-wit magician with a wand. "You can cast…" Dramatic pause. "A spell using the Orb. See if it actually does anything."

"I can do that?"

"Yes."

"Is it safe?"

"What do you think?"

"I think I'm playing with fire mixed with explosives and a side dish of stink bomb."

Sparky nodded. "Precisely. Perhaps while also rubbing jalapeño juice in your eyes."

"So you'll help me try? Please?"

"You asked nicely and you said the magic word. You know there are concerns and risks. You know there can be unexpected outcomes. What can I say? You're a big girl. You can make your own choices. It isn't exactly my job to tell you what to do. I'm just the hammer. You're the one swinging it."

"Right. Good. Thank you," said Eloise. "Let's get started."

"As you wish." And he saluted her with the tuber.

ЖЖ 70 ЖЖ

NOT SO ALLEGED

Eloise settled herself against a wall of Sparky's lair. "How do I start?"

"What did I say last time you were here?"

She thought back to their last conversation. "You spoke of intention. You said it was the force that drives the spell and gives it oomph. That it was different to making a wish, and that Melveeta had intention in spades."

"Good. You were paying attention. So what's your intention here?"

"To see and hear the truth."

"Right. You're touching both the Orb and the Star out there, wherever you are?"

"Yes."

"Then open your mind and cast your awareness outward with the intention of seeing and hearing the truth. Tell me when you're ready."

Eloise did as he said. She relaxed her body and mind and cast her awareness out into the world. "Ready."

Nothing. It was just like it had been before—Eloise concentrating and the smallest hint of a something from the Orb.

Then the naked mole-rat smacked Eloise in the middle of her forehead, right on the wisdom eye, with the chewed end of his tuber.

And the world opened up.

Sensations flooded into Eloise's mind in an uncontrolled, overpowering deluge, a crushing river of random insight and observation. A pauper giving birth in an alley, alone and cold. A couple saying, "I do" moments before soldiers broke in and slayed the bride. The half-brain sleeping of a dolphin. A wager between scoundrels. A herald crying that Eloise's grandmother had died of a broken heart. The scratch of a quill writing cryptic symbols that Eloise understood to spell out "Buy haggleberry futures." A sloth falling from a tree at the moment of death. An unknown noble counting the coins in his purse, disappointment searing his soul. Someone named Jorge hiding a cookie from his sister. A wag buying a joke engagement ring. A toddler's first steps. A bird's first flight. A girl's first kiss with the lass she'd long been sweet on. A magistrate's first conviction. A first drink of apricot nectar. A first punch in the face. An artist's first painting hung in a gallery. A first gasp of breath after nearly drowning. An arrow flying wide of a painted target and piercing a boy's abdomen. A bear tasting the first ripe blackberry of the season. The scent of bread lifted lovingly from an oven. A fall from a cliff. An aria sung with echoing reverence in a cavernous, empty devotional house. The cracking thud of a truncheon in use. A bishop's secret doubt in her faith. The transgression of a mayor to favor his daughter's idiot husband. The joy of a bee sipping a flower's nectar. The driven focus of a worker ant. A merchant cheating a supplier. An equine acolyte's first connection with the Purity. The fullness of grief. The fleeting joy of acquisition. The sloughing away of a shackled soul. The ache of an ague. A last breath.

Image after image, feeling after feeling, sound after sound, smell after smell. A waterfall splash of everything in the world, past, present, and, she knew intuitively, future.

Overwhelmed by the rawness and sheer volume of it all, Eloise broke down sobbing.

The naked mole-rat took her hand with a tiny paw and patted it with the other. "Loulou. Loulou. Loulou! Come back!"

Eloise looked at him and took several deep breaths, trying to get her crying under control. "Sorry. How long was I gone? It felt like a lifetime."

Sparky tilted his head. "Six, maybe seven seconds. Time is a bit strange around here. What happened?"

"The world. It was just so much. It's too, too much for anyone to take in." She swallowed back the lump in her throat.

"Did you see and hear what you were looking for?"

"No. It was like being thrown into the middle of the Gööödeling Sea during a tsunami and asking if I could see a particular drop of water or hear a particular splash."

"That makes sense," said Sparky. The naked mole-rat gave her hand a little squeeze. "So, two things."

"What?"

"First, it appears that the Orb of Alleged Omniscience is not so alleged. It seems that it does, in fact, possess some degree of magical quality that can be harnessed for the purposes of distant perception and knowing."

"That's good."

"Is it?"

"What do you mean?"

"Good, not good... After the fact, it's not always easy to tell which is which—whether something's good or bad. Often it is a confusing mix."

"Very philosophical of you. You said 'first' before. What's second?"

"I think I know what your problem is."

"Oh, good. What's that?"

"Scope."

"Scope? What do you mean by scope?"

"As in the scope of the endeavor. You can't know and see everything," said Sparky. "If you keep at what you were just doing, you'll end up a muttering, drooling mess." The naked mole-rat made a blank face and let a dribble of drool trickle, demonstrating his point. "You have to control the experience. You have to focus your mind on the specifics of what you're trying to find out. Use intention to narrow it down. Consciously seek out *precisely* what you need to see and hear. If you don't, you'll end up spending the rest of your life here with me. Not from my doing, mind you. You're the one who wants to do this. But mess this up and your fellow people out there, wherever 'there' is, will wish you were easier to feed and diaper."

"Oh."

"Exactly. So be precise about what you seek to see and hear, and then concentrate with all your might on seeing and hearing exactly that. And then get out of there."

"I'll try."

"'Try' will have to do." Sparky made an inviting gesture. "In your own time."

Eloise settled herself again, relaxed her mind, and spent a few heart-beats trying to work out which of the swirling mysteries she should attend to. She decided to pick one of the less confronting ones—what was going on with First Advisor Ligurian. "Ready."

Thwack! Chewed tuber against the wisdom eye and Eloise was off again, this time keeping her focus on the Ligurian situation.

Ligurian. Ligurian. Ligurian.

There was a rush of clarity. A rapid sequence of images and sounds—scenes, snatches of conversations, movements, emotions, thoughts.

There was an older woman being confined. She was unhappy, although not mistreated, and there was a section of her hair missing. Eloise felt the woman's strong connection to First Advisor. Sister? Aunt? No, mother.

There was a clandestine meeting. Ligurian and a low, shadowy figure. She felt First Advisor's disgust and fear. A demand made. A threat revealed. "There will be opportunities for you to pass on information. You will do so." She sensed his acquiescence.

Ligurian in his office, looking at dispatches from his intelligence network and burning them, rather than putting them into one of the royal boxes.

Ligurian presenting information to Eloise, but seen from First Advisor's point of view. His evaluation of her as clueless. His need to keep her that way.

Another meeting with the shadowy figure. And another. And another. And another. Information exchange. Demands made. Promises kept. The sense of betrayal. The sense of distaste. The sense of desperation. The sense of shame.

Eloise brought her awareness toward the shadowy figure, seeking clarity. The face was reptilian. The scales were a bright shining blue with white underneath. And there were three eyes.

Eloise barely had time to register that it was the Eastie trade negotiator Bosana de Coluber when the scene flicked on, this time jumping to the recent encounter in the Receiving Room where the Easties told her to hand over Flachberg.

Eloise had seen enough of Ligurian to understand his betrayal, but this took her in a new direction. What was going on with Flachberg? So she shifted her focus.

See and hear the truth of Flachberg. Flachberg, Flachberg, Flachberg.

The river of observation shifted.

The perspective became that of someone on a throne staring down at de Coluber. Eloise felt she was seeing this from the Eastie queen's perspective. A mission given. A mission accepted. The sense of creating diversion, disruption, and turmoil. The sense of sewing chaos, confusion, fear, and doubt. The sense of glee at doing so. The sense of creating cracks where there were none, and applying pressure to cracks that were there. The undermining of merchants. The fanning of dormant cultural flames and dissatisfactions.

The perspective lurched to a strange, disorienting, three-eyed viewpoint. The spreading of gossip, rumor, and slander. "She's not who her mother was." "She's hardly old enough to even look at the crown." "Don't expect much from her." "Do you think she'll live out the year?" "Her sister was the smart, capable one. Maybe we should move to the Half Kingdom." "Maybe we can get the sister back." "She's accident-prone." "Whatever she's taking for pain seems to have muddled her." "She looks tired all the time." "She keeps running off to the Bibliotheca de Records and Regrets to hide from her responsibilities." "Shirker." "Quarter-wit." "The shriveled pea in the pod." "The stunted bud on the rose bush." "A chipmunk as her champion? That tells you everything you need to know." Whispered phrases. Shouted epithets. Taunts leveled at her from public inns to market squares.

Then the dawning of an idea, a taking of initiative, a twist of thinking and the congealing of a plan that would please the queen much more than she anticipates.

The perception of Eloise being anemic, second-rate, and worthless was embarrassing, and Eloise felt something crack inside her heart. Of course she didn't deserve to be queen. She hadn't asked for it and hadn't been ready.

But the rush of insight moved on before she could come anywhere near to assimilating it.

The organization of provocative military exercises and troop movements. The infiltration of scouts and spies. A trickle of intelligence from the Western Lands and All That Really Matters toward the east. That trickle becoming a steady flow. Preparations to breach the

Adequate Wall of the Realms from the east, as well as sending ships to the coast. The operation shrouded in secrecy, but so large as to make that difficult. The measures taken to protect that secrecy, including an arrow through a nightjar's heart. The reopening of festering wounds in preparation. Flachberg as a symbol. Flachberg as a readied incursion. Flachberg as a conquest in waiting.

The audacity of it was staggering. The threat so clear. Eloise's obliviousness so complete. What a disaster.

She didn't know how much more of this she could take, but there was one other thing she had to face. She had to know how her mother had been killed.

TO SEE AND HEAR THE TRUTH

How could she best focus in on the cause of the late queen's demise? She couldn't just think about her mother. That was too broad. Maybe she could start with her mother dying and work backwards from there, except she wasn't sure she had that much control over what she was doing, and the reverse order might be confusing.

The fresh haggleberries. They were the key to it all.

So she brought her attention to haggleberries, in particular, the ones that took her mother down. She pictured them in the blueberry pie that hid them, mentally attached them to her mother, and allowed their pull to draw her toward them.

See and hear the truth. See and hear the truth. Mother's blueberry pie with hidden haggleberries. Mother's blueberry pie with hidden haggleberries.

A pie came into focus. It was carried from the kitchens by a goanna in a serving wench's outfit—Patrinia Tanche. Eloise felt the uncertainty in the servant's four-footed gait and an odd nervousness in the tight clutch of her stomach. She traveled along the hall toward the Salle de la Famille, but stopped at a sheltered alcove along the way. She set the serving tray on a table, lifted the silver dome covering it, and dug two raw haggleberries out of her pouch. Balancing the serving tray, the goanna slipped the berries through the blueberry filling and into the center of the slice of pie. Then she walked them into the Salle de la Famille and set the plate in front of Queen Eloise. The goanna slipped away, but Eloise stayed with her mother, and watched as she ate the pie. There was a brief wrinkle to her nose as she ate the fatal berries.

Her mother had no idea what was coming. The odd taste to the pie was just a blip to ignore.

But it wasn't a blip. It was a dagger. She just didn't know it yet.

The flow of knowing jumped forward. Eloise saw her mother vomiting and writhing in pain.

Jump.

Her mother, in bed, worried. Her father standing next to her, more worried. Eldridge the Apothecary, his back to them both, mixing a concoction of herbs and more worried than her parents put together.

Jump.

More vomiting. Her mother gaunt, her eyes sunken, her stomach sharp with pain, her life force ebbing. Ligurian standing in the doorway blinking back tears. Eloise focused on him. She could not perceive anything but love and grief toward her mother. Clearly, this had not been his doing, and he was suffering.

Jump.

Her mother talking to Ligurian alone. "She's going to need help. I need you to help her."

Ligurian nodding assent.

Jump.

Now she perceived the scene from her mother's perspective. Her limbs felt watery, her hands trembly, the ruin of her body almost complete. A painful, empty distress radiated outward from her disused stomach and ravaged her entire torso. There was a sense of resignation, an acceptance of the inevitable.

The door opened and Eloise saw her not-that-much younger self rush into the room looking road weary, travel worn, and anxious. Her hair was a disaster, her face a sun-darkened, dirt-streaked mess, and she almost certainly smelled like something a skunk would avoid.

Then something happened that absolutely staggered Now-Eloise. A delighted warmth filled her mother's chest, mixing with relief that Then-Eloise had made it back in time. There was a dying queen's concern for what she knew must lay ahead for the one who would replace her before she was ready. There was a mother's worry for the state that her daughter appeared to be in. But above all else, there was a deep flaring of love that filled the broken body and radiated outward toward her daughter. Then-Eloise was oblivious to it, but Now-Eloise could feel the pure, non-judgmental, unconditional, angelic, uninhibited love that her mother felt.

This truth, this unabashed, fulsome love completely defined her mother in that moment. It was so unexpected and so at odds with the stern manner that she'd always had with her daughters. Now-Eloise slowed the scene to a crawl and took it in, savored it, and let it reshape her entire sense of her mother, altering forever the lens through which Eloise viewed her past.

What a surprise.

What a gift.

Eloise let the awareness flow forward in time, this time speeding it up, knowing what was coming and not wanting to re-experience the full anguish of it. There was the talk of blueberry pie. The description of her mother's discomfort. The mention of the suiciding serving goanna. The self-inflicted death of Chef. A sip of water. The discussion of how the haggleberry could not have come from Johanna. The imparting of advice. Eloise taking her mother's bony hand in hers and kissing it.

And then, not long after, the shuddering final breaths, and her spirit leaving her body.

For the second time, Eloise bore witness to her mother's death. Even sped up, even knowing it was coming, it still hit her like a blow to the solar plexus. All she wanted to do now was curl up somewhere quiet and allow herself to grieve again.

She was about to try and extricate herself from the Orb's flow of perception when she realized she hadn't answered an important question—why did the goanna slip her mother the fatal haggleberries?

She focused her intention, seeking to see and hear the truth one last time.

Jump backward.

Patrinia Tanche, confused and worried, was being spoken to by someone deliberately hiding in the shadow of a barrel near the kitchens. Judging by the sight line, the person was not very big. The sense of a demand being made and pressure applied. The goanna refusing. More pressure. The goanna faltering, but continuing to resist.

Jump forward.

Patrinia alone in her tiny, barely furnished room in a far-flung, forgotten corner of the castle. She was crying—gut-deep, hiccuping, chest heaving, sobs. Unbounded anguish filled the tiny space. In the corner, her nest sat empty and cold. Two raw haggleberries occupied the space where her clutch of eggs had been.

Jump.

Once again, Patrinia Tanche walked the adulterated dessert toward the Salle de la Famille. This time, Eloise got a stronger sense of the goanna's emotional state. Yes, she was nervous and her stomach was tight. But there was also the sense of resolution. Dread had been pushed down, replaced by a fierce maternal protection.

The goanna delivered the hateful pie, then rushed away as quickly as she could.

Jump.

Patrinia was back in her room, once again sobbing.

The nest once again held her eggs.

They'd been broken. Deliberately. Dead, almost-fully-formed goannas lay in a gooey mess, just a few days before they would have emerged.

Jump.

Tanche stood on a stool and slipped a noose over her neck.

"No!" yelled Eloise.

But of course, the grieving servant couldn't hear her, since Eloise wasn't really there. Seconds later, the rope went taut, jouncing.

When stillness returned, a hidden voice hissed, "Good. One less thing to worry about."

The serpent slithered out from under a tarp, where he'd been secretly watching. Bright blue scales. White underbelly. Three eyes.

All three of them seemed to look right at Eloise.

She screamed again.

The snake languidly blinked his weird wisdom eye, then slipped away out of sight. She thought she heard him cough out a cold, hard, mirthless laugh.

It froze the blood in her veins.

If this was seeing and hearing the truth, she'd rather be deaf and blind.

I've seen enough. I've heard enough. Get me out of here!

❧ 72 ❧

INCINERATING REPUGNANCE

There was a small weight on Eloise's chest and a tapping on her face.

"El! El! Come back!"

Not tapping. More of a patting. An annoying patting, but a patting nonetheless.

"El!"

"Queen Eloise! Can you hear us? Can you open your eyes?"

She felt so tired. So spent. Overwhelmed by all she'd seen and heard. Sad. Angry. Gutted. Raw.

And hungry. Why was she so hungry? She could eat a mountain of scones. But old Chef's scones. Not so much new Chef's.

The patting got more insistent. She was probably going to have to pay it some attention soon. Maybe she could brush it away.

"El! El! For the love of Çalaht, come back! El!"

Pat pat pat pat pat pat pat pat pat.

She managed to mumble, "Cudditout. Lemmebe."

"Oh, thank Çalaht. El! Come on!"

Pat pat pat pat pat pat pat pat pat pat pat pat pat pat pat pat pat pat.

She waved an arm in front of her, trying to get the irritating patting to stop.

The weight came off her chest. There was a small thudding and an "oof."

Moments later, the weight was back and the patting restarted.

"Wheredascones?"

"What was that, Queen Eloise? 'Where's Dascones?' Tell us who Dascones is and we can find him."

"Could be 'her.' Or 'they.' Some people are 'they.'"

"Queen Eloise, where will find him or her or them?"

Whoever was talking to her sounded weird. She tried to get her mouth to work. "Wheredascones Where. Da. Scones. Wheredascones." Eloise waved her arm again, trying to point to her tummy. There was another thud and "oof."

"What did you say, El? 'Where. Da. Scones.'" The weight was back on her chest and the patting started back up. "Open your eyes. Come on."

Pat pat pat pat pat pat pat pat pat pat pat pat pat pat pat pat pat pat.

"'Where. Da. Scones.' Queen Eloise, are you saying, 'Where are the scones?' Are you hungry?"

"Yougodditwhoeveryouare. Wheredascones? Sconebiscuitmuffinwhaddever. Immastarving."

"Just a moment, Jerome. I'll send RoyLee to the kitchens. You keep trying to rouse her."

"Got it. This is worrying me. A lot. Is this normal behavior for someone who's had a bud or two of prattleweed?"

"No, it's not. But you see that?"

"What?"

"There's a seed on her mouth. I suspect she's had more than a couple of dried flowers."

"Do we need to send for Eldridge the Apothecary?"

"No. I'll handle this. Just... It won't be pretty. She's not going to be happy with me. And I'll probably have to restrain her. So you might need to stand clear. Have a mug of water ready. And that bowl."

Mercifully, the patting stopped and the weight came off her chest.

There was the sound of a wooden box hinging open and then closing again.

"Apologies, Queen Eloise."

Eloise felt a gentle pinch on her cheek and a wad of something was slipped into her mouth. A finger positioned it between her teeth and the inside of her cheek, well toward the back. Gauze, maybe?

Within moments, the whatever-it-was started to burn. It tasted like a soldier had gone on campaign for a month, spent the whole time tramping through swampland, come back and shoved his socks in her mouth, then given her a shot of straight jalapeño juice with a jalapeño juice chaser.

Horrid. Nasty.

Eloise tried to spit it out, but a hand clamped over her mouth, holding it in. She tried to turn her head away, but the hand stayed with her. Flinging her head back and forth did nothing.

Noxious. Scorching.

The flaming heat and disgusting taste took all of her focus. She had to get rid of it. Just had to. Eloise tried to stand up, but a different weight across her at the shoulders kept her in place. She was trapped. Trapped! Pinned down with the taste and heat of brimstone trying to blaze its way through her face.

Eloise bucked and tried to kick, but the heaviness holding her in the chair was relentless. She grabbed at the hand covering her mouth and tried to pull it away. No luck. Clawing at it did nothing. Pounding on it just made it press down harder. Seconds of misery stretched into a pepper-tasting, cauterizing hell of agony that seemed to last hours. No amount of thrashing made a difference, except to make her injured arm scream in pain.

The fiery, vile taste seared the inside of her mouth and burned through the muzziness in her head. Her muddled thinking washed away like the River Thurmond was flooded through it. Her eyes shot open to see that it was Lorch holding her down, one hand gripping the front of her face and his body positioned sideways across her to immobilize, while protecting himself from kicks, knees, and elbows. Through blurry vision, she saw that blood trickled from a scratch on his cheek.

Why was he doing this to her? She thought Lorch was her friend. Her champion. Why was he trying to kill her?

Eloise resumed struggling, putting all her might into trying to shove him off, but he was so much bigger than her and built like a stone dunny. She tried to wrestle, scuffle, pound her way away from him—anything to get the evil wad of misery out of her cheek.

Nothing worked. Lorch held her in place with the firmness of a polite boulder that had recently been shot with a crossbow bolt in its behind.

Eloise gave up. She'd die of the incinerating repugnance in her mouth. She resigned herself to her fate, went limp, and let tears flow.

"Good," cooed Lorch with an odd fuzziness. "Very good. I'm so sorry, Queen Eloise. It's the downer down. It's the only thing I could think of to do. I'm going to let go of you now, but I need you to not rush away. No flinging yourself out the window or anything. Sometimes people try to do that. Understood?"

Eloise nodded. Flinging herself out the window seemed like a good option.

"Jerome, hand me the bowl. Queen Eloise, I'll get you to spit out the downer down. Understood?"

She nodded again.

Lorch repositioned himself so that the bowl was near her face, then carefully eased off her, releasing her mouth.

Eloise snatched the bowl and spat, spat again, and spat some more. She scraped out the inside of her cheek with a finger and flung the sodden fluff away, over and over, until every last speck was gone.

Lorch handed her the mug of water. "Don't drink. Sluice and spit."

She did, repeating the action what seemed like at least ten thousand times, until the burning finally eased and the taste of soldier swamp footwear faded.

"By Çalaht's hateful hemorrhoids, that was the worst!"

"Apologies, Queen Eloise. I'm really sorry."

"I can't believe I did that to Johanna. I'm lucky she didn't murder me in my sleep afterward."

"Again, I'm sorry, Queen Eloise."

"If I ever, ever, ever suggest taking prattleweed again, just remind me of that. I will never, ever be a prattle head."

"No, Queen Eloise."

Eloise stopped talking.

Something was wrong.

❧ 73 ❧

AN EYE AND AN EAR

Eloise looked at Lorch, blinked a few times, then looked at him again.

He was fuzzy.

Not fuzzy, blurry.

No, not blurry. Half blurry. Blurry on the right.

She covered her left eye.

Blurry.

She covered her right eye.

Clear.

And there was a buzzing in her right ear.

She shook her head, but the buzzing persisted. Sticking her finger in there like she was trying to get out wax didn't do anything either.

She turned and looked at Jerome. The blur moved with her. Left eye closed—blurry. Right eye closed—clear.

The buzzing continued, loud enough to be noticeable, but not so loud as to deafen.

"What's the matter?" asked Jerome.

"There's something wrong with my eye and ear. They're not working right. This one is blurred. And I have a persistent buzzing."

"Is that new, Your Highness?" asked Lorch.

"Yes. Is this a prattleweed thing? Do prattlers get this?"

"No. Not that I know of, and I've been around a lot of them, including some desperately bad cases. They get other symptoms—losing their teeth, blood vessels in their eyes blow up so the whites go red, inability to tolerate direct sunlight, noses falling off. But not those."

"Strange," said Eloise. She hopped on one foot like she had just been swimming in a lake.

Jerome squinted at Lorch. "Did you just say their noses fall off?"

"In severe cases, yes."

"Ugh."

"Ugh, indeed," said Eloise.

"El, stop hopping." Jerome poured her a cup of haggleberry tea and held it out to her. "Do you need me to go get a healer? Or Eldridge?"

"No, not yet." She took the cup and saucer with one hand and, using the other, covered and uncovered her right eye to see if there was a change.

Nope.

And the buzzing! It was going to be a problem if it kept up. Fortunately, it was only in her right ear.

Eloise sipped. "How long was I... you know... out?"

Jerome and Lorch looked at each other and simultaneously raised an eyebrow each.

"Five minutes," said Lorch.

"Maybe four," said Jerome.

"Four or five minutes? Is that all? It felt like much longer. So why did you try to get me back?"

"It was the screaming," said Lorch.

Jerome nodded agreement with his tail. "So much screaming. Plus some rather indelicate language."

"Indelicate language? What kind of indelicate language?"

Both Lorch and Jerome looked down at their feet and said nothing.

"Fine. Don't repeat it back to me. Just give me the gist."

Lorch reddened. "There was... There were... Uh..."

"I got this," said Jerome. "There were unflattering references to some-one's parentage, a number of words that I wouldn't say in front of my mother that started with 'q,' 'w,' and 'y,' and several colorful, yet theo-logically unlikely religious admonitions."

"Did I really?"

"Yes, you did."

"How embarrassing."

Jerome gave his tail an indifferent flick. "Mainly it was the screaming that got us to do something."

"So, Queen Eloise," said Lorch. "How was it? Did you experience anything with the Orb of Alleged Omniscience?"

"There was no 'alleged' about the Orb. I'm going to have to change its name to the Orb of Actual If Painful Omniscience or something. And I never want to go anywhere near the thing ever again."

"What did you see?"

She told them, leaving out only her interactions with Sparky.

Jerome looked stunned. "That's... That's... That's almost too much to take in."

"But can we rely on it?" asked Lorch. "How do we know what you experienced was true?"

Eloise covered her left eye with her hand. The right eye's blur wasn't clearing. "It felt real enough. It seemed accurate. And the bits that included me, like seeing me come to my mother on her deathbed, matched my own experience."

Jerome shook his head. "But it's the same with dreams, though, isn't it? One moment you're having a very realistic and historically accurate conversation with your mother about that time when you were a pup and you threw up pumpkin soup on the bishop's cassock and the next you're dancing naked on a gargoyle with a pickle in your ear."

"That's oddly specific, Jer."

Jerome coughed. "Possibly a little too specific."

"So, Queen Eloise," said Lorch. "What are you going to do?"

"I'm going to assume it was true, unless I see evidence to the contrary."

"Which means?"

"Which means I want you to find Bosana de Coluber, that damned three-eyed snake, and throw him in a dungeon."

"Yes, Queen Eloise."

"And while you're at it, arrest Ligurian."

"Yes, Queen Eloise. Anything else?"

"Let's get ready to send troops to Flachberg. Lots of them. I think we might need them there."

"Yes, Queen Eloise."

Lorch rushed from the room.

Jerome looked from where Lorch had just been and then back to Eloise. "This isn't how I expected today to go when I woke up this morning."

"No."

Eloise took her hand off her good eye and put a finger in her ear to see if she could get the buzzing to stop.

She couldn't.

74

REUNITED WITH THEIR
CULTURAL HERITAGE

t the same time that Lorch was running from the Queen's Study, 2,437 strong lengths away, Kÿÿÿlïïïëëë Plööönqüüüëëër was sprinting like her life depended on it.

Which it probably did.

It was Kÿÿÿlïïïëëë's first day on the job as a wall guard at the Adequate Wall of the Realms. She had just come back from her first lunch break —a quick trip to the canteen, where she'd enjoyed a quite reasonable tomato and basil bruschetta with a smear of olive tapenade, plus one of the worst cups of haggleberry tea she'd ever tasted. But then, what else would she have expected in a far-flung, nowhere outpost like Flachberg? She'd been on the job for a whole five hours and 18 minutes, had another 12 minutes of free time before she was scheduled to subject herself to the admittedly dull process of learning the customs inspection element of her role, and couldn't keep the grin off her face.

She was so happy just to be alive and be a guard.

Kÿÿÿlïïïëëë slipped out the cloth badge from her pocket and traced a finger along the embroidered letters that spelled out her rank: Fourth Assistant Junior Trainee Wall Guard. They'd handed it to her at orientation that morning, and Kÿÿÿlïïïëëë could hardly wait until after her shift, when she'd have a chance to sew it onto her uniform's upper left sleeve. She'd also been given a "Welcome to the Adequate Wall" pin, which looked a lot better than the tinny, paint-faded one her mother had brought back from a business trip when Kÿÿÿlïïïëëë was five. She took a moment to pin the welcome message to her wrinkle-free, perfectly pressed uniform that still smelled brand new.

She'd always wanted to be a guard, as far back as she could remember. Her favorite bedtime stories when she was a girl were about guards. If she ever had to dress up for a costume party, she wore whatever made her look most guard-like. Her favorite toys were all guard figurines. When she got together with friends to play make-believe, she always made believe she was a guard. It seemed like such a noble profession, such a public service, and she loved how they looked in uniform. Plus, unlike certain jobs she could name (like lumberjack, lime burner, leech tutor, or treadmill operator), it struck her as a nice, safe, people-oriented job that had the benefit of not requiring exposure to stenches, sharp blades, heated chalk dust, mounds of guano, or teaching leeches to speak without a lisp.

Everything changed just as she was about to poke the pin through the top of her uniform pocket. Five hours and 22 minutes into her new job, a massive, flaming ball of what looked like (and reeked of) dried, burning ostrich dung flew overhead. She watched it land right in the middle of the guards' quarters.

The wooden shingled roof caught alight immediately.

Startled, Kÿÿÿlïïïëëë followed the arc of the projectile backward to see where it must have come from, and found herself staring straight at the Adequate Wall.

Surely not. How could it come from the wall?

The answer came at five hours, 22 1/2 minutes, when two more burning dung balls the size of washtubs came catapulting over the Adequate Wall from the Eastern Lands side.

Then another two.

All four crashed right into the middle of the guard compound, lighting up more roofs. They were followed by six more.

Bedlam erupted as guards rushed in all directions—some away from the flames, and some toward them. Within a minute, several bucket brigades had formed to try to douse the flames using water drawn at a painfully slow pace from the well in the center of the permanent encampment.

In shock, Kÿÿÿlïïïëëë watched her fellow guards, who were focused on saving their bunkhouses, canteen, armory, and offices, until a noise drew her attention back to the wall. Kÿÿÿlïïïëëë stared open-mouthed as, at exactly five hours, 25 minutes, a mass of soldiers from the Eastern Lands side rushed through the open gate in the Adequate Wall in perfect formation, drew out their weapons, and spread out, ready to advance into the heart of Flachberg itself. Dressed in dark olive-green battle tunics and breeks, they looked like some sort of ancient, invading horde.

Which, Kÿÿÿlïïïëëë reckoned, was exactly what they must have been. When five hundred of them had emerged from the portal and arranged themselves into perfectly spaced rows, they raised their swords, bows, and pikes in the air, and in one voice, boomed in exact unison, "Hello, people of Flachberg. We come to reunite you with your cultural heritage."

"What a strange thing for them to say," she thought.

Then the soldiers lowered their weapons and set out at a double-speed march, fatally mowing down any of the guards who happened to be in their way. It was cold, efficient, and effective.

Kÿÿÿlïïïëëë didn't need to see anything else. At five hours, 26 3/4 minutes, she fled the Adequate Wall, the bedlam of the fire, the fierceness of the soldiers—all of it.

It was clear that being a guard wasn't what it was cracked up to be.

At five hours, 27 minutes and 13 seconds, she was as gone as gone could be. Her Welcome to the Adequate Wall pin lay forgotten, dropped in a patch of dirt she'd never see again. Her Fourth Assistant Junior Trainee Wall Guard patch would never be sewn on.

She had more pressing things to deal with.

Like making sure she wasn't a casualty of an invasion.

75

LOUD AND SHOUTY

Eloise met with Lorch and Jerome in the Receiving Room. It was an informal gathering, so Eloise did not wear a cape, although if she had, it would have been the Livid Cape. Candles lit the hall, and a fire in the fireplace did what it could to beat back a late winter chill. The fact that her eye and ear were still acting wonky did nothing for her mood.

Neither did Lorch and Jerome's reports.

"I'm sorry, Queen Eloise," said Lorch. "We were only able to find one of them."

"Who?"

"First Advisor Ligurian."

"Former First Advisor Ligurian," Eloise corrected. "Where is he?"

"I've confined him to his house, and posted guards at each door and window to make sure he stays there. I assumed you didn't want him in the dungeons."

"No. Not yet. House arrest is fine, at least for now. Did he say anything?"

"Not really. He seemed unsurprised we were there. Resigned to it, even. His duplicity was an ill-fitting coat, but one he admitted freely enough to wearing."

"You should interrogate him," said Jerome. "See if the parts of what you saw with the Orb that had to do with Ligurian agree with what he says happened. If they match, it will increase your confidence in the truth of the rest, the other things that you didn't experience directly."

"Good idea, Jer."

"Thanks."

Eloise sat in silence, drumming the arm of her chair with the fingers of her cast hand and tried to master her temper. The cast itched worse than ever, and she wondered how much longer she would need to have it on. It hadn't really been all that long since she tripped at her Crown Plonking and re-fractured the poor thing. She looked around for something she could stick down inside it that would let her scratch the itch. A quill maybe? A jam knife? Nothing nearby seemed right. For now, she'd try to keep ignoring it. "What happened to de Coluber?"

Jerome cleared his throat and flicked his tail. Eloise knew that combination as a tell—she wasn't going to like what he was about to say.

"The snake seems to have disappeared."

"What do you mean 'disappeared?'"

"As in, vanished. As in, there's no trace of him. Nor Picholine Manzanilla, the Eastern Lands ambassador. Their quarters are empty. Their entire grounds are empty."

"Empty?" said Eloise. "What, their whole embassy?"

"It's like they were never there. Not a stick of furniture, not a scrap of scroll, not a pile of old coffee grounds, not a dirty sock, not a portrait of Queen Aglandau."

"How could they leave Brague without us knowing about it? Weren't there a lot of them?"

"Yes to the latter. I don't know to the former, but it is an excellent question."

A frantic thumping at the Receiving Room door interrupted them. "Please! Let me in! I must speak with the queen."

Eloise knitted her brow. "Isn't there a guard out there?"

More frantic knocking.

"I told the guard that she could have a break, since I'm here," said Lorch. He drew a knife from his belt, walked to the door, paused to ready himself, then snatched it open.

A bedraggled young woman fell into the room. She wore a disheveled Wall Guard's uniform, but without insignia, save the Gumball crest. Her hair looked like she'd come through a tsunami, and a mix of dirt and blood caked her face. "I'm looking for Queen Eloise," she gasped at Lorch.

He reached down and helped her up by the elbow. "Who are you and why do you need to speak to the queen?"

"My name is Kÿÿÿlïïïëëë Plööönqüüüëëër. I'm a guard at the Adequate Wall of the Realms, Flachberg Gate. Or, I was. I mean, I was a Fourth Assistant Junior Trainee Wall Guard. I don't think I am one anymore. Or at least not there, not at Flachberg." She put her hands either side of her head and pressed, closing her eyes. "Sorry, it's been a long few days getting here, and I'm a bit frazzled and brain fried."

Lorch gave her arm a gentle squeeze and spoke softly. "Why wouldn't you still be Fourth Assistant Junior Trainee Wall Guard at Flachberg Gate? Did you get fired?"

"More like fired upon."

"I beg your pardon?" Eloise stood and walked toward Plööönqüüüëëër. "What happened to you?"

The young woman looked at her and pointed. "I... It's... You're... I... You're the queen."

"Yes, I am."

Kÿÿÿlïïïëëë wasn't sure if she should curtsy, bow, or salute, so she wobbled into a contorted mix of all three. If Lorch didn't still have a grip on her arm, she would have crumpled to the ground again. "Your Highness. I'm so sorry."

"Sorry? For what?"

"Flachberg is lost."

Eloise felt the blood draining from her face. "What do you mean lost? Start at the beginning."

"It was my first day in uniform," she started, and went through everything from receiving her badge and pin to realizing that catapults were flinging flaming balls of dung into the middle of the guard compound, to the invading soldiers, including their odd chant of "Hello, people of Flachberg. We come to reunite you with your cultural heritage," and the slaughter of anyone who got in their way. "I'm… I'm ashamed to say, Your Highness, that I panicked. I ran. Even so, I barely missed having my head separated from my neck. It was only a bad trip that saved me. I smacked my head on the cobblestone road and blacked out. They must have thought I'd killed myself or wasn't worth the effort of skewering, but they left me where I was. It was night when I came to."

"And?" prompted Lorch.

"And when I woke up, the guard compound was nothing but a smoking ruin."

"What about Flachberg itself?"

"The town was… I'm sorry, but the town seemed to be celebrating?"

"What do you mean, celebrating?" said Jerome.

"Like it was a feast day. The Easties had brought table after table of food and drink and set it up in the middle of the town square. There was Eastie music, Eastie decorations (mainly olive branches), and the food was incredible Eastern Lands fare: olive bread with olive spread, sun-dried tomato and olive paella, an olive and grain salad with an olive-lemon vinaigrette, garbanzo and olive stir-fry, a chocolate soufflé tart with candied kalamata olives, black olive caramel, olive brittle, a sweet potato dessert with olive nougatine—"

"That sounds *awesome*," said Jerome, licking his lips.

"Jer!"

"Sorry, but it does."

"Not the point."

The chipmunk's tail drooped. "True. Apologies, Your Highness."

"And how did the people of Flachberg react to this?" asked Eloise.

"It was a mixed reaction. There were those who protested the intrusion. And there were others who were killed, so they didn't have much to say. But there were also those who welcomed the feast and seemed comfortable with the soldiers being there. More than one person said things like, 'This tastes like what my granny used to make.' And to be honest..."

"Yes?" said Eloise.

"It did taste like my gran used to make. I'm sorry, but I was so hungry and there were no barracks to go back to, so I broke down and had some of their feast food."

"It's OK," whispered Lorch. "A guard must take care of herself if she's going to take care of others."

Plööönqüüüëëër looked at him and tears spilled out, despite her furious blinking. "That's kind of you. I've not had a lot of kindness recently."

"So then what did you do?" he asked.

"Then it occurred to me that the queen ought to know. The guards were gone and Flachberg had been invaded and I had no idea if anyone else had been dispatched to deliver the news or what. So I said to myself, 'Kÿÿÿliiiëëë Plööönqüüüëëër, if you were queen, would you hope that someone might let you know what was going on if a platoon of soldiers took over your Flachberg?' And I answered myself, 'Yeah, I would.' Then I said to myself, 'Well, then why are you still here? Go tell her.' And I replied to myself, 'But I'm just a Fourth Assistant Junior Trainee Wall Guard.' So I said to myself, 'Stop talking to yourself and get going. Brague isn't going to come to you.' So here I am."

"I'm glad you are," said Eloise. She reached out and touched the other woman's arm. "You were very brave to come. I'll have more questions, but I have the gist. So, two things."

"Yes, Your Highness?"

"I want you to clean up and get some sleep. I'll get someone to find you a room, heat you a bath, and find you a change of clothes. We can talk tomorrow."

"A bath and a kip sounds divine." Kÿÿÿlïïïëëë hesitated. "And the other thing?"

"For your bravery and devotion, I hereby promote you to Third Assistant Junior Trainee Wall Guard."

The young woman gasped. "Really? Can you do that?"

"I just did."

"Oh, thank you." Plööönqüüüëëër did another contorted curt-sy/bow/salute, and again would have fallen if Lorch wasn't still supporting her.

Eloise raised her voice and said, "RoyLee, are you there?"

The wombat bustled in from a side door and skittered to a halt. "Of course, Princess Queen Eloise."

"Can you please fetch Lady Seneschal and have her find a place for Third Assistant Junior Trainee Wall Guard Kÿÿÿlïïïëëë Plööönqüüüëëër?"

"Of course, Princess Queen Eloise." He bowed to the young woman, said, "Please be following me," and led her from the room.

Eloise flumped back down onto the Receiving Room throne and put her face in her hands. "Çalaht sucking suppurating sores, this makes me angry and tired at the same time." She sat up straight, closed her eyes, took a long, deep breath, and blew it out. Then she did it again, trying to clear her head. "The Eastie queen didn't do this to my mother. Or my grandmother. Or my great-grandmother. Why does she think she can do this to me?" She imitated the snake's voice, but made it like a petulant child's. "'We want Flachberg. Just give it to us.' Well, stuff that."

"What do we do?" asked Jerome.

"Let's start by getting Other Places Advocate Bënnïë-Änn Thëjëts in here and see what she has to say."

"Right. I'll have her sent for." Jerome left in search of another page.

Eloise drummed her fingers on the arm rest, then covered and uncovered her left, then right, eye, and then, for the hundredth time, stuck a finger in her ear to try to stop the buzzing. She stood up, paced on the dais, then sat down again with a grunt and resumed her finger drumming.

Jerome slipped back into the room. "She'll be here shortly."

Eloise ignored him and tried her buzzing ear again, unable to achieve any change.

"Your Highness?" said Lorch.

Eloise didn't respond.

"Queen Eloise?"

She looked at him. "What?"

"We have to respond, Your Highness."

"No."

"No?"

"No. *We* don't have to respond," said Eloise. "*I* have to respond. I suspect they think I won't. I suspect..." Eloise stood again. "I suspect that Her Majesty, Queen Aglandau Gaeta Cerignola Ponentine thinks I'm too worm spittle to do anything about her soldiers sashaying into Flachberg, planting a flag, and handing out olive brittle."

"I suspect they'd be wrong about that," said Jerome.

"Damn right."

"And when you do respond, we'll be there to help you do it," said Lorch.

"Thanks."

More finger drumming. More eye covering and uncovering. More pacing. More unsuccessful ear clearing.

And then suddenly, Eloise stopped and stood very still. "Champion Lacksneck? Assistant Court Seer to the Court Seer Abernatheen de Chipmunk?"

"Yes," said Lorch and Jerome.

"I think it's time for something loud and shouty."

"Then loud and shouty it will be, Your Highness," said Lorch.

"What exactly would that look like?" asked Jerome.

"I have no idea. But I think it's time to figure that out."

The series continues with Eloise trying to work out how to handle the menace from the Eastern Lands. It'll take everything she has to keep her crown on her head and her queendom beneath her feet. **Read The Eastie Threat to find out what happens next.**

Want to read more about Eloise and Jerome? Six months before the start of *The Purple Haze*, they
played hooky from Court and headed out for a stolen adventure. It goes well. And then it really doesn't. **Claim your copy of The Wombanditos today to find out what happened!**

❧

And if you're wondering just what exactly happened at their Thorning Ceremony that caused Eloise and Johanna to go from being as close as twins can be to as estranged, then you'll definitely want to check out the standalone novel, *The Thorning Ceremony*. I promise you, you'll never guess what caused the rift.

THANK YOU

Thank you for reading *The Crown Plonked Queen*. Reviews are crucial for helping other readers discover new books to enjoy. If you want to share your love for Eloise, Jerome, and all the gang, please leave a review. I'd really appreciate it!

Recommending my work to others is also a huge help. Feel free to give this book a shout-out in your favourite book recommendation group to spread the word.

ACKNOWLEDGMENTS

It is a joy to get to say thank you to those who have helped me bring this book to the world.

Tamsin Dean Einspruch, our daughter, has from the word go been my first port of call for ideas, perspective, and thoughts on words. She is my first reader, and has been with this story every step of the way. Over and over she has helped me stay headed in the right direction. Thank you, sweetie.

Many, many thanks also to Cheryl Hannah, Olivia Martinez, and Brian Busby for their beta reads. Cheryl has been, for each of these books, the first person outside my family to read the manuscript, and her encouragement always gives me the heart needed to keep going. Olivia brings an always-keen eye to the words, and she and Brian provided very different perspectives to what they read. Valuable and valued input all.

Thank you to my editor, Vanessa Lanaway, and my proofreader, Abigail Nathan. Sharp eyes and red pens, both. Y'all rock. It's that simple.

Thank you to Maria Spada for the wonderful cover.

As always, a massive thank you to my bride, Billie Dean, who reads and gives incredible input on everything I write, who has encouraged me forever, and who believed in my creative soul much, much earlier than I ever did. I love you and I thank you. L^3.

And finally, thank you to you, whoever you are, for picking up this book and having a read. I appreciate it very much, and I'll see you in *The Eastie Threat*.

ABOUT THE AUTHOR

Andrew Einspruch is fond of the wordy, the nerdy, and the funny, which means that if you arranged for him to have lunch with Weird Al Yankovic, Tom Lehrer, William Gibson, and any of the Monty Python guys, he'd be your friend forever. Visit his web site for a complete list of his books at andreweinspruch.com.

Andrew is an ex-pat Texan living in Australia, and is the co-founder of the not-for-profit charity the Deep Peace Trust, which fosters deep peace and non-violence for all species. With his wife and daughter, he runs the Trust's farm animal and wild horse sanctuary. (You can see why there's the odd animal or two in his books.)

If pressed, he'll deny he ever coded in COBOL for a bank.

If you haven't done so yet, use the QR code below to claim your copy of the standalone prequel, *The Wombanditos*.